little brown dog

little brown dog

PAULA S OWEN

HONNO MODERN FICTION

First published in Great Britain in 2021 by Honno Press
'Ailsa Craig', Heol y Cawl, Dinas Powys, Vale of Glamorgan,
Wales, CF64 4AH

1 2 3 4 5 6 7 8 9 10

A catalogue record for this book is available from the British Library.

Published with the financial support of the Books Council of Wales.

ISBN 978-1-912905-43-0 (paperback)
ISBN 978-1-912905-44-7 (ebook)
Cover design: Kari Brownlie
Text design: Elaine Sharples
Printed and bound by CPI Group (UK) Ltd, Croydon, CR0 4YY

"He prayeth best who loveth best
All things, both great and small;
For the dear God who loveth us,
He made and loveth all."

Samuel Taylor Coleridge
'The Rime of the Ancient Mariner'

For Stanley, my very own Battersea boy
who was taken far too soon.

The Old Man

BATTERSEA PARK, AUGUST 2018

The sun reluctantly surrenders its red-hot grip on the park and slips towards the horizon. In its fading light an old man walks his small, brown, wire-haired terrier. Young Jake is of that age characterised by boundless energy and an insatiable appetite for misadventure. Occasionally, his master reflects that maybe adopting an older, more placid companion would have been wiser, given he's the one who has to walk him. But he is swift to dismiss such thoughts; he adores the rascal, despite the trouble he gets them both into. He is worth the odd grovelling apology to neighbours whose underpants Jake has yanked from the line and gleefully shredded.

It is late August, and the capital has wilted through a protracted, scorching summer, with no end in sight according to the Met Office. Everything is tinder dry. The grass is unidentifiable, its parched, crunchy shards working their way into the old man's open-toed sandals. The shrubs that the park is famous for – rhododendron, hydrangeas and oleander – gasp for cooler air. Their once vibrant hot-pink and poker-red flowers, now shrivelled and drooping, weep for the long-absent rain.

But the man's not grumbling: the evening's penetrating warmth seeps into his arthritic, eighty-year-old bones, easing the nagging pain that keeps him awake most nights. They plod along, one man and his dog, at the old guy's languid pace, the distant sounds of the capital providing the soundtrack.

This tranquillity is not to last. Jake is straining at his leash, yelping impatiently. A jerk jars the man's neck and he rubs at it, grumpy now, lamenting the money wasted on puppy training. He scolds the dog. But Jake's attention is elsewhere: a squat grey squirrel, chomping on a nut in a low branch of an elm twenty yards away. The old man relents; he'll not win this battle. He bends, fumbles with the catch, cursing his stiff joints. Eventually it comes free of the collar. 'There you go, boy.'

Jake's off like a rocket, and the squirrel, with a contemptuous flick of her magnificent bushy tail, flees toward the dense thicket. Beyond excited, Jake disappears into the undergrowth in pursuit. The man calls after him, but it's to no avail. Jake's yelps gradually fade into the background hum of traffic.

The old man trudges on in the direction Jake has disappeared, repeating his name, whistling, until his voice grows hoarse. He scours their favourite haunts, but Jake's nowhere to be seen – not at the Pump House, nor the café, where friendly staff feed Jake treats. He asks each passer-by. But it's hopeless – Jake is lost.

The sun creeps ever lower in the cloudless, cotton blue sky. The old man detects the faintest sense of a welcome chill in the evening air. He's beyond weary now. He wipes sweat from his brow, noticing the tremor in his hand is back. He cannot return home without Jake. Mary would be beside herself with worry. Anyhow, he'd not be able to live with himself if anything happened to the little guy – not on his watch. He calls the same phrases on repeat, anguish clear in his faltering tone: 'Jake? C'mon ol' son. Time to go home now, boy. Jake, please?' Nothing.

Stumbling across a decrepit, lichen-covered bench, he collapses into it, sighing heavily. Watery desperation leaks from his rheumy, storm-grey eyes. It's hopeless.

As his eyelids droop and exhaustion threatens to engulf him, he hears a distant yelp. He glances up, alert now, tapping his hearing aid in disbelief. There it is again.

The old man musters the last of his energy, rises with considerable effort, and hurries as fast as his aching body will carry him towards the source of the noise. It's an unfamiliar, less well-trodden section of the park – overgrown, with a neglected, almost sorrowful, feel to it. He glances around – there is not another soul in sight. He shivers, uncertain whether the chill is real or perceived.

Overgrown hawthorn, ivy and blackberry bushes make for slow progress. He snags his shirt on thorns, ripping a hole in the sleeve – reflecting glumly that it's another thing Mary won't be best pleased about. He soon rallies, though; the barking is definitely getting louder. He ploughs on with renewed purpose, despite the thickening undergrowth and paling embers of pink-streaked light.

He keeps calling, hope returning to his voice. Then halts, as an unwelcome thought bubbles to the surface. He's recalling clichéd TV crime dramas that inevitably begin with a hapless dog walker stumbling across putrefying human remains. He shivers, again.

'Don't be so ridiculous, Ian,' he scolds. After all, he's nothing but a rational, no-nonsense kind of fellow – forty-five tedious years of toil in an accountant's office made darn sure of that. He shakes off the ghoulish thoughts – of rotting bodies and accountancy alike – as he enters a small clearing. There, scuffing at the ground, barking with delight at the sight of his master, is Jake.

Overjoyed, the old man hobbles forward, then slows to a snail's pace. He's a tad reticent about getting too close to whatever Jake is pawing at under the crunchy leaf litter. He calls himself to order and bends down, creaking with the effort. His nose senses it first: that unmistakable, sharp, fetid stink of death. He swallows rising bile, but sighs with relief moments later. Jake hasn't uncovered a mutilated human carcass: just an eye-wateringly ripe, decomposing wood pigeon. He chuckles. How Mary will laugh. She's forever teasing him about his over-vivid imagination.

He retrieves a water bottle and bowl from his bag. Jake laps noisily, parched after his long adventure. The man feeds him a treat while gently admonishing him for running off.

The old man glances up. Ahead of him, gradually revealing itself through the gloom, is an age-weathered oblong block of grubby, off-white Portland stone, in danger of being swallowed by the

3

encroaching greenery. It's around five feet high, with a square slate inscription plate indented at its centre. The plate is dense with writing, in a font size he can't read without glasses. His gaze continues upward. There's something atop the plinth, but years of verdant growth have obscured it.

The old man unfurls and shuffles over, fumbling in his pocket for his 'readers'. He hooks them around his ears and brushes away thick, sticky cobwebs from the grimy inscription. He reads aloud the only words he can make out in the fading light.

> **"Men and Women of England,
> How Long Shall These Things Be?"**

His eyes all but disappear into the crease of a perplexed frown. The words make little sense. Curiosity piqued, he turns his attention to the mysterious shape above the plinth, hoping for a clue that will decipher the strange phrase. He scrapes back the dense ivy foliage; it crumbles at his touch. Peeking out appears to be a small, bronze head, with years of grime nestled in its folds. Still puzzled, the man licks his fingers to clean the face. He stands back to get perspective and starts when he finds himself staring into soulful, sorrow-filled eyes of a cowering dog. The dog stares back at him with a subdued, distrustful expression.

'Well, Jake, my boy. I'll be damned if this ol' fella don't look the very spit of you.'

ONE

The Rumour

BATTERSEA DOGS HOME, AUGUST 1903

Lena Hageby drops heavily onto a bench, blows out her cheeks and sucks a droplet of salty perspiration from her lip. A pained grimace gives the impression of storm clouds passing across her impish face. She's often described by society ladies, vexed by her casual beauty, as gangly. Her hair, worn in a messy chignon, is not in keeping with the expected style for a lady of some standing. Everything about her shouts of high breeding, but she appears to go to some length to disavow her privilege. Although fashioned from expensive fabrics, she wears her dress and footwear with a deliberate air of carelessness: an unbuttoned waistcoat; a white blouse opened a little too low for propriety, its grubby sleeves rolled up; scuffed, uncared-for boots. Her long-suffering mama, in exasperation, often laments about why her daughter feels compelled to push the boundaries of respectable dress so.

Lena's expression reflects her struggle with what she's just heard. She stares at the source of her distress, willing him to take back the story, erase it from her consciousness. Her words tumble out, tripping over each other in their eagerness to deny the horror.

'Are you quite certain? Surely not in this day and age? I will not, cannot, believe it. There are strict rules against abuse of this kind. You *must* be mistaken!'

Lena shares the narrow bench with Roger – the reluctant bearer of the news and a dog warden at the Home. He shifts awkwardly, slightly uncomfortable at being in such proximity to a woman who could never be mistaken for his wife. Roger is of a similar age, but one couldn't guess so: he wears each of his twenty-five years heavily. His seen-better-days, worn leather shoes are polished to within an inch of their lives. Overalls, although near threadbare at the knees and elbows, are starched and precisely ironed by Mildred, his adoring new bride. His general bearing reveals – in stark contrast to Lena's insouciance – a deep pride in his appearance. He's all too aware of his social standing and is intent on portraying at least a degree of respectability through his attire, even at work.

Roger, frowning, remains adamant the story he's told her is God's own truth. 'I've had it on good authority. It's happening, and it's widespread. Them medical schools, the doctors working there, they've no heart. Think they're above the law, can do whatever they like to 'em poor creatures, and it ain't right, Miss Lena. It really ain't.'

They both stare sightlessly ahead. A dozen dogs of various sizes, scruffiness and indiscernible parentage are bounding around the gravelled exercise paddock in a state of rampant over-excitement. Delighted to be in the open air, however sticky and humid, they stretch out their stiff limbs. They play-fight, chase their tails and snuffle one another's rear ends – a habit Roger always has found excruciating when in a lady's company. But the dogs, having no time for social niceties or decorum, continue their rough and tumble, loving their all too brief sniff of fresh air, freedom and each other.

Lena wraps her arms around herself, as if protecting herself from the horrors Roger has revealed. His words flaying her soul. Tears well up unbidden. She forces them down. Flushing scarlet, she exclaims, 'But there're laws against this barbarism! It can't be allowed. We must put a stop to it, for Chrissakes?'

Roger flinches at such blasphemy coming from the lips of a proper lady – the only lady he's had the privilege to speak with in such an informal manner. But Miss Hageby is different, that much he knows, and thus he surmises this is how even well-bred ladies talk when they're enraged. He shrugs, exuding an air of defeat.

'It's darn difficult to prove, that's the situation, Miss. Them medical fellows are so powerful, secretive. I ain't sure what can be done. Truth be told, they're untouchable. And this Doctor Bayling, he's one of the worst, by all accounts.'

Lena bristles, irritated by his pessimism – why are the working classes always so damn fatalistic? 'Well, I'll bloody well do something about it. There must be a way. We just need evidence to prove it's happening, then we can shut it down and get them debarred, defrocked, or whatever it is you do to so-called *doctors* who commit such atrocities.'

'Exactly, Miss!' Roger replies. 'And that's the thing we can't get. Proof.'

Lena mulls it over. 'But what if I went along? Attended one of these horror shows and saw for myself what went on? I'd be a witness. Then we'd have our proof.' Roger frowns, alarmed at what he's hearing, but before he can remonstrate Lena's attention is caught by yelping, the dogs are playing rough, snapping, growling at each other. 'Errol! Jasper! Cut that out now.' The dogs stop in their tracks, startled by her tone. She rises and strides over, grabbing each by the scruff – one a lively small, wire-haired terrier, the other a short, stocky, ragged-eared bulldog cross. Despite the discrepancy in bulk, it's the terrier that appears to have the upper paw. She leads them back to the bench and gives them a good talking to, before tousling their fur and planting kisses on their noses. 'Ooh, I can't be angry with my darling ruffians for long, can I? Now, be off with you, and no more fighting, you hear?' She lets them run off back into the fray, staring after them. A troubled frown invades her forehead. 'But where are they getting these wretched creatures from, Roger?'

Roger shrugs. 'Dunno, Miss. Stolen from families? From the streets? And I guess some folk, evil swine, just breed 'em for sale to these places?' Lena looks unconvinced, her frown deepens.

'So, what d'you reckon? You think we can get into one of these, these *demonstrations?*'

Roger, head cocked, observes her, his admiration barely disguised. But his eyes cloud as he works through the implications. 'Well, in theory, I s'pose you could. But you can't just waltz in, you know. Them places are only for students of medicine, and I ain't sure they even let the lady students in. You could get yourself 'rrested.' A shadow passes across his eyes as a worse fate occurs to him. 'Or manhandled by 'em navvy types they 'ave guarding 'em.'

Lena scoffs, a haughty nonchalance, not the slightest put off by his disquiet. To Roger's further consternation, she reaches into her skirt pocket and produces an enamelled cigarette case, flicks it open with a practised ease and proffers it. 'Care to join?' He feels obliged, even though he's never smoked – Mildred wouldn't approve. She lights them both, ponders a moment. 'You just bloody watch me, Roger! I've a knack for getting into places I'm not supposed to be!' She grins at him, then glances at her watch. Roger admires it: dainty, ladylike, rather at odds with her overall demeanour. A filigree gold bracelet encasing a porcelain, hand-painted watch-face bearing the legend 'Tiffany & Co'. A year's wage wrapped around her slim, elegant wrist.

'Oh shit, is that the time? Must dash. Jasper, Toby, Butch, c'mon old pals, your time's up too. Back to the kennels with you.' She squints through the curling smoke from the cigarette clamped between her lips as she struggles with their leashes. 'Same time next week ... as long as I ain't got myself 'rrested by then?' She winks back at him as she vacates the yard, three obedient dogs trotting at her heel.

Roger shields his eyes, staring after her silhouette, dog-leads in one hand, a gravity-defying tube of tobacco ash in the other. His face betrays his consternation at her latest profanity, but also awe and, truth be told, a latent desire for this fearless, gutter-mouthed lady, who doesn't baulk when dealing with dog muck or bathing the smelliest of their waifs and strays. His love-struck grin morphs back into a worried frown as he imagines what trouble she could get herself into. He scrunches his untouched cigarette into the gravel and, with a heavy sigh, begins the challenge of rounding-up a dozen exuberant hounds.

Lena turns the corner. When she is sure she's out of sight, she stops and leans against the yard wall, her mask of haughty confidence melting away. She kneels to better hug the dogs tighter and buries her face in their none-too-fragrant hair. When she looks up again, a solitary tear is wending its way down her perfect, apple-pink cheek.

TWO

Mrs P

ELMFORD MANSIONS, BATTERSEA, OCTOBER 1903
Eliza Blackwood, dog-tired after an interminably tedious shift, fumbles, all butterfingers and thumbs, with her key. Eventually it registers. She leans into the solid oak door, encouraging it to open with the dead weight of her shoulder. It reluctantly gives way with a weary groan that could have emanated from Eliza herself, and she almost topples into the flat.

The front door opens directly into the cosy, overstuffed sitting room, so there's no escaping what awaits her. Her eyes scan the aftermath of the supper party Lena hosted last night for the latest batch of Union recruits. Eliza retired when it was still in full swing, with the excuse of an early start at the library. She'd tip-toed out before dawn had forced its sleepy tendrils through the heavy velvet curtains, purposely ignoring the wreckage, hopeful Lena may see fit to tidy up a little when she arose from her leisurely, work-unencumbered, slumber. But no, of course not! What was she thinking? Lena has a convenient blind spot when it comes to recognising her own slovenliness. Eliza knows well enough by now her companion doesn't see, or *chooses* not to see, the chaos she creates around her. Expecting someone – be it her nursemaid, various nannies, mother, the *daily*, and now Eliza – to clear up after her. In all fairness, she couldn't claim she wasn't forewarned. She cringes as she recalls the gasp of horror that escaped her lips when Lena, with a proud flourish, first revealed her shambles of a flat. She hoped she'd masked it as a shriek of delight at the sheer size of the place – which was indeed a mansion compared to her own shoe-box-sized lodgings – but the queer, disappointed look Lena threw her suggested otherwise. Over the year they have cohabitated she has managed to instil a modicum of orderliness to their home, but, of course, Lena continues blithely in that exasperatingly messy way of hers, blissfully unaware of Mrs Rumble, their maid, and Eliza's efforts. Eliza has learnt to live with it – almost.

She removes her gloves and hat, and places them, with great care, in their allotted space. She shrugs off her coat, picking off a microscopic piece of fluff before hanging it. She still can't believe she owns such a beautiful garment – a velvet creation, midnight blue with a bold flower embroidered lapel. It's her pride and joy, given it would've eaten up a full month's wage. It is one of Lena's hand-me-downs, of course. Eliza always gets first dibs when she tires of items, often after only a few outings. But who is she to complain? Lena's cast-offs have transformed her meagre, threadbare wardrobe and Eliza remains quietly thankful for her friend's spendthrift ways.

It is the smell that assails her first, the lingering, sharp tang of stale tobacco. This is particularly exasperating as she has – *they have* – established a rule on not smoking inside. Lena must have passed the cigarettes round once Eliza was tucked up in bed, fast asleep. She favours a particularly punchy Turkish brand, flakes as black as sin with an even more pugnacious stench than the Capstans favoured by stevedores. The tendrils of smoke seek and claim residence in the deep velvet plush of the curtains and the cloth of the antimacassars. The only way to rid the whole flat of the tenacious odour was to remove the offending items to the backyard and thrash the very devil out of them with the carpet beater. The ferocity which she applies to the task helps to dissipate her frustration at Lena's repeated violation of the rule.

Next comes the assault on her eyes. There are – God help her – coffee cups, whisky glasses, *petit four* saucers everywhere: discarded on occasional tables, down beside the settee and peeking from behind the Hageby family portraits on the overmantel. There has been no attempt to clear them after Eliza bid the ladies goodnight, pointedly collecting the empty pudding bowls and taking them to the kitchen before retiring. What the blazes is she? Lena's unpaid skivvy? It damn well feels like it half the time.

Eliza slumps onto the settee. She valiantly tries to ignore it, but she cannot help herself, her eye keeps getting drawn to the chaos of the room. All the while she is growing more and more exasperated by her impossible housemate. She reaches to unlace her boots and release her swollen, aching toes. She must have covered five miles or more, up and down the stacks, the stock-take proving far more exhausting than she imagined. She massages her feet gently, tiredness now catching up with her. Her studies will have to wait awhile. But ... she can't settle, cannot relax, not with all this disarray colluding to destroy her peace of mind. Mrs Rumble is not due back until tomorrow, hence she knows the room will remain in this state unless she does something about it.

She struggles back up, feet throbbing in protest. Mumbling under her breath, she hobbles around the room, snatching up discarded pamphlets and scrawled-upon cards with sketched-out plans for forthcoming events. She rips and scrunches the paper, relishing the sound and feel of destruction. That'll ruddy teach her! She tosses the balls of ruined paper into the fireplace, ashy remnants of unburnt coke pellets still in the grate. The next time Lena flusters, searching for her ideas for the latest suffrage campaign, she'll deny all knowledge. It is a pyrrhic victory. She turns from the mantlepiece, resigned to dealing with the rest of the mess, hoping in doing so she'll dispel the grumpy mood that's threatening to consume her. As she passes an open doorway, something inside catches her eye. She reverses, pushes the door, and enters Lena's bedroom. She tuts in annoyance as she tiptoes across a floor littered with half-laced corsets, a grubby bodice and crumpled silk stockings to reach the closet. The wardrobe's doors are wide open, and there, nestled incongruously among the many dresses, skirts and a never-worn ball gown, are two sets of men's clothing. The formal attire hangs forlorn, awaiting warm bodies to give them life: well-pressed trousers with a knife-edge crease, matching jackets, white, starched work shirts, a tie, a cravat and two stylish waistcoats. She rubs at the fabric and frowns, at a loss to what Lena is doing with this implausible set of garments?

In all the time they've lived together, Lena has not *once* stepped out with a gentleman friend. Not once mentioned a man's name in a context that didn't involve a derogatory comment – her beloved Papa excepted, of course. In fact, Eliza would bet a farthing Lena's not once moderately indulged the advances of her legion of admirers, such is her level of disdain for the opposite sex. But... maybe she's wrong about her? Maybe she doesn't know Lena as well as she thought? They have never discussed the issue. It seems undignified, unladylike, to discuss men thus. Anyhow, Eliza would cringe to admit her ignorance, being the grand old age of twenty-six, and not even a chaste kiss on the hand from a suitor. Perplexed, she leaves, shutting the door on the mystery, and returns to continue the clear-up.

Eliza retrieves an empty tray from the sideboard, and scoots around the room, loading it carefully with the grubby evidence of last night's revelry; grimacing at the dainty bone china saucers, now despoiled with ash and cigarette butts. As she reaches for the coffee cups discarded beside the crimson velvet chaise longue, her foot connects with something solid beneath it. Puzzled, she kneels to peer underneath and freezes at the sight: a small earthenware dish. She catches her breath. She thought she had collected up all of Elgee's things weeks ago. She gently traces her finger along the name carved into the curved side of the bowl. 'Rest in peace, my dearest boy,' she whispers.

The very first time she glimpsed him, he had been snugly enveloped in Lena's arms. They were both waiting for Eliza to emerge from the Hansom that had just transported her and her life's possessions, contained within one battered leather trunk, from Tooting. She descended from the carriage, gingerly feeling her way down to the narrow metal step, a little unsure of its placing, that being the first time she had travelled in such a contraption. She would have happily taken public transport, but Lena had insisted on a cab, her words hitting a raw nerve: 'It's most unbecoming for a woman with aspirations to be lugging her most private possessions around in a trolley bus, Eliza.'

She had stood on the pavement, smiling and squinting up at Lena, trying to make out what on earth her new friend was cradling so delicately in a patchwork blanket. Eliza trailed the driver up the sweep of shallow, off-white Portland stone steps. He deposited her scant belongings outside the glossy, pillar-box-red front door of the mansion block and theatrically doffed his cap to them both, eyes cast down, shuffling foot to foot. Lena slipped something in his hand, and he was off, back down the steps in a thrice. It was deftly done, well before Eliza comprehended what had taken place. She frowned momentarily – she was perfectly capable of paying her own way! But her attention was soon diverted by the sight of a pale pink nose framed with delicate white whiskers, followed by a fluffy black head tentatively poking out of the colourful woollen folds. The cat, for he had not yet been named, had joined their new family the day before Eliza moved in. Lena had nursed him back to health after he was handed into the home by mud-larkers who'd come across a tied hessian bag washed up on the bank below Chelsea Bridge. Of the four kittens inside, only one was still alive – and barely. A bedraggled, half-drowned ball of black and white matted fur and gammy eyes, no one was hopeful the kitten would survive, but Lena was determined. She'd dried him off, kept him warm by opening her blouse and tucking him in to her bosom – laughing off the raised eyebrows and furtive lascivious glances of the men working there – and hand-fed him morsels of liver and milk until he was out of danger. Revived, he stared up at her with hazy olive-green eyes so full of gratitude that Lena was hooked. That was that: there was no doubt he was coming home with her. She had saved his life, she reasoned, so was beholden to protect him for the rest of it. It was fate, she informed Eliza that first day they were all together in the flat. In the space of just a week, she'd unintentionally gathered together a complete family: unorthodox it may be, but family, nonetheless. Little did Eliza suspect it at the time, but Elgee was just the first in a long line of surprises that made living with Lena so unpredictable, often infuriating, but never, ever dull.

Eliza sighs, smiles wanly, and straightens up, continuing her narrow-eyed scan for more malingering crockery. She spies several chocolate and almond sweetmeats sitting untouched and abandoned on a saucer; she pops a dainty looking morsel in her mouth. The intense saccharine chewiness of the marzipan centre causes her to blink rapidly, but the sweet sensation lifts her mood somewhat. She hums tunelessly while rounding up the rest of the dregs. Her tray now full, she navigates around a precarious mound of dinner plates and pans on their cramped kitchen table, and delicately places the porcelain into the already full Belfast sink. Reluctantly, she makes a start on the dishes, but she's distracted, her thoughts returning to the puzzle of the cloth magpies nesting in Lena's closet. A crack jolts her. She stares down at the fragment of sharp porcelain still in her hand and droplets of blood colouring the dishwater. Damn and blast. She turns, seeking a rag to stem the flow.

She starts as she senses movement in the flat. Returning to the sitting room, she is taken aback to encounter Lena, returned earlier than usual from the Dogs Home. Lena, equally surprised to see Eliza, quickly pushes the front door shut. Her attire is, as always, in disarray, grubby. Eliza eyes her with mild annoyance. She has such beautiful – not to mention expensive – clothes, but she is so careless with them, it breaks Eliza's heart. Lena glances over, quick to lose her cagey look, replacing it with a perfectly innocent grin. She adopts a cutesy, childish tone, a tone Eliza's well-acquainted with and one that puts her on high alert.

'Oh Liza, my dear, I'm thrilled you're here. I come bearing gifts. I've a surprise for you.'

Eliza smiles, cautiously. She involuntarily scans the room for evidence of this *surprise*. Nothing obvious, but then her eye snags on a half-empty gin bottle on the sideboard. She cringes at the image it conjures up. 'Lena, *cariad*, that's sweet of you, but last time you *surprised* me I ended up on a gin-palace stage, as inebriated as a Tilbury docker, warbling Lloyd George knew my father – woefully out of tune.' Her cheeks flush crimson. 'Thank heavens there was no one we knew. If anyone from the library had been there, my reputation would've been ruined.'

'Ah yes, still can't believe you'd never partaken of mother's ruin before then.' Lena chuckles. 'What a tedious life you led before you'd the good fortune to meet me.'

'That's hardly surprising if you knew my mam and da,' Eliza retorts. 'Mind you, a drop or two of the devil's brew in their tea now and then might've made life a tad more bearable.'

'Oh well, they don't know what they're missing,' Lena fires back.

Unwittingly, Eliza's mind's eye replays the still excruciatingly vivid scene of that debauched night at the Princess Louise. Against her better judgement, Lena had coaxed her up Holborn way for a civilised night out on the town, or so she had been promised, something to cheer her up after what happened to Elgee. The evening started so innocently. Eliza gasped when she first stepped inside. It was undoubtedly a beautiful place, as decorative and brightly lit as one of Prince Albert's famed Christmas trees. Its sparkling, jolly interior disguised its wicked secret: the most dangerous array of alcoholic concoctions that would pickle a navvy in two tots. It was her first, and, heaven forfend, last experience of that evil liquor – Hogarth got it right! Never again would gin pass her lips. Lena is still chattering.

'Anyway, you'll adore this. No gin involved, I swear. Unless you fancy a little Dutch courage before...?' Lena grins.

Eliza's face contorts in mock horror. 'Absolutely not! So, what is it *this* time?'

'Well, I know you'll think it's too soon, but she was in need, and

15

we've been so lonely without him and anyway, I couldn't resist, she's such a darling.'

Eliza, face hardening, cottons on to what Lena's eluding to. Her lips morph into a fine impression of a prune. 'But Lena, we've discussed this. It *is* too soon. Elgee's not long in the ground and losing him so young was awful. Only now I found his bowl. It brought it all back.' She takes a deep, determined breath. 'No, Lena. I forbid it.'

Lena's shoulders sag. Her head drops and her bottom lip protrudes. She stares imploring through impossibly long, dark eyelashes, her sapphire eyes brimming – she knows how to work it – but Eliza remains resolute. 'We're not rescuing another, not now, and that's final.'

Lena holds the look a moment longer, then shrugs, reaches to open the door, grinning back at Eliza. 'Oh dear, well, it's too late now. She's here, and she's staying.' With that she scoots out and returns with a wooden crate, used to transport marmalade oranges from Seville judging by the emblem seared onto its side. She sets it down, removes the hessian sack covering its top. They peer in. It is not oranges they are viewing.

Staring back up at them is a tiny, worried-looking kitten, no more than eight weeks old. A grey tabby, displaying all the shades of an ominous, storm-laden sky. Her eyes, not yet turned, are still a gorgeous, vivid cornflower blue. She sports a torn left ear and, when her short patchy bald tail shoots up, it becomes clear the tip is missing and has been crudely stitched. She silently mews a timid hello and with that one pitiful cry Eliza's rock-solid resolve deserts her as easily as the fine Gower sand that flowed through her childhood fingers.

Eliza gently lifts the kitten out, a mere scrap of fluff, skin and bone, weighing nothing. She feels her trembling and her heart is pounding rapidly. She cradles the kitten in her palm and, with a feather touch, strokes her tiny, fragile head. The kitten buries herself into the crease of Eliza's elbow, her heartbeat slowing and her

16

trembling subsiding. Eliza rocks her gently. In time, the exhausted kitten falls asleep.

Lena observes the scene with a self-satisfied grin. Eliza glances up at her friend, realising she has given in far too easily. She attempts to resurrect her most displeased frown, but fails miserably as a gentle snore breaks the silence. What a pushover she is! Eliza does not want to let Lena off that easily. After all, she has flagrantly disregarded her wishes. They had discussed this very subject just a week ago, when Lena agreed – at least Eliza thought she had agreed – they'd wait awhile before contemplating taking in another waif and stray. Now, Eliza reasons, it was an almost impossible restraint on her friend. Working at the refuge, Lena comes into contact with the most wretched consequences of man's cruelty and seeing those pitiful creatures, so appallingly treated, must break her heart. She has been volunteering there for almost two years now. It is the longest she's stuck at anything, and Eliza feels justly proud of her. She has got off lightly with just the two feline refugees, she concludes wearily.

'If we are to be keeping her, she'll need a name, I guess.'

'Well ... as you named Elgee, I hoped I might do the honours?'

'Mmm. I'm not so sure. Given you've gone against my wishes, I think you forfeit that right.' Eliza glares at her and Lena looks crestfallen. Eliza can't keep it up for long. 'I'm teasing, course you can name her. Are we keeping with the theme? Heroes?'

'But of course. We're nothing if not sticklers for tradition, are we not?' Lena reaches over and strokes the snoring fluff ball, careful not to wake her. 'I want to call her – wait for it – can you provide a drum-roll please?' Eliza obliges. 'She will henceforth be known as Mrs Pankhurst.'

The name takes Eliza by surprise, she emits an involuntary, and, to her horror, unladylike snort of mirth that momentarily disturbs the sleeping bundle. 'Oh, Lena, we can't call her that. It's too much of a mouthful, for starters. And it isn't, in anyone's language, a cat name.' She thinks for a moment. 'How about Millicent instead? Millie, now that's a lovely name as well as honouring an exceptional lady.'

Lena is indignant. 'Well, excuse me, madam! Did I complain when you chose that ol' duffer for a name? A sodding man at that. No, I bloody did not.'

Eliza grimaces. She hates it when Lena uses coarse language. There is no need for such profanities, especially given her refined upbringing. As usual, Eliza chastises her, and, as usual, it is water off a duck's back. 'Language, Lena, please. Elgee was a boy. What did you expect me to name him, Queen Victoria? And anyway, Mr Lloyd George is a fine, upstanding Welshman who, don't you forget, *supports* our cause.'

Lena shrugs, begrudgingly conceding her friend's logic. At that moment, the kitten stirs and opens one very sleepy eye. She squeaks another hello, more contented now. Eliza holds her up. Perversely, the sheer ridiculousness of the name is growing on her. Bringing her tiny wet nose, with its pinkish brown tip, closer to her own, she coos. 'Oh well. Looks like Mrs P it is then, little one, I'm sure you'll grow into it ... in time. But for now, you must be hungry, *cariad bach*.'

Eliza hands her to Lena so she can conjure up something suitable to eat. She enters the kitchen and is rifling through the larder when a thought strikes her. She turns on her heel and re-enters the sitting room, silently observing Lena. She has found a piece of loose wool, from one of her many expensive, now unravelling, scarves, and the kitten clumsily chases it around the sofa, spending more time on her back than on four paws.

Mrs P climbs up Lena and burrows into her neck, making a nest of her blonde curls. Eliza adopts an innocent, yet puzzled, expression. 'Oh, Lena, is there anything you might want to confess?'

Lena glances up, frowns quizzically. 'No, don't think so. Why d'you ask?'

'No special friend you've been keeping from me?' She nods towards the kitten. 'Animals aside, of course.'

Lena's eyes narrow. 'I don't know what you're blathering about. What the devil are you getting at, woman?'

Eliza fashions a lengthy pantomime stare, revelling in her friend's discomfort. 'So, you've not been sneaking the odd gentleman into your room on the sly, young lady?'

Lena snorts. 'No, I bloody well haven't. C'mon, Liza, you know me. I retain some decorum. Not much I grant you, but I *do have* standards. What on earth made you think...?' She trails off, her mind whirling like a dervish and leading her to the only obvious realisation.

'Then how d'you explain the men's clothing hanging in your wardrobe?'

Lena's expression wavers from enlightened to sheepish. Then she looks cross she's been rumbled and feigns indignation that Eliza's been sneaking around her bedroom. But Eliza knows, this time, for once, she has the upper hand.

Lena settles upon a penitent expression. 'Aaah! That. I *can* explain. I was about to tell you, truly. Remember my saying, some time back, about my conversation with Roger – from the Home? About the awful goings-on up at the university with that butcher – Bayling. Well! I've a plan to expose the devil.'

PARLIAMENT SQUARE, APRIL 1906 – THE PROTESTOR

To the casual bystander, we must appear a most incongruous army. I find the proximity of so many men, all tweed-caps and rolled-up shirt-sleeves, rather unnerving; as is the earthy, almost sour, aroma they exude. There's something – I sense myself blushing – uncomfortably arousing about their scent, a musky base-note that calls to an instinct; a deep-buried instinct that shall remain so. I adjust the angle of my parasol, to deflect one particularly ripe specimen, a ferrety-looking chap with week-old stubble and an unfortunate twitch, who had sidled up beside me. I flinch as his shoulder brushes mine; in doing so, I lose the grip on my banner. I struggle to regain my hold before the pole makes contact with my companion's forehead.

'Watch out, you nearly brained me,' she chides, but it is in good humour. And that's the thing. Observing the thousands that have joined – not just us ladies, but working men; mothers with children, and dogs, in tow; sneery anarchists, desperate to look sour, but who in actuality are rather obliging; Marxists; socialists; progressives; Latchmere Estate residents – I realise we form a motley bunch of comrades. And they all seem so positive, cheery almost, despite the sorry set of circumstances that have led to this day.

Strange, that on the march down they've been conspicuous by their absence, the 'anti-doggers' that is. Those so-called students with nothing better to do with their time than infiltrate our meetings and disrupt everything. It is strange they're not here, no sign of them at all. What are they up to? It makes me uneasy, this lack of heckling. I turn to her for reassurance. She squeezes my hand and smiles. Maybe they have given up. They should know by now they can't stop us, can't intimidate us into abandoning the cause. We will never give up; we will fight on until he is returned.

As we head up that last stretch the atmosphere is febrile, but contained – for now. It's noisy though; too loud for polite conversation. All clashing tunes and cloth-eared harmonising. I pick out anti-government chants, raucous sea shanties and, at a higher pitch, faint strands of our battle-song, sung to the tune of 'Onward Christian Soldiers'. It makes me smile. I join in, for once not shy of my inability to hold a note.

But then, inevitably, it begins.

THREE

The Demonstration

BLOOMSBURY, NOVEMBER 1903

Two smartly attired gentlemen hurry along a bustling London street. It's still officially autumn, but the evening feels distinctly wintry. A foggy dusk is falling fast and with it the temperature. The men are deep in discussion, their breath steaming, oblivious to all. Horse-drawn carriages trundle up and down the thoroughfare, cabbies swear at other road-users, all vying for space with the new-fangled electric trolley buses. Hansom cabs ply their trade in the warren-like side streets. Professional men, leaving offices late, dread the homeward journey on the recently opened, but already overcrowded, underground railway.

A closer examination of the young men reveals ... two women. Eliza shifts her tightly buttoned, starched shirt collar with an index finger. It is obvious to any passer-by that she's not at all happy to be there. Lena is talking in a grave, hushed tone.

'It's all true, Eliza. I've heard the same rumour over and over. It's an abomination. And this man, this Bayling, he's a sadist. We *have* to witness it, it's the only way to get evidence.'

Eliza looks furtive. She shivers, more from nerves than cold. Eventually, she replies. 'I don't know, it's risky. What if they catch us? We're trespassing after all. I'd lose my job if word got back, then where'd I be?'

'You're such a worrier. Nothing bad will happen for Chrissakes. We're here to attend a lecture, that's all.' Lena snorts. 'Albeit one where innocent creatures are tortured – and all in the name of *science,* allegedly.'

'Will you stop with the blasphemy? There's really no need.' Eliza halts, causing people strolling behind to draw up sharply. They issue loud, disapproving tuts as they deviate around. She glances down at herself. 'Just look at us. We won't fool no one in this get-up. We look more like bankers than students. And this ruddy thing is tickling my nose. I really can't be doing with it.' She tears off her moustache, squealing as it rips her delicate skin.

'Eliza! I took ages fixing it. It looked so authentic,' Lena exclaims. '*And* it's "we won't fool *anyone*". You do still struggle so with your double negatives, Liza.'

Eliza, her face puckering at the rebuke, continues undeterred. 'It's not like we aren't allowed in. It *is* the twentieth century, after all. Medicine's deemed a respectable calling for us nowadays.'

'I'm well aware of the bloody century we're living in, thank you. But we still don't have the blasted vote, do we, huh? Even with our supposedly liberal-minded king, we're *still* stuck in the dark ages, and these barbaric practices only serve to prove my point.'

She lets her words linger. 'Anyway, I think we look rather dapper. We'd make a pair of devilishly handsome chaps around town if we put our minds to it, don't you think?' Lena twirls and doffs her hat. Eliza stares back, unimpressed, but she cannot suppress a shadow of a grin forming. Lena completes a circle and replaces her hat, struggling to tuck the mass of blonde curls back under.

'Anyway,' Lena continues. 'It's not as if we're doing anything properly unlawful. We've mislaid our student passes, that's all.' She winks. 'Dressing as the male of the species means we'll attract less attention.' Her expression darkens. 'As you rightly point out, women may study medicine in this *enlightened* age, but I'll bet a guinea there'll not be a single one of our sex in that charnel house tonight.'

'Whatever way you want to phrase it, Lena, we *are* trespassing. We ain't invited!'

'Eliza!' Lena chides. 'It's 'we *are not* invited'. Standards please! Where *are* you picking up such *street* language? I'll not have you turn into a Cockney!' Eliza glares, annoyed with herself for such a slip.

They continue in silence, eventually turning a corner. Lena stops short. Eliza strides on, mumbling, still smarting at Lena's comments.

'Oh! Here we are. Too late to back out now.'

Eliza stops, turns, sighs, and lumbers back to where Lena stands. Both turn their gaze upwards; they stare in silent awe at the austere, flat-fronted university building. Its facade, comprising a severe, brilliant-white Portland limestone, looms over them, a Jurassic-age leviathan. Hordes of students push past a doddery old guard – seventy if a day. He's failing miserably to check their passes as they pile through the lobby into the brightly lit entrance hall.

Lena, absorbing the scene, whispers. 'See that group? Slip in behind. Keep your head down and let's be deep in conversation as we pass the old fellow.' Relieved, she sighs. 'Thankfully, there's no sign of those thugs Roger's so worried about.'

They adjust hats and scarves. Lena straightens, attempts a macho stance, deepens her voice. 'How'd I look? Manly enough for you?'

'My hero,' Eliza sighs, resigned to her fate. They take a collective deep breath, gird their temporarily manly loins, and set off. They're soon absorbed by the swarming, jocular crowd.

They join the tail-end of a noisy group. As they approach, the guard tries to stop the leader, a chap who goes by the name of Oscar. He's early twenties, expensively dressed, handsome in a boyish, sulky fashion, with that arrogant, almost cruel, air that often accompanies high breeding. Eliza dislikes him immediately. Oscar swans past, loftily ignoring the guard's impotent attempt to check his pass. His entourage follows in his wake but the others cannot mimic Oscar's natural-bred insouciance and push past the old man roughly. The women, although appalled by the students' attitude, take advantage of the guard's blustering and slipstream in behind, unnoticed and unchecked.

The throng carries them down a long, half-wood-panelled corridor, their tight proximity and odoriferous mix of beard wax, beef stew and ale belches repulsing the women. Above the panelling, dusty, cracked oil paintings clutter the walls, displaying countless portraits of identical medical men of yesteryear: all mutton-chopped solemnity and dead-eyed stare. The women ignore their uniformly disapproving glower, and glide by without a second glance. They unconsciously slow as the auditorium doors loom closer – the entrance to an ominous cave, filled with unknown horrors and cruel monsters. If they could turn on their heels and flee, they would, but the crowd's momentum makes escape impossible. Before they know it, they have been swept up and deposited within the inner sanctum of the building.

The auditorium is dimly lit, with feeble gas lights flickering at intervals along both sides of the sloping seated area. A typical university lecture theatre in style, its banality and solidity gives the women some short-lived reassurance. A faint whiff of ether and carbolic permeates. Wooden panelled from floor to ceiling, the room is windowless, with uncomfortable benches laid in curved rows. The benches fill from the back. This suits the women, who've reluctantly ended up in the front row. They slip into end seats with heavy hearts, a sense of dread engulfing them, so potent they can taste it.

Eliza fiddles with her muffler and tugs her bowler hat further down her forehead. She now laments her missing moustache, not least because of the throbbing. As she fidgets, she's noticed by a member of Oscar's group, seated behind the women.

Jack Forsyth doesn't pay much mind at first, glancing away. But then double takes, a nagging doubt alerting him to something about the twitchy young chap that does not sit right. He scrutinises him, then gasps. The smooth skin of the cheek, no hint of the day's inevitable stubble on the chin, long, delicate eyelashes and petulant, pouty lips all point to the 'chap' not being a chap at all. He stares now, making sure his eyes aren't deceiving him in the gloom. They are not. The person in front is, without doubt, a woman. But why would a female student feel the need to disguise herself? Women were allowed now and, if not exactly welcomed with open arms, at least they are not reviled or leered at, as was the case just a few years ago. So, what on earth would require a woman to conceal her sex? Fascinated, and determined to solve this enigma, he continues to stare, bewitched by her quirky attractiveness.

The room is filling fast. It resembles a fetid and smoky opium den more than a temple of learning. Packed with men – exclusively, as Lena predicted. The banter gets more boisterous as they swig from hip flasks, lighting cigarettes and cigars. As their jokey remarks about the evening's 'entertainment' become ever more visceral, Eliza shudders.

'Oh, Lena, listen,' whispers Eliza. 'It's awful. They're bloodthirsty thugs masquerading as men of science. How can they be so cruel? Please, can we get out of here? I'm not sure I can bear it. It's so much worse than I imagined.'

Eliza cannot stop herself from surveying the baying audience. In contrast, Lena's sole focus is the stage. A single electric lamp cuts through the cloying darkness and illuminates an operating table, positioned dead centre. Its presence dominates the room. The high altar to science, a potent symbol of the modern priesthood – the revered holy men of medicine.

Jack, mesmerised, continues to study Eliza. Oscar, sitting two seats away, notices he's distracted, not joining in with the banter. He leans over. 'Hey, Jack!' No reply. Oscar, unaccustomed to being ignored, shouts. 'Jacks ol' chap, what's up? You're quiet tonight. Cat got your tongue? Or should I say *dog*, what d'ya say, lads?!' Oscar, pleased at his witticism, looks to his gang for reassurance. They're more than happy to oblige. But before he can say more, the lights dim further, and his eye catches a movement.

Onto stage strides Doctor William Malcolm Bayling. The distinguished academic, physiologist and star of the evening's demonstration. He exudes a snooty, aristocratic air, but with no actual blue-blooded forebears, he's worked hard to cultivate this persona. His is a cruelly handsome face, with its aquiline profile and hooded steel-grey eyes that can, and often do, pierce a student's fragile confidence with a single, irritated glower. He takes position in front of the operating table. He demands total respect. The auditorium falls instantly silent. He nods, graciously acknowledging their obeisance. He scrutinises them in the manner of a lighthouse beam, sweeping his eyes over his audience, seeking his favourites, mentally ticking off a register. Eliza shudders, sinks further into the bench. He takes a minute to complete his survey, then lowers his head as if in prayer. As he raises it, he speaks. His voice a booming, classically trained baritone.

'Gentlemen. Welcome, welcome to you all. It's most humbling to see so many here. Foregoing, no doubt, a most glorious evening's entertainment in London's finest music halls and gin palaces.' He throws them a knowing smirk. 'Just to witness *my* simple little demonstration.'

Bayling executes a curt bow and nods in a manner that confirms he's not, in the slightest, humbled by his audience. He gestures to his technicians, waiting in the wings, who wheel on a tall metal trolley.

Upon it lies a small terrier dog, a young adult. He lies on his side, strapped down with leather leashes by the neck. His front and back paws are lashed together, his mouth muzzled. The technicians un-buckle him and unceremoniously dump him onto the operating table. They untie the limbs, place him on his back, and re-secure the leather straps to four metal rings at each corner of the table, placing his skull into a head-holder. Once satisfied the dog could not escape under any circumstance, the men leave the stage, shuffling backwards, almost genuflecting as they go.

Suddenly, the dog appears to shudder. The women think they hear a quiet, haunting whimpering. They glance at each other under lowered eyelashes, deeply unsettled. Eliza senses an all-too-familiar nausea building inside her. She feels the cold sweat trickling down her back, soaking her shirt. She scrunches her eyelids, focuses on her breathing. After a few minutes she feels sufficiently in control to risk opening her eyes, but the sight confronting her makes her wish she hadn't.

Eliza has a bird's-eye view of proceedings. She can see the wretched dog tightly strapped to the table. She observes vicious, painfully red, criss-cross scars of earlier operations on his shaved stomach and flank. From where she's sitting, it's almost as if he's staring right at her. There's a helpless pleading in his half-opened eyes, or is she imagining it?

'Without further ado I'd like to re-introduce you to our star specimen, dear Rufus here.' He gestures at the dog's prone body, unaware, or unconcerned, that the dog appears to be trembling. 'If any of you were present at earlier demonstrations, or my esteemed colleagues' lectures perhaps, you may recognise the little fellow. He's become quite the celebrity.'

Lena throws Eliza a told-you-so glance. Eliza's eyes, glistening with unspilled tears, dart around, horrified. She wants to be anywhere but here, now. Jack senses her distress. His puzzlement as to why she's attending such a morbid spectacle deepens. Even he, a medical student, doesn't want to be there, but it's expected of *him*.

As he talks, Bayling's exquisite Savile Row suit is being covered with a brown surgeon's apron. He proffers his hands to be encased in white surgical gloves. From their vantage point, the women can see the dog's not fully anaesthetised and is struggling weakly against its bonds. Bayling suddenly notices movement in the dog. He frowns slightly and gestures as if to recall the technicians. Glancing up at the clock on the far wall, he frowns again, quickly shrugs off any misgivings and carries on. He wields his scalpel aloft in his right hand.

'And now, gentlemen, to work...'

The audience shouts and claps encouragement. Eliza looks away, horrified. She swallows, fighting to contain the nausea that is winning the battle for control of her gut. Lena focuses on Bayling with a piercing, emotionless, intensity. She wills herself to watch, to witness his every move, whatever the cost.

'I'm now cutting into the abdomen. You may recall the earlier surgery where we ligated the animal's pancreatic duct. This new incision is to inspect that work and monitor healing.' He looks at his enthralled, wide-eyed audience with a satisfied smile. 'A warmup, shall we say, to the main act of the evening's performance.'

As he continues to cut, the body trembles. Surreptitiously, the women glance at each other. Their two faces, side by side, paint a reverse mirror image, the spectrum of extremes. Eliza's horror and disgust are played out on her face. Lena's shows no emotion. It's as if she's detached from reality, as if it is *she* that's anesthetised.

'Good,' he continues. 'I'm pleased to report the incision is healing well. So, gentlemen, let's begin tonight's experiment.'

The little dog's paws twitch, the whimpering audible now. His stomach is open, held by clamps left in place, the visceral, raw offal redness of his internal organs exposed for the crowd to gape at. Bayling does not replace the skin. Instead, he makes a fresh cut at the neck.

'I'm exposing the salivary glands and applying electrodes to the nerves here and here. This procedure demonstrating my hypothesis that there's a secretion of saliva in response to electrical stimulation of certain nerves in the neck.'

As he applies the current, the dog, feebly, strains against his bonds. Bayling continues, unconcerned by the movement, but becomes increasingly irate and clumsy as he's unable to initiate the reaction he expects. Time passes, Bayling continues to apply current. Finally, in frustration, he gives up. The dog ceases to struggle, now more dead than alive.

'Gentlemen, my apologies. It transpires tonight will not reveal any significant breakthroughs. The specimen is too enfeebled to provide an adequate reaction to my stimulations. I'll therefore dispatch him and, with regret, declare a premature close to our proceedings.'

He picks up the scalpel, pauses, thinks again, replaces it. 'But no, why waste the chance of practice? One of you will come and perform a further dissection. Mmm, shall we say ... removal of the pancreas? Before old Rufus shuffles off his mortal coil.'

Bayling surveys his audience, scrunching his eyes while peering into the gloom. The crowd is silent, holding their collective breath in anticipation of onto whom he will bestow this unexpected honour. Bayling focuses on a familiar face. 'Ah, Mr Latham-Ward, come, join me.' He beckons to Oscar, who is chuffed. He grins at his gang, and barges roughly through to the end of the row and joins Bayling.

Oscar takes to his task with a bloodthirsty enthusiasm, but not a corresponding amount of skill. It's excruciating to watch. The pancreas, a pink-veined, spongy, sausage-shaped organ, is hacked out and slithers, glistening, from Oscar's bloodied hand onto the marble table-top. The dog, mercifully, now appears lifeless.

Eliza sits with her eyes screwed tightly shut. She's desperate to cup hands over her ears but cannot for fear of revealing their presence. Lena sits motionless. Unblinking in her determination to witness and commit to memory every tortuous second.

The dissection is now complete, and, on Bayling's command, Oscar plunges the scalpel into the dog's heart. A final, dying whimper sees something snap in Lena. She leaps up. This jolts a hypnotised Eliza from her inner sanctum into a gruesome, visceral reality. Her eyes shoot open, she takes a moment to realise what has happened. Lena, incandescent with rage, has the look of a caged animal. The pent-up fury that's been building this last hour, the worst hour of her life, is violently regurgitated. She releases a howl of despair, a primal scream of anguish at man's inhumanity.

'You're barbaric. Evil. You saw he was conscious, suffering. Yet you kept on with your torture. Sadist! We'll stop this. It's illegal, and we've the proof right here. And witnesses.' She gestures with a manic, wild-eyed stare. The crowd boo and jeer.

Bayling, shocked into an astonished silence, belatedly grasps the situation. 'What the blazes? Have you completely lost your senses, man?'

At that moment, someone behind yanks her hat. As it is pulled free, her hair is released from its temporary prison and cascades down her back. Bayling baulks at the sight. 'Jesus wept, it's a bloody woman.'

As her disguise falls away, a gasp ricochets around the room. There's a moment of silence before the crowd erupts. Students gesture obscenely at Lena, and the jeering, sexist taunts, resume with intensity.

Eliza comes to in an instant. She gathers her wits and, with an almighty effort, she stands, turns to Lena, grabs both her arms and shakes her. 'Lena, we have to leave NOW! Do you hear me? They'll be coming for us. We've got to get out.' No response from a catatonic Lena. There is nothing for it: Eliza slaps her – hard. 'Now, Lena. Damn it, woman, run.'

Lena's hand flies to her smarting cheek. She looks agog at Eliza. The realisation of the trouble she has caused is sinking in. Eliza snatches their belongings, pushes Lena and they stumble out of the row and race up the stairs, as fast as they have ever run in their lives, aided, it must be said, by a lack of fussy, ankle-length skirts.

Also gathering his wits is Bayling. Veins in his neck popping, eyes narrowing to slits. He turns to Oscar, standing slack-jawed and gormless, and hisses. 'Get after her *now,* man. Teach that bitch a lesson she'll not forget in a hurry.'

The women are pawed and grabbed at as they pass. Luckily, the men are too inebriated to be a genuine threat. But then, one clamps a paw-like hand around Lena's ankle. She falters in his iron grip. She is trapped. His other hand snakes its way up her inner thigh. She kicks out wildly, her boot making contact with his groin. The man doubles over, shrieking in pain, loosening his grip, and she slips from his grasp. 'You vicious bitch! When I catch you, I'll rip you apart like that worthless hound back there.'

Oscar, always eager to please his mentor, leaps from stage, unaware he's still holding the bloodied scalpel. He gestures to his gang to give chase. Jack, still seated, stares after the fleeing women. He is bewildered, conflicted. He fumbles around, intentionally impeding his friends as they try to push past him. They eventually make it to the gangway and give chase, but the women have a good thirty seconds on them thanks to Jack. In the uproar and confusion, Jack slips away.

The women arrive at the door. It is shut fast. They grapple impotently with the heavy bronze handle, not helped by their sweat-soaked palms and a debilitating panic. The hall reverberates with obscenities of what the men will do to them when they catch them. Hysteria is rising, the drunken mob gaining ground. Eliza grabs her jacket, wraps it around her palms and with both hands twists the handle – back and forth, back and forth, it doesn't give an inch. The noise of the crowd is deafening. They aren't going to make it! One final desperate wrench and it gives. She yanks the door open and they flee the hall with the cat-calling and jeering ringing in their ears. Moments later, students tear through the hallway after them.

The auditorium slowly quietens. Oscar and his mob are off in pursuit of the women. The rest of the audience scatters like drunken beetles now it is clear the evening's bloodthirsty entertainment has come to an untimely end – *just like that unfortunate hound*, they snigger. The students emerge into a right pea-souper of an evening. The freezing, sulphurous smog envelops them in its claggy embrace as soon as they step outside. A sharp frost is settling underfoot. They are on the lookout for a convenient watering hole or a whorehouse – if they are in luck, both – to escape the chill and continue the evening's sordid pleasures.

Only Bayling is left in the auditorium, a solitary figure silhouetted in the shadow of the electric lamp. He reaches behind and clumsily unties and throws his gown to the floor, muttering incoherently. He storms off.

As the gaslights fade on the now-empty stage, a technician reappears pushing a trolley, its squeaking wheel echoing in the ominous stillness of the deserted hall. He unbuckles the leather straps binding the dog's neck and legs and grabs the still-warm corpse by its feet, showing him no more respect in his gruesome death than he did in his pitiful life. He tosses the body onto the trolley and begins his trek down to the bowels of the slumbering building. As he passes through dim, gas-lit corridors, the only sound is the trolley's rhythmic, high-pitched screech. He unlocks and throws open a back door leading into a narrow alleyway where the building's medical waste is discarded – the sordid remains of the day's experiments. It awaits collection by the army of dustmen, with their horse-drawn, tarpaulin-covered carts and strong stomachs, who appear after midnight to cleanse the university of its dirty secrets. As if by magic, they vanish the city's detritus away, though where to no one is sure, but out of sight, out of mind. No one cares as long as it is gone by dawn.

The technician gathers up the limp body, its fur now matted with blood and other bodily fluids. He curses as yellow-green intestinal bile from the gaping wound in the dog's flank oozes over his hands and soaks into his overalls. He dumps the carcass onto the apex of an already festering mound of body parts, a tangle of internal organs gleaming in the light reflected from the corridor behind. The man turns away without a second glance and re-enters the building; the door clanks shut. He bolts it securely and trudges back to his laboratory, seemingly without a care in the world.

The little dog, free of pain at last, appears almost peaceful, laid out on his makeshift funeral pyre.

FOUR

The Plan

ELMFORD MANSIONS, LATER THAT NIGHT

A door crashes open. The two women tumble into their sitting room, both dishevelled well beyond what could be called right and proper for ladies, or, indeed, gentlemen. Half-dazed still, they come to a shuddering halt; they take a moment to decompress, not quite believing they are now safe from their pursuers and the brutality they have just witnessed. Eliza tears at her overcoat's buttons, dislodging her hat as she struggles to remove her arms from the sleeves. To her fevered mind, the garment is infected with all the evils of that lecture theatre; she *has* to get rid of it. It crumples to the floor, where it joins the bowler hat. Eliza kicks at them. She gasps as her eye catches the wide-open door, she lurches towards it, slamming it shut. She fumbles with the bolt, finally ramming it home with a grunt. Pressing her back into the wood, she splays her arms across the door frame – defying anyone to enter. Lena stumbles across to the drink cabinet. She grasps the whiskey decanter and pours them both a generous measure. A significant measure of the amber liquid misses its target as an attack of the tremors invade her hand. She joins Eliza, who's now slumped on the settee, and hands her a glass. They sit staring into the fire's dying embers, whiskey undrunk, the cut crystal tumblers reflecting occasional sparks from the hearth. Lena shakily lights a cigarette, sucking on it with a frantic desperation. Eliza, for once, does not chide her. Each is caught in their own waking nightmare, remnants of adrenaline still pumping around their exhausted bodies.

34

Eliza is the first to break the silence with a mournful, primitive cry, her body quivering as despair overwhelms her. Lena reaches to console her friend, she herself a cauldron of emotions. Overriding everything is her aching sense of guilt for forcing her dearest friend to live through the horror. Yet, she is also abhorred by what she has witnessed in an academic institution with supposed strong moral codes. A temple of learning, where scientific advances sometimes required unpalatable decisions – but taken within the bounds of ethics, compassion and the damn law, for Chrissakes.

Into this commotion wanders a sleepy Mrs P, now a fluffy, confident adolescent, almost doubled in size in just two months. Alarmed by her beloved mistress's guttural sobbing, the cat jumps into Eliza's lap. She nuzzles her, bunting cheek on cheek, to all appearances wanting to smooth Eliza's anguish away. Lena cannot bear the sound of Eliza's misery and strokes her hair. 'Ssssh. Shush now, it's all right, we're safe now. I'll make this right, I promise.' She cups Eliza's chin, tilts it up and wipes away the torrent of tears. She holds her gaze. 'This barbarism cannot, will not, be allowed to continue.'

Eliza's crumpled, blotchy face tells its own story. Her voice rasping, almost incoherent. At last she stutters. 'But – What – Can – We – Do?'

'Stephen. Stephen Coleridge. I'll talk to him. He's a friend of Mama's, a barrister, *and* involved in the Anti-Viv movement. He'll know what to do.' She hugs Eliza, laying her head on her friend's shoulder. 'We'll get that butcher, bring him down, I promise.' She lifts her head, fixes Eliza with a contrite gaze. 'I'm so, so sorry you had to witness it. I'd no idea it would be that awful. If I'd known, I'd never have made you come.'

Eliza remains inconsolable, but much of the raw emotion has now been spent. Her tears are less angry, falling in trickles rather than a deluge, her anger replaced with a defeated, desolate air. 'But, what? What *can* we do, in all honesty? It was horrific, and so wrong, but we'd be taking on the might of an entire medical establishment, not just him – Bayling.' She turns, square on, to Lena. Their eyes lock. Eliza's despair is palpable; Lena can taste it in the air between them. 'They'd crush us, Lena. We're just two hysterical women who had no right even being there. We've no power, no influence, no *voice.*'

'What we witnessed is illegal, Liza. Bayling cannot deny that basic fact.'

'But why, how? Yes, it's barbaric, inhumane. Unethical, certainly! But illegal? This kind of experiment, it's allowed, isn't it?' Eliza's body sags. She hugs Mrs P tighter, burying her face in her soft silky fur until she mewls.

'That's it. What he did tonight, specifically *how* he did it, it's not allowed. That's the point. *And* he admitted it in front of the entire audience, for Chrissakes.'

Lena notices Eliza's grimace at the blasphemy, and steels herself for the usual reprimand. She finds herself disappointed when it doesn't arrive.

Lena rises and walks to the old oak bureau, which squats in the corner of the room. It serves as a dumping ground for her extensive collection of pamphlets and other literature – both Mrs Rumple and Eliza being *strictly* forbidden from tidying it. She delves into a piled-up heap, tossing irrelevant papers aside and creating a new paper mountain on the carpet. She mumbles. 'It's got to be here, I'm sure, Stephen gave it me ages ago, where the hell...? Ah ha, here.'

She brandishes a well-thumbed legal-looking document. It has a royal crest on the cream vellum cover, and the title: *The Cruelty to Animals Act 1876.* She flicks through impatiently until she reaches an earmarked page. She clears her throat.

'Researchers cannot be prosecuted for cruelty. *But* animals must be properly anaesthetised unless this would interfere with the point of the experiment. Each animal must be *used only once.* Although several procedures regarded as part of same experiment are permitted. The animal *must be* killed when the study is over, unless doing so would frustrate the object of the work.'

Lena glances over, her look urging Eliza to understand the significance. Eliza frowns, staring sightlessly into the fire's embers, absorbing the words, struggling to make sense of them.

'Can't you see? He's breached every part of this.' She pauses, steeling herself.

'For one, it was clear the dog was not anaesthetised properly. He was conscious, struggling, throughout.'

Eliza grimaces as the scene of torture seeps unbidden into her mind's eye.

'For two. He stated they'd used the dog before, Bayling and other brutes like him, *and* for separate experiments. It was obvious from the scarring he'd been repeatedly operated upon.'

Tears prick at Eliza's eyes again. She dismisses them. The time for tears is over.

'We have the bastard, Eliza.'

Eliza, more in control now, cannot let this pass. 'Language, Lena, please. There's no need for coarseness. We've witnessed enough of that tonight to last us a lifetime!'

A whisper of a smile plays on Lena's lips; she's glad to have her friend back.

'We do, though. He's breaking the law. We'll get him vilified, struck off even, or... Oh, I don't know. But, God help us, we can do something. We've proof – we witnessed it. Anyway, Stephen, Mr Coleridge, will know what to do, of that I'm sure.' She nods with the look of defiant confidence only the privileged can get away with when they are, in actuality, not feeling confident at all.

'But how do we prove any of this? We weren't supposed to be there, *and* you've just said the law states he can't be prosecuted for cruelty.' Eliza sighs. 'What grounds will we have to shame him, or anything else?' She trails off, lost in her own doubt. An elongated silence fills the room. Eliza glances up, puzzled. She's shocked by the expression on Lena's face.

'Lena, *cariad*. What is it? What's wrong... Lena?'

Lena remains silent for what seems a lifetime in her typical chatterbox world. She takes a long breath, sighs it out, steeling herself.

'It's just, well, you know ... you know when I lost control in there.'

'Mmm, yes, that took me a tad by surprise, I must confess. I thought we were keeping a low profile. *Not* drawing attention to ourselves!'

Lena frowns. 'Yes, yes. You don't have to remind me!' She hesitates, unsure of how and where to start.

'So, over the last months we've had these young men coming to Battersea, applying to adopt our dogs. There was a time, over the summer, when they were visiting regularly, a few of them a week. Sometimes the same chap would come back in a brief space of time with excuses about his mother, or sister, wanting a dog, too. I thought little of it, until... Well, until that conversation with Roger, it got me thinking. After that we were much more wary. So, when the rumours started increasing regarding what was happening at the medical schools, we clamped down. We're wise to them now, but they were convincing. We've tightened our procedures. They've to prove who they are and their residence, and we keep a record of them, so we know if they come back suspiciously soon, whoever's on duty.'

Eliza raises an eyebrow, looks warily at Lena. She hesitates before asking. 'What are you saying? That they take them for, for experimentation? No, please God, no one could be that heartless. After everything these poor creatures have been though. No. I can't, I won't believe it.'

Lena hesitates. 'Well, I'm not so sure, but that poor soul on the table tonight looked very much like a stray I cared for some months ago. One I became particularly fond of.'

'Oh, Lena. No, surely not.'

Lena stares into the fire as she recalls her time with him. In her mind's eye she is tending to a small brown terrier dog, who's eating lustily from a bowl, ravenous after their walk along the riverbank. When he's licked the bowl clean, he jumps up at her, and she scratches his cheeks, drawing him close to bury her face in his wiry fur. She recoils at the pungent odour. 'You need a bath, my boy,' she admonishes him gently. She throws a stick, he retrieves and diligently drops it at her feet, cocking his head to ask for a repeat performance. Lena flinches as she notices the raw whip-like scars on his leg; she picks him up, hugs him close. 'There, there, my sweet, nothing will hurt you again,' she whispers into his chewed-up, battered ear.

'Jasper, I called him, a terrier of some type. It was hard to tell which. Such a sweet, friendly little boy. Responded to the slightest kindness, even though signs of abuse were obvious. He was found lying in a road near Borough Market in an awful state, as if he'd been bait in a dog fight but was too wounded to be patched up so was just abandoned on the street. A kind soul found him and brought him in. I was there, so I took him on and bathed and looked after him until the veterinarian came to treat him.'

'Oh please, no, don't say it.'

'After some weeks of care, he was responding well and definitely on the mend. I thought maybe we could take him, but we still had Elgee then, and I didn't think he'd take kindly to us welcoming a dog into his home – although I wish to God I had done that now. Anyway, a few weeks later a young man came in and took him.

'A student type, well-to-do. The staff were a little surprised he chose Jasper, given he looked so beat up, mongrelish. I didn't get to say goodbye. I pray it wasn't him, but that's why I lost control. I convinced myself it was Jasper on that slab and couldn't bear it.'

Lena crumples, grabs at the bureau for support. For all her strength, retelling the story proves too much. Eliza rushes over and throws her arms around her friend, hugging her close, feeling hot tears of anguish and rage soak through her starched cotton shirt. They stand, rocking back and forth as if comforting a crying baby. Lena weeps herself into an exhausted silence. Eliza leads her back to the settee and takes Lena's hands in hers.

'Lena, *cariad*, I get it, I really do. And my heart breaks to think it might have been Jasper, but even if it wasn't him, it was some other innocent, tortured soul. So yes. I agree we must do something. And yes. I believe you might be onto something with the wording of the Act. But you're right: we need help, Mr Coleridge's help, to unravel this, to *prove* this legally.' Eliza's words seem to hit home, because Lena brightens somewhat. She smiles wanly, her eyes hinting at their true bright blue colour, the dull, cloudy hue of sadness washing away. She runs the back of her hand across her eyes, and blinks rapidly.

'You really think so? Truly?'

Eliza nods guardedly, her mind awhirl, her cautious nature fighting to be heard over this uncharacteristic show of resoluteness. 'Although we'll need statements from others there. Otherwise, it would be our word against his, and based on what I saw of those bloodthirsty rotters, that might prove tricky.'

Thinking of the men she encountered in the auditorium makes Eliza doubt her new resolve, but it's too late to waver now. 'But we have to try, otherwise tonight's horror show would've all been for naught and that would be unbearable.'

Lena, rather taken aback by this atypical boldness, claps her hands. 'I knew you'd understand. I couldn't live with myself if we did nothing.' She starts plotting, her brow knitted in concentration. Eliza glances over warily; she knows that look. More often than not, it means trouble for them both.

'Yes, but we must be careful,' Eliza counters. 'We can't just blunder into this as we've done in the past with protests. This is serious, Lena. Let's not be reckless. We'll be dealing with extremely powerful men who'll take a very dim view of outsiders meddling in their affairs. And let's face it, we're not just outsiders, we're *women*!'

Lena's not listening, she's scheming. She paces the length of the rug that covers the polished floorboards. She stops, spins around and pins Eliza with that look, a determined gleam in her eye.

'Sooo, how about tomorrow we confront Bayling? There's no time like the present. Challenge the devil direct. We'll demand he stop this cruelty or else we'll...'

Eliza looks up sharply, a shadow of foreboding darkening her eyes, but she says nothing. She hasn't the energy or wherewithal to argue, exhaustion now consuming her. She rises, disturbing Mrs P as she does. The kitten gives a disgruntled squeak and jumps off the settee in disgust. Eliza scoops her into her arms as she heads to her bedroom. She turns as she reaches her door, her tone weary, but not unsympathetic.

'Goodnight, Lena. Try to get some sleep, *cariad*.' She grimaces. 'I hope you don't have nightmares.'

FIVE

The Library

The following afternoon, a solemn-looking Lena hesitates at the entrance to Battersea's Central Public Library. A modern red-brick, three-storey construction, it features a fairy-tale turret to its right side, but, curiously, no match on its left. The overall effect being rather unsatisfactory and decidedly lopsided, as if the builders had run out of bricks, money, or both. Lena takes a steadying breath, then marches up the stone steps, passing under the red and cream lollipop-striped archway into the fusty smelling foyer. An air of obstinate determination trails in her wake as she makes her way down the gloomy, windowless central corridor, passing the newsroom on her right and the magazine reading room, packed with ladies absorbed in the latest *London Illustrated News*, to the left. She sweeps up to the first floor, accessed by a stone staircase winding around its balustrade of ornate ironwork and oak. Once there, she enters a double-height, galleried reference library with an open-timbered ceiling and a regiment of slim, tall windows that gives it a light, airy aspect. She pauses as her eyes adjust, slowly focusing on the swirling dust trapped within sunbeams, and it comes to her mind that the vision illustrates a perfect example of Brownian motion. Ooh, get me! Lena experiences a momentary flush of pride that she can recall anything from Miss Beale's chemistry lessons. She smiles fondly as she breathes in a familiar, comforting essence, all musky tomes and bees' wax polished into the reading desks. This place, the smell, reminds her of Eliza. Lena occasionally visited the library when the urge to appear bookish and intellectual took hold. It didn't last. She hasn't the patience for tedious stories of helpless damsels awaiting rescue by the inevitable ghastly prince, or, indeed, turgid accounts of kings past. Papa frequently chides that she has the attention span of a goldfish. She lets her fingers scuff over book spines as she saunters up and down the steep valleys of shelving in search of her friend.

Somewhat to her shame, she figures the last time she entered this space was well over a year ago, and that was to meet with Eliza, rather than for any more scholarly pursuits. It was the day after their fateful first encounter at the quaintly named Tooting Ladies' Tea and Debating Society. Her face clouds. She'd attended the event on a whim, and very nearly turned around and left, given the frosty reception she'd encountered on arrival.

She shudders involuntarily. It does not bear thinking about that she and Eliza might never have met, and that she might still be floating around her large, echoey flat, lamenting her – albeit self-imposed – solitude. She had never lived alone before and, truth be told, did not enjoy it half as much as she'd imagined. Not that she ever admitted as much to Papa, who was constantly coming up with the names of 'respectable young ladies with impeccable breeding' – his *exact* words – with whom she might consider cohabiting. She suspected his primary motive was to saddle her with a guardian, as she had refused the idea of a live-in maid. Someone of a temperament quite opposite to hers, who would curb – as he euphemistically put it – her more exuberant antics. She resisted these would-be chaperones as robustly as possible without causing undue offence. However lonely she felt, she had no desire to fill the void in her life with a frivolous creature of the type she'd encountered aplenty at Cheltenham Ladies College. She swore their only goal, the single topic occupying their vacuous minds, was to ensure they married well and began breeding as quickly as decorum allowed. They appeared nonchalant towards the fact they were receiving an education most of their gender could only dream of. She did so hate to disappoint Papa, but she had standards to uphold, and becoming a debutante, even belatedly, did not feature in her plans! Such issues are of no consequence now, as, since her serendipitous meeting with the remarkable Miss Blackwood, all thought of those ghastly women has been exorcised; even Papa has come round to her choice of companion. Eventually.

They met on one of those airless, oppressive summer days when it felt like London was suffocating beneath a city-sized candlewick bedspread. Lena was moping round the flat, conscious of that familiar, creeping sense of futility her position in society often evoked: an emptiness that threatened to turn her mood melancholic. There were no suffrage-related activities to occupy her and she wasn't due back at the Dogs Home until the following week. Bored or not, she certainly wasn't in the frame of mind to pick up a needlework, a twee 'Home Sweet Home' tapestry her mama had bought as a housewarming gift, and was fated never to be completed. Idly, she picked up the South London news-sheet. Nothing of interest stood out. She flicked through to the section 'Gentlewomen of the Parish' and there she spied it: a meeting to discuss the parlous state of girls' education, scheduled for later that afternoon. Tooting was an area of London she'd never had occasion to visit, but one she was curious to get a feel for, given its deliciously seedy reputation. And, although genuinely interested in the subject, what swung it was a promise of tea and cake to accompany the debate. Lena could never resist cake.

With a renewed enthusiasm, she chose her clothes carefully so as not to look too grand, dressed her hair haphazardly, shouted goodbye to Mrs Rumple and headed out. She had decided to forsake her usual Hansom and ride the tram for the sheer novelty. Everyone, it seemed, was riding the tram system these days, given the increasingly malodorous side effects of having so many horses pounding the overcrowded streets. Those equine by-products were the bane of the society lady's life. With multiple petticoats, and over-long skirts sweeping the floor as they promenaded, the likelihood of coming a cropper on a pile of steaming manure was as high as the stink it gave off in summer. *The Times of London* estimated, to a chorus of nervously rattling teacups, that within decades, the streets of London would be buried under nine feet of the stuff. Fortunately, the electrical tram network, trolley buses and the motorcar emerged just in time to save them all from drowning in excrement.

Lena endured a most uncomfortable ride down to Garratt Lane, where she'd been quite taken aback by the unseemly proximity of her fellow passengers, not to mention the riot of aromas emanating from them – nearly as unpleasant as the dung. She'd almost turned on her heel and fled on entering the venue where the meeting was to take place. Any place of worship tended to bring her out in hives, and this murky, airless Methodist Hall lived up to her low expectations. She was a mere rabbit's whisker away from aborting the plan and instead taking herself off to Regent Street for a spot of dress shopping, with an indulgent high tea at Liberty's to follow. But, to her dismay, the door had screeched open, alerting all to her arrival, and making an unnoticed, rapid exit impossible. She peered apprehensively through the gloom, glimpsing a gaggle of women in the far corner. They turned, as one, to examine the stranger in their midst. Lena smiled sweetly, waved a cautious hello, keen to show she came in peace. They took a long, excruciating moment to decide the measure of her. In due course, they smiled, a tight, downward smile that transformed into one amorphous, lace-frilled beast with many pinched mouths. Slowly it turned away and carried on with its gossiping. I'll not find many like-minded young women in here, that's for sure, Lena thought. She was writing the trip off as a dead loss when one of the coven, a leader with a Sergeant-Major-like gait, broke from the belly of the beast and approached with arms extended, trying her level best to appear welcoming, but not quite shaking off a distinct air of exclusivity. She introduced herself as Mrs Walker, the founder and chairlady of the Tooting Ladies' Society. Lena suspected she was of the type most comfortable in her own carefully curated clique and not so keen on interlopers upsetting the delicate equilibrium. But perhaps she was being harsh. After all, she was kind enough, offering tea and a scrumptious looking Victoria sponge. It was a treat that went some way to explain the uniformly plump physiques of the regulars, and Lena couldn't help but accept a generous slice. She politely excused herself and took off to a pew near the stage. It was there she noticed, seated directly in front, the shadowed silhouette of a woman she'd not spied earlier. She sported dark chestnut brown hair, in lustrous loose waves falling halfway down her back. The woman appeared to be in some kind of trance, mumbling to herself, gently rocking back and forth. Lena got the distinct impression she didn't want to be disturbed, so she sat, minding her own business, sipping rather-too-sweet tea and losing herself to the bewitching jammy creaminess of the sponge.

Twenty long minutes passed before Mrs Walker appeared on stage to call the meeting to order and then proceeded to witter on as Lena drifted off. She stirred only as sharp clapping sliced through her daydream. The woman in front had risen and was slowly climbing the steps to the stage, head bowed as if in penitence for heinous sins. Lena noticed the woman's hands were trembling violently. As she arrived at the dais, she gripped the lectern for dear life. Lena felt a stab of empathy, shuddering as the echo of a feeling long submerged invaded her body, that sensation of icy dread when first gazing out into a hostile sea of pimpled, bored faces. Adolescent girls can be the cruellest audience.

Slowly, the woman mustered the confidence to look up and out. Lena did her level best to catch her eye. When she did, she gave her the most encouraging smile she could summon, but truth be told, Lena was stunned. The sight fair took her breath away. That terrified young woman up on the stage was quite the most impossibly beautiful creature she had ever seen. And 'impossible' was meant quite literally. Her individual features made little sense. Her eyes, a deep chocolate brown, were a touch too close together. Her complexion olive toned. Her dark eyebrows untamed, far too luxuriant to be fashionable. Her broad, heart-shaped face housed an extraordinarily generous mouth, her full top lip moulded into a permanent pout, or so it appeared. A mismatch of curious features, when melded together, produced a perfect work of art. Lena sat bewitched. She could not take her eyes off her, and it appeared her encouraging gaze was giving the woman some comfort, boosting her fragile confidence. She gradually relaxed her white-knuckle grasp of the lectern, a grip so tight Lena half expected to see permanent imprints in the polished oak.

The woman, a Miss Blackwood, swallowed, cleared her throat and began speaking, at first with a slight tremor to her voice. Her accent, Lena could tell, did not have its origins in London, but she couldn't quite put her finger on it. It was melodic, almost sing-songy. She was lulled by its tempo. It was a touch coarse in tone, her annunciation and grammar not quite the ticket on certain words and phrases. Lena deduced, and it soon became clear, that Miss Blackwood had not received the privilege of a formal, lengthy education. However, as she spoke, her wide vocabulary indicated she was well read. Lena settled back to listen, to study that entrancing face, ponder its mystery, and applaud herself for her decision to stay.

Despite her tremulous start, Miss Blackwood eventually found her stride. Her eyes flashed with passion. She spoke with such outraged indignation it clearly emanated from personal experience. Her arguments were rational, coherent, persuasive. Even if Lena hadn't been supportive of the cause, she would've been a convert after listening to Miss Blackwood's impassioned argument. She stopped obediently when signalled to by the indomitable Mrs Walker. There was a round of clipped applause which petered out quickly. Lena's solitary clapping rang out in the otherwise silent hall. She craved the other woman's attention and was rewarded with a slight blush and a ghost of a smile as she made her way back to her seat. Lena heard the pointed clearing of a throat behind her and so naturally persevered for a few more seconds before tailing off with a final, defiant 'Bravo!' The proximity of the wonderful Miss Blackwood was too much for Lena. She reached forward and placed a gloved hand on her shoulder. The woman jolted at Lena's touch, head whipping around, eyes full of trepidation as if expecting to be reprimanded for some perceived misdemeanour. Lena was quick to compliment her, set her mind at ease. Then, on a whim, she invited her to dinner that evening. What on earth came over her? She did not make a habit of asking complete strangers to supper, but she knew she had to see the delightful Miss Blackwood again.

They saw much of each other in the week following that first evening, with Lena visiting Battersea Library the very next day to escort Eliza on the ten-minute walk back to her mansion flat. She experienced a frisson of joy at Eliza's obvious delight at the proximity to her workplace and the possibility of no longer having to endure the tedious omnibus journey from Tooting to Battersea each day. With that squeal of pleasure, a pact, mooted at their dinner the night before, was agreed. Eliza was to leave her shabby, shilling-a-week lodging-house off Garratt Lane and Lena, well, Lena was over the moon to be welcoming her first live-in companion.

She continues her search for the elusive Eliza. She must be in here somewhere, surely? Lena marches up and down and past countless bookshelves before eventually spotting her, wheeling a trolley, replacing heavy volumes as she goes. Lena waves, stage-whispers a greeting. Eliza starts, sighs on recognition and reluctantly tugs her misbehaving trolley, its wheel constantly pulling to the left, over to her friend.

'So? You ready?' Lena studies Eliza, sensing the reticence. 'You have arranged to leave early, haven't you?'

Eliza studies the floor intently. Finally, she replies, in a tone that respects the sanctity of the reading room. 'Oh, Lena. I had hoped you'd reconsidered. I'm really not sure it's the most sensible idea to –'

Lena interrupts, careless of such sanctity. 'For pity's sake, Eliza, what's got into you? You're always the same. You like to pretend to yourself you're this bold campaigner, a proud suffragist, but, when it comes to it, you're just a damn coward, scared of your own bloody shadow half the time.' This tumbled out with more malice than intended.

The senior librarian, overseeing her blissfully silent realm from the reference desk, glances over her half-moon spectacles. A pinched, spinster aunt figure, she undoubtedly rules her bookish empire with an iron grip. No regular crosses her more than once. She throws an irritated glance at the women. This hardens to angry incredulity when she recognises her young protégé as a co-conspirator in the disturbance.

Eliza returns the most apologetic, subservient smile she can muster and addresses Lena, whispering.

'One of us has to be sensible. Let's not be reckless. If we'd blundered into every foolhardy cause you've taken up, you'd have had us arrested a dozen times by now. And we know full well what happens to women who end up in Holloway!'

'Oh! So foolhardy now, am I? Reckless? Why not come out and say it ... stupid! That's what you think, isn't it?'

Eliza holds her hands up in an attempt to silence Lena. She is well aware of the glower penetrating the back of her head which, more than any words, perfectly represents her superior's displeasure. But Lena will not be mollified nor silenced.

'Since when did you turn into my bloody father, huh? I don't need lecturing on propriety for Chrissakes. I get enough of that at home, thank *you* very much!'

The librarian, enraged by this continued transgression, rises ominously and unleashes an unfeasibly long, steam-powered 'Ssssh'. Eliza grimaces, mouths a 'so sorry' and grabs Lena's arm. Lena, not best pleased at this manhandling, tries to wriggle free. Eliza holds tight and marches her out of the room.

Once they're out of the librarian's sightline, Eliza continues. 'Look, let's calm down, there's no need for unpleasantness. Arguing amongst ourselves won't help anyone. I've been thinking. Surely a safer move would be to write to him first, formally. An official legal letter.'

Lena rolls her eyes. 'Oh, how utterly splendid, a letter indeed. That's sure to rattle his teacup and no mistake!'

Eliza ignores the acidic tang of sarcasm. 'We'd lay out how we can prove he broke the law. How we witnessed it all, and how we'll not hesitate to take it to the highest level if these cruel practices don't stop – immediately.'

Lena's face adopts a sullen expression more suited to a spoilt, tantrum-prone two-year-old. Despite visual evidence to the contrary, Eliza remains hopeful she's getting through to her.

'We'll get your Mr Coleridge to draft it, in proper legal speak, and take it from there.' She pauses. 'I really don't see how barging in on him today will help. It'll just get us into trouble and forewarn him of what we're planning, ruining the element of surprise.'

Lena sighs. Eliza brightens. It's to be short-lived. 'But we agreed Liza, we agreed last night we'd confront that butcher. Now. Today.'

'We didn't quite *agree,* Lena. You just announced that's what we'd do. I didn't get much of a say in the matter, did I?'

'The last thing he'd expect is the *lunatic women* from last night to turn up and challenge him,' Lena continues, showing no sign of hearing Eliza's rebuke.

Eliza frowns. She opens her mouth to reply, but Lena is on a roll now.

'We'd *have* the element of surprise, now, here, today. It must be worth a go. Come on, for me. Don't be a coward; nothing bad will happen. He cannot touch us in his own office, in broad daylight.'

'That's really not the point. I just don't think it will help our cause.'

'Anyway, he hasn't a clue who we are, so you'll not get in trouble here.' She waves her arms around. 'If that's why you're fretting so?'

They stand glaring at each other, eye-to-eye, inches apart, neither willing to give in. Stalemate. Lena breaks the silence. 'Oh, forget it, suit yourself. Go back to stacking your precious books, because that'll make all the difference to the world. I'm going to confront the fiend, with or without you.'

She tears her arm from Eliza's grasp, turns on her heel and flounces down the corridor. Eliza sighs heavily, staring after her. She can't risk letting her go alone. God knows what trouble she'd cause for herself.

'Lena, wait.'

Eliza dashes back to retrieve her coat, hat and bag. She appeases the librarian with soothing words, promising she will make up the time twice over, mutters her goodbyes and rushes to join Lena who stands at the top of the stairs, drumming her fingers on the handrail. Eliza passes her and continues down the stairs. Halting halfway, she glances back up at her impossible friend. 'Well? Come on then, what you waiting for? Let's go confront the *fiend*?'

Lena, beaming triumphantly at Eliza's retreating form, follows her down and out onto the pavement with a renewed skip in her step.

SIX

The Confrontation

UNIVERSITY COLLEGE LONDON, BLOOMSBURY
The lift attendant silently glides the metal door open. Eliza and
Lena stand together. Lena motionless, chin held high. Eliza, try as
she might, cannot keep her foot still – tap, tap, tap. They face a
windowless vestibule, its gloomy aspect somewhat chased away with
fancy Art Nouveau electric lamps. Across from them, wedged into
a modest chair, a fierce-looking gatekeeper. Fifty-something,
matronly, her meagre desk out of proportion with her heavyset
frame, Miss Ethel Dunratty represents a formidable psychological,
and physical, barrier to her master's office beyond. The women
shuffle out, stop dead as Dunratty raises an accusatory eyebrow.
Lena is temporarily flummoxed, her brain racing. She takes a breath,
then with an astonishing arrogance born of entitlement, strides up
to her. Eliza, always vigilant to potential trouble, trails in her wake.

'Good afternoon, Miss...' Lena trails off. 'Is he in by chance? My
friend and I were passing, and I thought, what the hell, I'll drop in
on my favourite uncle.' With that, Lena sweeps past and is at
Bayling's door before Dunratty, who in twenty years working for
the good doctor has never heard mention of a grown-up niece,
objects. Lena knocks and, without pausing, opens his office door.
'Uncle Bill, you old fox, it's been ages, how the devil *are* you? Mama
sends her fondest, but complains she's utterly forgotten what you
look like.'

Eliza, slack-jawed at Lena's audacity, scoots in behind her. She shuts the door in Dunratty's scowling face with an innocent yet victorious grin.

It takes a moment for their eyes to adjust. The floor-to-ceiling windows provide ample natural light and panoramic views of the busy London streets below. The office is half wood panelled, the walls above groaning with framed certificates and degree scrolls and interspersed with grainy, sepia-tinted daguerreotypes and modern black and white photographs of Bayling smiling, shaking hands, with a roll call of medical dignitaries. There are no family photographs.

Bayling lounges in a green Chesterfield chair behind a large, well-organised, buffed mahogany desk. The room exudes an unmistakable academic aura. He stares sightlessly, fingers steepled, deep in thought. He is torn from his musings as the door swings open.

He is startled, but not displeased, to see two attractive young women enter. His pupils widen then disappear into slits as he recognises Lena, but he cannot quite disguise his appreciation of her obvious charms. Dumbfounded, he takes a moment to calculate how to deal with this unforeseen turn of events. Deciding on a dignified approach, he greets them with a grace that, in turn, throws them off balance.

'Ladies. What an unexpected pleasure. Come, take a seat. May I offer some refreshment, perhaps?'

Dunratty's spherical profile is visible through the half-glazed office door. He notices, smiles, and turns to Lena with a conspiratorial wink. 'And how is my dear sister? Well, I trust?'

The women approach, pointedly *not* sitting and mutely refusing the offer of tea. A faint aroma of bees' wax blended with expensive sandalwood cologne helps soothe their disquiet – for the moment. A stand-off plays out, neither side knowing quite what to say next. Bayling, impatience a virtue, rises, unfurling to his full six foot two. He emerges from behind his desk. To Eliza, he is reminiscent of a tiger prowling, eyes steadfast on its prey, nostrils slightly flared, absorbing their essence. She swallows hard. He's intimidating close up, something they hadn't fully appreciated from viewing him on stage. Even Lena – until this moment resolute – is having second thoughts about the wisdom of confronting him directly. Although she'd never admit it, a letter of legal intent feels an attractive alternative at this moment.

His impervious grey eyes scan the full length of them, from boot to bonnet. He's getting the measure of both, but concentrating on Lena. The women instinctively recoil, having the sense that they, too, are being flayed, visually peeled open and intimately probed. Bayling, satisfied, concludes his examination. In a quieter, amused tone, he addresses Lena.

'You're the interloper from yesterday, are you not?'

Lena opens her mouth, but discovering it suddenly parched and uncooperative, makes do with a curt nod.

'I can only assume you're here to apologise. To make amends for that... Mmm, how to put it? That *performance* last night. Am I right?'

A charming, yet obsequious, smile. He pauses, anticipating her fulsome apology. She's still incapable of speech.

'I, of course, am gentlemanly enough to accept your *mea culpa*, Miss...?'

He executes a tight, theatrical bow. His eyes lock onto hers, goading her, not knowing what to expect. This was turning out to be deliciously entertaining. Lena remembers a trick from her time in school plays, bites her cheek to lubricate her mouth, and finds her voice.

'Dr Bayling, what an absolute dis-honour to meet you, finally. Albeit a relief to be here, rather than watch you torture defenceless creatures.'

Bayling, caught off-guard, inwardly winces. 'Madam! Less of the hysterical language if you please. I see, like many of your sex, you're inclined towards melodrama.'

'On the contrary, sir, I'm *restraining* my language; manners don't allow me to articulate what I really think.'

'There was no torture on display last night, be assured,' he replies, smiling condescendingly. 'I've licences to prove everything I do is sanctioned, humane and beyond reproach.'

'I'd heard so much told of your barbarism, I made it my unpleasant duty to see for myself if it could be true.' She glares at him. 'What we witnessed proves it. You should be ashamed. *Sir.*'

He adopts a patient, weary expression. 'I appreciate how it may appear that way to the uneducated, overly sentimental eye, but you *are* mistaken, my dear. Your outburst perfectly shows why the fairer sex should be discouraged from attending such procedures. Women are far too susceptible to squeamishness.'

'Please desist with your patronising tone, sir. You're a butcher, no more, no less, masquerading in a medical gown.'

Eliza swallows an incredulous gasp. Lena's surely gone too far. Bayling drops the mask.

'Oh! I see. That sweet, innocent face of yours belies your delusion. You're one of those! Your lot have been causing us much, shall we say, irritation lately.' He snaps his hand, as if flicking a persistent fly.

'You would do well not to be so dismissive. We can prove you acted illegally last night, and we *will* act on it.'

Eliza stands a step apart, wary of the interplay unfolding between them. She has the distinct sensation of being once removed from the action, an understudy viewing, from side stage, a two-handed play.

'You're misguided, of course. But I cannot blame you. You are disposable pawns in a complicated game. Unwitting foot soldiers for a bunch of ignorant fools who view vital scientific experimentation as paganistic ritual.'

'Doctor Bayling, please don't make the mistake of underestimating us. We're not credulous, uneducated or whatever other fallacies you and your cronies perpetuate to keep us *little women* in our place.'

Maddeningly, Bayling finds himself increasingly enticed by this cocksure young woman. Her stubborn petulance, the proud jawline, blue eyes blazing with passion, is arousing his ardour, despite himself.

'Is that so? Then here's your chance to prove you're worthy of intelligent debate, Miss...' He pauses. 'You have me at a disadvantage, I don't know your name.'

Lena glares back. Bayling shrugs nonchalantly, but his eyes betray him.

'You and your comrades are marauding vandals – nothing more. Prime examples of modern-day Luddites. And just as misguided, misinformed and doomed to fail as their namesakes.'

Lena moves to disagree, Bayling raises a palm to silence her. 'They, you, can't stop progress, it's as inevitable as the tide.' He sighs. 'Tell me, how on God's earth can you live with yourselves? Valuing a lesser creature's fleeting pain over human suffering, when the former can easily help reduce the latter?'

'We don't value one form of pain over any other, sir. All suffering should be eliminated, but humanely. What we demand is that you stop your cruel practices and now. You may have your precious licences, the morality of which we aren't here to debate. But all the licences in the empire do not give you a free pass to inflict unnecessary suffering on defenceless creatures you've strapped down, sliced open...'

'Enough!' Bayling barks. 'It's despicable how these anti-vivisectionists behave, and you, young lady – whether you are one of them or not – proved yourself no better by your embarrassing overreaction last night.'

'There are ways and means Doctor Bayling, and you were the one behaving despicably last night, sir, not us.'

They face off like bare-knuckle fighters sparring in the moments before contact. Their physical inequality receding as two equal and opposite forces of nature lock horns.

Eliza glances towards the closed door. She spies Dunratty, ear pressed against the glass, and watches her silhouette scuttle away as the volume in the room rises. Eliza frowns, sensing trouble, but her attention is drawn back to centre stage.

Bayling sighs. 'May I beg an indulgence? Allow me to persuade you my intentions are pure, worthy even. That I'm not the monster you perceive me to be.'

'I fail to see how you can possibly justify your torturous practices.'

'Listen without prejudice. If you are capable. Then judge me as you will.'

'We'll hear your argument, sir, if you, in turn, will entertain ours.' Lena straightens her sagging shoulders, puffs out her chest, girds herself for the next round.

Bayling nods. 'My life's purpose has been to contribute to easing man's suffering. Whatever you think of me, I don't relish inflicting pain on my specimens. It's regrettable, of course, when they suffer. But it's for the greater good. Can you not see that?'

'No, Doctor Bayling, I really can't. I cannot see why you must inflict unnecessary agony to achieve your ends, however honourable you believe them to be. The end can never justify the means when there's abject misery, torment and inhumanity at its core. That's the classic torturer's excuse. There's no justification. What we witnessed was deplorable. And to what end exactly? Your experiments were ultimately pointless. Just hours, weeks even, of torture for that poor creature. All for the sordid entertainment of those heathens who have the barefaced cheek to describe themselves as students of medicine.'

'I strive to help my fellow man – rich, poor, I don't discriminate. It's that simple. How can you resent – despise me even – for a lifelong vocation to relieve suffering?' The women glower, unmoved. Annoyed his performance isn't having the desired effect, he changes tack.

'Are you a woman of faith by chance? Do you read scripture?'

'I cannot see what religion has to do –'

'Book of Genesis, chapter one, verse twenty-six?'

Lena, not a diligent student of any subject that bored her, and religious studies fitted that bill, has no clue to his reference. Eliza, the victim of a strictly Calvinistic Methodist childhood steeped in Old Testament fire and brimstone, knows the passage instinctively.

She steels herself, steps forward, clears her throat and recites in a clear, confident voice which belies her inner terrors.

'And God said, Let us make man in our image, after our likeness: and let them have dominion over the fish of the sea, and over the fowl of the air, and over the cattle, and over all the earth, and over every creeping thing that creepeth upon the earth.' Her smile is saccharine sweet.

Bayling tears his gaze from Lena, stares at Eliza as if noticing her for the first time. He nods sagely, welcoming her words.

'Exactly. Thank you, Miss...? You make my point succinctly. Man was given dominion over *all* lower forms of life. Therefore, it's our God-given right to use the Earth's resources, in any way we so choose, to assist humanity in its struggles.'

'Oh?' Eliza feigns surprise. 'Do excuse me, but I beg to differ. I suggest you are interpreting scripture in far too narrow a fashion.' His smile fades, eyes narrow.

Eliza continues with a boldness she doesn't feel. 'God also instructed man to be the *steward* of his creation. Forgive me, I cannot quote the exact passage, but I believe it instructs us toward the humane management of all creatures that walk the earth, to care, to tend to them kindly. We contend your abuse of that poor creature last night puts you in direct conflict with God's will. Would you not agree, sir?'

She exudes a familiarity with the subject that surprises her; the tedium of Sunday school comes good at last. Bayling's forehead creases into a chevron; her superior knowledge of Old Testament teachings discombobulates him. A topic, truth be told, he knows precious little of except the selected passages memorised to serve his purpose. His eyes flash annoyance at being outplayed by this meek slip of a thing.

'My research efforts have already led to the most extraordinary breakthroughs. They will, if I may be so bold to say, revolutionise medicine.' Bayling gestures to his wall of fame in what he considers a self-effacing manner. 'Saving thousands of lives, relieving the suffering of millions more. It is I who's on the side of the angels. *I* who am fulfilling God's will, protecting the one, the only, species He fashioned in his own image.'

He addresses them as a head teacher would speak to naïve, over-sentimental pupils.

'So, dear ladies, I'm afraid it's inevitable more animals will need to be sacrificed, God's will or not. Your futile disruptions will not, cannot, be allowed to sabotage progress.' He cannot contain a condescending smile invading his face.

'I enjoy the support of the medical establishment. Add to that His Majesty's Government and, of course, the not inconsiderable matter of having the law on my side.' He smirks, adding. 'You've the backing of a sprinkling of cloth-eared *progressive* politicians, hot-headed radicals, over-sentimental suffragists, simple-minded trade unionists and ragtag groups of animal rights lunatics. We, ladies, will see who triumphs.'

'Yes, indeed Doctor Bayling, we *will* see who has the law on their side. The Honourable Mr Stephen Coleridge QC will have plenty to say on that score,' Lena adds. Bayling's eyes momentarily cloud with recognition.

'Jesus wept! What would you have us do instead? Experiment on the destitute, cripples in their hospital beds, the shackled lunatics in Bedlam, the old and discarded? Well, would you?' His tone leaks exasperation. 'Sometimes unpleasant choices have to be made if we want to progress.'

'I'm certainly *not* against medical advances, far from it.' Lena admits. 'My mother was cured with an experimental treatment that, I've little doubt, was first tested on animals.'

'Then, by all that's holy, woman, you should appreciate more than most the value, the necessity, of my work.'

'But this, your careless methods, the needless cruelty, this is not the way to achieve it. The manner in which we treat, respect, *nurture* other species defines our humanity, and your vicious, *unnecessary* cruelty last night clearly defined yours – sir.'

Lena gestures towards Eliza. 'We were there, we saw. You hide behind virtuous words, licences, your certificates and accolades, but you can't disguise it. You felt his pain, saw his suffering and continued, regardless. I swear, we'll shut you down. *We will stop you.*'

Eliza, sensing Lena's exhaustion, takes over with that unfamiliar sensation of boldness she is beginning to savour. 'Doctor Bayling.'

Reluctantly, he moves his focus from Lena's perfectly enraged face to Eliza's serene, dispassionate one. 'You seem very calm, considering.'

Bayling, bemused, raises an eyebrow. 'Considering?'

'We've eyewitness evidence you operated on a semi-conscious creature. You admitted, in public, to using the same animal in multiple vivisections. You continued your experiment for over an hour when it was clear he was suffering throughout. Your actions contravened multiple clauses of the *Cruelty to Animals Act.* There's no defence in law for ignorance. Especially from such an experienced practitioner.' She draws breath. 'You, sir, will be hearing from our lawyer.'

He turns away, concealing the wave of concern flooding his face. He frowns as he recalls his actions from last night, slamming the desk in frustration. Damn and blast. Bayling commands his face into a neutral expression and pivots to face them.

Before he has a chance to speak, the office door bursts open. Dunratty's heavy frame fills the doorway, legs akimbo, hands disappearing into generous hips. Behind her, two burly, sneering guards lurk. Bayling slams his palm out, they are not to enter yet. He looms over Eliza, index finger jabbing inches from her face.

'A word to the wise, young lady. I would not waste your time threatening me. I've many friends in exceedingly high places. Life will become extremely difficult for you and your pretty, nameless friend here, if you even dream of causing trouble for me.'

He snorts. 'Who the hell d'you think you are, anyway? I'll tell you, shall I? As you seem to have cultivated delusions of self-importance which need cauterising. You've the audacity to waltz into *my office*, threatening me, and, by implication, challenging the authority of the entire medical establishment. Seriously? Pah! No wonder you haven't secured the vote yet. Delusional, the lot of you. If it came to it, which it will certainly not, it'd be my word against yours, and who'd believe two *women* over a *celebrated* man of science?'

A dismissive hand flick. 'Now, if you please, you've wasted enough of my time. I've students to teach, *lives* to save. Good day to you both. *Dunratty*!' He turns his back and stares out of the window.

Dunratty smirks malevolently, moves aside to allow her henchmen entry. The women turn to leave, flanked by the guards. When they reach the door, Lena turns, eyes blazing. 'Trust me, Doctor Bayling, you've just made a big mistake. You've no idea what you've unleashed.'

The taller, crueller-looking of the guards grabs Lena with a roughness that causes her to gasp. The other tackles Eliza with equal force and a lewd intimacy. Eliza struggles, disgusted by his touch. They are manhandled out of the office.

Outside, Oscar, Jack and two others sit, awaiting their tutorial. They arrived in time to overhear the tail end of the exchange and peer curiously at the medley of bodies crowding the doorway. They stare, speechless, as they come to recognise the pair as the women from last night.

Jack gapes, fuming at the sight of the thug pawing the young lady that so entranced him. He's on the verge of challenging him, but refrains, realising there's precious little he can do to defuse the situation. Embarrassingly, he's also aware of his physicality; although no lightweight, he's not a match for these two meatheads. Instead, he's overwhelmed by a compulsion not to be noticed by her. He keeps his face hidden as she is frogmarched past and thrown into the lift. Lena follows and is unceremoniously shoved in. The lift door is closed on the women's red, infuriated faces, imprisoning them within its metal cage.

From the doorway, Bayling barks at his students. 'Well? What are you waiting for? I don't have all day.'

SEVEN

The Idea

ELMFORD MANSIONS, FEBRUARY 1904

Lena and Eliza pore over documents spread across their dining table. Towers of leaflets, boxes of pamphlets and haphazard piles of posters have colonised the sitting room. For once, Eliza seems unbothered by the mess. A poster hangs lop-sided on the door, declaring:

On Illegal Practices & the Plight of Laboratory Animals
A Public Meeting, Battersea Town Hall
Tuesday March 9th

Mrs P jumps onto the pile of event posters lying on her favourite spot in the window recess, and settles down to clean her nether regions in her typical, languid style. The words *"Dogs welcome"* are visible through her swooshing tail. Lena holds a pamphlet at arm's length, admiring the artwork of the cover.

'My, don't they look the part? The Society has done a splendid job. You'll take a supply for the library, Liza, won't you? The posters too? Put some up in the lobby.'

Eliza's frown deepens as she reads its content. 'Mmm, I'm not sure. They might be a little too controversial for the *powers that be*. Remember all the fuss over the suffrage leaflets I tried to distribute? They took serious umbrage. That last warning's *still* hanging over me. I can't risk more trouble. I need this job. After all, it's not like I've independent means like...'

Eliza slaps her palm over her mouth. Her last comment was not meant for airing. Lena glares, eyes narrowed, self-righteous indignation spreading like wildfire. She puffs up in that way of hers that can only mean trouble. Eliza braces herself.

'Well, that's rich,' Lena stutters. 'Let's not forget who keeps this cosy roof over our heads, Eliza. If it weren't for Papa's generosity, and mine come to that, you'd still be festering in that bloody hovel down in Tooting.' A crimson flush creeps up Lena's neck, threatening her cheeks. She can't stop herself. 'After all, a squat isn't quite the place for an aspiring lady to reside, is it? Some would say handing out leaflets is a small price to pay.' Lena studies Eliza's face and knows her words have touched a nerve. She curses herself for bringing such things up. But subtlety was never her strong point, the tone being set from that first visit to Eliza's digs.

The evening heat was cloying, the humid air plagued by clouds of insects; the women's conversation was interrupted by the need to keep their mouths clamped shut. Once out of danger of ingesting a gnat-based supper, Lena listened entranced as her new acquaintance chattered on. Her language was odd, an unusual, awkward formality to her words, as if carefully chosen in an attempt to disguise her normal diction. But what was that accent? Lilting, musical somehow, Lena really couldn't place it. Northern perhaps? She'd not had much exposure to provincial accents.

As they strolled on, Lena noticed the surroundings getting shabbier. Eventually they turned into a street comprising dowdy, three-storey, semi-detached houses with small front gardens that had become dumping grounds for all sorts of detritus. Rusty bicycles with twisted wheels, splintered wooden crates, and worn-through dockers' boots littered the place. Eliza came to a sudden standstill outside a particularly down-at-heel example. Her face scrunched into an expression that Lena perceived as embarrassment.

'Well! Here we are. My humble abode.' Eliza stood aside, opened the creaking iron gate and with a nervous sweep of her hand invited Lena through. A grimy black and white, geometric-tiled path led the way to a shallow entrance portico, its sootied white surface flaking so badly that, if it were human, a doctor would have diagnosed psoriasis.

Lena stood, hesitating, at the threshold. She was taken aback by the property, but at pains to hide her shock. She was aware of, and sensitive to, her privilege. She had not earned, either by graft or intelligence, the advantages she so freely, carelessly even, enjoyed. She was unfairly blessed, through an accident of birth, and so tried her damnedest not to judge others for where, and how, they lived. Oh, but this ... this was truly something.

To be fair, Lena could tell that 72 Crawford Road had once been a proud, handsome family home. But now, the property had fallen into almost terminal disrepair, from its dull, black front door pleading for a fresh coat of paint to the windows thick with the everyday grime of a London street. The neglected rose bushes were remarkably still clinging to life, but were almost beyond recognition, just vicious-looking thorny twigs and wilted blooms, bowed as if shamed by their reduced circumstances.

The houses on Crawford Road had been built around sixty years earlier, desirable residences for lower-middle-class families 'on the up'. Sadly, over the intervening decades, that original veneer of exclusivity had worn off. The working classes began colonising the area, it being close to the factories where they toiled all hours. Petty crime and vandalism rose and the well-to-do decided they could do better elsewhere; those that could afford to upped sticks for the more upmarket districts of Streatham and Wimbledon. So, it transpired that a certain Mrs Edith Carruthers saw an opportunity to make a tidy sum for herself by entering the now considered semi-respectable occupation of private landlady.

Mrs Carruthers had lost her husband, Arthur, prematurely, aged just forty-two. A glum looking fellow if his true likeness had been captured by the faded daguerreotype claiming pride of place on the mantlepiece. Fortunately for the avaricious Edith, Arthur – a cautious, tight-fisted man in life – had left her a generous legacy in death. She, being a practical, no-nonsense type and not one to dwell on her loss, shed her widow's weeds as soon as decorum allowed and wasted no time in buying number 72, filling each floor with poor but respectable working families, sometimes up to six to a room.

The attic was let to Eliza only because even the canny Mrs C couldn't fit a family in, such were its meagre dimensions. As her old-fashioned sensibilities prevented her from taking in a bachelor, she reluctantly took Eliza's shilling, all the while viewing Eliza's twenty-four-year-old spinster status with a permanent, suspicious side-eyed stare.

As they entered, Lena struggled to still her tongue, to not embarrass – or worse – humiliate her new friend. The first thing that struck her was the distinctive aroma of many-days-old sweat mixed with stale, rough-cut tobacco. It caught the back of her throat and she faked a coughing fit to cover up her watering eyes.

Eliza hurried Lena through the dingy hallway, their heels clicking on the encaustic hall tiles, once a vibrant pattern of sky blue, brick red, beige and off white, now dull and grimy, impacted with decades of dirt from lodgers' boots.

The stench faded somewhat as they climbed. The stairs appeared endless, a threadbare, grubby runner leading them ever upwards. Lena imagined she would run out of oxygen if they climbed any higher. Suddenly Eliza stopped and unlocked a mean little door that was set back in the eaves. She pushed it open. Lena had to duck to enter. It was garret space turned into servant's quarters, and one of the lowest rank judging by the size. How Eliza lived in such cramped, miserable conditions was beyond Lena's comprehension, but she forced her face into what she hoped passed for a neutral expression as she surveyed the interior. She vowed then she would make it her mission to release Eliza from this desolate, cell-like existence.

Eliza feels the words as a slap. Her inherent sense of inferiority, unworthiness, always lurking just below the surface, rises like bile. 'It wasn't a squat, Lena. Please don't exaggerate. I paid good money to live there. Just because it didn't live up to your exalting standards...' She pouts. An awkward silence descends, neither woman wanting to give ground. Eventually, as is usual, it's Eliza who relents, realising this could escalate into one of their petty feuds which have a tendency to fester if not nipped in the bud. 'But, yes, you're right, I'm sorry, that wasn't fair. It was wrong of me to bring up your situation. Neither of us can be held responsible for what God has deemed our respective paths in life.'

Lena glances warily at her friend. She always feels uncomfortable when Eliza brings God into the conversation, never *entirely* sure if she's kidding. But Eliza shoots back a teasing grin and Lena cannot maintain her sullen glower.

'I guess a few pamphlets can't hurt. I'll try a poster too; if it's removed, then so be it. I'll just have to throw myself at their mercy.'

'That's my girl; you're growing a backbone at last. Must be my influence.'

Eliza scowls, pokes her tongue out. She returns to the pamphlet, finishes reading, lays it down and stares sightlessly at its cover. She mulls over its words.

'Besides, the library's readers are quite the radical bunch, if their borrowing habits are anything to go by – even if management isn't. I'm sure I'll entice a few of them along. I'll drop some off at the Anti-Viv when I'm next passing, too.'

The National Anti-Vivisection Hospital, to give it its full title, was founded by one Mrs Theodore Russell Monroe. It had opened its doors to patients a year earlier on Prince of Wales Drive. Established *for the relief of human suffering by physicians and surgeons opposed to vivisection,* it swiftly became popular with Battersea's poorer residents, who had heard disturbing whispers of unethical goings-on in the mainstream hospitals.

There'd been rumours circulating for years that the sick and homeless were taken from the streets, with the promise of food, shelter and free treatment in the so-called *charity wards* of hospitals across London. Alarmingly, some awoke to find they'd become unwitting *volunteers*, used for experimentation by cack-handed medical students. Or by unprincipled physicians hell-bent on making a name for themselves, whatever the human cost. The patients of the Anti-Viv, as it became known locally, were comforted by the knowledge the medical staff there had proven themselves to be ethical, trustworthy, and had sworn a public oath never to involve themselves in such practices. Indeed, the impoverished of the borough, of whom there were many, would go nowhere else, preferring to suffer at home untreated rather than risk becoming unwilling human *guinea pigs* at the hands of those they viewed as butchers masquerading as men of science.

Eliza had once had cause to visit the hospital for a burn on her hand that looked in danger of turning septic. Their professionalism and care impressed her. Since then, she'd regularly donated magazines and books that were surplus to the library's requirements. Although the reality being, she reflected sadly, many of the hospital's patients were not in a position to take advantage of her offerings.

'Talking of the meeting, I've finished my speech at last. It was the hardest thing – reliving the whole wretched experience. I'd done such a thorough job of burying the memories, dredging them up was like being there in that torture chamber, feeling his pain all over again.' Lena exhales, a tear pricking her eyelid. She shakes it off. 'But it's done now, and after this I'll dig a hole so deep the memory will never, ever, be unearthed again. But till then, I need to rehearse. May I practise with you, Liza?'

Eliza throws her an empathetic smile. She was relieved when, at the planning meeting, Lena volunteered to retell the events of that night, suspecting that, if asked, she would not be physically or mentally up to the task. She would freeze up there on stage, in front of God knows how many people, just like she did at the Tooting Ladies' meeting. It's a vision so awful she feels nauseous each time it resurfaces. For unlike Lena, she has been unable to bury the memory of that terrible evening. Eliza has not admitted this, especially not to Lena, but she continues having nightmares. They haunt her so badly she has begun to dread sleep's insistent, inescapable siren call.

Night after night, the dog appears to her. Fully conscious now, eyes bulging in fear and pain, staring straight at her, willing her to do something – anything – to stop this. Frantic, she scans the room, but there is no one else in the auditorium; it's eerily silent, just her and the little brown dog, desperately pleading for release. But Eliza finds herself immobile, frozen in her seat as if by some invisible force. She looks down. To her horror she finds her arms bound with the same coarse black leather restraints cutting into the dog's shaved limbs as he lays prostrate on the slab. She shouts for help, but no sound emerges. She cannot count the times she is woken from such ghastly visions, drenched in sweat, but conscious enough to stifle her screams, so as not to alarm Lena. Eliza knows her memories will render her incapable of verbalising the horror. It is the least she can do to help her friend rehearse. 'Of course, Lena. Although can't say I relish reliving it either, no offence.'

'None taken.' Lena nods solemnly. 'I've persuaded Stephen, Mr Coleridge, to speak from the legal perspective, which is a real coup. But, what about you, are you minded to say something? I wish you would, you're such an engaging speaker. I'll never forget your speech at the witches' coven.' Lena smiles wistfully. She loves reminiscing about that afternoon about as much as her friend hates it being brought up, yet *again*! Eliza cringes at the mention of her first and, in *her* view, mortifyingly amateurish attempt at public speaking.

The hall had been sparsely populated when Eliza arrived. In due course, the meeting was brought to order. She was barely conscious of her name being called, but, with sharp applause ringing in her ears, Eliza's eyes snapped open. It was time!

She gripped onto the lectern for dear life, sensed the sweat collecting at the top of her high-collared blouse. It felt clammy and cold. She thought she might faint. She couldn't speak. But then her eye snagged on a young lady. Her friendly grin was a salve to Eliza's rampant nerves, alleviating her tension – and queasiness. She took a moment to gather her wits, then began.

She'd been invited to speak on the right of girls beyond ten years of age to an education, with no subjects banned. This being a cause close to Eliza's heart, she had leapt at the chance. The current Education Act was hailed as a landmark in legislation when it first appeared, being the first to enforce elementary education for all. However, weak, inconsistent implementation meant that poorer children, especially females, often slipped through the net. A loophole allowed them to be removed at ten, or younger even, if they met the 'expected standard'.

That was where Eliza's bookish nature worked against her, as she was deemed well above this 'standard' – especially for a mere girl. The assessment gave her mam and da the gift they'd wished for: an excuse to remove their daughter from what they saw as a pointless waste of her time, and, crucially, their hard-earned money. They ripped her from her beloved school at the tender age of nine and placed her in service at the Big House as an apprentice maid-of-all-works where she'd learn a *useful* trade. Why waste time on the 3Rs when she could be mastering the essential skills of collar starching and bodice tying?

Up on stage that afternoon, her indignation, all that pent-up anger, found its voice at last. And, after initial hesitation and a horrid dryness of mouth, she relished the opportunity to expunge it, vomit it out as she had her earlier nausea in Mrs C's outside privy.

'I ask you, what use are piano lessons to the inquisitive young girl captivated by physics? The art of needlework to the woman passionate about law, or deportment classes for the would-be engineer? Ladies, in this new century, I believe we can and will make great strides. Women will force entry into all remaining professions closed to us. We'll dismantle the last bastions of gender discrimination and prove ourselves equal. They can no longer justify keeping us in our place, because our rightful place is by their side, as equal in the workplace as we should be at the ballot box.'

She scanned her audience. Was she convincing them? She sniffed a distinct air of scepticism. Except for that one enthusiastic young lady, they appeared tight-lipped and dubious. But she wasn't done yet.

'Let's consider the venerated field of medicine, forbidden to our sex just a few years ago, yet now considered a respectable career choice.' She paused. 'Who could have imagined such progress? And that's within my short lifetime.' A few nodding heads. 'Witness Mrs Garrett Anderson. The first women to be accepted by the medical establishment, albeit grudgingly, as a fully qualified physician. Not content with that achievement, she's set up her own school of medicine for women. *Just for women*! Ladies, this would not have been imaginable ten, even five years ago. This is genuine progress.'

As she warmed to her theme, Eliza became transfixed by the young woman. Her stare was hypnotic in its intensity. So much so, at the close of her allotted ten minutes, she imagined she was addressing her, and her alone. As the applause came to an abrupt close, there was a lone clapping still, echoing sharply through the hall. It was, of course, the young lady, displaying the signs of blatant disregard for social norms that would come to define her.

Eliza has spoken publicly, on behalf of the Union, several times since. With Lena's encouragement she has gained in confidence and poise so much that the idea of speaking no longer fills her with morbid dread, but there's still a lingering trepidation. Eliza sucks in her lower lip, steels herself. 'Well! I wasn't planning to, but a germ of an idea's been growing, it's been nagging at me for a while now. So, I've changed my mind. I think I will ... speak, that is. Just a *few* words, mind you, to test it, see if there's any appetite ... for such a thing.' Lena's expression urges her on.

Eliza takes a breath, nervous about how the idea will come across. 'So, how about we propose some memorial, to him, Jasper, but representing all wretched creatures who've suffered similar fates? A statue, perhaps? Something that'll endure, remind us of our duty of stewardship, humanity, towards other species.' She falters, unsure now the words have been aired, she glances over at Lena, curious of her reaction.

'I thought I might propose it at the meeting. If it's popular, then we could start raising funds.' She pauses, winces. 'That's if anyone turns up, of course.'

Her uncertainty hangs heavy between them. Lena, sensing her friend's growing pessimism, gently chides her.

'Don't be daft, woman, of course they will. I've been promoting it through the local WSPU for weeks, and they are rallying groups right across London. Then there's the Anti-Viv societies, they're on the case too. It'll be full to the rafters.'

'I'm just not so sure enough people care. After all, they've too much worry in their own lives to spend time fretting about the fate of other creatures. What if it's a flop, Lena? What if nobody comes? I'll feel as if we've failed him, failed them all, and I couldn't bear that.'

'Have faith, woman. You'll be surprised at the strength of feeling. There are decent, caring people out there, Liza – they aren't all brutes like Bayling and his ilk. It *will* be packed out, standing room only, I promise. And yes, let's propose a memorial, that's such a wonderful idea. You're so damn clever. I'd never have thought of that.'

Lena gazes at her with that unfathomably fond look of hers that Eliza finds mildly disconcerting, though she can never quite put her finger on why. She shrugs and turns back to her reading, oblivious to her friend's ardent stare.

BLOOMSBURY, APRIL 1906 – THE STUDENT

Of course, I've heard the rumours; they have been circulating for weeks. This is going to be the big one, much larger, better organised than their previous efforts, and word is the Antis are planning something equally big, equally as disruptive. I try not to get involved; after all that has happened, I'm best well out of it. But there is something about this event that makes me nervous. Nervous for her, as she will undoubtedly be there, right at the front more than likely. I sense I have to be there, to ensure no harm comes to her. The Antis have been getting increasingly bullish in recent times, with their childish antics – hurling eggs at speakers, letting off stink bombs, drowning out meetings with their pathetic chants – infusing all with an increasing degree of viciousness. Worryingly, they have been supplementing their ranks with paid-for muscle, including the coarsest of men – ruffians, layabouts, dockers, pickpockets and the like – to do their dirty work for them. The kind of man who, I fear, would have no compunction about hitting a woman if it came down to it.

I'm left with no choice; I have to attend. Their final gathering point, the culmination of the march, is apparently where the trouble is to kick off. I'll head straight there.

I dress neutrally, not wanting to be identified as supporting either side if I can help it. I choose a well-worn pair of houndstooth trousers held up with braces, an open-necked, collarless shirt and just a light cotton jacket, as the day had dawned unseasonably warm for early spring. As I pass, I scoop a tweed cap from the coat rack, only realising, when I'm halfway down the stairs, it's the exact same one I'd worn to the meeting all that time ago. The meeting that heralded the start of it, and the genesis of my fall from grace. I pause mid-step. Should I go back, change it? It being a bad omen and all. But I'm already running late, so I shrug off my superstitions, tug it down over my forehead and head out the front door.

As I emerge from the Underground station, I hear faint chanting and shouting in the distance. I take the stairs to the surface two at a time, my heart racing, fearful as to what awaits me at the top.

EIGHT

The Public Meeting

LAVENDER HILL, MARCH 1904

Outside, the bright day is fast losing its battle with the encroaching evening gloom; the sun's last-gasp rays glint off the bronze weathervane that projects skywards from the central turret of an expansive red-and-cream-coloured building. At pavement level, a local lad by the name of Thomas Riley, flat capped, shirt-sleeves rolled up to non-existent biceps, is enthusiastically wielding a horsehair brush. A bucket is wedged between his feet. He's plastering paper strips embossed with *TONIGHT* across posters advertising a public meeting. Gobbets of paste splatter in an arc around him. Folk hurry past, weary after a back-breaking day at the factory. They give the boy a wide berth, paying no heed to his message.

The lad pastes his last strip. He steps back, pushing his cap back on his head to better admire his handiwork. His work now done for the day, he scoops up the bucket and makes his way up the curved stone steps of the entrance portico. He enters the spacious lobby; it never fails to impress – the new-fangled electrical lamps dazzling to his eye. He takes the left-hand corridor, boots clattering harshly on the mosaic. He passes through the Octagonal Hall, noticing how its yellow-stained, glass-domed roof glows with the remnants of the sunlight. His eye is drawn to the wide-open doors that expose the interior of the *big* hall. Inside, he spots two young women placing leaflets on the plush velvet-covered seats. He pays them no heed. He's focused on depositing his bucket and brush with the gaffer and collecting his hard-earned penny. The penny will remain in his hot, gluey palm for only a few moments before he impatiently proffers it to the taffy seller down by the Junction.

Battersea's new municipal town hall, built at the apex of Lavender Hill, is a much more grandiose affair than the public library, situated a little further down. This despite the fact they were built within years of each other and boasted the same – by now celebrated – local architect, Edward Mountford.

The frontage displays a symmetrical design built in English Neo-Renaissance style. It boasts a central wood-and-metal bell tower, balanced on either side with brickwork chimneys, that dominates its silhouette. London red brick makes up its upper storey, and warm, beige-hued Bath stone is used for the ground floor, pillars and colonnades. Its grand entranceway is a semi-circular, Ionic portico feature with shallow steps leading to heavy, ornate oak doors, which open onto a colourful gem of an entrance hall. Seven marble pillars separate arched walk-throughs, with a vibrant turquoise-blue and cream mosaic-tiled floor, edged with colourful flower garlands and its famous bee motif. The jewel in the crown is a bifurcated grand staircase, with its pink marble balustrade, that astounds visitors upon entering. It rises to a first-floor gallery, flooded with light from the glass ceiling above. Everyone who climbs its gently sloping staircase, from councillor to humble labourer, experiences a tiny glimpse into what it must feel to be royalty.

Built primarily to house the proliferating number of staff in the new, autonomous council which has recently uncoupled itself from the yoke of neighbouring Wandsworth, it has rapidly become the spiritual hub for the bold, radical thinking which the parish of Battersea is becoming infamous for. The town hall welcomes contentious meetings and opens its doors as the rendezvous point for demonstrations; it has become *the* destination for fire-brand campaigners to hold court on a variety of issues – from the rights of workers and demands of trade unions, disputes with landowners, to the ongoing fight for female suffrage. Thus, the building is the obvious choice to host Lena and Eliza's meeting, run in conjunction with the Anti-Vivisection Society, to bring publicity to the plight of laboratory animals in general, and to whip up moral outrage at the abominable actions of certain medical researchers in particular.

To the rear are situated three public halls. The largest, the Grand Hall, accommodates up to 800 people at a pinch. It boasts an arched ceiling rising to thirty feet, and is adorned with dense, decorative plasterwork and ornate ventilation grilles. Decorated woodwork fronts the platform stage, with an organ centred on the floor in front of it. Its impressive pipes act as bookends to the stage itself. Wide corridors run along both sides, above which towering arched windows bathe the hall in natural light. This magnificent room is to be the venue for the evening's meeting, although Eliza still has severe doubts about how they will fill such an enormous space.

Inside the Grand Hall, Lena and Eliza busy themselves, like the bees in the entrance mosaic. They fuss over chairs, pamphlets, the placement of the VIP seating – anything to distract from what can only be described as a disturbing lack of an audience. The grandiose wall clock, set out in the hallway, mocks them as it cheerfully chimes a quarter to the hour. The hour it is alluding to is seven: the advertised start time of the meeting. A few locals wander in, but there's no disguising the hall looks distinctly empty. They glance at the clock, then at each other. Neither speaks. Doubt spreads like a rash. No one's coming, no one cares. They continue their fussing, neither wanting to accept reality by voicing their concern.

Silence is broken as a door slams at the far end. They spin around, glance upward. A well-dressed, ruddy-cheeked gentleman of indeterminable middle-age approaches. An aura of exceedingly fine breeding and a large smattering of privilege envelops him. He strolls along the edge of the room. Eliza is none the wiser, but Lena hoots with pleasure, cracks a wide grin and waves. 'Mr Coleridge, sir. Over here.'

The Honourable Mr Stephen Coleridge squints at two fuzzy

female-shaped figures. He is too vain to admit to it, but as the years have crept up on him, he has an increasing need of spectacles. He recognises Lena only when she speaks. He quickens his pace, and is a little out of breath when he reaches them. He takes Lena's proffered hand and kisses it. 'Miss Lena, my dearest, dearest girl. What a pleasure it is to see you again. You look more like your delightful mother every time we meet.'

Lena, lowering her eyelashes, elegantly accepts his compliment. 'It's wonderful to see you too. And thank you, and the Society, so very much for agreeing to sponsor this meeting, and for speaking. It's such an honour to host you, sir.'

'You must call me Stephen, please.' Coleridge bows his head bashfully, still clasping her hands. He is as entranced by Lena as he has been by her mother for the thirty-odd years of their acquaintance; it saddens him to this day he couldn't win her heart over the attentions of the rakish, debonair Reginald Hageby. Lena politely extracts herself.

'But heavens, where are my manners? Please let me do the honour of introducing my dearest friend and companion, Miss Elizabeth Blackwood. Eliza, please be acquainted with Mr Coleridge, Stephen. He of the genius legal mind and fearless champion of all creatures – great *and* small.' He nods, a ghost of a smile acknowledging the reference.

Coleridge turns to Eliza, takes her hand, bows. 'Charmed, I'm sure, Miss Blackwood. It's a privilege to make the acquaintance of any friend of Miss Hageby.'

He raises her hand to his lips, and with a flourish, kisses it. Eliza blushes crimson, rather shocked by the brazenness of the man she's only just met.

Suddenly Coleridge's face darkens, the charming demeanour fades, to be replaced by a stern expression typically reserved for recalcitrant witnesses. 'But ladies, back to this dreadful Bayling business. There's a genuine risk I must warn you of before we take to the stage tonight.' His conspiratorial tone takes them aback.

They huddle in muted conversation. As Coleridge speaks, Eliza's face clouds. Although focused on his words, both women's eyes flicker between the auditorium and the clock. A few people trickle in, but it still looks deserted. No one is coming.

The clock's hands show one minute to seven. Then it strikes the hour. All three glance up; the room is still three-quarters empty. The women look crestfallen.

As Coleridge continues his warning, the back doors burst open, and people flood in. At last, an audience. It's a mixed bag, comprising local men and women, some still in grimy work clothes, many with dogs in tow, young, keen activist types with a self-assured confidence and shiny pink cheeks, demurely dressed suffragists, a smattering of local councillors with an unmistakable whiff of self-importance trailing them, and members of the London press, complete with obligatory notebook and pencil, accompanied by photographers. The women emit audible sighs of relief, while Coleridge, in his typical fug of self-confidence, smiles contentedly.

The women smile and wave as they recognise friends, colleagues and fellow volunteers. Lena spots Roger seated some rows back, and winks. He grins and gives her a thumbs up, recalling their conversation all those months ago and her determination 'to do something'.

'Well, she was good to her word,' he says to his companion, a fellow Battersea worker. 'Woe betide anyone that underestimates the formidable Miss Hageby, and no mistake.'

In no time, the hall's full, and, just as Lena predicted, there's indeed standing room only.

Starting later than intended, all three are positioned on stage. Coleridge and Eliza sit behind a small table to the left. They look a little lost on so large a platform. Lena is at the lectern. If she is nervous, gazing into a chattering sea of faces, it doesn't show. Her speech is laid out before her: pages of scribbled, almost unreadable scrawl. But it is there more for comfort than necessity. Lena has rehearsed so often that every painful word is seared into her soul.

As if an invisible conductor has tapped his baton, the audience suddenly ceases their chatter.

'Ladies, gentlemen, and not forgetting the dogs. Welcome all.' She scans the crowd before grinning at the sight of scruffy mongrels sitting at their masters' feet, intermingled with pampered lapdogs perched contentedly in their ladies' arms.

'It's humbling to see so many have made the effort to be here this evening. To bear witness to this true-life horror story I'm unfortunately compelled to relate.'

Lena swallows. The sudden realisation that she is about to relive every gruesome, tortuous detail, in front of hundreds of people, hits her like a tornado. An unexpected wave of stage-fright overwhelms her. She grasps the lectern, fumbles for the glass of water, panicked by this unfamiliar feeling. She struggles to get a grip, and, with a tremulous tone to her voice that shocks her, momentarily goes off script.

'Ladies, gentlemen, I apologise in advance if I become a little overwrought during this talk. To be frank with you, I've practised endlessly but, as you will soon come to understand, it doesn't get any easier. The horror isn't numbed or dampened by repetition. And sometimes my emotions let me down. So, please, I humbly ask you to bear with me.'

Her sincerity has them hooked. She takes strength from their apprehensive, but supportive faces. A final glance back at Eliza.

'Let me take you back to a cold, foggy evening, late last year. Miss Blackwood and I, with heavy hearts, attended a live demonstration, performed by one Dr William Bayling, lecturer and research fellow at the London Medical School, part of the University College. Persistent rumours had been circulating for months regarding his particular style of barbarity, and we determined we had to discover whether there was any truth to these stories.'

She catches herself. She glances at Coleridge, recalling his earlier warning not to use inciting language when referring directly to Bayling. He throws her a stern 'be careful' look, she nods acknowledgement.

'Do pardon me, I meant to say *alleged* cruelty towards laboratory animals in his lectures.' She pauses. 'Now, the medical establishment is a close-knit, secretive community and, try as we might, it had proven impossible to substantiate the rumours in any conclusive way. No one would talk, no one would break rank – not staff, not students, and certainly not the academics themselves. There was only one course of action left. We had to infiltrate one of these lectures, witness the *alleged* brutality first-hand. Then, and only then, would it be possible to tackle this man directly. To expose him for what he is.'

She stops short, realising she is in danger of losing control of her emotions, and language. Deep, slow breaths calm her.

'What follows, ladies and gentlemen, is a true and accurate account of what we both witnessed that night.'

She is a vivid storyteller, leaving no gruesome detail to the imagination. She peers out into an audience of women openly sobbing, the roughest of grown men wiping 'dust' from their eyes, others hugging their dogs just that little tighter. Journalists scribble furiously.

At the back of the hall, a group of working-class lads stand – late entrants to the event. Threadbare greatcoats and flat caps make them almost indistinguishable from the assembled throng. However, closer examination reveals a familiar face, a face that's turning a quite remarkable shade of purple – Oscar's. Next to him stands the hapless Jack, fearful of attracting attention, desperately trying to calm him. The rest of the gang are close by – some tasked with taking notes, much to the suspicious bemusement of the locals. The students' faces are a picture of indignation as Lena continues her verbal lashing of them, and all they stand for.

Lena concludes her story. Mercifully, her eyes remain dry throughout. Her relief is palpable to all in the front rows. Seconds of awkward silence ensue as the audience works out whether it is appropriate to applaud such a tale. Inevitably, British good manners prevail, and the clapping begins, followed by shouts of 'bravo' and support. She attempts to fan down the applause as it continues too long for her modesty to bear.

'Thank you. Thank you all for listening.' She shouts to make herself heard above the din. 'I appreciate it's not the easiest story to hear, just as it's not the easiest to tell.' When the applause eventually peters out, Lena resumes.

'Now it is my very great honour to introduce esteemed barrister, and Chairman of the National Anti-Vivisection Society, the Right Honourable Mr Stephen Coleridge. He's agreed to share his views on how we can, through legal, *peaceful* methods, stop this unlawful butchery from ever happening again.'

She turns to encourage Coleridge to centre stage. They pass halfway. He clasps her hand and winks. Lena takes her seat and Eliza squeezes her arm. They lock eyes. An emotion only they could ever share passes between them. They turn to study Coleridge, his entire demeanour changing before their eyes as he takes control of the lectern and then the room. His warm, welcoming persona flips, as if someone has flicked a switch, into a much stiffer, foreboding presence. He seems to have grown several inches. The audience catches a collective breath as they wait. He absorbs the tableau before him. Each attendee has the sense his every utterance will be for them and them alone. Coleridge pauses for what seems a lifetime. He begins in a deep, distinguished baritone, careful to annunciate, to lay each word before his audience as if they were precious gemstones.

'Ladies, gentlemen, what you have heard spoken of tonight... Is this not enough to make your blood run cold? If this is not torture, then I call on Bayling and his cronies to tell us, in Heaven's name, what torture is?'

First an astonished gasp. The audience were not expecting such blunt words from such a learned gentleman. Then applause and cheering erupt like a gun salute, ricocheting off the walls. It takes a while to quieten, but Coleridge is in no hurry. He stands and absorbs their enthusiasm. He has a growing sense of conviction that what he has belatedly decided to do – something he warned the women against earlier – is the right course of action, despite the risk to himself and his professional reputation.

'There stands in Gower Street the University College of London. Within the walls of that University there is a laboratory licensed for vivisection, and into its dark portals there passes a never-ending procession of helpless dumb creatures – dogs, lost or stolen from their homes, where they had known nothing but affection, follow one another down that shameful corridor into a scene of nameless horror, where man degrades his race and his manhood, and brings upon the university a smirch that time itself will never erase.'

Oscar and his gang, noting every word, stifle indignant outrage at this provocation. To their disgust, they are being encouraged to shout support. Their neighbours are eyeing them ever more warily as the evening draws on, curious to why they are not clapping, suspicious of the notes they're taking, given they're definitely not *press*.

'Sadly, my friends, I've little faith in the law to provide any form of justice for this violated, pitiful creature and the many hundreds – thousands – like him that suffer in similarly horrific, and let's not forget, illegal, ways.'

Another gasp emanates from the crowd, subdued this time. This was not the message they wanted to hear from an esteemed defender of the law. The sense of hope in the room diminishes like air leaving a deflating balloon. The mood darkens. Coleridge pauses, sensing it. He is working his audience with consummate skill. Settling on his alternative path, mentally ripping up his prepared words, he gathers himself up.

'Therefore, ladies, gentlemen… Let me instead take matters into my own hands.' He pauses, then with a determined, solemn tone. 'I hereby, publicly, and without hesitation, name Dr William Malcolm Bayling as a brutal, sadistic torturer who knowingly committed multiple offences under the Animal Cruelty Act.' He brandishes his well-thumbed copy of the Act. 'On not one, nor two, but three separate counts.'

The women, reflecting the audience, swallow a collective gulp and stare at him in disbelief. Just an hour earlier he'd been categorical in warning them off accusing Bayling directly. And yet here he is, in front of the assembled London press, denouncing a respected medical researcher and renowned academic as a sadist and torturer. Coleridge, revelling in the shock wave he's created, puffs up into full barrister pomposity, and lays out his case.

'For one, we have unequivocal eyewitness accounts, from these fair ladies here present, that the dog was conscious, struggling, and visibly distressed throughout the long, torturous procedure. This is illegal practice, my friends.'

He's building momentum now; he has the audience hanging off his every word.

'Count two – we have it from Bayling's own lips that he, and others like him, had vivisected this poor creature multiple times, over an extended period, and for different purposes. Again, *illegal*.'

The cries of disgust from the crowd spur him on.

'Finally, he forced an incompetent, unlicensed student to dissect, then kill the animal, in front of a bloodthirsty, baying crowd. For a third time *illegal*.'

Coleridge, out of breath, falls silent. Again, a hiatus before the audience erupts. At this third point the students, as one, turn to Oscar. Oscar reddens, swallowing, the last statement catching him off-guard. He had no idea that what he did was unlawful. He is suddenly growing hot under the collar, feeling faint. The desire to get out of that room overwhelms him and he abruptly motions to the others they should leave. As ever, they follow his lead, except Jack, who shuffles awkwardly, reluctant to go before the object of his desire and growing obsession, Eliza, has taken the stage.

Jack shouts to Oscar. 'I think I'll stay.' Oscar throws him a sharp look, put out by this uncommon act of disobedience. Jack needs a plausible reason why he would want to hear more of this, in Oscar's eyes, blasphemy. 'It's best if one of us does. Bayling wants a report on everything said, remember, and that other woman's yet to speak.

'I'll be fine, don't fret. After all, as you remind me, I'm working-class stock myself. I'll blend in seamlessly.'

Jack flashes his disarming grin. Oscar's face darkens, but then he nods sagely. Acknowledging the sense of the plan, he slaps Jack's shoulder.

'Fine, yes, marvellous idea, Jacks, my boy. But don't forget, our meeting's *first thing* tomorrow, so we must be prepared. And Jack.' He regards him with a theatrically ominous look, risks a wary glance around, and whispers, 'Be careful, won't you? We're in enemy territory here.' With that parting shot, Oscar and the rest slope out, their departure eyed with increasing suspicion. Jack fades into the scrum, moving closer to the front, and returns his gaze to Eliza.

Eliza rises and shuffles over to the lectern. Unbidden, memories of her first speech slip into her consciousness. However, to her relief, the old anxiety that crippled her back then is conspicuous by its absence. Admittedly, she is well-rehearsed, but the lack of nerves surprises her. Nonetheless, she is grateful for the large stand to hide behind. She grips it and looks out, expecting the familiar butterflies to make a reappearance, and yes, there they are. But it is not unpleasant. She smiles at her audience and summons the spirit of her heroine, Mrs Millicent Fawcett, any residual anxiety slipping away as easily as an otter slides from a bank into the river.

'Good people of Battersea, fellow suffragists, animal lovers, members of the press. Allow me to conclude on a positive note, rather than send you home with heavy hearts.'

Murmurs of support build in the crowd, grateful for a change in tone after Coleridge's tub-thumping dose of brutal realism.

'I end this meeting with a request. A plea that the barbaric fate of this nameless, homeless, helpless little brown dog is not forgotten. That his plight be a reminder to us all – compassionate, caring human beings, men *and* women, equal in the eyes of God – that we're not powerless.'

More 'hear, hears!' echo, bouncing off the walls.

'The medical establishment may appear too great an adversary, too powerful an authority to challenge. But I believe we here tonight, every one of us, can do something, however small, to help stop this horror. Let that dog's suffering not be in vain, lost in a fog of countless other pointless acts of torture. Let his death herald the start of the fight to end such practices.'

She gauges the audience; she still has them. 'I, if I may, would like to propose a memorial, ladies and gentlemen. Yes, a memorial dedicated to this one dog, but representative of every wretched creature that's suffered at the hands of man's thoughtless cruelty. A statue to remind us we have a duty to show compassion, kindness, to all living things.' She hesitates, unsure of her next point, as it has just occurred to her.

'I would like to repeat something Miss Hageby here once said. Something that resonated with me deeply, something I feel perfectly sums up the cause we're here tonight to support.' She smiles back at a puzzled-looking Lena.

'She said, "Our very humanity, or indeed a lack of it, will be defined, judged, by how we treat, care for, and nurture all other species we share this wondrous planet with. Not just our fellow man." Now, I'm no longer of any particular faith, but I do believe that God will be the judge of us, come the day of reckoning. And he will find wanting those of us who defy his command to be good stewards, to nurture and protect all of his creation.

'So, what do you say, proud residents of Battersea? Are you with us? Are you on the side of the angels?'

Silence. Eliza's mouth dries. They're not interested – she knew it. What a fool she's been! Then a low murmur builds. One voice amplified tenfold, a hundredfold. In no time, the room is in noisy agreement. Jack surprises himself by shouting support too, before looking around, anxiously checking that Oscar and his lackeys *have* left.

Eliza stands, allowing herself a flicker of a smile, absorbing the applause. She unclenches her fists and glances back at Lena, who is clapping wildly, sporting the broadest grin. She is quite taken aback by the level of enthusiasm, stunned into a comfortable paralysis, unsure if her legs will support her back to her seat. Slowly the crowd silences and, taking her words as a signal for the end of formal proceedings, people shift their chairs, huddle in groups, catch up with friends, or drift off home. Some approach her with offers of a penny, tuppence, a shilling from the well-to-do. Eliza, unprepared for such an eventuality, descends from the stage to join people funnelling out the door, gratefully taking their contributions. The pile is growing fast, and Eliza juggles the cascade of coins being flipped to her. Coins are slipping through her fingers. Flustered now, she struggles to contain them.

From nowhere, an upturned tweed cap appears before her. Grateful, she pours the coins in and takes possession from the hand proffering it. She raises her gaze to discover who her saviour is and finds herself staring straight into the cool blue eyes of a sensitive-looking young gentleman. She smiles coyly, taken with both his handsomeness and the intensity of his expression. When she gathers the wherewithal to fashion a sentence, the unfamiliar, coquettish tone surprises her.

'Oh, my, thank you. I was in danger of losing our first batch of donations, and that would never do.'

'No, it certainly would not, Miss Blackwood.' Jack nods, and grinning, performs a jokey salute. 'Mr Jack Forsyth at your service, ma'am. It's a pleasure to be of help.'

They gaze at each other, neither knowing what to say next. Each is shy of the other, sensing an immediate, unmistakable spark of attraction. Jack, having only briefly glimpsed Eliza close-up, is now seeing her in detail. He's transfixed – more so because she's not pretty by any conventional measure. Her chocolate brown eyes are deep set, with strong, dark, almost masculine eyebrows framing them in a half moon. Her chin is pointed, and her nose, rather too small for her large heart-shaped face, is home to a field of freckles she shows no sign of disguising, as is the fashion of the day. It's her mouth, however, that ultimately captivates him. It's her most striking feature. No ladylike rosebud lips for her. Hers are full, pouty, almost juicy in appearance. Her top lip is noticeably larger than her bottom and pronounced, which gives her the appearance of always being about to speak. Jack resists an unbearable urge to reach out and touch her mouth, trace the contours of her lips, experience their softness. Instead, he forces himself to break the silence, with no idea of what will come out of his mouth. He just needs something – anything – to distract himself from Eliza Blackwood's impossibly beautiful face.

Lena, with Coleridge in tow, is chatting to a gaggle of ladies when, struck by a vague feeling of disquiet, she glances across. She stiffens as she notices the intimate exchange between Eliza and a man. Even from a fair distance, she senses something out of the ordinary is happening. Her body tenses, a wave of unease washes over her as she squints at the stranger. She excuses herself and approaches them, keenly observing their body language. Jack is speaking, but failing to produce coherent, intelligent sentences. He's relieved when the tension is broken by Lena's arrival, but not for long. Lena draws level, and, ignoring Jack, addresses Eliza. He frowns, sensing her hostility.

'I say, Liza, Mr Coleridge and I are off to supper soon, to celebrate. Do say you'll join us.' This is presented more as a command than a request. Eliza's face drops. She hesitates. In her heart of hearts, she would prefer to stay, get to know this charming young man a little better, but she feels reluctant to refuse Lena, especially under the circumstances.

'Oh, please Miss Blackwood, I wouldn't dream of keeping you. But would you allow me the honour of calling on you again? At the library, perhaps? I'd like to help with the appeal if I can.' He pauses, grins. 'And, of course, retrieve my cap.'

Eliza starts, her eyes widening. She stares quizzically at him. How on God's earth did he know where she works? It wasn't mentioned when she was on stage.

And she is sure they've not met before. She would have

remembered him, this boyishly handsome, self-effacing young man. So how...?

Jack senses Eliza's sudden wariness and curses himself for being so careless. He has nearly given himself away.

The truth is, he followed Eliza and Lena that evening after the lecture. He hung back after Lena's outburst and slipped out of a side entrance to avoid joining Oscar and the rest in their pursuit. As he turned the corner, he spotted the women fleeing from the building, and on impulse followed them down a side alley. There had been no rhyme or reason for it, just instinct. He shadowed them, his cloak-and-dagger tailing aided by the murky fog, all the way back to Battersea. He only turned back when he saw her put a lamp on inside the sitting room.

After that night Jack returned to the area whenever lectures and practical work allowed, hoping against hope for another glimpse of the mysterious, cross-dressing woman. One morning, weeks later, after several uneventful visits and fading hope, he struck lucky. He was strolling along when the front door to the mansion block opened. Who should step out, but the woman herself? She was in a hurry, dressed in conventional attire this time; sky-blue jacket with an impressive corsage, a candy blue striped skirt, neat cloche hat, a small black patent leather bag and matching lace-up boots. She had turned left and hurried down the street. Jack spun on his heel, crossed, and followed her, keeping his distance, all the way to the Battersea Public Library. She slipped into the building and skipped up the stairs. Jack waited before following her up. He loitered in the reading room, idly thumbing dusty, musty-smelling old tomes, desperate to locate her, but she was nowhere to be seen. How could she have disappeared? After some time, just as he was leaving to get to a lecture, he spotted her wheeling a trolley. He was delighted at this sudden change in his fortunes – she worked there!

The next challenge was to discover her name. He had hung around the library as often as he could for weeks afterward, watching for her, but being careful not to be spotted by her. He was all too aware that his behaviour could be considered a little odd! He knew he had to summon the courage to talk to her, and soon, lest he be thought of as a lurker. But courage had been conspicuous by its absence – and he cursed his own cowardice. One afternoon, as he watched her leave, he overheard a colleague call out she had left behind a book. 'So, she's Eliza,' he whispered, vocalising it to see how her name felt in his mouth, on his lips. He repeated it, over and over, as he approached the same colleague a moment later. 'Oh, excuse me, you couldn't say if that was a Miss Eliza Cooper I just saw leaving? It's just she looked so familiar; I was wondering if she was the same Eliza I went to school with?'

'Ah! No, sir,' the librarian replied. 'She's an Eliza Blackwood, sir, not Cooper.' Her forehead creased momentarily, then she added. 'And she ain't married, so Blackwood's her maiden name.' She shakes her head decisively. 'It can't be her.'

'Oh well, thank you very much, my mistake, eyes deceiving me.' Jack floated out. A newfound optimism carried him. He was chuffed with his newly discovered powers of detection – Sherlock Holmes would be proud. In one fell swoop, he had discovered her full name. *And* that she was not married. All was well with the world.

'But, how, how on Earth do you know where...?' Jack flinches. He will find the question exceedingly difficult to answer with any semblance of honesty.

Luckily for him, Eliza is distracted by an impatient Lena who hands over her coat and handbag and encourages her towards the exit. Eliza allows Lena to lead her, but keeps her eyes trained on Jack, his expression shifty as he desperately tries to conjure up a plausible reason for his knowledge. He breathes a sign of relief when he realises he's being spared by Lena's desire to remove Eliza from his presence.

At the door, Eliza turns; despite her misgivings, she wants to see him again. 'Yes, yes, of course you may call on me. You'll find me at the library every day except weekends. I look forward to it.'

Jack shouts after her retreating figure. 'I'll call tomorrow afternoon then. Perhaps we can take tea afterwards?' He waves until she is out of sight. The night couldn't have gone any better: he has an appointment to meet her again, and twenty-four hours to fashion an excuse for knowing where she works. He grins, shrugs on his overcoat, turns his collar up, lopes off up the corridor and steps out into the invigorating spring night air.

As he saunters down towards the railway station, lamenting the lack of a cap to keep the chill from his ears, his thoughts rewind to the magnificent woman he watched on stage just half an hour since. Her passion, the fervour in her eyes and commitment to her cause gives him pause for thought, and to lament his own failings, his own cowardice. He could see the poor wretch of a dog was not adequately anesthetised and was suffering – horrendously. Where was his compassion, his bravery, his moral compass then? Why was he so afraid of what Bayling, and the others, would think of him? Why didn't he speak up at the time? Or afterwards? He had always feared he was weak, lacking a backbone when it mattered most. After all, he had never stood up to his father, or his grandfather for that matter. And Eliza, through her fearlessness and courage, had brought it home to him. He is suddenly overcome with a deep sense of shame, but also a conviction that he can, he will, change. Especially if he has the brave, beautiful Miss Blackwood by his side.

NINE

The Legal Challenge

The following morning finds Bayling in his office, muttering angrily under his breath. Spread across his vast desk are the day's papers. He's holding the *Daily News*, its front-page splash responsible for the crimson flush invading his face.

The silence is severed by a hesitant rap. The silver-cloud head of Miss Dunratty appears around the door. She's wary of her boss' moods and doesn't care to disturb him when he's in one of his tempers. He's a habit of taking it out on her if there's no one else around to absorb the bile. She nervously announces there are students to see him, expecting a barked instruction to make them disappear. To her surprise, he motions her to show them in, a deep frown burrowing into his forehead. The men are fidgeting behind her; she senses their anxiety. She falls back to allow them entry, relieved not to be in the firing line for once. Dunratty returns to her desk with a nagging sense she's just abandoned these two young men to their fate.

Oscar and Jack reluctantly cross the threshold, sensing the tension in the air. Bayling scowls over wire-framed reading glasses as they shuffle closer to his desk. He rises, leans across the desk brandishing the newspaper at them.

'Well? What've you got to say for yourselves? Seen this, have you?'

Oscar is very well aware of what the headline says.

'Dr Bayling, Sir, we did as you requested. We've a record of everything said last night.' Oscar opens his notepad, shakily rifling through the pages.

Bayling, his simmering fury now brought to full boil, cuts him off with a roar. 'I don't need your pathetic notes, boy. I've read it in the bloody papers this morning.' He tosses the paper aside with disdain. 'That blighter Coleridge will rue the day he crossed me. And those damned women, they're like blasted terriers themselves, they just don't give up. What impudence to accuse *me* of torture, call *me* a butcher, in public, with the bloody press crawling all over it. That man's taken leave of his senses.'

The students side-eye each other, they've not seen him this incensed before, even though his reputation for temper tantrums is legendary. Bayling is now such a deep shade of scarlet they worry he might burst a blood vessel.

Bayling drops heavily back into his chair. His mind is awhirl with the consequences. His reputation, what will this do to that? All sullied by a man he attended school with! The shame of it. Was there no loyalty left in the world? Bayling continues ranting, retreating into himself, barely aware of the students hovering nervously.

'I'll crush him, the swine. His name cannot protect him. Coleridge and those bitches will pay dear for their slander. How dare they tarnish my good name over some worthless, flea-bitten hound? I'll get a retraction. Force him to apologise, eat his blasphemous words in public, if it's the last thing I do.'

Bayling thrusts his chair back and stands. He glances up, surprised to see the men still there, silent as statues. He moves from behind his desk, and in three strides he's looming over them.

'Tell me, Mr Latham-Ward, what good did it do, me sending you and your chums along last night, huh?' He pauses, but his glower informs Oscar it would be unwise to respond. 'I'll tell you what: none. Absolutely no good at all. Why didn't you speak up, man? Tell the truth of what happened? Oh no, of course not. You just stood there, mute and lily-livered, scribbling your feeble notes while they spouted lies about me.'

Oscar opens his mouth but is silenced by a glare. 'I pulled strings to get you a place here, boy! Only did it out of stupid, misplaced loyalty to your father, begged me to take you, he did. But what good's it done me? You constantly disappoint with your dim wit and stupidity. Without my help, you'd have failed every bloody exam, for heaven's sake.'

Bayling returns to his desk and sighs as he sits, he's now flat out of that furious head of steam. 'I give up on you, Ward, I really do. From now on, you'll have to get through without my help. I'm done, finished with you.' He dismisses them with a withering glower and an imperious flick of his hand. 'Go, get out of my office now, and don't show your faces again till you come up with something that'll help sort this, this travesty. You hear me?'

Jack doesn't need telling twice, he's out the door like a shot. Oscar, wounded, opens his mouth, then closes it again. He slumps out. Dunratty stares at their retreating backs, a rueful expression splitting her granite façade. She has some empathy with their plight, even the obnoxious Oscar.

The lift door closing obscures her view of them when she's startled by a command.

'Miss Dunratty, could you come please? I need you to take a letter.' She reaches for her pencil and notepad, stands, adjusts her crumpled skirts and pats her candy floss hair. 'Today please, God damn it, woman.'

She rushes in, concern etched on her face. Her boss is seated with his back to her. He's gazing out of the picture window that dominates the wall behind his desk. The view from this fourth-floor aspect is nothing special, just a typical, busy London street, a haphazard mishmash of Georgian and Victorian properties that litter central London, built up erratically over the preceding centuries with no masterplan or cohesive design.

Every available nook and cranny in this patchwork of buildings is cluttered with ramshackle construction sites. Men are crawling all over them like worker ants: sweating, swearing and labouring over the next generation of townhouses and office buildings, doing the bidding of avaricious developers keen to meet every demand of the cash-rich social climber eager to build monuments to their wealth. Bayling is staring at the busy scene unfolding below, but he's barely taking it in. He's too deep in thought, constructing sentences.

Dunratty knows better than to disturb his concentration and waits patiently. Eventually her employer snaps out of his musings, swivels his chair around. She relaxes somewhat. He appears calm considering the earlier rumpus.

'Ah, Miss Dunratty, thank you for coming so promptly.' His tone is softer than before, grateful even. She doesn't mention she's been standing there for five minutes. He gestures for her to take a seat. 'Please, be so kind as to take a dictation. I require this letter delivered this afternoon to a Mr Joseph Tomlinson of 6 The Strand.' He places his fingers together as if in prayer, bows his head, closes his eyes and begins.

'My dear Joseph, it's been a while since we last had occasion to meet. I hope this correspondence finds you and your delightful family well.' He pauses, ordering his thoughts.

'I am writing to request your professional services once again, to ask you to turn your exceptional legal brain to a most unfortunate, unsolicited turn of events that has befallen me. I believe my good name, and my, hitherto, unsullied reputation, have been damaged by a series of slanderous, inaccurate remarks – lies, in fact – that have been rendered libellous by the unfortunate, wide reporting in today's press.' Dunratty notices his colour rise. Her mouth tightens imperceptibly.

'You'll be shocked when you hear the author of these unfounded falsehoods is an alumnus of our *alma mater* – a Stephen Coleridge. You may recall from our school days that his character was already rather maverick and his views radical, but, bluntly, with this slander, he has gone too far. I wish to discuss taking action against him, and, if possible, the two women who are the source of the lies he's spreading.'

'If I may call on you at your convenience to discuss my options, I would be indebted to you, sir. I remain your obedient servant, etc., etc.' He pauses for a moment. 'Got all that?' Dunratty nods, eyes glued to her notebook, still writing furiously. 'Jolly good. Once it's done, please have it delivered by messenger, and instruct them to wait for Mr Tomlinson's response. I want to arrange the meeting as soon as possible, to nip any more of this nonsense in the bud. Is that clear?'

'Yes, Doctor Bayling sir, all clear. I'll get this typed for your signature and send one of the university boys with it.' She backs out, eyes fixed on him, noting with relief his change in mood, bending into a slight curtsey on her way out the door.

Bayling, for the first time this morning, allows himself a satisfied half-smile, one that almost reaches his eyes. 'I'll teach that blighter a lesson he'll never forget. And those bitches; they'll damn well rue the day they crossed William Malcolm Bayling, and that's a promise.'

WHITEHALL, APRIL 1906 – THE OBJECTOR

The lions have just come into view – majestic and serene, glinting in the hazy spring sunshine – when our nostrils are assailed by an all-too-familiar stench. It's reminiscent of rotten eggs, but much, much worse. The sulphur waters the eyes and causes retching all about me. I gag, hold my breath and fumble blindly for my handkerchief. The air is tinged mustard yellow. Then we hear them. As one, disciplined, rehearsed – unlike our lot – chanting their war cry. It's that damned rhyme again. The words spat out, dripping with vitriol, malevolence. It makes me shudder every time I hear it.

> As we go walking after dark
> We turn our steps to Latchmere Park
> And here we see, to our surprise
> A little brown dog that stands and LIES
>
> Ha ha ha, hee, hee, hee
> Little brown dog, we don't love thee
> Ha ha ha, hee hee hee
> Little brown dog, how we hate thee
>
> If we had a dog that told such fibs
> We'd ply a whip about his ribs;
> To tan him well, we would not fail.
> For carrying such a monstrous tale.

They appear, from left and right. I freeze at the sight of them. They look so full of hate, loathing. So, they did have a plan to disrupt us. We both dared to believe they may not appear today, given it's been so quiet all the way from Hyde Park. Oh, how foolish are we?

They have really pulled out all the stops by the looks. There were hundreds of them, piling in from all directions. At their head, leading the procession, a typical specimen. A stiff, poker-faced young gentleman *dressed as if for church in a morning coat and black-silk top hat. He holds aloft, on a six-foot-high pole, a crudely stuffed effigy of a dog – its fur skinned from a coarse-haired terrier by the look of it. Behind him, a horde of ruddy-cheeked, suited student types, exclusively male, intermingled with a rougher breed, bought for the day for a shilling no doubt – an unholy alliance in normal times; but these are anything but normal times.*

TEN

The Statue

PICCADILLY, APRIL 1904

Eliza and Jack sit in Lyons' tea shop, at a table near the bay window, a popular spot for observing the frenetic pace and sights of Piccadilly Circus, although they appear oblivious to their surroundings. The café is decorated in the typical Arts and Crafts style. Walls adorned with a variety of copper kitchen utensils try a little too hard to give the impression of a quaint, country-style kitchen. Dozens of hoop-backed wooden chairs flank round tables covered with floral patterned cloths. Each has a centrepiece of fresh cut, fragrant sweet peas in a twee vase. The room is dominated by small covens of society ladies, daintily sipping tea: little fingers cocked as if they too were listening in to the banal conversation of their owners.

An overabundance of waitresses bustle around the dozen occupied tables, in fierce competition as to who can take the most orders. They're dressed in the traditional Lyons' uniform, starched white pinafores over the black twill, long-sleeved dresses that must cause huge discomfort on such a humid day, topped off with neat white caps sporting a frilled edge.

The couple are far more intimately acquainted than at their meeting in the Grand Hall in March. They remain blissfully unaware of the waitress's repeated enquiries as to whether they require 'More tea, cake, the bill perhaps?' They're far too caught up in each other to notice the comings and goings of 'café society'. In their mutually besotted state, there are just the two of them. Now and then they tear their eyes away to stare at a technical drawing Eliza unfolds, tea things carelessly swept aside to accommodate it.

Outside on the busy thoroughfare, with the gait reminiscent of a plump, waddling goose, Miss Ethel Dunratty comes into view. She's been sent on an errand by the good doctor, an assignment she believes beneath her position, judging from the irritated scowl clouding her doughy, world-weary face. She carries a wicker basket concealing a regiment of wooden toy soldiers in a tin. A birthday present for Bayling's son. 'Not the role of a senior secretary – must have words,' she mutters under her breath as she trundles along, knowing full well she'll not find the courage to confront her boss with such a trivial grievance, or any grievance in fact.

Dunratty, lost to a world of her own griping, casually glances in through the tea shop window. She sneers at the ladies within. Women with nothing better to do than drink cups of over-priced tea and talk twaddle about silks, exotic feathers for their ridiculous hats and, she scoffs, getting the vote. Just as she turns away in righteous disgust, she spies amongst the tables of anonymous chattering heads, a familiar face. Her granite face brightens as she recognises young Master Jack, one of her favourites of Bayling's current cohort. He's always so courteous, enquiring after her health and that of her bed-bound mother. Not like his arrogant tyke of a friend, Oscar Latham-Ward – a nasty piece of work if ever she's seen one, and she's seen quite a few over the years. The smile soon vanishes as she catches sight of his companion. She double takes, unwilling to believe what her eyes are showing her.

There's Jack, smiling, chatting in a most inappropriately chummy manner to one of those appalling women who gate-crashed her office all those months ago. Ethel never forgets a face, and it's her, there's no doubt. If she recalls correctly, this was the quieter of the two she-devils, riding the coat-tails of the first young madam who lied barefaced about being the doctor's niece. She bristles at the memory; conscious her employer has inhabited a rather discombobulated frame of mind ever since. Ever since that rotter, what's his name again? Something to do with poets? Wordsworth? Shelley? Coleridge? Coleridge, that's it, besmirched his reputation. What the blazes is Jack doing with *her*?

She moves on, for fear of being spotted gawping. As soon as she sees an opportunity, she takes up position behind a conveniently parked milk cart. The milkman is fitting a nosebag to his horse, so Dunratty is confident she has at least a few minutes to make sense of the scene. As she observes them – she prides herself on razor-sharp eyesight even into late middle-age – expressions of confusion, curiosity, dawning enlightenment, then cunning, flash across her face.

By the time the milkman packs up, she's seen enough. Her mind awhirl, she hurries off, smirking. This should win her credit in his eyes, a few words of gratitude, a smile even – now, that's a currency that's been in short supply recently.

In the café, Eliza is chattering on, gazing up coquettishly at Jack, but something out of the corner of his eye bothers him. He drags his attention from Eliza and glances through the window. He frowns, distracted by the silhouette of a vaguely familiar, stout figure waddling along. He racks his brain, annoyed he cannot quite make out who it is. He shrugs and focuses his attention back to the object of his desire, quick to dismiss the sense of disquiet, concentrating again on her voice, lulled by its lilting musicality.

'The granite for the plinth has been found already. It's being donated by one of Lena's family connections. She's well acquainted with so many useful people. And is *most* persuasive when it comes to getting them to agree to things.' She beams at the thought of her friend's refusal to take *no* for an answer. 'And a local stonemason will be fashioning it for us, he's donating his time, so that didn't cost nothing neither.'

She pauses, their eyes focus on the table which displays a rolled-out drawing of a statue. It's a pencil sketch of a circular stone pedestal around five feet in height, according to the scribbled dimensions, with the outline of an inscription plate. A dog sits atop the plinth, looking out with a distant, otherworldly expression. 'And the bronze is being cast now, as we speak.' Eliza's voice takes on a sorrowful tone. 'It's modelled on a Battersea terrier Lena thought looked most like him, Jasper, bless him.'

As she talks, Jack's love-struck gaze morphs into a worried frown. His misgivings over the memorial are growing. The more he hears, the more he fears Bayling's reaction to this reawakening of the debate. The rumpus over Coleridge's *alleged* slanderous words seemed to have quietened down in recent times, hopefully forgotten. But a *statue* dedicated to the dog could reopen old wounds. And that's the last thing Jack wants, given his blossoming friendship with Eliza, and his overwhelming need to come clean about a little white lie that's been festering away all this time.

Not that Eliza notices his pained expression. She has also retreated into herself, her memory recalling a fragment from that awful evening, the images *still* haunting her through sweat-drenched night terrors.

Across from her, Jack fidgets. He needs to confess, and soon, so they can put it behind them. He's desperate to do the right thing, but in doing so he knows he may very well lose her before they've even a chance to explore a future together.

The kernel of his predicament is buried deep, wrapped inside one regrettable, stupid untruth. Since then, inevitably, more layers of half-truths and obfuscations have only entrenched the deceit. That poisonous seed was sown on their first tryst – if he could even call it that – the day after the town hall meeting, when they met at the library. He panicked in that moment, and to his eternal shame let slip a lie in answer to an innocent, four-word question: 'What are you studying, Jack?'

In fairness – and as he rationalised at the time – he'd no choice. To tell Eliza the truth, when they'd spent just one, delightful hour together, would have killed any chance of continuing their acquaintance, and he couldn't risk that. His had been a Hobson's choice – to lie and retain a slim chance of happiness, or tell the truth and end up with nothing, nothing except the furious contempt of the woman he was falling in love with.

Over the weeks, he and Eliza have become much better acquainted and, to their mutual delight, find each other most agreeable company. Each subsequent meeting amplifies their attraction. Frustratingly, neither is prepared to declare their feelings for fear of dragging upon themselves the unbearable weight of rejection. So, to protect their fragile hearts, they continue in the same shy vein, painfully *proper* in all interactions. Each longing for the other to break the logjam and allow the pent-up emotion to flood out so they may bathe in its waters. For now, they are making do with the ongoing drought, while ever hopeful of the rains.

'Eliza, I, ah, really, um. I need to tell you something.'

Eliza isn't listening, still caught up in her own world, the visceral memory of that poor dog threatening to steal a tear. She doesn't want to appear weak in front of Jack, prides herself on her 'stiff upper lip'. Her sensibilities and level-headedness, a true librarian's demeanour, are her proudest traits. Once she's confident her eyes will remain dry, she recalls her train of thought.

'And, you know the really clever thing? We've included a water fountain in the plinth. Two, in fact. One for us and another for animals at the bottom. There, can you see?' She points at the drawing, and sure enough, at the base of the pedestal a couple of pencil strokes represent a small trough-like protrusion. 'Isn't that something? Beauty and utility combined – William Morris would be proud.'

Eliza smiles, absentmindedly placing her hand over his, breaking his wretched trance. Jack loses his nerve at the touch of her cool, elegant fingers. He looks discomfited, his guilty conscience clear to anyone willing to see. Eliza stares up at him. He cannot quite meet her open, trusting gaze. For the first time, Eliza notices something's amiss with her beloved Jack. She ducks her head, trying to catch his line of sight, but he resolutely avoids her eye. She frowns, becoming irritated by his attitude. She thought he'd be delighted with the progress they're making with the memorial. What on earth is causing him to act in this sullen manner? She shrugs. He'll come out with it soon enough if it's important. Not put off by his strange mood, she has something she needs to ask him, and ask him she jolly well will!

'So, it's all going to plan, I'm relieved to say, given we've not attempted nothing like this before, me and Lena I mean.' She hesitates. 'But there's one important task left. And, Jack, I, we, could really do with your help. Given you read Classics.'

Jack pales, swallows visibly. There it was, his lie given form by her own innocent lips, swirling in the ether between them, an invisible fog of deceit that will prove his undoing. He gulps. Can he tell her now? Does he have it in him? *Tell her, man!* He is hardly aware of the words leaving his mouth.

'Of course, Eliza, you can ask me anything. If I can help, I will. You know that.' He falters, dismayed at the sounds flowing from his mouth, appalled at his own cowardice. That was his chance, and he's blown it. Not only blown it, but sunk just that little deeper into the quagmire.

Eliza half-smiles at his bowed head. She's somewhat heartened by his words, but still perplexed by his demeanour; he appears cowed, defeated almost. But what the issue is, she has not a clue. 'Well, almost everything's sorted, we've even potentially found the statue a home. It's a little off the beaten track.' She frowns. 'But getting permission at all is challenging, so it will be a coup to get the council to agree.' She taps her nose conspiratorially. 'It helps that Lena's rather friendly with, shall we say, the more radical representatives on Battersea Council.'

'Now, why doesn't that surprise me?' Jack smiles weakly, but his expression remains one of a condemned man.

'So, it's all falling into place, except for, well, the most important aspect of the whole endeavour really, you could say.' He still hasn't a clue what she is getting at. 'You see, we're yet to settle on the inscription. Can't agree on what it should say, how radical it should be?' She pauses, smiles fully this time, willing him to cotton on. The penny drops. He gets it, but isn't ready to admit it to himself, or her, so continues to stare blankly.

'I just mentioned to Lena that you study literature and that maybe we could ask you, with an outsider's objective view, to help us with some appropriate words. And Lena thought it a splendid idea. So? What do you say? Will you help us?'

Jack swallows hard, registering the unbearable irony, but doubting Lena's apparent enthusiasm for his involvement. Reluctantly, he's forced to agree. What else can he do?

'Of course, I'll help if I can, but to warn you, I'm not blessed with any great poetic talent you know? So, I'm not sure how useful I'll be.' He attempts a nonchalant, apologetic grin.

Eliza grins at him. Now, that's the old Jack. She pushes his arm teasingly. 'Oh, stop with the false modesty. Your letters are always so beautifully written. You've a magical way with words, Jack. And it's the words that count after all, for it is they that'll inspire people – move them to do something about this horror.'

He summons the nerve to meet her eye, to grin back at her. The deceit will have to live a little longer. Anyway, he reasons, if he can, by some unholy miracle, come up with words that inspire – but not offend – then maybe Eliza will find it in her heart to forgive his lie. Maybe? In time.

'Fine. You win. Consider me at your disposal. Where have you got to so far?'

They huddle, heads together, reviewing the scraps of paper Eliza produced from her over-stuffed carpet bag. Jack is grateful for something – anything – that distracts him. Even though this is *so* inappropriate, he almost laughs out loud at the incongruity of it all. They lose themselves in the jumble of words, arranging potential epitaphs, once more oblivious to all.

The café door swings open and a breathless Lena dashes in. She scans the busy room, ignoring the society chatter, and spots Eliza;

she still feels that tingle of delight at that first sight of her, even after all this time. She waves and bustles over, her progress slowed by the number of occupied tables she must manoeuvre around, the ladies eyeing her dishevelled state with snooty disapproval. The angle of the front door, and her circuitous route through the café, means she only spots that Eliza has company when she's almost upon her. A fleeting grimace. She isn't best pleased to see *him*.

This was to be *her* private time with Eliza. Her treat of a famous Lyons' afternoon tea to celebrate the memorial finally being granted a location. Now here he is, like a bad penny, turning up out of the blue, spoiling her plans, *again*. Jack has become a persistent thorn in Lena's side; it is obvious Eliza is becoming ever more attracted to him. It fractures Lena's heart every time she has to endure Eliza eulogising his supposed virtues. She prayed it was a passing phase and tried her damnedest to pour cold water over this virtuous Jack-shaped flame Eliza's been tending. So, it's a kick in the teeth to see her rival sitting there, bold as brass, smiling and plotting with *her* friend, *her* Eliza. She's swift to disguise her displeasure.

'I'm so sorry I'm late, I know how it riles you. But you simply must forgive me. I know you will when you learn why.' She smiles at the thought. 'A litter of puppies arrived just as I was leaving, and I just couldn't tear myself away. They're so sweet, bless 'em. But I see you've been well entertained in my absence.' She turns to Jack and flashes the biggest smile she can muster. He recognises it for what it is. She proffers her hand.

'Jack, what a surprise. Eliza didn't mention you were joining us.'

Jack rises and takes Lena's extended hand, with an equally forced enthusiasm, and just the faintest touch of insincerity.

'*So* delighted to see you again too, Lena. This wasn't planned, I can assure you. I was passing by and spotted Eliza sitting here alone. So, I popped in to say hello, then we just got chatting.'

'How serendipitous!' Lena eyes him suspiciously. She doesn't believe it for a second. Eliza, oblivious to this undercurrent, cuts in.

'Jack's agreed to help with the inscription, Lena, isn't that splendid?

'Oh, that's utterly marvellous. Given your obvious talents in the writing department, Jack, we'll have this settled in no time.'

Her smile is acid sweet. That distinct whiff of sarcasm is lost on Eliza, but not so Jack, who winces, aware, but mystified, by Lena's growing antagonism towards him.

Lena orders a cream tea from the hovering waitress, and they settle down to the task at hand. All is progressing harmoniously, considering, Lena begrudgingly accepting Jack's suggestions, and Jack sensitive to Lena's thoughts on phrasing. Eliza sits back and observes them, bickering over a minor point, but it's a light-hearted exchange. She smiles. All she wants is the two people who mean more to her than anything, to get on, to be friends. And it looks as if, at long last, they might be making some small progress.

Jack looks up from the word jigsaw he's been studying and glances out of the window. He freezes, then recoils from the figures he has spotted out on the busy street. He turns his face toward the interior, he swivels his back to the window. He rues the fact Eliza had picked a table so visible from outside, but there was nothing he could do when he joined her. Now it could cause him no end of grief. He has to get out of there, and fast. He tries to think, praying his back isn't too distinctive to anyone looking in.

Across the road, Oscar and two of his gang are striding towards the tea shop. They are speeding along, and in seconds they will be parallel with the window. Jack jumps up, upsetting a not-quite-empty teacup over the papers. The women exclaim and start dabbing the plans with their napkins, averting any lasting damage. He mumbles an apology as he scrabbles, all fingers and thumbs, for his jacket. He consults his fob watch.

'Oh my, oh my. I've lost track of the time. I've a lecture at three, and I will be so terribly late. Ladies, please excuse my rudeness, but I must dash.' He almost knocks over his chair in his haste. Both women gape in mild bewilderment. His progress is hampered by his clumsy navigation around the cluttered tables, but eventually he disappears from view. Eliza stares open-mouthed, looking exceedingly put out. Lena battles to hide her delight.

'Hmm, typical bloody student, didn't even pay for his tea. I guess I'll settle his bill then. Never mind, we'll get on better, just the two of us, hey?' She smiles at her friend, who scowls at her.

'No, don't.' Eliza snaps back. 'I'll pay for Jack's. It was my treat anyway. He always pays when we are out and it's not right. We're equals after all.'

ELEVEN

The Ask

Jack wrenches open the café door, stumbles onto the pavement. He glances across to check he's hidden from the women's view, leans against the door, closes his eyes and breathes a heavy sigh of relief. He then scans the surroundings for the men. They've made rapid progress, he spots their backs now fifty yards down the street, he'll have to be quick to catch them up. A nonchalant wave to Eliza as he saunters passed the tea shop window; she barely acknowledges him. When he's convinced he's out of her sightline, he breaks into a sprint.

'Oscar, Hugh, James, hold up. Where you off to? There's no lecture this afternoon. What's the rush?'

They stop, turn, wait for him. Oscar's in a cheery mood, joking, larking around. As soon as Jack draws level, he pounces and grapples him into a bear hug, ruffles his hair, puts a chummy arm around his shoulders.

'Hey Jack, where've you been all day? When I rose this morn, you'd already gone. What ya been up to? Anything you need to confess to your uncle Oscar, huh?' Jack flinches under Oscar's curious gaze.

'Hardly morning, Oscar. I didn't leave 'til midday, and there were still no signs of intelligent life emanating from your malodorous pit. Big night again, was it?'

Oscar taps his nose. 'A gentleman *never* tells, dear chap, and I, if nothing else, at least have the pretensions of being one.' He bows, doffing his hat, and, with an exaggerated gait, prances in the manner of a dandy. They take turns scoffing at him as they motor along.

107

Jack, still none the wiser as to why they're so keen to get to college, presses them.

'We're off to see Bayling.' Oscar adopts a deeper, melodramatic tone, a vague impersonation of the good doctor. 'We've been summoned by his Lordship. He wants to see us. It's urgent, apparently. And I, dear boy, have an inkling we might be out of the *doghouse* at last – if you'll excuse the expression. Hoorah!'

'Oh?' Jack replies, frowning at the recollection of their last encounter over the *Coleridge* issue. Bayling has been distant with them ever since, their tutorials turning into frosty, awkward endurance tests. 'How come? He was mad as hell at us after last time.'

'He's something important to announce,' says Oscar. 'And our humble services are once more required. God knows why, but it sounds promising, and if it helps me get in his good books again, then splendid – what with finals round the corner.' Oscar stops, turns to Jack, puzzlement clouding his eyes. 'And you, dear friend, were specifically asked for. Why, I cannot say, but you'd better come. Don't want to piss the esteemed Doctor off, do we? We've done far too good a job of that already.'

Jack looks as quizzical as Oscar. What on earth could Bayling want with him? He's never taken the blindest interest in Jack in the years he's been his tutor. He shrugs it off, falls into step and gets carried along by their laddish banter. They hop onto a passing tram, each pulling the other up. In no time, they arrive at the university building and cram into the lift to the fourth floor.

They tumble out, laughing and joking, but fall into a respectful silence as they sense Dunratty's annoyance at the intrusion. She's, as ever, at her desk, stiff and upright, her ample bottom wedged into the chair, glaring at them as if they've just openly insulted the King in her presence. In their imagination, she's taken on the form of a mythical dragon, hell-bent on guarding the entrance to her master's lair. They learnt swiftly it doesn't pay to invoke the ire of the fearsome Miss Dunratty. The students shuffle up to her desk as one entity, safety in numbers. Oscar announces, rather too insolently for her liking, that the Doctor was expecting them and she should inform her boss *post haste*. His manner, while not disrespectful, has that whiff of haughty superiority Dunratty finds so irksome in the boy. She scowls but does as she's told.

Dunratty rises, not taking her beady eyes off Oscar until she turns to knock. She pops her head around the door to announce them. Bayling's demeanour changes with the news, and in a cheery tone he instructs her to 'show them right in.' Dunratty smiles, assuming this jovial mood has emerged from the curious intelligence she brought him earlier, combined with the news he received via telegram that morning. She is hopeful this mood will last, she's had more than enough of his unpredictable black moods over the last months.

Dunratty signals the young men to enter. Jack passes her and nods politely. She returns a suspicious frown. He's taken aback; what on earth has he done to deserve such a malevolent glower? They'd always been on civil, almost friendly terms, despite his association with Oscar.

All four shuffle gormlessly into the office. Bayling stands facing the window.

'Gentlemen, gentlemen, how good of you to come, and so promptly too. Please be seated.' Bayling slowly pivots to face them, eyes scanning each of them before settling upon Jack, who fidgets under his unrelenting stare. Oscar's gaze follows Bayling's to Jack. Bayling hasn't given Jack the time of day before. What's going on? Oscar clears his throat.

'Our absolute pleasure, sir, but how can we be of...' Bayling ignores him, still focused intently on Jack.

'I'm pleased to report some exceedingly good news I've received regarding that wretched dog incident of some months ago.'

Jack jolts as if hit by lightning, every sinew and nerve in his body tensed. He consciously unclenches his jaw and fists, desperate to look nonchalant under his tutor's unblinking gaze.

'You'll recall I requested a public apology from the man who defamed me, Coleridge.' They nod in unison; how could they forget? Their jovial mood is evaporating. 'In return for said apology, and a full retraction, I would allow his slanderous comments to pass with no further action. A gracious offer, you'd agree?' All four heads nod vigorously. 'Oh yes, sir. Absolutely, sir.'

Jack brightens, optimistic this news heralds the end of the whole sorry incident, and an end to his torment. Coleridge has seen fit to apologise, and all is forgiven. Thank God! He's puzzled the women mentioned nothing of it earlier. They can't have heard yet, he reasons. His body, pumped with adrenalin a moment earlier, deflates. He disguises a perceptible sigh of relief with a cough. Bayling's face suddenly darkens.

'Sadly, no such apology has been forthcoming and although I am, by my very nature, a patient man, that patience is now spent. He's left me no choice. His gross impertinence has forced me to issue a legal writ against him.' He pauses, curious as to what effect his next sentence will have on Jack. 'And, of course, against the lunatic women that started all this nonsense.'

Jack's short-lived optimism comes crashing down around his ears. He can't quite comprehend what he's hearing. A legal challenge? Not only against Coleridge, but his precious Eliza too. This will break her, she'll not cope with the shame of it, the damage to her reputation. In his distress he doesn't notice he is being studied. Bayling allows himself a tight smile. It was only Coleridge he'd pursued the defamation against. The case against the women was not strong, or so his solicitor advised him, but Jack's horrified reaction confirms Dunratty's earlier gossiping. Somehow, for an unfathomable reason, Mr Jack Forsyth is in league with those confounded women.

'Well, gentlemen, I'm pleased to say I heard this very morning that my case against them is deemed to have merit and will be heard, later this month. And I imagine Stephen Coleridge Esq. is receiving the news...' He takes out his pocket watch with a melodramatic flourish. 'Just. About. Now.'

110

He shuts the watch with a snap that jolts Jack out of his stupor. Jack, his complexion turned deathly pale, tries his damnedest to remain poker-faced under Bayling's relentless scrutiny. He'd never been a good card player. The other three, oblivious, mutter their congratulations.

Oscar vies for attention again. 'Well, that's splendid news, sir. It is a travesty, what that man accused you of. At last, justice will be served.'

'It is indeed good news, but let's not get ahead of ourselves, Mr Latham-Ward. I've not won the case – YET. That's where you four fine gentlemen come in.'

Three puzzled faces stare back at him. How the hell could they help with a court case? Jack's mind is racing, he's got an inkling of what Bayling requires, and the thought makes him bilious.

'Gentlemen, gentlemen, please don't look so befuddled, it's very straightforward. All I require, when the time comes, is you testify in court that the mongrel in question was adequately anaesthetised throughout the procedure. It's that simple.' The ground gives way beneath Jack's feet.

'To ensure my victory, we must undermine the testimonies of the two women. Yes, they were in the front row, but you were also seated close to the stage. So, I'm counting on your combined, *consistent* evidence outweighing theirs. Are we clear?'

Three men nod their agreement. Oscar beams, delighted with the outcome. Jack looks stricken as he realises the enormity of what Bayling is asking: stand up in court and give evidence *against* Eliza. The thought mortifies him. He'd be calling her a liar, to her face, in a public court. Knowing full well she is telling the truth.

'You will testify to what you saw that evening. A dog rendered completely unconscious; any movements perceived by the women were involuntary muscle spasms. You heard no whimpering *what-so-ever*. Clear?'

All three continue nodding like over-enthusiastic pigeons. Jack, desolate, but conscious of the doctor's unyielding gaze, executes a slight movement of his head.

'Gentlemen, I appreciate your cooperation. It will be noted, have no doubt on that score. This whole unhappy incident will soon be history and we can return to more important matters, such as saving lives. Good day to you all.'

Bayling returns to his desk. They turn to leave. Three men relieved it's over and that they've got off lightly, the fourth in a state of turmoil. They reach the door, Jack leading the retreat. He desperately needs some air. He grasps the door handle.

'Oh, Mr Forsyth, I almost forgot. May I detain you a moment longer? There's a minor matter I need to discuss with you.'

Jack's hand freezes on the handle, he tenses, then releases his grip. What the hell does Bayling want now? He reluctantly turns back into the room, catching Oscar's quizzical eye. The others pile out and the door clicks gently into place. To Jack, it sounds like a cell door clanking shut. He's now alone with Bayling. He attempts to lick his parched lips, but his mouth is as dry as the desert. Bayling stares back at him, unblinking: an unreadable, bland expression.

'Mr Forsyth, Jack. I may call you Jack? Please take a seat. This won't take long.'

Good to his word, Bayling does not detain him long. Less than ten minutes later, an ashen-faced Jack emerges. He passes Dunratty, oblivious to her presence. She stares after him, concern clouds her cold green eyes. She has no idea what her boss said to the young man, but she's experiencing a rare tweak of conscience for her likely role in it. Whatever Bayling has threatened, it appears to have devastated young master Forsyth, and Jack doesn't deserve that, no matter what dubious company he keeps.

THE MALL, APRIL 1906 – THE PROTESTOR

Loutish, sweating testosterone, itching for trouble, they've obviously been biding their time, amassing out of sight, lurking in doorways and recesses. Now dangerously fired up, with naught to do except swig from flasks and goad each other. They, too, have placards and banners, and children's toy dogs, speared through, to taunt us.

A flash. A crack, like gunfire. Several more. They're lobbing Chinese crackers into the crowd. Our tight-knit battalion suddenly shatters into a hundred splinters. Ladies and anarchists scatter, shrieking in terror. Mothers scream, panic-stricken, yanking their children from danger.

The dogs are going spare, driven to a state of terror by the sparks and explosions of the Chinese crackers, barking, straining against their leashes, some breaking free. Those that do, lunge at the students, all bared fangs and spittle. I gasp in horror as they are kicked, beaten senseless and stamped on. Many lie in the gutters. I try to block out their dying yelps and the sound of children screaming for their pets.

Our men, incensed, charge at them; wooden banners are now makeshift weapons. We watch fearfully as pandemonium grips what had been a tranquil Sunday afternoon.

The police arrive – I recognise some of them from the Dog Patrol – but they provide sparse comfort. They are, as ever, hopelessly outnumbered. Their feeble whistles are drowned out by the cacophony. They pile in to separate the warring factions. As soon as they subdue one fight, three start in its place. They look on, resigned – they've witnessed this so often that they appear almost nonchalant. I want to scream at them, but what's the use?

I squeeze her hand tightly; she returns the pressure. It gives me some small comfort.

TWELVE

Mr Hageby

THE HAGEBY FAMILY HOME, MAY 1904

Lena perches on the edge of a russet-brown Chesterfield settee. Her eyelids are lowered in a penitent's hooded gaze; her hands clasped in her lap to stop the tremor. She surreptitiously glances up at the whip-thin figure of a man before returning her attention to an almost imperceptible heart-shaped blood stain in the rug at her feet; a reminder of one of many childhood misadventures, this one leaving Lena with a nasty gash in her scalp. She unthinkingly raises her hand to touch the scar.

Shafts of refracted light flicker through the stained-glass picture window of the stylishly understated drawing room; the rays bathe her father in an unearthly, multi-coloured glow. Reginald Hageby Esq. personifies the archetypal upper-middle-class, middle-aged gentleman. That's to say he dresses in conventional, formal attire at all times, even when relaxing. One can imagine him sleeping in such garb, it is so much a part of who he is. However, his austere countenance cannot totally erase the glimmer of a younger, carefree Reggie evident in his world-weary, yet still twinkly, eyes. Emergent laughter lines hint at a well-used sense of humour, but he's in no mood for laughter today. Quite the opposite.

Reginald stands at the cream and pink-veined marble mantlepiece that dominates the room, staring over at his errant daughter with frustrated concern. He draws absentmindedly on his pipe; the fragrant tang of expensive Turkish tobacco permeates the air. Its aroma only heightens Lena's craving, but she dare not indulge in front of him; her father heartily disapproves of ladies smoking. Oh, the hypocrisy! The atmosphere feels distinctly frosty – unusually so for such an otherwise affectionate pair. They both appear unsure of what to say next, like two strangers who have exhausted polite small talk and find they've nothing else in common. The tension is fractured by a rap on the door, their heads swivel in unison. Whoever is on the other side does not wait to be summoned in by the master of the house; so not a servant.

A handle turns and the door creaks open. Lena's mother, Daphne, pops her head around. Her delicate, softly defined features, only recently hinting at the first cruel touches of aging around her jawline, are framed by the narrow gap. She motions as if to speak, but on sensing the sombre mood, hesitates, mumbles her excuses and retreats, easing the door shut with care. Tea can wait, she concludes, a worried crease marring an otherwise porcelain-smooth forehead. She waves away Maisie, a shy sixteen-year-old maid-of-all-work, who is hovering nervously behind her with a tray laden with tea and still warm scones.

'Papa, I –'

'Enough.' His curt tone reverberates sharply around the room. 'I've heard quite enough of this nonsense, Evelina. You have gone too far this time.' She stares at him, open-mouthed. The unpalatable truth is slowly dawning that her beloved Papa's seemingly infinite tolerence regarding her *antics* has finally been breached.

She was undoubtedly a 'daddy's girl' – her poor Mama hardly ever got a look in. Father and daughter had always enjoyed an unusually close, affectionate bond – a relationship somewhat disapproved of by *society*. That's not to say she wasn't in awe of him, however. She craved his approval, whilst simultaneously testing his indulgence to the limit.

An only child, her melodramatic entrance into the world was accompanied by life-threatening complications, but much fanfare, given her poor mother had endured the agonies of years of miscarriages. Consequently, her parents considered Lena something of a miracle baby and she was cherished, and indulged, to an unhealthy degree, allowing her to explore her frequent flights of

115

fancy. Unfortunately for the Hagebys, this level of familial freedom, combined with Lena's strong will, contrived to thwart what little hope they clung to for a conventional lifestyle for her. It was always the plan to prepare Lena, from the nursery onwards, for a *suitable* union. The coming out of a demure, refined debutant, swiftly married off to a gentleman, from a fine upstanding family, who could pass muster in Papa's eyes and take on the mantle of the Hageby estate when the time came. She, of course, had other ideas.

Lena had been allowed free rein through her formative years, becoming almost feral in her endless outdoor pursuits, her faithful red setter Charlie forever by her side. Growing up in the genteel surroundings of her ancestral home – a country pile founded on the proceeds of a long-distant, now unmentionable, sugar plantation –she had tried her parent's patience with increasingly outlandish escapades. Often described as *headstrong*, a euphemism for 'spoilt' in polite circles, her behaviour was certainly deemed unbecoming of a lady-to-be. But through it all, whatever trouble she caused, she could always rely on her Papa to be her most loyal defender. Until now, it seems.

'But Papa, please, if you'd witnessed what we did, you couldn't ignore it either. It was sheer barbarity. There's absolutely no need for it, not in this day and age, and it wasn't as if it's a one-off. That man, that butcher Bayling, is renowned for his cruelty. Someone has to stop him.' Her pleading finally breaks through his brittle façade. His gaze meets hers; his lips turn upwards in a whisper of a sad, indulgent smile.

'Oh, Evelina, my dearest girl. That might very well be so, but why did it have to be you? And *Elizabeth*? It's her I'm more disappointed with. She ought to know better.'

Lena feels a pang of pure jealousy, as sharp as if it were a slap. 'Excuse me? But I don't see why you're bringing Eliza into this.'

'You I can understand being reckless, it's in your nature, I'm afraid to say, and I'm half to blame for it, I know. But I had faith in Miss Blackwood. I'd hoped, when she became your companion, she'd help keep you from sniffing out any more trouble.'

Lena bristles, her blood rising. She is no longer contrite. 'So! You imagine *you* recruited Eliza. As my chaperone? Well, that's bloody rich! *I* seem to recall you were more than a little reticent when I introduced her to you!' She puffs her chest and her chin juts out imperiously. She clears her throat, practising her baritone. '"Are you *quite* sure Miss Blackwood is of an appropriate social class, Evelina? And is that a *Welsh* accent I detect?"' She glowers at her father, her impression of him uncannily accurate. Reginald's face betrays a modicum of shame at her reminder of his earlier prejudice – of which he is not proud. 'Eliza's not my moral guardian, Papa. I'm twenty-bloody-six. I don't need nurse maiding, for Chrissakes.'

'But you never seem to learn, child. You can't blunder into situations like this, with no thought for the consequences. These are powerful, dangerous men. You cannot interfere with them; they have the entire establishment on their side. You could've been seriously hurt. I shudder to think what may have happened if those brutes had caught up with you. You are not just disrupting a local hunt here, Lena. These people mean business.' He falters, gripping the mantle for support. Lena's jealous outrage evaporates as she observes the distress in his expression. It's only because he cares so much, she thinks. He still loves me. She will make him see why they did it.

The young Lena had no time for trivialities such as dolls, prams and frilly dresses, all of which laid scattered, unloved and untouched, across her playroom floor. Her passions were for nature, caring for wounded or orphaned wildlife, making dens and chasing Charlie through muddy fields and clear running streams alive with tiny silver fish and frogspawn. An early manifestation of such passion was her youthful disgust for the locals' enthusiasm for fox-hunting – an activity she was unfortunate to witness, by chance, on one of her and Charlie's unchaperoned excursions into the endless Sussex countryside bordering the estate. The horror of viewing, close up, that exhausted, pitiful creature being torn to bits by a ravenous pack of dogs, haunted her. The look of utter terror in the dying fox's eyes became the focus of her nightmares for years.

Ergo, from the tender age of ten, she was a noisy, tenacious and vociferous campaigner against any form of blood sport. She was a persistent thorn in the side of the local gentry and gained quite the reputation as a *saboteur*. This was much to her father's vexation, given his status in the village. To his credit, he steadfastly refused to curtail her protests, whatever his outraged country squire neighbours demanded. Secretly – and he'd never admit as much to Lena – he admired his little girl's bravery in the face of such opposition, marvelled at her self-developed moral code.

Her father seems to have retreated into himself. An invisible barrier has sprung up between them. She cannot resist the urge to smash it, reach through and make him understand she had little choice but to fight for that poor, tortured creature and the countless others that suffer at the hands of Bayling and his ilk. He shares her innate love of animals and an abhorrence of their mistreatment, of that she is certain. Not wishing to distress him further, she's equally determined to make him see her side.

She takes a slow, deep breath, steeling herself to utter words, any words, to unlock this dreadful stalemate. When she speaks, the voice reverberating in her ear is a shock. It's her own seven-year-old voice: whiney, pleading, pathetic. She's mortified to hear it tumble from her mouth, but now she's started she cannot stop.

'Papa. I understand your concern for my safety, I do, truly. But if not us, then who? Who will stand up for these wretched creatures? They have no voice of their own, no defences against the men intent on doing them harm. Their teeth, claws, are no match for the whips and chains that bind them, the chloroform that chokes them and scalpels that slice them. No rights, no defence. Stephen says –'

'Do NOT talk to me about that bloody man. That fool, Coleridge. I hold him entirely responsible. He'd no right to use you like that. His reputation may withstand such humiliation. Yours will most certainly not.'

'Don't blame Mr Coleridge, Papa, he's been a rock. He's taken this court case upon himself, organised everything. Without him, I don't know what we'd have done.'

'Balderdash. Without him, and his reckless, slanderous words, you wouldn't be in this bloody mess.'

'There was nothing slanderous about what he said that night, in fact –'

'Enough. Do you hear me? You seem utterly incapable of growing up. Or taking responsibility for the ever more outrageous antics you get tangled up in.' His frustrations boil over.

'That expensive education was a total waste. Of your time and our bloody money. Good God, they couldn't even instil the most basic common sense in you, for Christ's sake. I've a mind to demand my money back, so help me. Your grandfather was right, God rest his soul. Educating girls is a waste of time and effort. I should've just concentrated on marrying you off and been done with it. God help us all if you lot end up getting the vote.' He has gone too far. His words taste of bitter ashes; he regrets each one. Lena gasps in shock.

'Papa. You don't mean that. How can you say such terrible things?'

Lena was not academic by nature, something she'd freely admit – not that it mattered of course, her being a girl, and wealthy. She developed a passing interest in science and mathematics, more so than for deportment and domestic science. She excelled at French, but pondered what use this could be, apart from the odd shopping trip to Paris. What she lacked in academic ability, she more than made up for in other ways, however. The young Evelina developed an advanced level of emotional intelligence, and an all-consuming – some would describe as foolhardy – devotion to any cause that touched her heart.

Growing up, Lena could be defined as a governess's worse nightmare, an accolade she cheerfully accepted as a badge of honour. From six years old, she fastidiously worked her way through an impressive number of them. By the age of thirteen, she had depleted even her parents' bountiful patience. With heavy hearts, they sent her away, kicking and screaming, to the most prestigious school for girls they could find: Cheltenham Ladies' College.

Her unconventional upbringing exerted a powerful influence over her fledgling personality, for good and ill. On the plus side, she was fiercely independent, imaginative and self-reliant, born from years of playing alone in the woods. On the downside, she was somewhat selfish by nature, a fault she freely admitted to anyone who challenged her behaviour. After all, she'd never had cause to share her toys, treats, her parents' love. Why start now?

So, imagine her shock when, after the turmoil of an emotional farewell, she was shown to a dormitory. The horror at the realisation she was expected to share her most intimate space, with not just one, but a gaggle of strangers. She counted at least six beds. This indignity, forced upon her just as she was entering her most sensitive years, overwhelmed her and, she's not proud to admit, she threw a full-blown tantrum there and then, as her peers looked on in shocked amazement.

There was one bright spot on the troubled adolescent's horizon, however. The only thing in those early tumultuous days that helped soothe her disquiet, and that was her blossoming crush on her headmistress, a Miss Dorothea Beale. Miss Beale had built a reputation as an outspoken campaigner for women's rights. She was a fearless critic of the powers that be. It was Miss Beale who awoke and sustained Lena's faint interest in the topics of mathematics and science, she who nurtured that unconventional streak she identified in this pouty, spoilt, yet ultimately kind and tender-hearted young woman.

To justify spending more time in the company of her idolised Miss Beale, Lena developed an obsession for the cause of female suffrage. She undertook extracurricular lessons to both deepen her understanding of the issue and indulge her overwhelming infatuation. Over the next five years she also gained important life skills in sharing and patience, reluctantly honed her French, scraped through her other subjects, and acquainted herself with just enough knowledge of the societal niceties required of her to pass muster as an educated lady – of sorts.

In her time at Cheltenham, she'd become even more outspoken: teachers used the term 'recalcitrant' to describe her, but that wasn't entirely fair. She'd find herself in no end of sticky situations in defence of the causes she held most dear. On many an occasion she was only saved from expulsion by the over-protective, if rather guilt-ridden, Miss Beale herself.

These remembered fragments from her adolescent life, all the subtle influencers, have, Lena now realises, unwittingly led to the predicament she now finds herself in. In this tension-filled room, with her dearest Papa regarding her as if she were an unwanted intruder, a recently discovered cuckoo in the nest.

'Oh, my dearest child. I can't count the times I've bailed you out of trouble. At the hunt, in school, and now your run-ins with the authorities at these suffrage meetings. And I've defended you, to the last, as I've seen the point of it, the injustices you're battling, the causes you adopt. But this ... this is on a completely different scale. It's a High Court case, Evelina. It is national news for Christ's sake. Your reputation, such as it is, and our family name, could be ruined if they find Coleridge guilty. Did you really have no clue as to the trouble you'd cause by organising that damned meeting?' He throws his hands in the air, his expression a mix of hopelessness and dismay. It breaks Lena's heart to see him like this. She rises, takes a few tentative steps towards him, hoping proximity will break down this emotional divide.

'Please, please don't be angry with me. I'm so sorry, I truly am. I, we, never dreamt it would come to this. How could we?' She reaches for his arm. He shrugs it roughly away.

'Come to this, you say, and all over one stray mongrel. I despair, I really do. You've brought shame on this family. Your mother will struggle to bear the disgrace, you know damn well how weakened she is.'

'Papa, please. You can't mean it? I know you don't. I'm scared, I really am, I don't know what to do.' She cannot force any more words out – tears are the only thing she can produce; they stream down her cheeks. To her horror, her stony-faced father appears impervious. She dries her eyes on her sleeve.

'They're making us testify, Papa. It will be our word against theirs, and they'll have a dozen witnesses who will bare-faced lie to protect Bayling's savagery.'

'What, exactly, do you think I can do about it? I can't smooth this away like I've done before. What do you want of me, child?'

'Say you'll be in court? I need you; I can get through it if you're there.'

He stares at her, his face the mask of a stranger rather than the loving father she knows is in there somewhere. They've reached an impasse. He's not budging. She tries one last tactic. 'I swear once it's over, I'll never get in trouble again. I'll take up knitting, embroidery! I promise I'll be respectable, behave more like a lady.' She pauses, realising that may sound a little facetious. She prepares for her final, do-or-die strategy, one she knows she will not honour – but what the hell, if it wins her father around, then it's worth it. 'I'll even *try* to secure a husband, if that's what you *truly* want for me?'

She trails off, not quite believing she has vocalised it. The idea repulses her the instant it is out of her mouth. That is it: she's played her last card. She stands staring at his proud, unyielding profile. He's turned away from her now, gazing into the cold, dark hearth that hasn't seen a fire in months. She stares at him for the longest time, detects no movement or softening of his stance.

Eventually, aching with sadness and despair, she makes to leave, dragging her feet over the faded antique oriental rugs which cover the polished oak floor. Her father's gaze is fixed, knowing if he looks up now, he will relent, call her back to him, forgive her. Lena reaches the door. With a hand on the handle, she turns.

'If it's the last thing you do for me, please be there, Papa. I'm not sure how to get through this without you.'

He looks up at the sound of the closing door, stares at the space she occupied. His proud face is a study in pain and regret.

Her mother is hovering, listlessly rearranging already arranged flowers in an elegant Wedgewood jasperware vase. She's heard everything, yet says nothing. Lena rests against the oak door for support and quietly breaks down. Mrs Hageby rushes to enfold her sobbing child in her arms. They stand, hugging, rocking back and forth, not speaking of what's passed. Lena clings to her Mama for just a little too long, hugs a little too hard, hears her whisper, 'There, there, my dear. Hush now, he'll come around. He always does. You'll get your own way; it just might take a touch longer this time. He's angry, and scared for you, but too proud to admit it, that's all. It'll pass, I promise.'

Eventually they part. Her mother holds her at arm's length to get a look at her tear-stained face. She dabs at her eyes with a dainty white lace handkerchief. She gently chides her. 'Oh Evelina, it's a good job you don't bother with rouge, it would be all streaked by now, and you couldn't face the world like that.' She smiles and Lena attempts a feeble smile back. She sniffs and wipes her nose on her silk sleeve, leaving a glistening slug trail behind. Mrs Hageby, unable to disguise her look of horror, takes the handkerchief, one unlikely to have experienced anything as unladylike as snot before, and forces it into Lena's hand. 'Here, take it, you need it more than I.'

Her mother wipes Lena's tears away with her thumbs. Once Lena feels calm and in control, she prepares to take her leave. They hug and kiss goodbye. Maisie rushes to hand Lena her coat and hat, the maid desperate to give the impression she's unaware of the emotional scene unfolding in front of her, then she hurries to open the door. She curtseys clumsily, eyes averted, as Lena passes by her. Lena drags her reluctant feet down the grand stone entrance. Mrs Hageby watches from the window as her daughter crunches her way along the gravel driveway, cutting such a forlorn figure that her mother's heart breaks. She stares until Lena disappears into the brougham's carriage, then turns with a heavy sigh. She starts as she spies her husband, standing several feet away, holding onto the banister as if he would fall over without it. 'Oh, Reggie! My darling!' She is shocked at the sight; she has never seen him looking so old and careworn as he appears right now.

THIRTEEN

The Promise

ELMFORD MANSIONS, SAME AFTERNOON

Eliza busies herself plumping already-bulging cushions, rearranging carefully positioned ornaments and putting the finishing touches to an already impeccably uncluttered sitting room. She's been at it for hours, having dismissed the maid early to ensure she wasn't still loitering when her guest arrived. In truth, Eliza was never really satisfied by the *daily's* efforts anyway, regularly griping about Mrs Rumple's slap-dash approach to household chores. She wouldn't have lasted five minutes at the Frobisher's residence! It fell on deaf ears however, as Lena wouldn't have a word said against her beloved Gertie. Mrs Gertrude Rumple is a sixty-ish – she never divulges her exact age – widow who, to be fair, would happily admit to not being the world's greatest maid, nor cook for that matter. She has a round, open face, with a fine criss-cross of broken veins scattered across her permanently ruddy-coloured cheeks. Her expanding torso is carried around on short, stout legs and her ample bosom has soothed away most of the woes in Lena's world over the years. When she first moved in, Lena won the hard-fought battle with her father to not have a live-in maid, as she suspected – rightly – that any residential help could be recruited as a spy for her father. Instead, they'd compromised on a respectable, retired housekeeper who had recently been bereaved and was looking for a little extra cash-in-hand income to supplement her late husband's meagre savings. Lena and Gertie had soon come to a mutually beneficial understanding that, if Gertie didn't report back to her employer on any of Lena's more questionable pursuits, then Lena would turn a blind eye to Gertrude not turning up on occasion, usually when she'd given the gin bottle a little too much attention the night before. After all, Lena didn't much care anyway, never worrying about a little dust, or a messy sitting room; it was only Eliza that got herself into a lather about it. But even Lena has to admit that Mrs R's absences are becoming more frequent in recent months.

Eliza's humming to herself, content with the state of the sitting room for once, taking time to give Mrs P's soft, jagged ears a much-appreciated scratch. She murmurs to her purring cat. 'Now Missus, you will be nice, won't you? No uncivilised behaviour. You hear me? And definitely no hissing. Or there'll be no liver for tea.'

Mrs P languorously stretches out, taking in the armchair's length, arches her rear end, then cocks her nose in the imperious manner that reminds her human companion who, exactly, is in charge. A shrill ring startles her. She scoots off the chair and under the sideboard. Eliza starts too, then smiles. She glances in the large mirror in the overmantel, pinches her cheeks until they flush pink, and frowns at an unruly curl that will not stay put. She gives up trying, smooths her crinkled silk skirt, re-buttons the sleeves of her best blouse, heads into the vestibule and opens the front door with a flourish.

There Jack stands, shuffling nervously and clutching a small posy of pansies and sweet peas framed with ferns. He always relishes that first sight of her, all rosy-cheeked and perfect. Her rich brown eyes, with their flashes of gold and black glinting in the afternoon sun, leave him lost for words.

'Oh, Jack, it's so lovely to see you. Please come in.' Jack crosses the threshold. They stand facing each other in the wide hallway, not sure of what polite etiquette demands of them. For propriety's sake, they settle on a stiff handshake. Formalities over, she leads the way into her sitting room. Mrs P has resumed residence on the back of the settee and is evil-eyeing Jack. 'Take a seat.' Eliza gestures and Jack sits, shuffling to the opposite end of the settee to the cat. He has already heard the stories. Eliza bustles around, but it doesn't quite mask her nervousness at this unorthodox assignation. She smiles warmly, but her mouth is edged with sadness. 'Thank you so much for coming. I need the company today.'

Jack sits back, trying to make himself comfortable, but something's bothering him, and it's not just his proximity to the cat. He is jittery, on edge. His eyes scan the room. It's his first visit, and it surprised him to receive the invite, given Eliza's such a stickler for etiquette. A spinster entertaining a gentleman friend in her home is certainly not the *done thing*, even in these enlightened times. In particular, as it seems – unless his eyes are deceiving him – without a chaperone. 'You're on your own. No Lena today?' Eliza nods. His entire body visibly relaxes into the cushions.

'She's gone off to the country. Parental visit. She's desperate for her father to be there. In court, I mean. But he's steadfast refusing, so she's on a crusade to win him round.'

'Ah, so she's got some humble pie to eat then. Bet that's choking her.' The last few caustic words tumble from him. As they air, he instantly regrets them. They come across as churlish, petulant, and he does not want her to think of him like that – not at all. Eliza throws him a concerned frown.

'She likes to appear tough, but she's Daddy's girl at heart and his reaction has really shaken her. Her legendary charm doesn't seem to be working, not this time!' Jack finds it hard to conjure up any sympathy for his nemesis, but tries his best.

'From the little I know of Lena, she's used to getting her own way – so not doing so must hurt.'

'Mmm, yes. Usually, she winds him round her little finger, he dotes on her. But I've never known him this cross before, and trust me, from the stories Lena's told, he's had just cause over the years. I suspect it's more the publicity surrounding the court case, it's brought his family's hitherto unblemished name into disrepute, and it "simply won't do". He's a very proud man, is our Mr Hageby.'

Jack winces. It was bound to come up, but he was hoping to avoid the subject of the trial for as long as possible. He eyes her with concern. Close up she looks weary, worn down by the stress of it all – the faint outline of worry lines framing her eyes. 'And you? How are you coping with it all?'

Eliza crumples down beside him with a deflated air. She's carried herself with composure, but now her face collapses and she exudes a long, mournful sigh. 'Oh, Jack. If truth be known, I'm struggling. I try to be strong for Lena as, despite appearances, she's not coping well. But I've no one to support me, and it's tough sometimes. I've never been in trouble before.' She pauses, reflects on the veracity of that statement, which she has to admit – since meeting Lena – isn't wholly accurate. 'Well, nothing serious. Not like this.'

'Hey, silly. You've got me. I'm here, you can talk to me anytime. You know that, don't you?'

'The odds are stacked again us. If we lose, there's a potentially huge financial cost – notwithstanding our reputations. We'd be branded liars and troublemakers. God knows if I'll keep my job. Then where would I be? I've no other means except my wage packet.'

She leans toward him, resting her weight against his arm. He tentatively places an arm around her shoulders. She doesn't flinch or offer resistance. Buoyed by this, he gently buries his face in her hair, surreptitiously breathing in the very essence of her, savouring it.

'I'm sorry you're having to deal with this. It's not right. All over a few unfortunate words. He could have brushed them off, shown he was the bigger man, and it all would have been forgotten in days. Yesterday's news. But no, that Bayling wants his pound of flesh for the sheer hell of it.' He chokes on that last sentence. Flushing red, he splutters. 'God, I'm sorry, that was tactless, forgive me.' Eliza looks at him, puzzled, not comprehending the irony; she soon cottons on.

'Don't be daft. I know you didn't mean it cruelly. And besides, we haven't lost yet! You never know, we may even beat the swine.

127

That'd teach him!' She's distracted by something out of the window, points. 'And look, there's pigs flying over Lavender Hill.'

They attempt a chuckle, but it's hollow mirth, neither feeling optimistic. For Jack, the burden of his ongoing deception weighs especially heavily.

Into this melancholic scene jumps Mrs P, square onto Eliza's lap, demanding attention, or food, probably both. The cat and Jack eye each other with suspicion. But she moves closer to give him a tentative sniff. Eliza and Jack hold their breath, Mrs Pankhurst's chequered history with the male of the species precedes her. Extraordinarily, she bunts his arm, deciding he's friend not foe, and hops the short distance into his lap. Eliza stares open-mouthed, stunned by this atypical behaviour from her adored, but temperamental, feline friend.

'Well, I'll be damned! You *are* honoured. Mrs Pankhurst rarely tolerates men. Our poor old postman is terrified of her. She'll lay in wait on the bay window and if he dares venture up the steps, she carries on like a she-devil, hissing and spitting. Once she got close enough to cause him a nasty scratch on his hand. Lena used all her feminine charms to persuade him not to report us.' The cat is now cheek-rubbing Jack's chin and purring. Jack's face betrays his nervousness.

'When she arrived at Battersea, she'd only let women near her. She'd hiss and claw at the men. They feared for their lives she was that feisty, even as a tiny kitten! I suspect that's why Lena adopted her. She's a real man-hater,' Eliza adds with a mischievous glint. Jack grins, they share an unspoken understanding.

She smooths the cat's head. 'Kindred spirits, you and Lena, aren't you, Missus?'

Pleased with the stamp of approval, Jack tentatively scratches Mrs P's chin. She graciously allows it. 'Ah-ha!' he says. 'Her name makes sense now. I was wondering!'

They fall into an amused, comfortable silence. Eliza's eyes dart up to meet Jack's, then glance away shyly. Jack, still unsure of Eliza's intentions, opens his mouth, but no words emerge. He shuts it when he catches sight of his gormless reflection in the glass of the display-case. There's a palpable tension in the air that might explode at any second. And then, it does. Jack can resist no longer, he reaches over and gently presses his lips against hers, she doesn't move away. The moment feels unbearably elongated, until, without warning, they melt into each other. All the pent-up emotion regarding the court case is unleashed in Eliza. Jack, taken aback by her force, willingly surrenders to the urgency in her kiss. They allow themselves to fall back onto the plumped cushions, lost in each other's passion, kissing so deeply it feels as if they are merging into one.

Their mutual lack of experience causes much nervous mirth amidst the fumbling. They're clumsy in their impatience to liberate each other's bodies from their cloth prisons: the corset, many hooks, uncountable buttons, braces and garters. Mrs P, dislodged by this coupling, looks on, her feline sensibilities disgusted by the undignified sight unfolding before her saucer-like pupils.

Suddenly, the door flies open and a distressed Lena stumbles in. She comes to an abrupt halt in the middle of the room. She stares, mouth slack, for several seconds. Long enough for the would-be lovers to comprehend the situation they find themselves in. Lena bellows in a tortured, raw tone that both Eliza and Jack have heard only once before – in that wretched lecture theatre – and never want to hear again.

'What the blazes is *he* doing here?' The two recoil as if struck by lightning. Eliza, mortified at being discovered in such a compromising position, scrabbles to cover her half-undone blouse. Jack, blushing crimson, mis-buttons his shirt and fiddles clumsily with his braces. Lena stands, silently watching their humiliation play out.

'As soon as my back's turned, you're sneaking *him* in. What's wrong with you, Eliza? We've court in a matter of weeks and you're entertaining men without a care. How dare you treat my home like a... like a bloody brothel!'

With a guttural sob, she spins on her heel and storms off to her bedroom, slamming the door with as much force as she can muster.

Eliza's flushed face screws up into a silent 'sorry'. Jack stares at the bedroom door, mortified. He finishes dressing in silence and makes to take his leave. 'I'm so sorry, I'll go. It's obvious it's not a good time. You need to go to Lena. She looked distraught.' He adds with a wry look. 'And I don't think it was just seeing us!'

'Oh, Jack, I'm sure she didn't mean it, I've never seen her like that before. I've no idea what's happened, but it doesn't bode well. She's never back this early from visiting her family.'

They reach the front door of the mansion block. Jack turns to say goodbye.

'Jack, may I ask something of you?' Eliza cuts in, her foot tapping away.

'Yes, of course. What is it?'

'It's more a favour, really.' She pauses, composing herself. 'Well, you know I was saying I've no one? No family to speak of, to be there for me. Lena's got her mother, and father – well maybe – but I've nobody. So, I was wondering...'

Jack visibly wilts, his colour drains.

'... if you'll be there? When I take the stand, I mean. Of course, Lena's there, and Mr Coleridge, but I need someone just for me. Will you? Please say yes. Jack?'

Jack grabs at the railing to steady himself. He's sinking deeper into that all too familiar quagmire. He feels sick to his stomach, but looking at her hopeful, pleading face, he cannot refuse her. He takes a deep breath. The lie tastes of bitter poison as it falls from his lips.

'Yes, yes. Don't fret, you won't be alone, I'll be there. Now, go. Go see to Lena. She's distraught and I don't think it's just seeing my ugly face.' He wants the earth to open and consume him. He's in torment, but unable to see any way to make things right. Make them right and keep Eliza's respect, that is.

Eliza throws caution to the wind. She wraps her arms around his neck and kisses him, straight on the lips, in public. Jack cannot reciprocate. She senses this frigidity and pulls away, confused. She looks at him oddly. 'You don't know how much it means to me, Jack. Thank you.' She chances a tentative smile which doesn't quite make a return volley. He turns from her, his face burning, mumbling as he trips down the steps as fast as his feet can carry him. 'My pleasure, I'll see you in the courtroom.'

Eliza, frowning now, stares after him, mystified. She's always worn her emotions close to the surface. She's at a loss to explain his coolness after their moment of unexpected passion. Yes, Lena walking in on them was unfortunate but, perversely, it was a relief. At least now her feelings for Jack are out in the open, and Lena will just have to get used to it. She and Jack are a couple, and Lena's insidious sniping will have to stop.

She focuses on his slumped, defeated figure until he disappears. Her face is a battleground of emotions – confusion and elation fighting for dominance. She shakes herself out of her reverie, turns and scoops up Mrs P who's wandered out, curious to see what the fuss is about. She re-enters the flat and pads towards Lena's bedroom. Outside the closed door, she sighs, steels herself, and taps softly.

ST MARTIN'S LANE, APRIL 1906 – THE RINGLEADER

It's getting effing tedious now. I 'preciate 'em toffs paid us, and well at that; better than I'd get for a shift down at Tilbury, that's a cert. But for 'eaven's sake fellas, give us some sodding action! They said to be yer by twelve sharp, but it's gone two and still not a peep. And to cap it off, it's turned out bloody hot. I'm sweating turnips in this 'ere coat, but 'ad to wear it. Handy for hiding my 'tools of the trade', shall we say.

My lads are restless. I sense their frustration at not having nuffing to do. I'm the same. It's bollocks, that's what it is. A farthing's a farthing, but its value expires after an eternity of kicking our heels. Anyhow, we drunk our fee some hours ago, partaking of the finest selection of ales available in The Chandos. So, it's pretty fucking pointless us waiting round any longer.

I glance around the tavern, my boys are scattered hither and thither, some asleep on benches, others standing in groups, getting tetchy, I can tell. I shout across the bar. 'Aye, lads. Let's call it a day, shall we? No mongrel-loving lunatics out today.'

'Awright there, Sid. If you say so. We'll be off then,' replies Jim, my best boy. He turns to relay the message, 'aving to kick some of 'em awake. And, dutiful as a bunch of soldiers, they soon dissolve into the crowd like they were never there.

I step out the ale house, intent on getting me omnibus 'ome. But wait, hang-on a second, summat's happening. Summat's definitely going down on the south side.

I sense that familiar thrill, adrenaline pumping, the rush I get just before we pile in. At last, we'll earn our money! I put fingers to lips and give a sharp whistle to get the men's attention. Once rounded up, we skulk along the side of St Martin-in-the-Fields church, keeping out of sight for the moment, sussing out where to focus our efforts.

In the distance, skirting round the worst of the fighting, I spy a gaggle of women. Ladies by the looks, those suffras that're making such a nuisance of themselves all over town, with all their fluff and bluster about getting the vote. Like 'ell they will, we ain't even got it yet, never mind giving it to bleedin' women! I signal the lads to fall in behind the plinth, the one that is missing its statue, I've never known why. We watch them draw closer, their voices getting louder, singing those stupid suffrage tunes. I make a split-second decision. I signal to the lads to follow me and we move away from the plinth and into view.

FOURTEEN

The Trial

The court case is scheduled for late spring. The day dawns bright and sunny, bringing with it all the hopefulness and joy that the season is celebrated for. But this optimism is not shared by the two women making their way along the Strand that morning. Eliza and Lena – their faces in matching granite-set frowns – march in step, as if part of a funeral cortege, drawing ever closer to the famous courthouse that is to determine their fate over the next days. Each is imprisoned in her own private hell, a claustrophobic anxiety that had rendered them mute. Both suffer similar symptoms: a rising nausea that never quite reaches a peak of merciful, if violent, release; ice cold sweats – on such a warm day – making their prim, high-necked blouses and light jackets clammy; and mouths so parched they did not see how they'd be able to utter a word when in the witness stand.

As they approach, desperation to delay the inevitable slows their pace. Try as they might, they cannot ignore the ominous gothic frontage of the Royal Courts of Justice. The brilliant white stone of its ornately carved facade glows in the morning sunshine, its glare too much to take with the naked eye. It exudes an ethereal halo which separates it from the griminess of the surrounding buildings.

Alas, they can delay no longer. As they draw close, they pick up their pace again, eager to bypass the hordes of waiting press who are jostling for position, calling to the women. Eliza halts briefly, unnerved by hearing her name shouted out, but hurries on as the pack approaches. They are demanding comments, words which will be mangled into tomorrow's salacious headline, no doubt. The women run the gauntlet of hundreds of keen eyes and sharp tongues as they skirt an endless snaking line of people, at least thirty yards long: this is the queue for the public gallery. It is, for all its mawkish intent, a scene of true democracy in action. Ranks of rough-and-ready working-class types, waiting cheek-by-jowl with prim, well-to-do society ladies. Both share the crowded pavement with gaggles of young, rowdy males – by the look of them, students of the law.

There is no favour awarded to the 'better heeled' of society. All-comers have to wait in line, equal for once. They queue patiently, eager to witness the already infamous, hotly anticipated court case that has been the talk of the chattering classes for weeks. The case's notoriety is amply demonstrated by the sea of papers, pages flapping gently in the morning's breeze, all headlined with a variation of the front-page splash *Daily News* headline: *Bayling vs Coleridge – legal case begins*.

The women navigate the human hurdles unscathed and come to an abrupt stop outside the main entrance. They stare at the ornately carved stone arched open doorway, set back from the two imposing turreted towers that flank it. Shallow steps lead up to a set of two identical arches that contain the doors leading to the lobby.

Before they enter, they take turns scanning the length of the broad thoroughfare, hopeful of spotting a familiar face. The street is busy at this time of the morning, but squint all they like, there's no sign of either Lena's father or the errant Jack – who Eliza hadn't seen since that fateful afternoon. After minutes of fruitless scanning, they admit defeat, turn to head into the dark, imposing vestibule of the court.

A mature, deep male voice booms Lena's name; they stop in their tracks and spin around. Lena brightens, smiling for the first time that week, then slumps somewhat when she recognises the owner of the voice. Bustling towards them, waving and out of breath, hurries Stephen Coleridge. They wait the moments it takes for him to draw level. He dabs at his forehead with a silk handkerchief and beams at them. 'My dears, I'm so glad to have caught you. We should have a quick briefing before we enter, just to make sure we are singing from the same hymn book and all that.' He cuts off, chastises himself. 'But, heavens, where are my manners? I haven't asked after you. How are you both?' They mumble the expected pleasantries, but their faces cannot disguise their despair.

Coleridge, attuned to reading expressions over his many years in court, empathises. 'It has been exceedingly wearisome, I confess. I didn't imagine Bayling would see this farce of a case through. I'd taken it for bluff and bluster, given he hasn't a leg to stand on. The evidence is unequivocal: he broke the law! Any half-competent jury will see that immediately.' Seeing anxiety still etched on their faces, he smiles at them, offers a reassuring pat on the arm. He is not in luck and they remain resolutely glum.

At that moment, Bayling and his legal entourage sweep past them up the steps. Bayling turns to regard all three of them from his vantage point. Exuding a smug, confident air, he nods and doffs his hat. 'Mr Coleridge, sir. It's been a while.' Coleridge coolly acknowledges him with a detached grace. Bayling turns to the women, he bows. 'Ladies, what a pleasure it is to see you both again.' He smirks. They scowl. 'But what a shame it's to be in such sorry circumstances. All of this... What shall we call it? Mmm, *unpleasantness* fits the bill well. It could've been so easily avoided with a ... simple. Straightforward. Apology.'

Coleridge emits a loud, indignant snort.

Bayling turns his gaze to Coleridge. 'Instead, you'll soon be paying dearly for your foolhardiness.' He shakes his head in mock sympathy, all the while his eyes displaying intense amusement. 'It's all so very, very unfortunate, and the expense of it too. My, oh my!'

Bayling pauses, anticipating the forthcoming retaliation. He was relishing an angry tirade from the delightful Miss Hageby. But... nothing. Both women stare beyond him, faces impassive, neither willing to give their nemesis the satisfaction. Annoyed, he returns his gaze to Coleridge, daring him to speak. Coleridge is delighted to oblige.

'Dr Bayling. *Sir*. Why, in God's name, should we apologise? In a civilised society one rarely feels the need to excuse oneself for speaking the truth, does one, however inconvenient?' Coleridge, unblinking, regards him blandly, unnerving Bayling. 'How could we retract what's a wholly accurate account of pernicious cruelty, illegally inflicted on a conscious animal? Hmm?' Coleridge neither requires nor waits for a reply.

'And to what end, might I be so bold as to ask? It's clear the whole sorry charade had no scientific merit whatsoever. It transpired to be entirely for the puerile entertainment of your bloodthirsty disciples.'

'How dare you, sir! What damned impertinence. You're making yourself look foolish, simply compounding your slanderous nonsense.'

'Sir, if we were to forsake the truth now, and deny that wretched creature the justice he deserves, I put it to you we would be more deserving of contempt than even the perpetrator of that savagery.' Coleridge puffs himself up like a peacock.

'Our day in court is welcomed. Not lamented, as you seem to suggest. It will prove us the moral, and legal, victors. And you, sir, will be exposed for what you truly are: an amateur, a sadistic butcher's boy masquerading as a medical professional.'

Bayling's calm demeanour dissolves before their eyes. His face turns an unfortunate, livid shade of purple as his blood pressure rises to dangerous levels. 'Well,' he splutters. 'We've not long to wait to see which one of us will be left licking their wounds. I'll see you in court. Good day to you all.' He whips round and disappears into the murky gloom of the court building. His legal team is left scrambling in his wake.

The women wide-eye each other, then turn to stare, open-mouthed, at Coleridge. He grins, a mischievous twinkle in his eye. 'Ah, well, ladies, you know what they say, "in for a penny" and all such good stuff.'

After a final, futile scan of their surroundings, they follow Coleridge into the darkness of the narrow entrance lobby and through into the central space. When their eyes adjust, they gasp at the lavishness of the wide, airy Great Hall. This space has been constructed entirely of Portland stone, the floor colourful patterned caustic tiles. Leaded glass windows, positioned high in the walls, depict magnificent, painted displays of various coats of arms and, above them is an impressive, vaulted stone ceiling. The women look up in awe, executing a three-sixty degree turn as they absorb the confident grandeur of the place, and for a brief, exquisite moment forgetting their troubles. Coleridge looks on, amused by their childlike wonder. This being his workplace, he takes as much notice of the magnificent decoration as a shop worker would notice changes in a window display as they hurry, head bowed and indifferent, to and from work each day.

Then, with reluctance, they move towards their allotted courtroom, Court Number Two. The location of the courtroom has been upgraded in the weeks leading up to the case, given the increased, indeed frenzied, interest. The pomp and splendour of the central lobby are left at the courtroom door, however. Inside is a pared back, modest room, clad in a rich brown oak, which welcomes natural light through a series of landscape windows skimming the ceiling across two of the four walls.

The court opens to the public and press corps. The room is packed in no time, court staff having to turn away disappointed latecomers. Lena, Eliza and Coleridge sit at the front, just behind their counsel, Mr George Walton, and his team.

The women keep their eyes forward, staring at the judge's empty wooden throne, with its royal crest looming above it. They summon the courage to glance up to the gallery, eyes like lighthouse beams washing over the bobbing sea of anonymous, hostile faces. The crowd stares down at them, curiosity at fever pitch. The women's scan is in vain – there is no one they recognise here. But, on further scrutiny, Lena gasps, spotting a familiar face. Her mother smiles down at her, signalling discreetly with her fingers, shy of drawing attention to herself in this vulgar crowd. Lena smiles gratefully and, with renewed hope, glances either side for a glimpse of her Papa. It's to no avail; he's not present. Lena's face crumples at the realisation. Mrs Hageby's expression soon mirrors her daughter's deflated look: it's not enough that *she's* there for Lena and she knows it.

Bayling sits on the opposite side, equally close to the front. He's leaning forward, conferring with his team, issuing instructions and barking orders to his harried-looking barrister. Oscar, Hugh and James sit some rows behind Bayling. Next to Oscar, there remains an empty seat.

Once the court's declared to be in session, they announce the jury. Everyone turns to stare at the parade of twelve impassive figures. They enter single file, like monks gliding into prayer and take their allotted seats, protected from defendants by a high solid wooden barrier: the dozen white, middle-aged males whose random, undeserved, and temporary hold on power will, over the course of the next days, decide the women's fate. In Lena's fevered imagination, they merge into one amorphous mass of heartless, callous judgement. The jurors display a common skin tone of a pallid ash grey, as if they rarely glimpse daylight. Their identical, dour demeanours give them a uniform, humourless look. She shivers, sinks further into the uncomfortable wooden bench.

There's a low, constant, but not disagreeable hum in the room, the sound of hundreds of conversations taking place among the press, public, the prosecution and defence teams. No one's voice is discernible above the discordant chatter. Eliza muses the overall effect as being what she imagines the Tower of Babel sounded like in its day-to-day business. A sensation sweeps through the room that foretells the show's about to begin. The hum dies away. An expectant silence fills the space.

With a sombre tone, the clerk announces the judge, ordering court to stand to show due respect. Lord Justice Alverstone enters through an almost invisible door in the panelling to the left of his high wooden chair. He strides in, a majestic air to his gait. But for all his pomp he has the appearance of a kindly older gent. Eliza estimates him to be in his early sixties. He has wise, penetrating, milky green eyes and grey whiskery, pork chop sideburns that almost reach the edges of his thin, wrinkled lips. After taking his seat and making himself comfortable, he acknowledges the room, the jury, legal counsel, the defendants and litigant. He executes this with such a sense of authenticity and courtesy it has the effect of convincing the audience they're in the presence of an honest, righteous man. A man they can trust to deliver justice. He welcomes the jury, calls court to order, and the proper process begins.

First to take the stand are the expert witnesses, called to help judge and jury understand the disputed technical points the case hinges upon. Veterinarians, anaesthetists, and other independent medical experts give their professional opinion on the opposing accounts – provided by the women and Bayling – regarding the dog's state of consciousness. The court watch as a succession of interchangeable, bland medical men espouse their often-conflicting views. After a time, their submissions become a confused blur of dissenting voices.

'My Lord Justice. It is my professional opinion that the anaesthetic administered would not have been adequate to ensure full sedation. Hence it was more likely that the dog would have been semi-conscious throughout the procedure.'

'My Lord, gentlemen of the jury. In my considered view, too large a dose of the anaesthetic would be entirely consistent with the explanation as to why the subject didn't respond to the electrical stimulation. I believe this to be the most viable explanation for the facts as they were presented to me for analysis.'

'M'Lud. The gas administered was of an obsolete formulation, no longer in common usage because of its proven unreliability. Hence it is my professional view that it's entirely feasible the dog was conscious throughout the procedure.'

The expert testimonies conclude, serving only to emit more heat than light on the subject under discussion. The judge, jury, press and public remain none the wiser as to the dog's condition. A frustrated Justice Alverstone, his patience stretched by the muddle of conflicting evidence, calls an end to proceedings. They are to resume after luncheon with the testimonies of the medical students.

The women's insides are far too churned up to contemplate eating a single morsel, so they endure the unedifying sight of Coleridge and his counsel Walton devouring a hearty meal of lamb stew with suet dumplings, washed down with an amber ale, and rounded off with a squat, smelly cigar each. They avoid talk of the trial. It's not too difficult as no one is any clearer after the morning's ramblings.

The men conclude their meal with grunts of satisfaction aimed at the waiting staff. They declare themselves replete and ready for battle. This is where the fun and games begin, they inform the women, who cringe at the flippant language. Walton declares himself loaded and ready for action, fully intent on decimating the student's evidence, line-by-line. Lena remarks that shouldn't that be 'lie-by-lie'. His self-belief in his abilities is infectious. They return to their unyielding wooden seats with a refreshed enthusiasm.

Hugh, James, and then Oscar, are called to the stand. Their evidence is suspiciously similar, not just in content but in tone and delivery, as if they'd been rehearsing their lines together. When placed side by side, their words tell an identical story, a sentence read out by each witness.

'I swear by almighty God that the evidence I shall give...'

'We were sitting three rows back and to the right of the women...'

'I had an uninterrupted view of the stage.'

'The animal in question was fully sedated; there was no question of there being any conscious movement...'

'No, sir, there was no sound whatsoever coming from the dog; the ladies must have been mistaken.'

Hugh and James are dismissed by the increasingly irritated judge.

It's clear to him the men have been coached, and – given their careful use of words and phrases – that legal experts had advised on language. As much as it frustrates him, there is nothing he can do. Such practices are not illegal, even if their ethics are morally dubious.

Oscar, much to his dismay, is kept on the stand for longer than his companions. The prosecution gently coaxes him through his account of his actions that evening, the actions proceding the dog's eventual death. He delivers, word perfectly, the lines he has been rehearsing for weeks. He visibly relaxes when Bayling's barrister nods to the judge. 'I have no further questions for this witness, M'Lud.'

But Oscar's ordeal is by no means over yet. He is still to be cross-examined by the defence counsel. Walton rises, whispers to his assistant, who nods assent. He walks over to Oscar, eyeing him all the way.

'Mr Oscar Sebastian Latham-Ward, can you confirm to the court your status as a third-year medical student at University College London?'

'Yes, I confirm that is my current status.'

'So, still an undergraduate indeed. Not yet a qualified practitioner. In fact, it will be several years before you do become fully qualified. Is that correct?' Oscar swallows and nods. 'Mr Latham-Ward, for the benefit of the court you must verbalise your agreement.'

'Yes, sir.' Oscar squeaks.

Walton continues. 'So, we can agree, that – on the night in question – you were not qualified to perform public dissections on living specimens, in front of an audience. Is that correct?'

'Yes, sir.'

'And, as a matter of *fact*, this was, therefore, an unlawful act undertaken by yourself on the specific request of your tutor, Dr William Bayling? Correct?'

Oscar is flinching under the unwavering scrutiny of Walton, who isn't giving an inch. He glances across to Bayling. This is unchartered territory. The lawyers hadn't coached him on this angle, and he is struggling with what's acceptable to admit. He fears implicating Bayling further, and the inevitable consequences of such a slip.

Bayling, equally uncomfortable with the way this is headed, avoids Oscar's stare. He shuffles nervously in his seat. One part of him, the small pocket of conscience that still experiences compassion, feels guilt for placing the youth in such an invidious position. However, the dominant, self-serving Bayling is much more concerned with the damage Oscar could do with the odd, carelessly spoken word. He stretches over to his counsel, seated in front of him, whispers. The barrister doesn't turn, but nods in agreement.

'Isn't that correct, Mr Latham-Ward?'

'Yes, I now believe it to be the case. However, in my defence, at the time I'd no idea...'

'Thank you, Mr Latham-Ward, that will suffice.' He turns to face the judge. 'No further questions, M'Lud.'

Next, the clerk calls a Mr Albert John Forsyth to the stand. There's no response, no movement in the witness seats. An interminable pause ensues, before the usher works his way to the front and passes a note to the judge. He reads and nods, that being the signal for the clerk to call the next witness, Doctor William Bayling.

Oscar and the men glance at the empty seat and then each other, shoulders shrugging. Their attention is diverted to the sight of Bayling being sworn in. Tall, proud, haughty, he is a formidable sight. His testimony is revealed to be identical to that of his students.

'I swear by almighty God that the...'

'The animal was fully sedated...'

'Absolutely no sounds were coming from...'

'No movement whatsoever...'

The line of questioning by his barrister is no more than a slickly rehearsed advert, devised to promote his adherence to the highest ethical practices in the realm of medical vivisection.

Lena audibly scoffs at what she is hearing until the judge throws her a stern look. She picks incessantly at the skin around her fingernails; Eliza places her hands over hers, stroking them. She relaxes only when Walton rises to start his cross-examination, even allowing herself a fraction of a smile at the thought of Bayling's forthcoming flaying at his hand.

'Dr Bayling, can you confirm the specimen used, the terrier dog, had been used on many previous occasions, by various researchers, for different dissections?'

'I can.' He pauses. 'But for a perfectly logical, humane reason.' He absorbs the murmur of surprise emanating from the gallery. 'If you'll allow me to elaborate?'

Walton feigns a coughing attack. 'Humane? Why, Doctor, do continue. Please, enlighten us here today...' He throws his arms around to illustrate the court is all ears '... as to how the repeated unlawful torture of a helpless animal can ever, in any civilised society, be described as humane?'

'Mr Walton, I will not tolerate such emotive language in my court, if you please,' the judge reminds him. Walton demurs, albeit reluctantly. He gestures for Bayling to continue.

'Sir, surely the use of fewer animals in such vital experimentation is to be welcomed, encouraged, is it not? Particularly in this modern, so-called enlightened age, where the feelings of lower forms of life are put on a level with the suffering of human beings?' His palms are held up to the heavens in despair as he addresses the jury directly. 'Hence it baffles me why I'm being vilified for reducing that suffering. Using just one specimen when I could have legally, justifiably, used two, three, more!' The jury remains unmoved, impassive, absorbing the proceedings without emotion. No one displays the slightest reaction to anything revealed so far.

Walton continues in the same combative vein, challenging Bayling on each point Coleridge called him out on. Bayling's answers are careful, measured, in each case appealing to the greater good resulting from his actions. Finally, the verbal volleying between the men falters: they have both run out of steam. Walton fails to make a distinct dent in Bayling's defences. Bayling, however, after repeated, unflinching questioning, has to admit failing to follow established legal procedures. He reluctantly acknowledges the unlawful multiple use of one specimen, the possibility of the dog being under-anesthetised, and – most unequivocally – the use of an unqualified person both in the vivisection and euthanasia of the creature.

Next, it is the women's turn to take the stand. They give coherent statements of what they witnessed. In contrast to the students' carbon-copy accounts, each gives their account from their unique perspective, with their distinctive voices. There is no hint of rehearsal or calibration of their stories. Indeed, there hadn't been. The women couldn't bear the thought of reliving their experience yet again. There was no need anyway: each had every minute of that evening's horrors seared into their memory. Inevitably they saw, felt and experienced a different truth to the other, but their combined testimony is watertight. They know what they saw, heard, and nothing, no amount of aggressive – the sympathetic newspapers would argue intimidating – cross-examining by prosecuting counsel can poke holes in their accounts. To the contrary, they appear to grow stronger, more resolute, the more rigorous the interrogation.

Eliza handles it with more self-control than Lena, but even so, Lena surprises herself by holding on to her composure. She keeps her fiery temper in check. She is excused and strides back to her seat, head held high. Her mother, who did not dare take a breath throughout her testimony, smiles down at her daughter, prouder of her in that moment than she has ever had cause to be.

Finally, Coleridge is called to the stand. He is asked by the prosecution to reiterate his exact words from the public meeting. He obliges, with a distinct lack of remorse, delighted with the opportunity to fire every acid-filled word at his adversary directly. He pauses to secure his recently acquired spectacles around his ears.

He catches Bayling's eye and holds it: unwavering, unblinking, unashamed. He repeats each of his accusations, verbatim. Bayling sits, pinned to the bench under Coleridge's piercing stare. He wills every muscle, every sinew in his body to be still, but finds he cannot control a slight twitch to his right shoulder. It is imperceptible to most, but not to Coleridge, whose lips curl ever-so-slightly upwards. Bayling's counsel offers him the chance to recant and apologise for such slanderous slurs on an innocent man's otherwise spotless character. To no one's surprise, Coleridge imperiously refuses to entertain such a ludicrous request.

There is nothing more to add, or to be revealed, by drawing out this tetchy questioning any further. Coleridge is dismissed from the stand, struts back – jaw set firm, nose in the air – to his seat. He winks encouragingly at the women. Judge Alverstone confirms, via a raised eyebrow to the clerk, that the day's proceedings are done. He moves to stand down the jury. Once the sombre procession of grey-suited, bowed jurors has filed out, he dismisses the rest of the audience.

Eliza glances around, idly watching as the court empties. Pressmen chattering noisily as they shuffle out, society ladies gossiping behind cupped hands, with not a care in the world; it was simply a day's free, deliciously scandalous entertainment for them. She sits quietly, unbothered by the hubbub of the emptying courtroom, the disruption glancing off her like raindrops hitting a drum. Well, it's done now, she concludes. Our fate lies solely in the hands of twelve unreadable, sallow-faced strangers. She feels a peculiar sense of calm, a serenity that takes her by surprise. And more unexpectedly, even the non-appearance of Jack hasn't distressed her *too* unduly, she'd been too preoccupied with proceedings to really notice. What will be, will be. The absence of emotion, the disappearance of the constant, churning dread she'd lived with for the past week, is slightly disconcerting. She side-eyes Lena, curious to view her friend's reaction. Lena is stretching across, whispering with Mr Coleridge. He pats her arm affectionately. She returns a weak smile, but Eliza can tell it's not genuine. Lena turns back, her doleful eyes scan Eliza's greedily, searching for reassurance that everything is going to be alright. Eliza takes Lena's hands into her own.

'It's over, Lena. We did well. *You* did well. If they don't believe us after that, then so be it. We couldn't have done more, we've done *him* proud, and that's all that matters.' Lena nods, summons up a sad grin and Eliza feels Lena's hands tense. Her shoulders unfurl and her chin juts out in that quaintly pompous way of hers.

'Yes, Liza. You're absolutely right. We bloody well did. And we aren't done yet. We've still got the not insignificant matter of a memorial to deliver, don't forget.'

The last to vacate the court, Eliza, Lena and the two men leave the building together, forming a tight clique, to better repel the relentless pursuit by the press. The press pack finally gives up hope of getting a comment and its members scuttle away to file their copy for the morning's headlines. The women bid Coleridge and Walton a pleasant evening and head for home, their perfectly aligned steps a lot lighter than they were on arrival that morning.

FIFTEEN

The Verdict

The following day dawns in similar fashion to the one before: cloudless, warm and full of promise. The women, their worst day behind them, set off with more of a spring in their step. They travel to court on a packed, suburban electric train from Clapham railway junction, battling through the throng of city workers, all of whom have the same intention: to get to their workplace with as little interaction with their fellow commuters as possible. It is a futile hope, thwarted daily, given the train is stuffed like a sardine tin before it has pulled into the platform; it is filled as it passes through the new commuter suburbs of Wimbledon, Sutton and beyond. On reaching Victoria, they swap to the underground train to emerge, somewhat sooty and crumpled, from a bustling Holborn station.

Relieved to be back in the open – if not exactly fresh – air, they retrace their steps with a brisk walk down Chancery Lane towards the Law Courts. Both are in a talkative mood, mulling over aspects of the case, tentatively weighing up their chances, but careful not to mention what really preys on their minds – the conspicuous absence of a certain two men.

They reach the courthouse to be confronted by an identical scene to yesterday's: a snaking queue of people chattering away without a care in the world. The majority are back for a second chance to gawk, discuss the finer points of the arguments, eager to witness, first-hand, the hotly debated verdict.

Many are devouring the write-up of the previous day's drama in the morning papers. The inevitable press pack is in attendance again, its number swelled dramatically overnight. They are well named, Eliza thinks, their behaviour reminiscent of a ravenous pack of wolves, tracking down their desired prey, desperate to be first to the kill, by whatever means. Unfortunately for the women, they are the tasty morsels the pack currently has its eye on, and it is not so easy to avoid them the second time around. In an instant, they are spotted and encircled.

The journalists bark their names from all directions, disorientating them and bringing on an unexpected panic attack in Eliza. The sensation she is about to be crushed overwhelms her. A blackness descends, she is sure she will faint right there. She grabs at Lena, silently mouthing 'help'. Lena's protective instinct toward Eliza overcomes any personal jeopardy. Standing her ground, she articulates in a clear, loud voice, that the journalists present – if they indeed consider themselves civilised gentlemen – should please have a care and make way for two ladies to proceed unhindered. The demand is so formal, the order so authoritative and calm, the men fall back instantly. Shamed by their uncouth behaviour, they allow the women passage with no further harassment.

Eliza rushes up the steps and flees into the central lobby area. It is a space that, to her, represents calm, tranquillity and safety. She stands, panting, leaning for support on one of many statues of bygone royalty, slowly regaining her composure. Lena joins her, concern etched into her flawless pink and cream complexion. Eliza smiles weakly, gives her a reassuring nod, straightens up and without a word they march, heads high, back into Court Number Two.

Again, the court is soon packed and the press gallery has standing room only. The women scan the public benches. No familiar faces. To Lena's regret, not even her mother is here today. They both feel the sharp stab of betrayal. A last glance only serves to locate Oscar – a smug grin on his face – leering down at them. Their attention is taken by the clerk of court calling order.

'All rise.'

The room shuffles to its feet. Lord Alverstone emerges once more from his secret door, and, with that regal air of his, takes his seat at the head of the room.

'Members of the jury, ladies and gentlemen of the court, please be seated.' A scraping of chairs and rustling as the court sits.

'We've heard evidence from all parties concerned.' He acknowledges the barristers, the jury, then nods and turns to the women with a benevolent smile.

'The two young ladies gave unequivocal, coherent accounts of their experience on the night in question. I've no reason to doubt their sincerity and compassion for the plight of that animal. And, indeed, for laboratory animals in general. Nonetheless, their evidence was directly contradicted by the accounts of the men also in attendance and, I may add, from similar vantage points. One may argue that medical students, given their education and experience, are in a better position to assess the condition of the animal, however well-intentioned the young ladies may be.'

He pauses, scans the jury. They stare back at him, unblinking, inscrutable.

'We've also heard expert testimony from a variety of veterinarians and anaesthetists. Their testimony has not much helped clarify my thinking on the aspect of the dog's level of consciousness, and ability to experience pain, such was the level of disagreement between them.' His face scrunches with irritation. 'However, it is incumbent upon you, gentlemen of the jury, to consider that expert testimony, to consider whether you are able, on the basis of it, to form a reasonably certain view of the dog's level of consciousness.

'What *is* clear, however, is the fact – verified by the Plaintiff himself – that he, and others like him, used the wretched creature on more than one occasion, and for multiple experiments. This, gentlemen of the jury, is a clear transgression of the Act as it stands.' Lena dares to glance at Eliza, a shadow of hope hovering.

'Also not in dispute is the fact an unqualified medical student was encouraged – again by the Plaintiff – to remove a body part from the animal, before being instructed to kill it. This also contravenes the Act.' The women raise a hopeful smile.

'Finally, we have heard the testimony of Mr Stephen Coleridge, the defendant. A man whose father, for the court's record, I knew both as a friend and colleague when he held this position of Lord Chief Justice before me. The defendant is charged that, in a public place, with witnesses present, he did defame and damage the professional reputation of the Plaintiff, Dr William Malcolm Bayling, with accusations of premeditated torture and illegal practices contrary to the *Cruelty to Animals Act of 1876*. He refused, when given the chance here in court, to retract these comments.'

With the summing up of the evidential phase of the case thus closed, Lord Alverstone takes a moment, adjusts his glasses, then clears his throat.

'I'm obliged to instruct the jury that it would be considered a complete defence of the accusation of the original slander if Mr Coleridge, and his counsel, were to prove that the allegations are substantially true. That being whether the Plaintiff had indeed performed an operation on an animal that was not fully anaesthetised and had thus committed a criminal offence. This accusation had been publicly made by the defendant; whose case was that he had exercised the public right of criticising the system of licensed vivisection in general and had not exceeded the fair bounds of criticising what was a fair subject for public comment. And it is to this specific legal point I direct my comments.' Coleridge bends to look over at the women, smiles encouragingly.

'Normally, a case of this nature would attract limited public interest. However, it has been reported upon so widely that, regretfully, it has become a story of fevered national obsession. This unfortunate situation must not be allowed to influence your discussions or your decision today.'

Alverstone regards the twelve men sternly, some shift awkwardly in their seats.

'Gentlemen of the jury, I call on you not to dwell too long, or too

151

deeply, on the general case for, or against, vivisection *per se*. That complicated, contentious debate is for another time, another place. It *will not* be deliberated upon in this court.' A flicker of emotion might be detected in one or two.

'I, myself, a dog owner for much of my life, am extremely fond of my own hounds. You may well be too. But any such personal affections are to be put out of mind today. It is your solemn and legal duty to weigh the balance of evidence set before you, and only that evidence, to determine whether you believe the defendant, Mr Stephen Coleridge, was within his rights to besmirch the plaintiff. If, in your judgement, his words were justified by your belief in the veracity of the women's testimonies, then you must find for the defendant. This case pivots on that one crucial point. I urge you to focus your deliberations on that, and that alone.'

He lets his words settle. 'I call on you all now to retire to debate where the burden of proof lies and consider your verdict. Court is dismissed.' The jury leave the room, then the rest of court empties.

The women, Coleridge and Walton, are ushered out of the courtroom and deposited in a small ante-chamber off the main lobby. It is sparsely furnished with a long oak table and uncomfortable, high-backed wooden chairs. The only comfort afforded is a clutch of flaccid cushions to soften the ache, which would become a painful eventuality if holed up here for too long. Coleridge and Walton take their chances and sit, whispering across the table. Lena stands at the only window, staring out, contemplative and distant. Eliza paces, her cool demeanour now stripped away. Her worries come tumbling out.

'So? Mr Walton, Mr Coleridge, what are our chances? I was watching them, the jury. They were so emotionless, devoid of pity. All carbon copies of Bayling, I'd swear to it. It would be a different story if they allowed women on juries. We're going to lose, aren't we? They didn't believe us. After all, we're just silly, hysterical women with no clue about medical matters.'

Lena snaps. 'Oh, shut up, Eliza. Why shouldn't they believe us?

We were credible, genuine, much more believable that those clones that had rehearsed every single word that came out of their lying mouths. Bayling admitted he re-used the dog, and that clown of a student admitted he unlawfully killed him. How can they *not* believe us?'

Coleridge rises and takes Lena by the shoulders, leading her to a chair. The last thing they need is an altercation now.

There is a sudden short, urgent rap at the door. The clerk pops his head around, addresses the men. 'Jury's reached its verdict, sirs.'

Coleridge frowns, takes out his pocket watch, then risks a cautious smile. 'Mmm, that was quick. Barely thirty minutes. This must mean a unanimous verdict. If there was any dissension in the ranks, they'd be locked away for hours. On balance, I feel this works in our favour.'

Walton smiles at the women, picking up Coleridge's strand as he sees their puzzled expressions.

'You see, they had to weigh up whether they believed you two fine ladies. If they did, it's a straightforward decision. All else falls away, as the judge rightly implied: Stephen is vindicated and Bayling has lost.' Walton's grin widens.

'Otherwise, they would have had to consider the students' evidence and the conflicting testimonies of the expert witnesses. That would inevitably take longer and be more divisive, more argumentative. They then would have to weigh up where the balance of evidence lay – with you or with them – which would surely take some hours. Yes, ladies. I believe we've done it. '

They look to each other, their eyes reflecting a growing hope. Coleridge inflates his chest and grins. Walton sits calmly, confidence oozing from every pore.

Heads held high, they troop back into the courtroom and resume their seats. The court is brought to order. The jury is the last to be called. They slope in, sit stiffly, eleven pairs of eyes staring into the middle distance, not catching anyone's gaze. The jury foreman then takes his place at the far end of the group, seated nearest to the

153

judge. Lord Alverstone addresses them.

'Gentlemen of the jury, have you reached a unanimous verdict?'

'Yes, we have, My Lord,' the foreman replies.

'And how do you find the defendant, Stephen George Coleridge?'

'We find the defendant guilty as charged, my Lord.'

The world stops turning. The women sit, paralysed. They had taken Walton's words to heart, they'd felt confident of victory, thought his reasoning so watertight it was not to be questioned.

A hushed moment as the court takes in a collective breath, then it is bedlam. The public gallery, the women now see, is packed with medical students, whooping, clapping and back-slapping Oscar, who wears a smile as broad as the Cheshire cat.

At the back of the public gallery, standing in shadow, a familiar figure. It is Reginald Hageby, his proud Roman face a portrait of pain and regret. He turns and leaves the courtroom, unnoticed by his desolate daughter.

The women face each other, their faces blank. Walton turns to console Coleridge who, to be fair, does not appear overly surprised or upset. He gazes dispassionately at the retreating backs of the jurors, now filing out of the courtroom with undue haste, their unpleasant duty discharged.

Lord Alverstone calls for order, but the court is in uproar. The pressmen are clamouring, but are efficiently, and roughly, restrained by a small army of court officials. Order's restored, silence resumes.

'Mr Stephen George Coleridge, the jury has found you guilty of the charges laid against you. I therefore order you to apologise to the Plaintiff and to retract your comments in a public sphere. You will, in addition, pay a sum of two thousand pounds to Dr Bayling, in recompense for the damage to his good name. As well as all legal costs arising. Ladies and gentlemen. Thank you for your patience. I now dismiss the court.'

The room empties, except for the principal opposing parties. Coleridge, with a defiant flourish, produces his cheque book and gold-inlaid fountain pen. He slowly writes out a cheque, waves it for a few moments to dry the ink. He rises and walks over to his adversary, who is laughing and back-slapping with his legal team. The men eyeball each other. Coleridge, without a word, much less an apology, hands over the cheque. Bayling, stunned, recovers his composure sufficiently to accept it with a smug, exaggerated grace. Coleridge turns on his heel and departs the courtroom without a word, pompously ignoring the press who hound him out of the building.

Court is eerily silent, a triumphant Bayling having swept out after bidding the women an effusive and patronising farewell. Lena and Eliza are the only two left in the echoey chamber. The court clerk, having popped his head around the door, observes their distressed state and decides against asking them to vacate. He is only too aware of the rugby scrum press pack that awaits them. It is a fate he wouldn't wish on anyone, particularly not these two fine young ladies who – in his humble opinion – have been treated badly in this whole sorry process.

The women sit hunched, broken, staring at the empty judge's chair.

'He didn't come, Lena. He promised he would, but he didn't. Not a word.'

'Nor did Papa. I so believed he'd relent ... be here for me. He always has. No matter what, he's always stood by me, defended me against everyone.' She breaks into gusty, loud sobs – a two-day dam of pent-up anxiety breached at last.

They hug, each wallowing in their personal betrayal. Finally, emotion spent, they gather their belongings and leave. Thankfully, the press have given up hope, surmising the women have sneaked out through a back exit, and so have sloped off back to their smoke-filled offices to write up the story for the morning's covers.

The women reverse their earlier journey in a near-empty train, but they do not notice nor care for the improved comfort. They disembark at Clapham Junction and continue on foot. They amble up Lavender Hill, without purpose, a cloud of despair hovering about them.

They turn into their street. In the distance, a figure sits on the low wall that borders the flower bed outside the bay window. Lena gasps. Eliza, eyes trailing the pavement, shuffles along oblivious, her shoulder brushing the street railings as if she needs them to stay upright. Her face is expressionless, worn like a mask, almost shielding her misery from the world. Lena nudges her, gesturing towards their flat.

Eliza halts, taking a loud gulp of air as she processes the scene. A hint of optimism crosses her lips, but it does not last. Just as rapidly, her face darkens as a storm of fury engulfs her, her pupils narrowing to snake-like slits.

They close in, Eliza unable to take her eyes off the figure. He seems in deep conversation with somebody, someone unseen, and does not notice their approach. They are close enough now to overhear his words. He is conversing with ... their cat.

'Hey, Mrs P, at least you're still talking to me. I doubt anyone else in this house is.'

The women approach.

'Hello, Jack.'

Startled, he whips his head round. 'Eliza. Lena. You're back.' His eyes dart from one to the other and back again to Eliza. 'Oh, Eliza, I'm so, so sorry. I've just heard. I'm devastated I couldn't be there, I really am, but you see on the way to court yesterday I...'

Eliza cuts him dead with a glare. She is on the verge of a tirade when she notices two wooden sticks leant against the gate. Her gaze shifts further along Jack's prone body. He is sitting with his left leg at an angle, foot on the ground. His right leg is stretched out in front of him, resting along the length of the wall, encased – from knee to big toe – in a plaster of Paris cast. Jack follows her gaze, winces as he shifts the imprisoned leg. She gasps, a flash of clarity dawning. She skips the last steps, bends down and awkwardly throws her arms around him, all the while laughing and crying, relief writ large across her face. Lena looks on at the joyous reunion unfolding in front of her. She cannot disguise her dismay: it illuminates as surely as a lighthouse beam.

TRAFALGAR SQUARE, APRIL 1906 – THE STUDENT

I take the final stair of the Underground station into the dazzling sunshine of the square. I stand, dumbfounded by the scene of chaos unfolding in front of me. The protestors are piling in from the southern side, there is a river of them flowing along Whitehall, as far as the eye can see. There seems no end to their number. Their folly was to contain themselves to one massive line, rather than approach from multiple directions. They were sitting ducks for the Antis who have been lying in wait either side, amassing up the Strand and along the Mall. It was an ambush, plain and simple, and they blithely walked straight into it, the fools. The Antis pick off the frontline marchers and corral them into one space in the middle of the square. Fights are sparking across the open ground. As I watch, I see two roughs with cudgels relentlessly battering a crouching man sheltering to the side of Nelson's Column. The chanting is at fever pitch now, with the protestors' banners being used as weapons or lying in the gutters, being stamped on furiously by the Antis.

I break into a sprint, pushing men out of my path as I rush towards the epicentre of the violence, which was culminating between the two fountains. I need to find her, reach her before she gets hurt. They'll be looking out for them, theirs would be the ultimate scalps for the mob to claim. Oh God, I couldn't bear it if anything happened to her. All this is my fault. If I'd been braver from the start, told the truth. Suddenly I hear an all too familiar voice at my back.

'Jack! You traitor. You've got a fucking nerve.'

I spin round. He stands before me. Eyes wild but glazed, nostrils flared, he's high on the thrill of the violence happening around him. He holds aloft a short wooden baton.

SIXTEEN

Bayling

THE BAYLING FAMILY HOME, LATER THAT DAY

William Malcolm Bayling strolls along the garden path, an air of smugness about him. If one did not know him better, you could almost imagine a skip in his step. He pauses to appreciate his elegant, red-brick villa, situated in the most fashionable and, as he often slips into conversation, expensive area of Highgate. Situated to the north of London, its elevation and distance away from the noise, pollution and hoi polloi of the city make it a sought-after address.

He notices an over-enthusiastic wisteria has scrambled across the bedroom windows and makes a mental note to enquire into the services of a gardener to wrestle it back into order before it plunges them into a perpetual purple darkness.

He breathes deeply, taking stock, admiring the mature, if rather neglected, garden. Borders of unruly lavender spill onto the path. The gnarly old crab apple drowns under a vigorous purple clematis. A camellia has cast off its frowzy petals, scattering them confetti-like across the lawn. He realises – given the distractions of these last months – that this is the first time he has seen his garden, properly seen it, this year. But that is the past. Today he has won. He's been vindicated by twelve men good and true. He feels energised, reborn, rediscovering an optimism he was convinced had deserted him for good. That fool Coleridge can crawl back to his kennel and lament his rash outburst and – he grins as he taps his breast pocket – diminished finances.

The minutes tick by; he is lost to the heady scent of spring flowers, at peace, at last. This is something he would not have dreamt of doing before today, but he vows to make time to just *be*, not to be in such a tremendous rush all the time. Reluctantly, he returns to reality and skips the last steps to his front door, eager to share his news with Agnes. The hour will surprise her. At their breakfast that morning, he had solemnly informed her not to expect him until evening, such was his uncertainty of how long the deliberations may take, and what the verdict might be. How he laughs now, chastising himself light-heartedly. Why was he not confident from the off? With hindsight, there was only ever one verdict possible.

He enters the cool, rose-scented hallway, meticulously placing his hat and cane in their rightful positions in the polished mahogany and ironwork coat rack. He checks his appearance in the mirror and nods in admiration; a gentleman and scholar nods back at him, radiating that unmistakable aura of victory. Only then does he call for his spouse, in a somewhat brusque, formal tone.

In a heartbeat, his wife comes hurrying. Agnes Bayling is in her mid-forties, a gaunt woman with a brow-beaten expression permanently etched into her pale visage. She represents the epitome of a society lady. Her hair, styled by her maid into a severe chignon, causes her face to appear stretched. Her attire comprises a multitude of layers: undergarments, torturously tight corsetry – which may go some way to accounting for her sour look – petticoats, and an overskirt of silk and taffeta that rustles as she moves.

Bayling married this humourless woman, not for her winsome looks or sparkling wit – of which she displayed neither – but for a rather more mercenary reason: her family name. Agnes was born a Worthington, an old family of some repute and not inconsiderable wealth. She was the eldest – mercifully for her long-suffering mother, her father gave up hope of a son after the fifth daughter – but she was the last to be married off. One can only imagine her parents' relief when the charming doctor, by then in his mid-thirties, showed a passing interest in their aging spinster daughter. With a more than generous dowry waved in front of the ambitious but relatively impoverished Bayling, he snapped up the opportunity to climb a rung or two up the social ladder.

They married within six months of Bayling first calling on the embarrassingly keen Agnes. Some in polite society whispered in mischievous tones of the unseemly haste, predicting the 'early' arrival of Bayling junior. But they were much mistaken, as there was not to be a visitation from the stork for several long, barren years. Even if it were not a love match – from Bayling's point of view, at least – it was a perfect match of ambitions and intellect. For what Agnes lacked in womanly virtues, she more than made up for with a keen, intelligent mind and a naked ambition that was to be realised, second-hand, through her husband's blossoming career.

Agnes exclaims when she realises it's her husband calling; she was not expecting him so soon. And he *does* looks rather cross. 'William, dear, you're back early. I wasn't expecting you for hours. Do you have the verdict already? Did you win? Oh, *please* say you won.'

Bayling holds what he regards as his poker face, which indeed looks cross, for a few moments longer, relishing the suspense and the concerned look on her face. But then breaks into a wide smile.

'Of *course* we won, woman. Was there any doubt? Oh, ye of little faith!' Which was a little rich considering that morning Bayling himself had little faith to speak of. He reached into the pocket of his exquisitely tailored, black cashmere frock coat and retrieved the cheque.

'And look, he wrote this out immediately.'

Agnes takes it from his outstretched hand and, as she reads, her eyes widen. In a rare display of emotion, she squeals and attempts to embrace her husband. This is met with a stiff reception by Bayling, who clasps his hands instead.

'My, oh my, two thousand pounds! That must have stung. What on earth are you going to do with all this money, my dear?'

'Well,' says Bayling, smiling wryly. 'I've a mind to set up a research

160

fund: the Coleridge Endowment for the Advancement of Vivisection.' He titters. 'That would serve the old fool right. But I feel that would be a little too malicious, even for me. And I've decided to be magnanimous in victory.'

Agnes purses her already meagre lips. 'But after all he's put you through. The damage to your reputation. It's only right you take revenge. I say do it.' She pauses. 'Did he recognise you, after all these years?'

'No, I don't think so. At least, if he did, he hid it well. It's possible he may not know me; I don't recall we interacted much. He was five years above, and older Carthusians rarely acknowledged the younger boys' existence, unless you were their fag, of course. Speaking of boys, where's young Henry? Is he home?'

'Yes, in the garden with Nurse. Rosemary brought Oliver around. As you're back so early, maybe you can play with them? He'd love that; he's always mithering me about when you'll be home. His bowling's coming on, you know. I think there's genuine talent there.'

Bayling frowns at the news that one of Agnes' endless sisters is visiting. He had wanted to spend his victory afternoon in peace, to savour every memory.

'Ah, Rosemary, how is your lovely sister? And that tedious husband of hers, Humphrey, isn't it? Don't tell me he's here too?'

Agnes looks aghast, glances back. 'Ssssh, she'll hear you. She's just here, in the drawing room. Please try to be pleasant. And it's Herbert, as you jolly well know. There is no need to be rude, especially on such an auspicious day.'

With that, a slight, blonde, blue-eyed, seven-year-old boy comes careering down the hallway. He is dressed in the typical well-to-do boy's fashion for the season: sailor-necked striped shirt, necktie half undone, short navy-blue trousers in a brushed cotton, and knees scuffed green and brown. He jumps up and down at the sight of his Papa. His Nurse follows closely behind, fruitlessly attempting to control his wholly inappropriate, buoyant behaviour.

'Daddy, Daddy, you're home. You're back early! Yippee! Please come, come play with us. You can bat first; I'll bowl for you. Please, Papa, come play.'

Henry attempts to throw his arms round his father's legs, but is pulled back by Nurse. Bayling reacts awkwardly to the boy's affections. He pats his son's head, ruffles his hair perfunctorily. He does not drop to his son's level, hug him tight and engage with him in a way Agnes hopes for – as does Henry himself. Bayling throws him an apologetic, but slightly irritated, smile. 'Perhaps later, Henry, Papa's rather busy right now'. Bayling glances up at Nurse, silently instructing her to deal with him.

Henry looks glum, deflated by his father's dismissal, but he's getting used to it. He steps back and stares up at his Papa with disappointed, teary eyes, shrugging off Nurse's attempt to lead him away. Just then, a golden spaniel comes bounding down the hall. On spotting his master, he makes a beeline and jumps at Bayling. The change in the man's behaviour is marked and wryly noted by Agnes. Bayling's face lights up. He kneels beside the dog, wrestles him gently, allowing him to lick his face. 'Hello, Sandy old chap. How've you been, fella? Missed your daddy, have you? Huh? Good boy. Down you go now. Come on down with you, boy.'

Bayling continues to play, the dog is loving having his tummy tickled. Henry tugs on his father's sleeve, bottom lip protruding, desperate for a crumb of attention. 'Come, Papa, please. Ollie's here, too. And he's brought his new dog, Lucky. Sandy and Lucky have been playing together. Come, come and see.'

Bayling, with a resigned sigh and a sharp look from Agnes, reluctantly allows his son to lead him along the corridor. He is frogmarched into the deep, narrow back garden with its long, narrow lawn, deep, bushy herbaceous borders and fruit trees shedding the last of their blossom. The ebullient Sandy bounces along at his side, licking at his hand. Henry continues to tug at his father, calling his cousin to come say hello. Oliver, practising his batting with an imaginary ball, turns. When he spots Bayling, his face falls; he just about conjures up a half-hearted wave.

Without warning, a dog shoots out of the dense, lush undergrowth and pelts full speed toward Bayling.

'Lucky! Lucky, my boy, come here. Heel.' But Lucky's in no mood to listen to his young master.

Bayling pulls up short, causing Henry – who still has grip of his father's sleeve – to jerk to a halt. He stares, transfixed by the uncanny resemblance. The dog has stopped and is staring straight back at Bayling. He backs away, not taking his fearful, dark eyes off the man. He growls, a low, guttural, savage sound, baring his teeth in fear and warning. Oliver looks on, dismayed; he has not previously seen his new companion act in such a manner.

Bayling registers the faintest flicker of remorse, guilt even, as he imagines he is staring into the hauntingly familiar face of that little brown dog.

SEVENTEEN

Jack

Eliza arranges an early finish at the library. Unexpectedly, and to her relief, the powers-that-be had not dismissed her after the verdict went against them. She suspects the erstwhile unknown dog-loving tendencies of the usually taciturn Chief Librarian, Mr Phipps, had been influential. He took her aside one day, not long after the trial, and in a conspiratorial tone declared it 'a dreadful miscarriage of justice how that butcher, Bayling, didn't get his comeuppance'. Eliza smiles wryly. How wrong you can be about a person.

To celebrate release from his plaster of Paris prison, Jack has invited Eliza on an excursion to the West End. Thrilled, she accepts immediately, the trip being her first unchaperoned 'stepping out' with a man.

They have seen each other occasionally during the intervening weeks, six unseasonably hot weeks of Jack hobbling around on crutches. But his incapacity meant their meetings were limited. Eliza offered to visit him at his lodgings, but he always point-blank refused, which deflated her somewhat. Is he *that* ashamed of her? His excuse being, on the contrary, it was *he* who was ashamed of his student digs and would be mortified to host a lady in such shoddy surroundings.

'Oh, Jack. You must know I cannot be shocked. I've told of my situation before Lena rescued me from Madame Carruthers' squalid attic. No place can be worse than that, surely?'

'Eliza, please. Indulge me in this one, small thing. You'd surely think less of me if you saw how I lived.' Jack squirmed. She most definitely *would* think less of him. But it wasn't so much the squalor. There'd be no way to disguise his true identity – and no way to hide *who* he lived with. Perish the thought.

'But –'

'I'm sorry, Eliza, but that's my last word on the subject. I promise, as soon as I finish my studies, I'll move into more salubrious accommodation, and you will receive the first invite.'

She pouted, she cajoled, she teared up. But he was steadfast: she *was not* to call upon him. Reluctantly, she respected his wishes, although it irked her. Instead, they communicated via letter in-between times, and Eliza felt she had got to know him just as well through his beautifully written, and subtly romantic, missives.

Eliza rushes back to bathe and dress in peace, ideally before Lena returns from her WSPU meeting. She wants to avoid her if she can. Lena has been so crotchety of late, particularly so when Eliza dares to mention her forthcoming evening with Jack, and seeing her now would only spoil Eliza's buoyant mood. She encounters Mrs Rumple on her way in; she frowns as she scans the sitting room with an ex-maid's critical view. Her eyes lock on the whiskey decanter, triggered by a familiar aroma coming off a shifty-looking Gertrude as they say their goodbyes at the door.

After trying on everything she owns, she eventually plumps – as it is promising to be a warm evening – for a pale violet, shot silk dress that Lena had most recently tired of.

She rolls her hair in rags; then prepares her bath. The steam will help give it more of a curl. Jack likes it curly. She lowers herself into the warm lavender-scented water and lays back against the cushioned headrest. She closes her eyes, releases a contented sigh, and allows her mind to wander.

After the initial shock of seeing Jack and his plastered leg perched on their garden wall, Eliza, and a reluctant Lena, helped him up into the flat. The story Jack told was that, on the first day of the trial, he'd been rushing to catch the Underground train to Chancery Lane. In his haste, he slipped at the top of the ticket hall steps. The next thing he knew, he found himself spread-eagled at the bottom of the staircase – leg twisted at an unnatural angle – a fog of anxious, disembodied faces floating above him. He vaguely sensed staff calling for a stretcher to move him out of the path of the commuters, impatiently pushing past. Then the pain cut in and that's the last he remembered.

They rushed him to nearby University College Hospital. The break was bad: a clean slicing of his left fibula, or calf bone to the uninitiated. Jack relished describing the level of gory detail so much that eventually a rather squeamish Eliza had to request he desist. Although his hastily assembled knowledge on the subject impressed her. Quite the expert suddenly! The upshot was the pain was excruciating. They placed him on a high dose of morphine, and, as he phrased it, he was 'pleasantly out of it' for the next twenty-four hours. He was in no fit state to send word. As soon as he could, he discharged himself, intending to hobble over to court somehow, and was on his way when he heard news of the verdict. Hence, he instructed his Hansom to take him straight to the women's flat instead.

Of course, Eliza forgave him the moment she clapped eyes on the plaster cast, but she would not let him off the hook too easily.

The water, now tepid, encourages Eliza out of the bath. She dresses leisurely, keeping corsetry to a minimum to avoid overheating. She even attempts a modest amount of make-up, but nothing that would show. It wouldn't do to look like she's just stepped off the *stage*, heaven forfend! A little powdered rouge, a rim of kohl round the eyes, and the matt tawny brown-red Coty lipstick which only comes out on high days and holidays.

Mrs P sits slyly observing her, fascinated by Eliza's uncharacteristic display of vanity. Before she leaves, Eliza sneaks into Lena's bedroom to liberate a squirt of the expensive French perfume – Worth of Paris – that her friend is so fond of and refuses to share. Mrs P admonishes her with a disapproving yowl. Eliza wags her finger. 'What Lena don't know won't annoy her. So, no telling, or you'll forfeit your fish supper, missus.' Eliza steals one last look in the mirror and declares herself as good as she'll get. On a whim, she snatches up Lena's silk parasol, grinning mischievously at the cat as she slams the front door.

They have arranged to meet at Charing Cross. Eliza takes the train into Victoria and then rides the underground District railway. They are meeting under the station clock at five sharp. Eliza emerges and excitedly scans the concourse, butterflies taking flight in her tummy. Ah, there he is. His head down, frowning, pacing, three limping steps one way, then the other. Eliza frowns. He doesn't look too thrilled at the thought of their imminent reunion. She creeps up behind him and cups his eyes.

'Surprise!'

'What the fuck?'

Jack rips her hands from his eyes and swings around, clutching her wrists tightly. He freezes, cognisant of Eliza's view on expletives. His neck reddens. Eliza stares silently down at her captive wrists, then up at him, taken aback at his reaction. Jack, mortified, releases his grip, runs his hand through his hair.

'Eliza! I'm sorry. That was terribly uncouth of me.'

'Oh, Jack, please don't fret. It's my own silly fault – one shouldn't sneak up on people like that.' She smiles reassuringly, but her forehead wrinkles as he turns to lead the way out.

Any awkwardness is smoothed over; and they make polite conversation as they stroll. They salute the magnificent bronze lions as they saunter toward the Mall. There they exchange pleasantries with the legendary milkmaids, plying their trade with penny glasses of milk, as they had done for as long as anyone could remember. The most endearing, and surprising, eccentricity of the two sisters are the cows – Maisie and Daisy – they bring along with them each day, ensuring the milk is as fresh as can be, albeit a tad cloying on such a warm day.

As they bid the ladies good day, Jack lowers his voice.

'Apparently, there's a plan for a semi-circular building – just here – that'll be so enormous it will span these two roads.' As they pass the eastern entrance to the Mall, Jack stops, his finger tracing an arch in the sky from the park over to Trafalgar Square. Eliza follows his curve, eyes widening at the immensity of the structure. The area marked for development undoubtedly includes the ladies' pitch, which is currently open land, perfect for grazing a few cows.

'But whatever will happen to them?' Eliza frowns. She couldn't quite imagine the milkmaids, their Friesian cows and ramshackle old milk cart being allowed to pitch up in front of such a grand new building.

'Well, that's the controversy,' Jack replies. 'They've apparently been given their marching orders. But word's got out and the good folk of London are none too pleased.'

'And rightly so,' retorts Eliza, indignantly. The sisters are an institution, adored as much for their batty eccentricity as their tasty beverages.

'The maids claim an ancestral right to sell milk from that very spot, but they haven't yet produced any legal documents to prove it.' Jack shrugs. 'Without evidence, it seems unlikely they'll be able to stay. Although, rumour has it the King's got involved, it seems he enjoyed their milk as a child, and has made his displeasure be known. So, I guess we'll have to wait and see.'

'Well, if good King Bertie can't resolve it, I'm sure Lena would take up their fight; it's just the thing she gets puffed up about. She needs a new cause to lift her spirits, she's been so down lately,' Eliza muses, a mischievous grin spreading across her face. 'She'd think nothing of marching on Parliament with an entire herd of cows in tow to make her point.' They chuckle at the absurd imagery her words throw up.

They have been strolling for some time. Eliza is not paying much attention to where they are heading, her thoughts dominated by the old maids' plight. She has to concentrate as they reach Oxford

Circus's fright of a crossroads. They take their lives in their hands, navigating between the multitude of omnibuses, trams, carts, delivery vans, Hansom cabs and bicycles coming at them from every direction, horns blaring. Each vehicle, it appears, is in the most dreadful hurry to be somewhere else.

They are walking on, up Regent Street towards Langham Place, when Jack comes to a halt. Eliza glances around, non-plussed, before recognising the Royal Polytechnic Institution. She had visited the theatre within, on Lena's insistence, a year or two earlier, to witness, of all things, a train pulling into a station! The effect on the audience of this minute-long film was nothing short of astounding. The sight of a life-sized steam locomotive bearing down on them in the inky blackness, only at the last moment veering left off screen, caused several ladies to scream in terror – a few even fainted. Eliza heard grown men cry out in disbelief, but she was proud she'd kept control of her sensibilities and rode out the entire journey in a dignified silence. Although she'd been impressed by the ingenuity of it, she commented to Lena that she failed to see then how this would ever take off and hasn't been tempted back into a moving picture theatre since.

She raises a quizzical eyebrow.

'Mmm? What *am* I letting myself in for? More trains hurtling towards my head at fifty miles an hour?'

Jack chuckles. 'No, not at all. It's just a little something to make you smile – at least I hope it will. It's a tale of a rather clever dog that saves the day; I thought it might be fun. Rather unimaginatively it's called *Rescued by Rover*, but let's not hold that against it.'

'Sounds marvellous, do lead on.' She grins and brazenly threads her arm through his as they head towards the box office.

They enter the dimly lit auditorium and settle into generous, cushioned seats. The room plunges into darkness, and the chatter falls away. There's breathless anticipation for what the enormous screen – the length of a trolley bus – will reveal. The orchestra starts up. A dramatic drum roll, then violins join in, in lively accompaniment to the title and credits. A lone piano takes over when the action starts proper. The scene opens in a nursery where a young child plays with a handsome collie dog. A gasp ricochets at the clarity of the picture. Eliza grasps Jack's hand in amazement. He squeezes it tight, intertwining his fingers with hers. She smiles to herself in the darkness, an unfamiliar tingling sensation spreading through her.

Jack gazes at her, the film forgotten for the moment. In profile she looks majestic, almost haughty. Her straight, proud nose with just the slightest uplift at the end; and that mouth, the juicy fullness of it, still entrances him. Her tongue darts across her lips, moistening skin that's become dry from her quickened breath. His memory of *that* afternoon swims into view; the moment he first tasted their sweetness. Embarrassed by the obvious swelling in his closely cut suit trousers, he brings his hand onto his lap, praying she will not notice. She does. The sight causes an aching sensation between her legs. She shifts awkwardly, her cami-knickers feel damp against her thigh. She feels her colour rise and feels grateful for the darkness.

Mercifully, the extraordinary action unfolding on screen soon diverts their attention. The child is taken out for a stroll by her nanny. As soon as the nanny's back is turned – she seems a bit of a trollop, flirting with a soldier when she was responsible for the youngster – an old hag snatches the child from her pram and scarpers without the courting couple noticing. The nanny returns home, full of shame and remorse, and naturally the parents are distraught. The family's dog – the Rover of the title – witnesses this and runs off. What follows is a series of extraordinary scenes where the dog follows a scent, crosses busy roads and swims streams, emerging to shake the water from his fur. Eliza, to her embarrassment, ducks, so powerful is the illusion of water droplets spraying the auditorium. Jack, amused, glances across at her. Their eyes lock, but the action on screen lures them back, another moment lost. Rover arrives at a slum street where he checks every house until he, miraculously, discovers the kidnapped child. After an altercation with the now inebriated hag, he makes the return journey home.

This clever dog persuades the father to follow and leads him straight to the child. They are reunited. All is well with the world. *The End.*

The film is seven minutes long; Eliza swears she hardly took a breath in all that time. They sit in mesmerised silence. Eliza changes her mind and decides moving image films are truly something. She gradually returns to reality, glances down, smiling coyly at their still tightly entwined fingers, savouring this elicit closeness, his faintly carbolic scent.

'I guess I'll need my hand back at some point,' she whispers. Jack obliges, reluctantly. She stares at her empty palm. It feels bereft, as if missing an essential part of itself. She frowns into the darkness, her longing for him still fresh. How can they move this friendship into something deeper, something more physical? She's shocked to realise she desperately wants it to, despite the opprobrium it could bring, but has no idea of how to make it happen.

EIGHTEEN

The Restaurant

Eliza and Jack emerge, blinking, from the theatre. The thoroughfare is still bustling, the low evening sun creating a shadowy other world of dark figures following the living to their evening's entertainment. The couple stroll towards Soho in a comfortable silence. Both still overwhelmed, overtly by the spectacle they've just witnessed, but privately by the realisation of the extent of their mutual, barely disguised desire. Their hands brush as their arms swing, but neither is brave enough to entwine them once more. Not here, in the light, for all the world to gawp at.

They are to dine at an intimate Italian restaurant on Berwick Street that Eliza had visited some months earlier. Lena had heard good things about *La Bella Vita* and brought Eliza along to try it out. Eliza smiles; this was yet another aspect of her life that had changed for the better. She had not set foot in a restaurant before the evening she first met Lena. After they'd escaped the clutches of the Tooting witches' coven, and *she* had recovered from the embarrassment of Lena's impromptu visit to her digs. What a portentous evening that turned out to be!

Eliza flopped heavily into her seat. It was done. The ordeal of her first speech was over. A wave of relief engulfed her and her body melted into the unyielding wooden pew. Her eyelids drooped. Suddenly, she felt a presence at her back. Her head snapped round. She was taken aback to see a grubby, cream silk glove gripping her left shoulder. She sensed warm, sweet breath on her ear.

'You're an inspiration, Miss Blackwood, truly! I'd be keen to discuss this issue further, if I may? Please, take supper with me this evening.'

The young woman's stage whisper caught the attention of the sour-faced ladies flanking them. They turned as one, and glared at her, but that having absolutely no effect, they shifted their evil eye onto Eliza instead.

Eliza mumbled an acceptance, before abruptly closing down further chat for fear of the wrath of Miss Walker and her lavishly petticoated lieutenants, whose ranks included one Edith Carruthers.

The proceedings wrapped up within the hour, and the young women skulked out into the fading, pale embers of the day. The sky streaked with the beginnings of what would turn into a delightful, salmon-pink sunset. Eliza was relieved to emerge from the dusty gloom of that Methodist Hall, crammed full of unhappy reminders of her own miserable childhood.

'Well, Miss Blackwood, I should introduce myself, as I have you at a disadvantage. I know a lot more about you than you of me.'

'Yes, I'd like that.' Eliza smiled back. 'But please, call me Eliza. It's Elizabeth really, but that always sounded too fancy for the likes of me.'

'And I'm Evelina Hageby, Lena to my friends. I'm honoured to make your acquaintance, Eliza.' She executed a short, gentlemanly bow and removed an imaginary top hat.

Eliza took her cue and dipped into an exaggerated curtsey. 'And it's my very great pleasure to make your acquaintance Miss Hageby.' Lena threw her a disapproving look. 'Lena.' Eliza shot back.

They started to giggle, for no good reason other than the sheer joy of it, and it quickly built into hysterical, raucous guffaws. This unmaidenly behaviour was too much for the Tooting ladies. Their snooty displeasure only heightened the young women's mirth and kept them chuckling long after they observed the last of their over-plumped bustles waddle off into the sunset.

'Come.' Lena took Eliza's elbow and threaded her arm through in a rather over-familiar fashion. 'Let's find somewhere fun to dine. I'm not familiar with the area, so I place myself in your capable hands.'

'I believe there are a few restaurants that serve a decent tea. Although, I confess, I haven't yet visited any,' Eliza replied, then hesitated. 'But can I beg an indulgence first?'

'Of course you may. What is it?'

'I became rather anxious before my talk. As a result, I perspired in what can only be described as a most unladylike manner.' Eliza blushed at her admission, but had a growing sense that Miss Hageby would not be offended. 'I'd feel more comfortable at dinner if I changed beforehand. Would you be kind enough to accompany me to my lodgings? I promise not to dilly dally.'

Lena chuckled. 'Why Miss Blackwood – Eliza – I see you're not a dilly dallier in any respect.' She wrinkled her dainty snub nose in mock disgust. 'And we wouldn't want to scare off our waitress with disagreeable odours before we sample our first course now, would we? Do lead on.'

The women arrived at Eliza's attic room quite breathless. Eliza unlocked the door. 'Well, here we are. Please, come in, make yourself at home.'

Lena hesitated a moment too long before ducking to step inside. She said nothing for the longest time. Eliza followed Lena's gaze, a lighthouse beam sweeping the entirety of her life's possessions. Assessing them, doubtless finding them wanting, shocked how one could live in such cramped conditions for a week, never mind six long, lonely months. To her creeping mortification, as they strolled Eliza had gradually come to realise that Miss Lena Hageby was, despite initial impressions, of solid upper-middle-class stock! And there was she, Elizabeth Sian Blackwood, ex-lady's maid herself, taking a lady of some standing to her meagre, shilling-a-week matchbox of a lodgings. She was now sorely regretting her earlier request.

'Well,' Lena eventually declared, 'it's certainly *bijou*.'

Eliza had no idea what this meant, but given Lena was smiling as she spoke, she could only assume she was not being derogatory. Eliza conjured a weak grin. 'It's small, I know, but suits me well enough. And it's convenient for the library, of course.'

'Of course,' Lena echoed, still distracted by the room's meagre dimensions. 'But come, let's get you changed so we can continue our evening. I'm ravenous.'

As she spoke, Eliza took the step over to her wardrobe and rifled through, searching for something suitable. In truth, what she had on was her best and only formal-wear, reserved for high days and holidays, or that rarest of beasts, an outing to the theatre. In frustration, she settled on a work blouse, a little worn around the cuffs from shelving books. The collar was also frayed but it would have to do. She ducked behind the papier mâché dressing screen to change.

Minutes later, Eliza re-emerged. She did not want Lena in that room a moment longer than necessary. Curiously, Lena appeared flushed, agitated almost, and in an almighty rush to leave. Eliza glanced around, puzzled at what could have caused such a change in Lena's mood, but put it down to the paltry surroundings that were so unbecoming for a lady. They retraced their steps and were soon back on the pavement, relieved to be gulping the cool, fresh air after the gloopy heat of the house. A soothing breeze accompanied their walk to the restaurant, Le Chat Noir. Eliza commented she had always thought it a rather rude sounding name. Lena, between stifled giggles, enlightened her that *chat* was French for cat!

Following a theatrically raised eyebrow from the maître d' at the audaciousness of two women requesting to dine without a chaperone, at Lena's stubborn insistence they were eventually shown to a table.

Lena ordered for them both, batting away protestations after announcing the evening was her treat, and Eliza was not to put a hand to her purse. Eliza felt a stab of embarrassment, suspecting

Lena had surmised the parlous state of her finances: the truth being a meal in Le Chat Noir would cost Eliza almost a week's wages.

They dined well on what was a first for Eliza: cold soup. Who'd have thought of such a thing? She took one sip and promptly embarrassed herself by exclaiming they had forgotten to heat it up. The maître d's eyebrow took another excursion skywards. Lena explained, through bouts of uncontrollable guffaws, that it was supposed to be served that way, was made from potatoes and leeks, and had a complicated name that Eliza couldn't master however many times she tried. Their main course comprised vegetables, yet more potatoes, and a lush creamy sauce. As they sat down, Lena had defiantly declared herself a vegetarian. This was too much for the maître d', who looked utterly befuddled. With an exaggerated huff, she explained the concept in fluent French, which left Eliza open-mouthed. This revelation resulted in his eyebrow travelling so high it was in danger of escaping his forehead. It transpired there were precious few dishes which did not entertain part of a dead animal on their plates. For her part, Eliza thought it ill-mannered to expect Lena to watch her eat meat and so vegetables it was.

Eliza still cringes at her naïve reaction to the 'vichyssoise incident', as Lena insists on calling it, although now she can see the funny side – almost! How much Lena has taught her over their time together. She can just about pronounce that ruddy soup's name now. And she certainly knows how it, and a whole host of other foreign dishes, should be served. A sudden wave of guilt washes over her. She's been too preoccupied with her feelings and concern for Jack, to realise how she's been neglecting her friend over the weeks since the trial. Blithely oblivious to the fact that Lena needs her too. Oh lord, how selfish she's been! She'll make up for it, and that's a promise. Starting tomorrow, she will make up for her self-absorbed behaviour.

As Jack and Eliza arrive at the restaurant, her thoughts return to her hidden agenda. Although she feels they have become well acquainted over the past months, there remains an aspect of Jack's life which is still a mystery. Her curiosity is now overwhelming her, and she's on a mission. Tonight, she decides, is to be the night. She *will* get the truth out of him.

They tuck into a meal of spaghetti in a deliciously rich tomato sauce and a glass or two of a splendid Chianti. Eliza, as well as frequenting foreign restaurants and learning to appreciate the delights of cold soup, has become quite the wine expert, courtesy of Lena and her pilfering of the Hageby's well-stocked cellar. They take an age to decide upon a dish from the sweet trolley. The choice is overwhelming and Eliza, who has sampled most of the delicious creamy concoctions on offer, feels the need to explain each one. Eliza has to stop herself correcting Jack's description of it as dessert. Honestly, Eliza, who do you think you are? With all these airs and graces? She'd only known Welsh cakes and *bara brith* before moving to London, but now she's extolling the virtues of *tiramisu* over *panettone* to a rather bored looking Jack. She can still taste that first sweet pastry Lena recommended in Le Chat Noir, as clearly as if she'd eaten it yesterday.

The whole meal was accompanied by what was, Lena declared, an exceedingly palatable claret. This was another first for Eliza. The deep juicy flavours went straight to her head and made her quite giddy. Afters, or 'pudding' as Lena insisted on calling it, was a revelation. They scoffed a glorious mix of Yorkshire rhubarb and almonds, baked in a tart, and served with Chantilly cream. After they'd eaten their fill, or as much as their discreetly loosened corsetry would allow, Lena ordered coffee. She then did something so shocking, so unbecoming of a lady, Eliza almost fell off her chair. Without a care, Lena reached into her embroidered satin handbag and withdrew an enamelled box. Eliza watched, stunned, as she flicked it open, retrieved a slender, brown cylinder with a gold tip, tapped it sharply on the lid. She gestured to Eliza, but she just shook her head, mutely. Lena then summoned the maître d'. His appalled face mirrored Eliza's. With grudging obedience, he proffered a

177

flame. She cupped it, and, with languid, practised ease, lit the offending item. She breathed out a slow stream of sharp, fragrant smoke, winked at Eliza, and smiled sweetly up at him. He shuffled off with a backward glance of disgust. Eliza forced a neutral look; she didn't want her new friend to think her old-fashioned.

Lena then regarded her with a most peculiar expression. She took a deep drag on her cigarette, tapped off a precarious column of ash. A furrowed brow formed a chevron in her forehead, and a look of almost maternal concern took possession of her eyes. She reached across and covered Eliza's hand with her own.

'Eliza, my dear. I've said nothing for fear of offending you, but I feel we've become much better acquainted now. And so, well, I hope what I'm about to say will be taken in the manner it's intended, that is with absolutely no judgement nor snobbery.'

Her tone took Eliza by surprise. Although the wine had dulled her senses, she was still sensitive to this abrupt change in manner.

'Please, continue. I assure you nothing you can say will offend me,' replied Eliza breezily, but inwardly steeled herself for whatever humiliation was to come.

After their bowls are cleared away, Eliza, hoping the wine may have loosened Jack's tongue, takes the bull by the horns.

'So, Jack. I'm curious. You've never mentioned your childhood, or family even.' His head jolts up. He shifts awkwardly in his chair. She pierces him with her stare. 'Is it a state secret?' He will not be let off the hook, not tonight.

'Umm, no, course not.' He blushes a deeper red than the rosy glow bestowed by the wine. 'It's just not that interesting and, well, I don't want to bore you.'

'Oh heavens. You won't bore me. I'd love to know more about what made you, well ... you.' He still looks reticent, so she offers a trade.

'How about if I start? We can do a family history swap.' He nods, his mind racing.

178

'So, you know the story of my education – such as it was – and being placed in service at the Frobisher's, but not how I ended up here, in London, lending books for a living.' His face relaxes, grateful to be given a few moments' grace. The glance she shoots back assures him he will not wriggle out of it when his turn comes.

'Well, one afternoon I'd finished my chores early, and was desperate to continue the book I'd started – *Vanity Fair* it was. It was quite a challenge, some of the writing was beyond me, but I simply loved the story, so I snuck into the library before anyone did spot me and add to my list of tasks. I so loved being in there, the smell of beeswax and paper dust intoxicated me. I was so absorbed in Becky Sharp's world that I didn't hear the door creak open. To my horror, the Dowager almost tripped over the mop and pail I'd left by the door.' Eliza's face clouds at the memory.

'Of course, given I was somewhere I had no absolutely no right to be, *and* being caught red-handed with Mr Thackeray, I expected instant dismissal.' Jack attempts to disguise a lewd grin – not well enough – as Eliza throws him a puzzled glance. 'But, unbeknownst to me, my choice of reading material was to be my saviour. The novel just so happened to be one of my lady's favourites and, on questioning me, she realised there was more to the petrified girl trembling in front of her than your average illiterate skivvy and decided to take me under her wing. In time, she even promoted me to be her lady's maid, even though I wasn't that skilled at needlework. Lucky for me she wasn't much bothered by fashions, she'd been in widow's weeds for a decade and appeared in no hurry to forsake them, but I learned fast, and picked up quite the knack for it. She was far more interested in my love of books, and we passed many a pleasant afternoon discussing the latest novel she'd chosen.' Eliza's eye mists over. 'She was so kind. She taught me much that I had missed through my meagre schooling, even helping with elocution lessons.' She smiles fondly. 'My valleys accent often mystified her, her being an Englisher. She was more family to me than my own parents, who were much more concerned with the well-being of my brothers.'

179

Jack cocks his head, eyes rounding in surprise. Eliza had not mentioned siblings before.

'Ah yes, sorry, I guess I don't talk about Huw or David much. They're both passed on, you see. Huw, the eldest, twelve years older so I hardly knew him, was killed in the First Boer War. He was just sixteen – far too young to have been sent to that hellhole, but sent he was, and he survived a few months, before the battle of Majuba Hill saw him with a bullet to the chest. He died instantly.' Jack reaches for her hand and she relishes his touch. 'And David, he was two years younger than me, was injured in an accident at the pit. He was a miner, naturally. What else is there to do in the valleys if you're poor and don't do well at school? It was quite the job just keeping our Dai in the classroom, which was ironic as my folks couldn't get me out of one fast enough. Got himself trapped under a cart's wheel while underground and it broke his back. They got him out, but probably did more damage. He survived for a while, but I think he just lost the will, knowing he'd be paralysed for life, and slowly slipped away. That was the final straw for my mam and da. It was as if they'd lost everything. Even turned from their chapel for a time.' She raises her eyes to his. They are dewy, but tears are conspicuous by their absence.

'I don't speak about it as it seems remorselessly bleak, but that's how it was. They seemed to forget they had a child still living.' She shrugs. 'But I guess to them girls didn't count for much, just a burden to be offloaded.' She wipes away a single rogue tear.

Jack places his other hand – cool, smooth to the touch – over hers. Eliza smiles sadly up at him. 'But it was all for the best, in the end I mean, as I spent eight contented years with my dear Dowager Lady Frobisher before she passed on. Eighty, she was. Unbeknownst to me she had left a small bequest, with the instruction I should spend it on bettering myself and doing something I love. So, being true to her wish, I did just that. I took myself off and became apprenticed to the head librarian in town. When I qualified, I moved to London to further my ambitions. It was a scary thing to do, but my lady hailed from here originally and told the most wonderful stories. So, I thought I'd see it for myself. After all, my parents weren't interested, and I'd no other family. After six months, I met one Miss Evelina Hageby, and, well, you know the rest.' She takes a sip of her wine, eyeing Jack expectantly over the top of the goblet.

Jack clears his throat. There is no wriggling out of this. 'Fine', he croaks. 'Although I warn you, mine's not a very uplifting tale either.' Eliza says nothing, tilts her head and smiles encouragement.

'Home is South Yorkshire, the village of Cawthorne. My mother was the eldest of three sisters, born to the local landowner. So, her family was relatively well off and respected in the town.

'My father on the other hand was known as a bit of a chancer, a local Jack-the-lad. He was handsome, with a reputation for the ladies. They met by chance at the local village fête and fell in love. Well, at least my mother did. My grandfather disapproved but my mother, always strong-willed, disobeyed her father and ran off and married him, anyway.

'Her disobedience outraged grandfather, and he washed his hands of her. It broke her heart, but she'd made her choice: her future was with her husband and she was nothing if not stubborn. My parents moved down south soon after I was born, so my father could find work. My sister was born four years later.

'We were happy for a while, but money was tight after they'd sold all my mother's jewellery. My father resumed his dubious methods of earning a crust, and mother turned a blind eye. What else could she do? Just after I turned ten, he was involved in an altercation over money. It turned violent, and he was dealt a fatal blow to the head.'

'I'm sorry, Jack. It must have been hard, a boy growing up without his father.'

Jack shrugs, he appears peculiarly nonchalant. 'After father's death, all was forgiven, and they summoned mother home. The prodigal daughter and her offspring were welcomed back into the protective custody of my grandparents. But the shock of my father's death had a detrimental effect on my mother's health, and on her mental state in particular. She retreated into herself, became reclusive, prone to unprovoked, sometimes violent, outbursts. Specialist doctors swarmed over her, as they couldn't find anything physically wrong. They eventually pronounced her a lunatic, much to my grandfather's embarrassment.' He sneers. 'They hushed it up and – to keep her out of the mental sanatorium – my mother and sister were set up in a remote worker's cottage on the family estate. There they could live a quiet life, out of harm's way, and beyond the inquisitive eyes and flapping ears of neighbours.' He takes a long gulp of wine.

'They packed *me* off to a provincial, middle-ranking boarding school. My resemblance to my father disturbed grandfather's sensibilities, apparently. So, out of sight, out of mind. Life, for my grandparents at least, got back to normal. I visit mother when I'm able, but it's not that often. And when I do, well... I feel such an overwhelming sense of guilt I leave as soon as I can.' He swallows hard. 'It's my poor sister, you see. She's stuck in limbo. Her life paused indefinitely because of circumstances beyond anyone's control. But here am I, enjoying myself, free to live my life as I wish. And the only reason I'm here and she's there is because I'm a man, and she had the misfortune to be born a woman.'

Eliza now regrets her determination to force his family history out of him. He looks so forlorn, so guilt-ridden. She has no idea what to say to help ease his guilt, as, fundamentally, she agrees. It was simply an accident of gender that saved him from a virtual prison sentence, trapped out there on the moors, with a wretched, damaged mother and uncaring grandfather. His sister is paying the price for being born female. Eliza changes the subject.

'I've some marvellous news, Jack.' He glances up, curiosity piqued. The vaguest shadow of a smile teases the corners of his mouth.

'Oh, yes? What would that be?'

'We've, at long last, arranged a date for the unveiling in

Latchmere Park.' Eliza smiles hopefully at him, but to her dismay, his nascent smile vanishes. Jack now appears positively miserable.

'Oh! I thought you'd be pleased, after all the time and effort we've put into this.' He snaps to attention, his sorrowful expression replaced by a bright smile, one Eliza knows is not genuine as it doesn't come close to reaching his eyes.

'I'm sorry, Eliza. I'm thrilled for you, of course I am. It's just ... talking about my family has brought up painful memories. But I'll buck up. We're here to enjoy ourselves, after all. Let's toast.' He makes a tremendous effort to smile, authentically this time, and raises his glass. Eliza matches him, and they clink a toast.

'To the dog memorial, may it be the start of a humane revolution.'

Eliza gazes up at him, experiencing a fuzzy, warm glow that comes partly from the wine but mostly from the growing intensity of her feelings for him. She thinks, for the first time in an age, maybe in her entire lifetime, that all is right with the world.

THE NATIONAL GALLERY, APRIL 1906 – THE PROTESTOR

The crackers and stink bombs cloud the air with a yellow tinged haze. In the chaos of the fighting, I lose my grip on her hand and find myself swept along by the tide of protestors desperate to escape the violence. I end up deposited on the pavement outside the Clarence. My head spins, my eyes scanning for a familiar face, her face. It's hopeless, I'm separated from her and the rest of my companions. A ball of fear lodges in my throat, I am adrift in a morass of strangers and it isn't easy to distinguish friend from foe. I peer into the crowd, continually searching a blur of anonymous faces, turned ugly, animalistic, and now a fog of fists, blood and spittle. Where the hell are they? A rising sense of dread. What if they are caught in the middle? But then I spot one, then another, and then her, on the other side of the wide thoroughfare. I signal to them to move back, get away from the violence. I take a deep breath and dive back into the mob, battle my way across the road. I signal to them to follow me and we regroup in a recessed doorway off The Mall. I wait until she has reached the doorway safely and only then do I feel my tension release slightly. The women look to one another, and then at us two expectantly. I decide we will continue with our original intention.

'Okay, ladies. Let's head for the Gallery as planned. We'll skirt around the Square and get these banners hung.'

Once we've left the violence behind, we feel brave enough to resume singing. I glance over and she smiles. A warm, encouraging smile that speaks to things maybe being normal between us again. I hope so, but then hope's in short supply these days.

From nowhere our path is blocked by a dozen men wielding sticks, bars, cricket bats. Coarse-looking, brutish, definitely not students. We stop dead, instinctively forming a tight knot. They advance on us. My blood runs cold. I reach for her hand again.

NINETEEN

The Unveiling

LATCHMERE PARK, SEPTEMBER 1904

The event to welcome the memorial to the borough is turning into quite the grand affair. Lena and Eliza, the crushing disappointment of the court case now fading into distant memory, throw themselves into organising the unveiling ceremony. To their delight, many local dignitaries have responded positively to the invite. Their guest list includes the mayor of the parish, a swathe of Battersea councillors, alongside notable radicals, liberals, and famous literary types. The London press is also sniffing around, eager for the next salacious chapter in the court case that sold so many extra newspapers back in the spring.

It is a few days before the unveiling and the women, accompanied by Coleridge, are in Latchmere Park. The council created the recreational ground, to give the rectangle of greenery its official status, to provide much-needed outdoor space to serve the new Latchmere Estate. The estate itself comprises parallel streets of identical two-up two-down cottages. The houses were built for the area's workers, many of whom were forcibly evicted from their slum dwellings, which were levelled to make way for housing earmarked for the middle-classes – those with plenty of money and the desire for a central London address.

The park's grassed areas are divided by a criss-cross of pathways that dissect it into quadrants. Saplings, planted around the perimeter, supplement the mature trees, such as a magnificent willow that survived the nearby building works and the sturdy oaks that appear centuries old. The perennial flower beds display the last of their droopy blooms before starting their hibernation.

The three stare, captivated by what's unfolding in front of them. There is a hive of activity and, to the disproving wrinkling of Eliza's nose, much coarse language emanating from the centre point of the paths. Labourers are lowering something onto a circular stone base. A final loud thunk, and it is in place.

The base is a granite plinth. The object being lowered is the bronze statue, protected by a short cotton shroud, its bottom half glinting in the afternoon sunshine. Eventually, the noise diminishes as the workmen finish off for the day. The park reverts to a peaceful oasis; Lena, Eliza and Coleridge are its only occupants. They solemnly march over to the memorial. Lena is the first to cut into their awed silence.

'Who'd have thought this day would arrive? After the horror of the trial, I'd almost given up hope. But here we are. And there *it is*.'

Standing seven feet tall, the memorial already looks as if it has been there forever. The plinth has been polished to a glistening, smooth perfection. The workers have turned on the fountains and, for the first time, water is trickling from the copper piping. The spray catches the sun and causes prisms of refracted light to sparkle in a halo of primary colours. The higher fountain, created to quench human thirst, encircles the dog statue, a moat protecting him from all horrors. The lower fountain, for use by dogs, horses and any other passing creature, incorporates a small bowl protruding about six inches from its base.

Lena stretches up and tugs on the cotton shroud. It falls to the ground revealing an image of a terrier dog looking solemnly into the distance, soulful yet proud, with a dignity in death which was denied to him during his brief life. Eliza cannot prevent a tear from forming. Lena is struck by the uncanny resemblance to her Jasper.

Coleridge takes a drink from the fountain, the first living creature to do so. Lena reaches to stroke the dog's paw. Eliza reads the polished metal inscription that wraps around the smooth curved surface of the plinth.

In Memory of the little Brown Terrier Dog
Done to Death in the Laboratories
of University College, after having endured
Vivisection extending over more than Two Months
having been handed over from one Vivisector to
Another...

Till Death came to his Release.

Also in Memory of the 232 dogs
Vivisected at the same place in just one year.

Eliza pauses. Lena and Coleridge glance up at her, concerned. She fights to maintain her composure with a grace that impresses her companions.

'Men and Women of England, how long shall these Things be?'

'Amen to that,' concludes Coleridge, bowing his head.

This seemingly simple last line – so agonised over – swirls around Eliza's mind. Its many tendrils unfurling, slowly revealing themselves in an insistent, whispered reproach. *How long? How long? How long, Eliza?* How long indeed? How long before mankind understands its dues to the earth? How long before humans comprehend they *cannot* abuse God's creatures without a reckoning of sorts? How long will women be treated as inferior, feeble-minded, of use only as playthings, servants, or for breeding? How long, in fact, before she and Jack can be together – openly, no ring required, without shame, judgement, or rebuke from *society*? Eliza glances over to Lena; her friend's expression is unfathomable. Lena's become increasingly distant of late. Ever since the verdict and Jack's accident, in fact. Eliza smiles hesitantly at her friend. She realises, with a sudden stab of remorse, that she has continued to be neglectful, even after her resolution at the restaurant. She's been far too preoccupied

187

with her deepening relationship with Jack, and the plans for the unveiling. But this is done and she determines to try harder, make time for Lena, to involve her more. She glides over and slips an arm around Lena's waist. Lena tenses, but then Eliza feels a relaxing and a reciprocal arm snakes around her own waist. Lena tilts her head towards Eliza's, and they draw close.

'But ladies, come, we cannot stand here dawdling,' Coleridge chides them. 'We still have much to organise before tomorrow's event. Indeed, I've had word from Mr George Bernard Shaw, no less. He's expressed a desire to attend, and is keen to say a few words, which is most gratifying. Most gratifying indeed.' He puffs himself up in the manner of a pompous pigeon. The women's eyes widen: a genuine celebrity, attending their humble event. How utterly thrilling!

'Come now, lots to do. We've not discharged all our duties to this little chap yet.'

Coleridge raises his hat to the bronze terrier and ushers his brood from the grounds, in much the way a mother duck corrals her young. As they leave, two workmen reappear with a large black canvas shroud and cloak the entire structure, securing it with sturdy hessian rope.

The day of the inauguration dawns. It is a cool, bright September morning, a Saturday. The cotton-blue, cloudless sky combines with the autumnal chill that invaded the air overnight and is now refusing to leave. Lena and Eliza are up early. There's lots to prepare before the official activities start. They load banners, leaflets and pamphlets into a Hansom carriage and set off.

When they arrive, they take a moment to enjoy the peace and tranquillity of a perfect autumn morning. Surrounded by the natural sights and sounds of this small green paradise, it is hard to believe they're so close to a bustling, noisy, polluted city. The overnight frost frames the scene. A gradual thawing has produced rows of dewdrops, trembling on the myriad of webs that glisten like silver threads in the weak sunlight. The hydrangea's blowsy, defiant blooms are losing the fight to retain their vibrant summer hues of pink and blue, surrendering to the inevitable browning of their petals. The deciduous trees, the grand old oaks, elegant sycamores and mighty horse chestnuts, are reluctantly releasing their grip on their scarlet-red and russet-brown leaves to the season's persistent gusts of wind. The signs of autumn's inevitable approach give the surroundings a melancholic, brooding feel, in keeping with the bittersweet theme of the day.

The women are absorbed in their preparations; they are soon joined by an army of volunteers and time flies. Before they know it, it is half-past eleven and early bird arrivals are flitting in. Within the next thirty minutes, the grounds fill up. It is a rich mix, similar in make-up to the town hall meeting. The Latchmere residents are out in force, joined by the radical campaigner types for which the borough is becoming notorious. There is a smattering of Liberal councillors wearing smug expressions, eager to inform anyone who asks – and many who don't – that it was they who were responsible for obtaining the necessary permissions. Many of the women's suffragist friends are in attendance. To Eliza's disquiet, the press is out in force. She hoped the unveiling of the statue would not be *that* newsworthy – but there again, what does she know?

The memorial itself is out of view, hidden under the tarpaulin cloth. They have kept its design a secret, so there is much anticipation. Many in the audience have donated to the cause, so feel a strong sense of ownership. They are proud to be part of this – the statue belongs to all of them.

Eliza scans the crowd for Lena. She spots her, talking to Battersea resident and formidable anti-poverty campaigner, Mrs Charlotte Despard. Eliza smiles, knowing it will thrill Lena to be meeting Mrs Despard, with whom she is very much in awe, at long last. The two women have little time to enjoy together, however, as a swarm of journalists are descending like locusts and bombarding Lena with questions. Her picture is taken by a photographer. Eliza frowns, experiencing that familiar feeling of misgiving. She prays Lena is not saying anything out of turn. The last thing they need is more legal trouble.

Eliza hands out pamphlets to the thickening crowd, all the while keeping a wary eye on Lena. Her attention is captured by the familiar, portly figure of Coleridge striding across the grass. He is in the company of a rake-thin, grey bearded, stern countenanced gentleman of about fifty. She experiences a flicker of recognition, but is equally sure they've never met. Then it dawns on her: this is their special guest, and the reason so many literary and intellectual types are here today. The man is Mr George Bernard Shaw. Coleridge is in his thrall, hanging onto every word as they stroll along, Coleridge executing a slightly comedic double step to keep up with his companion's long-legged stride. Shaw's gauntness only serves to emphasise Coleridge's rotund physique.

Coleridge acknowledges her, but, to her chagrin, does not come over to introduce his companion. She can only watch, disappointed, as they walk toward the shadow of the shrouded statue. She peels her eyes away for an instant to scan her surroundings. Suddenly she feels a firm hand on her shoulder. She spins, a broad smile brightening her face. 'Oh Jack, you made it,' she begins, her smile fading somewhat when she realises it's not who she thought. Lena's wide smile disappears too, replaced by an irritated scowl.

'Looking for lover boy, are we?' Lena huffs.

Eliza glares back, trying not to rise to the bait. Instead, she turns, and attempting a nonchalant air, resumes her scanning. Lena has the whip-hand now and will not let it lie. She continues, in a mean tone that does not become her. 'Face it, Liza, he didn't turn up last time, did he? So what's different now? He surely cannot break another bone, however accident prone the poor chap might be!'

'He said he'd be here, and he will be. I've faith in him. He couldn't help it last time, could he? Anyhow, I don't recall your beloved Papa proffering a reason for not being in court. And where's he today, huh? Too busy to come support his only daughter?'

Eliza's words hit their target. A sharp intake of breath and Lena turns away, stung. Eliza, remorseful, grasps at Lena's arm. She does not get the chance to apologise, as Coleridge chooses that moment to call for order, shouting to be heard above the general throng.

'Ladies and gentlemen, may we have some quiet? We're about to begin.' A hush falls upon the gathered crowd. 'Good people of Battersea, thank you for coming along this fine afternoon. As you'll be aware, these last six months have been, shall we say, *eventful* in our fight for justice for all imprisoned creatures. Tortured at the hands of so called *doctors* under the pretext of evolving scientific progress.'

A cheer erupts and there are shouts of 'hear, hear!'

'And, yes, there've been times where we've been close to giving up, so vociferous have been the howls of protest from the medical establishment. The cost to our cause, and to me personally,' he smiles ruefully, 'has been high. But nothing in society will change if we, my friends, surrender to the bullying tactics of the over-privileged, corrupt, self-serving powers that be.' More cheering. Coleridge is settling into his familiar, bombastic groove.

'And so, we find ourselves here today. A day, to be frank, my friends, we thought might never arrive. The unveiling of our memorial to this one dog who represents all creatures that are done wrong by humankind.' He pauses for reflection. 'And let us not forget that this wouldn't be possible if not for the generous donations from citizens of this borough *and* beyond. People, like yourselves, who care so deeply. I thank you all.' He acknowledges the applause. 'Today also wouldn't be possible without the dogged, if you excuse the term, and fearless determination of my dear friends and colleagues – Misses Hageby and Blackwood here.'

The women blush, their tiff forgotten for the moment, lost in the clapping and cheering.

'Finally, I'd like to thank our most distinguished guest for being here today. Ladies and gentlemen, it is my honour to introduce Mr George Bernard Shaw. Respected playwright, activist and humanitarian, who has agreed to unveil our memorial and say a few words.'

191

Mr Shaw steps forward, acknowledges Coleridge and his audience. He tugs on a rope; the black cloth falls to the ground. The crowd gasp at the sight of the statue, over seven feet-tall, bronze sparkling in the midday sun. The proud terrier's face looking out over their heads, beyond pain now. They cheer with even greater enthusiasm. Shaw waits patiently until they run out of steam, then begins.

The audience is mesmerised by Shaw's oratory; there is not a sound except his sonorous voice. Into this silence Jack arrives at the gate. He is out of breath from rushing, anxiety framing his face; he's late! He pushes his way through the throng with a refrain of 'I'm so sorry, please excuse me'. On tiptoes he peers over the amassed top hats and exotically feathered headwear, his head swivelling, desperate to locate Eliza.

He spots her at the front, to the left of the statue, which he pauses for a moment to admire. It *is* an impressive sight, not done justice to by the drawings. He ploughs on, parting the crowd as he goes, waving at a mesmerised Eliza, who remains oblivious to his presence.

Jack's progress slows the nearer to the statue he gets. Those close to the front are less happy to make space for the interloper trying to usurp their prime viewing position. One last push through, and he is within touching distance. He raises his hand to grasp Eliza's shoulder when, to his shock, a hand grabs his arm roughly. He spins, not sure what to expect. There, standing behind him, frowning, is Oscar. Jack is stunned, lost for words. Oscar is the last person he thought he would see here. In fact, he was counting on it. He finds his voice, a hiss.

'Oscar. How? What on earth are *you* doing here? You've your exam resit. How the hell did you get out of that?'

'I could ask the same question. What the hell are you doing here, Jack? You've not shown the slightest interest in this damned dog issue since the trial, yet here you are. Bold as brass.'

Jack's panicking now. What if Eliza turns and catches him, all chummy with Oscar, of all people? He glances back at her. She is still enthralled by Shaw. He moves back, putting as much space between them and Eliza as possible. Oscar seems content to follow Jack's lead, trailing him out from the nucleus of the crowd, talking all the while.

'Anyway, Bayling fixed it. He excused me from the resit, quid pro quo I come here and report back on what went on. To ensure Coleridge and those bitches aren't up to their old tricks again.' He snorts and gestures towards the statue. 'Looks like Coleridge's got that tuppenny playwright Shaw doing his dirty work instead. What a load of old codswallop he's spouting – huh?'

Jack is walking backwards, his eyes fixed on Eliza, fearing she will turn at any moment. She half twists at one point. Jack ducks as if to tie a shoelace. But it is momentary, she turns to the front again and he sighs with relief. Finally, the men are engulfed by the swarm, hidden from Eliza's sightline. It is fortunate as, at that moment, she glances back, frowning, scanning the crowd behind her, as if she'd sensed something.

Shaw concludes his speech and turns his attention to the inscription. He reads it as if it is poetry, his deep, commanding voice has all in his thrall. Oscar, his attention now caught by the man's words, turns pale. Jack, although intimately familiar with these words, still stops in his tracks. He watches warily, as Oscar turns from white to blush to scarlet in quick succession.

'What the blazes…? How dare they? The damned impertinence of it. Sentimental bloody nonsense. Oh hellfire. Bayling will not take well to this.' Oscar looks fearful, realising he will be the harbinger of bad news – again.

'Oh, fuck it. Jack, come, get a sodding move on. We've got to get to him before he reads it in the damn papers again.'

Oscar leads a reluctant Jack back through the outer ring, arrogantly charging through the crowd, only just avoiding an altercation with some swarthy types he inadvertently elbows.

Jack is conflicted, desolate, helpless. Eliza will think he's let her down *again*. He'd promised he'd come – hell or high water, he'd said

– and he'd seen no reason to steer clear, as he'd been so sure no student acquaintances of his would be present. But what could he do? There was no excuse that would allow him to return to the statue, to her – nothing, at least, that would not raise Oscar's suspicions further.

They clear the crowd and leave the park, the distant clapping as Shaw concludes, reverberating. Jack throws a final glance back into the throng before chasing after the rapidly retreating Oscar.

An hour later Oscar and Jack arrive at Bayling's office. They emerge from the lift looking identically downcast. Dunratty glances up, surprised. She checks the schedule, to satisfy herself she hasn't overlooked something – but no, course not, the doctor does not see students on a Saturday.

'Gentlemen! This is a surprise. Do you have an appointment?'

'No, Miss Dunratty, we do not. But it is of the utmost importance we see Dr Bayling.'

Dunratty, about to dismiss them out of hand, senses the panic in Oscar's expression, and the desolation in Jack's eyes.

'He's in his laboratory but doesn't care to be disturbed when he's operating.'

'Trust me, Miss Dunratty, he needs to hear what we have to say.' She has never seen Oscar looking so humble, contrite even.

'Very well, on your heads be it.' She sighs, knowing it will not only be them who suffers if he is annoyed by this intrusion, which she expects he will be. She gestures to the corridor. 'It's the third door on the right-hand side'. The men reluctantly make their way along a windowless passageway and knock on the door.

Bayling, in blood-splattered medical scrubs, glances up from the operating table. On that table a medium-sized cat is splayed, his whole abdomen pinned open. Bayling is removing part of his stomach. The cat is clearly semi-conscious and emitting a low guttural howl of despair. Annoyed at the disturbance, he scowls at his technician, who shrugs. Bayling glances up. He sees the vague outline of two figures through the glass. He growls at the closed door.

'Damn and blast. What on earth is it? Did Dunratty not make it clear I'm not to be disturbed?'

Oscar takes a deep breath, and, with a tremor to his voice, calls out. 'It's us, Dr Bayling. Oscar and Jack. We need to speak with you urgently, sir.'

'Can't it wait, boy? I'm in the middle of a very delicate procedure.'

'Sir, we're terribly sorry to disturb but ... but it's about that dog and its memorial, sir.'

Bayling freezes mid incision. He exhales and puts down his scalpel, wiping his bloodied hands on his apron. 'You'd better come in then.'

The men open the door and timidly shuffle in. They have never before been granted access to the laboratory, Bayling's inner sanctum, and what confronts Jack chills him to his core. The far wall is lined with small, bare-metal cages, dozens of them piled up on top of each other, floor to ceiling. They contain various species of animals – dogs, cats, rabbits, guinea pigs. Most are silent, staring dead-eyed past him. Some, recently operated on, are whimpering, shaved torsos roughly stitched up, with wounds still visible. The place has an almost visual stench of pain, suffering, hopelessness, death. Jack is sickened by what he is seeing. He glances at Oscar, who stares around the room – wide-eyed in horror. Oscar takes a deep gulp, steels himself, and concentrates on what he must relay to Bayling, whose expected reaction is frightening him much more than this visceral, demon's abattoir he's entered.

On another table, behind the one Bayling is working on, lies a dog. It is flayed on its back, strapped down, abdomen sliced open from breast to groin, still conscious. His mouth is muzzled, but a low moan can be heard. Electrodes are attached to the exposed veins in his neck. Another technician is attending to the controls and is shocking the animal, recording his reactions. Jack stares open-mouthed. Oscar, eyes rolling, takes in the scene, recovers his composure with difficulty.

Bayling stares at them with undisguised irritation. 'Well, what's so urgent? Out with it, man. Can't you see I'm busy?'

Oscar gulps, ready for the inevitable tirade. 'Sir, that dog memorial down in Battersea, it's, well, there's an inscription on it ...'

Bayling is exasperated at Oscar's ineloquence. 'For the love of God, just spit it out, boy.'

Another deep gulp from Oscar. 'Sir, this inscription. Well, its words are rather impertinent, you might say.'

Bayling's head jerks up; he pins them with a piercing stare.

'Go on,' Bayling murmurs with a quiet calm that sends a chill through the men.

TWENTY

A Call to Arms

UNIVERSITY COLLEGE MEDICAL LECTURE THEATRE
The fusty air is thick with swirling chalk dust that catches the throat.
Before he dismisses class, Bayling reaches for a newspaper on the
table beside him. The *Daily News* front-page feature is dominated
by a photograph of the memorial. Bernard Shaw and Coleridge are
shaking hands while peering up at the gleaming bronze dog. Lena
and Eliza, visible in the background, are looking on proudly, the
onlookers flanking them too many to count. The inscription itself
is not clear enough to be read, but the newspaper helpfully
reproduces it in full. Bayling brandishes the paper aloft. The
students are well aware of the headline; it was the talk of the
common room. A hushed silence sweeps the auditorium. Oscar
cringes. Jack, dismayed at the sight, holds his breath. What now?

'Gentlemen... Ladies.' Bayling nods to the solitary group of
women present, huddled in a small clique at the back. 'I assume
you've seen the travesty adorning the front pages of our less
reputable newspapers this weekend.' He shakes the paper away from
himself as if it were a rancid carcass requiring disposal. The crowd
murmurs affirmation. After all, the story was impossible to miss,
displayed, pride of place, on every newspaper stand in London.

'After the humiliation of the court case, one might expect
Coleridge to have learnt his lesson. To desist from causing me, and,
by implication, the entire research effort, further irritation.' He fixes
them with an accusatory stare. The audience shifts. They are feeling
a little uneasy as to where this may be heading. Bayling reddens, he

can feel that insistent throb in his temple, his blood pressure rising, but cannot stop now.

'But hell no, not a chance. That cur doesn't know when to give up. More fool him, that's all I can say. He *still* doesn't comprehend who he's dealing with. The medical establishment must show its teeth, unite in outrage against him and his deluded disciples. We need to erase this stain on our profession once and for all.' He crumples the paper and tosses it away in disgust. Tentatively, a few students voice their support. Calls to *'bring him down'* and *'crush the philistines'* echo around the wood-panelled chamber.

'It's you and I who devote our lives to the alleviation of disease, of suffering. Selfless to the last. We, ladies and gentlemen, have our priorities straight – not these mongrel-loving fanatics. Good God, they'd rather endure their own families suffering unspeakable agonies and avoidable deaths to protect a handful of strays who'd have died of malnutrition on the streets, anyway. At least if they come to us their pitiful lives will have meant something, served a higher purpose.' The wider audience finds its voice now, eager to display loyalty. Strident calls of agreement, clapping, cheering, calls of 'hear, hear!' ricochet from student to student, filling the room with discordant noise. Bayling silences them with a gesture.

'If you will indulge me for a few moments longer, I'd like to recite the lies that people will read, for many years to come; for as long, in fact, as that infernal statue remains on display. These words, gentlemen, are a travesty.'

Bayling reads the epitaph in its entirety. The last declaration he spits out, loathing clear in his tone.

'Men and Women of England, how long shall these Things be?'

Jack slips down further in his seat, his eyelid twitching uncontrollably; he covers his face. This was Lena's doing. Each time he suggested a softening of tone, she would suggest an even more provocative phrase. He should have known the words would be incendiary. God! If Bayling only knew he had had a hand in its creation. Oscar, sporting a washboard brow, leans over, stage whispers. 'Fucking hell, Jack. What the hell is Bayling up to?'

'How *dare* they?' Bayling roars. 'How dare they spout such malicious nonsense? Gentlemen, we cannot tolerate such venomous sentiment. If you feel slighted, denigrated by these words, you must not, cannot, remain silent. You must drown out the feeble squealing of these Luddites. Let's silence them once and for all.'

Jack observes through his fingers. Those last words send a shiver down his spine; someone's walking over his grave. Who is he wanting to silence, exactly? Bayling's arrogance appals him: a man drowning in privilege, who demands to be heard, to be obeyed, at all times. What right does he have to muzzle the already disenfranchised? Eliza's face appears in his mind's eye. He gulps, suddenly fearful. Is he *actually* inciting his students to violence? He's lost his mind, surely! Jack's palms are clammy against his cheeks. His thoughts are spinning out of control; he feels light-headed, weak, helpless.

The audience is on its feet, clapping and cheering, shouting support, decrying both the statue and the inscription. Working themselves into a frenzy of indignation on their lecturer's behalf. There are calls for it to be toppled, destroyed. Once the chant is in full throttle, Bayling smiles. He eagerly absorbs their fury for a moment, before holding his hands out in the manner of Caesar.

'Thank you, gentlemen. Thank you. You're too kind, indulging me in this matter. That's all for today.' He turns to leave, takes a few steps, then, as if an afterthought, saunters back to the lectern. The room is again silent.

'Gentlemen. If you believe we have been dealt a disservice, I urge you to do whatever you consider right and proper to redress this travesty. Search your conscience. Unleash your righteous outrage. The future of medical research, of progress itself, is under attack. Gentlemen, your *own* professional futures are under threat if we don't address this persistent thorn in our flesh. I leave you with that

199

thought. Good day to you all.' Bayling sweeps off stage, content with his performance. Whatever happens next, however it unfolds, his hands will be clean. And his conscience? A ghost of a frown skits across his face, then disappears beneath a satisfied grin.

TWENTY-ONE

The Attack

The memorial rapidly gains notoriety across the capital. In part, because its unveiling was attended by well-known liberals, celebrities and radicals, an audience that guarantees extensive press coverage. The other reason, ironically, is the sustained vocal outrage emanating from the medical establishment itself, up in arms at the very audacity of the existence of the statue, and, in particular, its epitaph. Its members' hysterical carryings-on ensure that the effigy of a stray dog, displayed in an out-of-the-way, modest patch of greenery in a working-class area of south London, remains in the public eye for far longer than would otherwise be the case.

The monument receives many hundreds of inquisitive Londoners in the weeks following its inauguration, keen to indulge their curiosity and scratch their heads at what all the fuss is about. As word spreads regarding its provenance and contentious inscription, they come from farther and farther afield to read its incendiary words for themselves.

The inhabitants of neighbouring Latchmere Estate quickly develop a peculiar attachment to the inadvertently controversial centrepiece of their park. Bemused by the sustained interest, local women take turns to make sure it appears pristine for all its visitors. They scrub the granite plinth when passing birds bless it, and are often to be found up stepladders, polishing the bronze until they see their faces reflected. They ensure the little dog always looks his best, proud and gleaming, watching over them all. He becomes their lucky emblem: the unofficial mascot of the estate.

Eliza and Lena visit their 'Jasper' whenever their schedules allow. They stroll the easy ten-minute walk over to the park, take a seat on the nearby bench and sit in contemplation, staring up at his soulful, wise face, desperately trying *not* to evoke memories of that awful night. The controversy surrounding the sculpture is not diminishing as they imagined, and desperately hoped, it would. If anything, the debate is getting more heated, and this troubles them.

Medical academics and students, egged on by Bayling and his supporters, persist in decrying the statue. It is an affront to their profession, their standing, and *will not be tolerated*. They have looked into legal means of getting it removed but found, to their immense chagrin, they have no case: the memorial is staying put. The wider debate surrounding live animal experimentation is also becoming a hot topic, causing furrowed brows and much wringing of hands in the laboratories and lecture halls across the land. Anti-vivisectionists have been getting bolder, disrupting live vivisection demonstrations across the capital and generally making a nuisance of themselves.

A common refrain of '*something must be done*' rings out in the private members' clubs that medical men, such as Bayling, frequent. And, indeed, something is being planned. It is whispered about in university tea rooms. Surreptitious, scribbled notes are slipped between students during class. Pertinent, heavy glances pass between lecturers and their tutees in corridors. The fightback has begun.

It is late October, just past midnight. A cool silvery light reflects off the eye of the gleaming bronze dog. All is calm. The workers' cottages are swathed in a gentle darkness, inhabitants tucked in for the night, off to the land of nod hours ago, given their excruciatingly early starts. The faint hooting of the tawny owls in the ancient oak is the only sound to break the velvety silence. The silhouette of a cauldron of bats glides past, the darkest of shapes clear against the grey-white disc of an extra-large moon.

There is a rustling in the undergrowth, most likely a fox snuffling for some easy prey. The sound intensifies, a vixen with cubs perhaps? It soon becomes plain that, whatever is moving in there, it is much larger than your typical urban wildlife.

Out of the bushes, a shape appears: human, adult, male. Dressed in black, face blackened with soot. Then another, and another. A mob of a dozen men assembles, as quietly as a bunch of lads are able, near the statue. A closer look reveals familiar faces. Oscar, Hugh and James, all three twitchy, nervous, and looking like they want to be anywhere but here. The mob sways slightly, as if on board ship: they had imbibed a barrel load of ale beforehand, to provide the Dutch courage required. Now the alcohol is making its presence felt.

They encircle the monument, armed with hammers, crowbars, bats. The ringleader gives a silent signal, and they begin, quietly, to attack it. They try their best to lever off the metal plate. They pelt it with paint, glue, beer bottles, eggs, whatever they have been able to find to deface the loathed monument. They soon forget the need for stealth as they become emboldened. They coax each other on, ignoring warnings from their relatively sober leader. The banter grows louder and rowdier, shouting encouragement, cheering every time paint, or an egg, hits its target.

Soon the commotion attracts the attention of nearby bobbies on the beat. The drunken mob is also doing a sterling job of jolting the neighbourhood from its slumbers. Sleepy men yank bedroom windows up and shout profanities. The moonlight pours light on the tableau below them, and inhabitants with strategic viewpoints soon realise their statue is under attack. Their angry, desperate cries reach the police who stop their dawdling, crank up the speed and sprint as fast as their middle-aged legs will carry them. They home in on the source of the noise, whistles blowing, truncheons waving, the peace of the night well and truly shattered.

The two bobbies reach the park boundary, shouting, creating an unholy racket in an attempt to scare the blighters off. Simultaneously a gaggle of residents, hastily robed in plaid dressing gowns and slippers, armed with shovels, fireside pokers and whatever else they had to hand, also descend on the park.

The mob freezes. They have been rumbled. Their leader makes a sign to scramble and they disappear back into the undergrowth just before the first wave of defence arrives. Women, their hair in rollers and rags, dressed only in their nightwear, overcome their modesty to see what all the commotion is about. Their faces sport a ghoulish grey glow in the moonlight, and all wear the same dismayed look as they survey the level of carnage inflicted.

The following morning Eliza, Lena and Coleridge stand in the same vantage point as they did before the unveiling, once again looking towards the statue. Instead of joy, this time their faces are a perfect study of dismay, all three close to tears. At the memorial there is a hive of activity. Residents, pails and brushes in hand, are scrubbing furiously at the plinth, elbow grease eating away at the brightly coloured vandalism.

The monumental stonemason who put so many hours, so much effort and so much passion into crafting the base, is surveying the damage, his distress clear. The dog, although splattered with a range of dubious substances, looks otherwise unharmed. He is being meticulously cleaned by women balancing precariously on rickety stepladders. Already parts of his body are emerging from the stiff coating of paint, egg yolk and hardened glue, and he is beginning to gleam again.

Lena walks up, places a consoling hand on the shoulder of the stonemason. Her initial dismay is displaced by a rapidly boiling fury. 'Who'd do such a dreadful thing? It's just a memorial. How could anyone be so angry, so violent, towards a simple statue for Chrissakes?'

Eliza, close behind, responds with an uncharacteristic venom. 'Oh, I don't think it takes much to work out who's behind this,' she growls. 'Winning the damn court case wasn't enough for him.'

Coleridge joins them, looking thoughtful, doubtful. 'I'm not so sure, Elizabeth. Common vandalism isn't quite Bayling's style.'

'Well, if it wasn't him, he'd have encouraged it, incited it, of that I've no doubt.'

At that moment, Jack appears. He had heard whisperings at college about a plan to attack the statue, but declared he wanted nothing to do with it. This was much to Oscar's annoyance, who had not spoken to him for days as a result, hence Jack had only just got wind they'd *actually* gone and done it.

He reaches the throng of people, taking it in, observing the clean-up, every step increasing his sense of guilt. But what could he have done? He could not have warned them, it would have raised too many awkward questions about how he knew. Besides, he truly didn't believe they would go through with it. He imagined their threats to be bravado and bluster that would blow over, everything forgotten in a matter of weeks. At least, he prayed that would be the case. How wrong he was, again.

The sight confronting him is appalling, the statue is a war zone. Red and blue paint splattered from top to bottom, left to right. Smashed eggs stuck to the granite surface, resembling the burst cysts he had witnessed in hospital wards. They have attempted to jemmy off the inscription plate, but have not got far, such is their ineptness at any kind of manual labour. There are chips in the granite where it has been hit with iron bars.

He approaches Eliza tentatively, conscious she has not forgiven him for his absence at the unveiling. He reaches her without her noticing and touches her arm. 'Eliza. Eliza, my dear, I'm so sorry, I've just heard. I can't imagine who'd do such an awful thing.'

The lie sticks in his throat somewhat, but there, he's said it. She doesn't react at first, but slowly turns to face him. He sees the sore redness of her eyes, the drooping of her shoulders. She looks defeated, spent of any fight. She hasn't even the emotion spare to continue being cross with him.

The sight of her like this crushes him, and he reaches to take her in his arms, envelop her, keep her safe from harm. She lets him console her, arms hanging loosely at her side. She slumps against him, allowing herself to be cocooned. His banishment because of the second no-show is forgotten for the moment. Slowly, she laces her fingers around his neck, and, burying her head in his chest, greedily breathes in his scent – reminiscent of carbolic soap. Oh, she has missed him. Lena turns, shocked to see him there. She can't help but stare, the unwilling witness to this tender embrace. Another little piece of her heart breaks at the sight.

Moments pass, Jack and Eliza oblivious to the commotion surrounding them, lost in their own private miseries. Eliza feels the weight of the world, the force of the establishment, weighing down on her. She knows how Sisyphus must have felt, with his impossible boulder and never-ending mountain. This incident is crushing the last of her resolve. She just wants to crawl back into her dusty world of books, safe in the literary bosom of the library. Jack is locked in his own prison of lies, trapped, with no way out of the quagmire which would not destroy everything that's precious to him.

When Eliza eventually feels strong enough to emerge from the safety of Jack's embrace, she sees the crowd has multiplied. It's working itself up into a collective fury as people take in the extent of the damage. It is not long before they get themselves organised. These folk are nothing but practical, resilient under fire, and they are damned if they're allowing this outrage in their own neighbourhood. As a group of women busy themselves with the clean-up, and the men repair the inscription plate, another group of no-nonsense matronly types organise their menfolk. They are arranging a rota, organising a night-time watch schedule, to protect the statue from further attack.

TWENTY-TWO

The Confession

They watch from the side lines: Eliza, cosseted in Jack's arms; Lena, stiff-backed and tense standing beside a concerned Coleridge. They are taking solace in the touching acts of kindness people are displaying for 'our little bronze mutt', as the statue has become known. As befits Battersea, the locals resemble a swarm of worker bees. Each is designated a job and accepts their role with enthusiasm, demonstrating an inherent pride in their work.

On realising there is nothing more to do that isn't already being well attended to, the four pool their dwindling resolve and plot their next move. Once they have agreed on a plan, they walk out together, separating at the park gates. Lena and Coleridge travel into town to call upon sympathetic journalists. Eliza and Jack head to the flat to compose a leaflet that tells of this outrage.

Jack, a mournful expression overshadowing his face, lounges on the chaise longue in Eliza's sitting room. He's absentmindedly dangling a string for a playful Mrs P, their unlikely friendship still going strong. The cat, Eliza thinks, with a touch of jealousy, behaves almost flirtatiously around him. She emerges from the kitchen with a tray of tea and cake. She pours two cups and passes one to Jack. She cuts into a *bara brith* loaf, thickly butters it and offers a generous slice. Jack declines with an apologetic shrug: he has no appetite. He has resolved his shameful subterfuge, his web of lies, cannot continue. He'll tell her the truth today – this very minute – and hope that somehow she can find it in her heart to forgive him. Jack stares at her with such an unreadable look it takes Eliza aback.

'What? What is it, Jack? Won't you try my fruit cake? The recipe's handed down through generations. It's renowned throughout the valley. It's my only inheritance, you must try some.' A ghost of a smile lingers.

He is on the verge of blurting it out. *But where on earth to start?*

'Eliza, I, I need to tell you ... to confess something. I only pray you can find it in you to forgive me.' He falters. The smile is gone and curiosity now clouds her face.

'What? What on earth is it? You can tell me anything. I won't judge you, silly thing. What can be *so* bad it's making you sweat like this?' She smooths away a drop of moisture beaded on his brow; her gentle touch almost makes him swoon. She smiles, a picture of innocent concern, encouraging him to continue. He swallows hard.

'I haven't told you that much about myself, have I?' She stares, a worried frown taking root, not wanting him to relive more of the sad childhood he confessed to at the restaurant.

'I suppose not much, 'cept your father's death. Your poor mama's illness, how she, and your sister, live up north.' Shut up, Eliza. 'But there's no need to dwell on such things, 'specially as it causes you pain.' Her smile so sweet, her face so full of concern, love even, it's eating him up, but he's committed now.

'I haven't explained why I'm here, in London. Why I study, my motivations, values, what I believe in. None of it. In fact, you hardly know me, the real me.'

She shrugs. 'I guess not, but there again, you know little of me.' Her expression is now becoming coquettish. 'And I like it like that. We can be deliciously intriguing with one another, can't we?' She trails a finger slowly down his cheek. He shivers.

'We've all the time in the world to discover the details,' Eliza continues. 'Why not let our histories unravel slowly, or even make up new ones?' She reflects, liking the sound of that. After all she's not proud of hers, so why not invent a better, happier past? 'Who cares what we were, Jack? It's who we are, and what we'll become that counts, isn't it?' Her chin juts in a defiant, daring look he's not seen before.

Jack gazes at her, intrigued, sensing something different. She seems bolder, braver, as if the attack on the statue has smashed something in her too. Gone is the strait-laced, prudish lady librarian, and into her place has stepped a bohemian, a liberated, devil-may-care woman.

What to do, though? He senses they are at a crossroads, and her brazen demeanour has awoken an animal instinct he's finding difficult to tame. He cannot spoil this moment; confessions will have to wait. He moves closer. Closer still. Kisses her. There is no tenderness this time. There is a force, a coarse desire powering his actions. She does not resist. She meets his kiss, returns it with an equal, a greater ferocity, willing him, daring him, to go further – much further. He needs no encouragement. He scoops her into his arms, carries her to a bedroom door. As he manoeuvres to open it, she shrieks with mirth.

'No, not this one. It's Lena's.'

'Crikey, that would be inappropriate.' A grimace temporarily replaces his lustful look. He locates her bedroom, and they almost fall into it, Eliza still cocooned in his arms. He traverses the room in three easy strides and lays her on the bed with perfect gentleness, as if handling a Ming vase. At her wordless invitation, he lays down beside her. They lie facing one other, no words spoken, or needed, there is an understanding of what is about to unfold.

With trembling fingers, she unbuttons her blouse. He watches, paralysed by an overwhelming desire. Exuding an intoxicating mix of innocence and raw sensuality, she unhooks her corset, peels back her layers.

He lies enraptured, gazing at her unblemished, olive-toned skin. His eyes follow her gentle curves downwards. Her champagne coupe breasts with their brown-pink nipples make his lips ache. Her waist curves in before veering back out into unexpectedly voluptuous hips. He carries on his visual journey, feasting his eyes on the neat forest of dense, curled, chocolate brown hair, nestled in the crease at the top of slim, muscular thighs.

Shyly, but with determination, she turns her attention to him. Her dilated pupils render her eyes coal black. He surrenders to her, still unable to move, such is his mesmerised state. It takes a long while – too long – to divest him of waistcoat, tie, braces, shirt, vest, trousers, and undergarments. She gapes, incredulous, as she finally unbuttons his cumbersome long johns.

Jack finds himself struck by a sudden, unexpected bashfulness. Although not unfamiliar with the act of lovemaking, he has never been *in love* before, and this breath-taking passion renders him, to his mortification, helpless.

Untroubled by any such stage fright, Eliza, the curious ingénue, stares unabashed. She reaches down and caresses him gently, catches herself gasping when she comprehends how large, how solid, this erstwhile mysterious part of the masculine body can become. She'd not seen the male member in any state except flaccid, and they were made of marble, belonging to lifeless Greek gods displayed in museums. She'd also spied the odd pencilled line-drawing in the whispered-about special library collection but had dismissed those as sordid fantasy, being so ridiculously out of proportion. The thought of that inside her terrifies and thrills her in equal measure.

Her exclamation breaks Jack's inconvenient paralysis. He reaches up, chilled fingers brushing against her painfully erect nipples. She shivers, gasps in delight at his long-awaited touch, arching backwards and thrusting her breasts towards him, the prim shyness that once defined her now cast aside. He needs no further prompting: taking her nipple into his mouth, his hot lips making a perfect seal, he darts his tongue over the nub as she quietly moans in delight.

She reaches down blindly, fingers tracing down his taut chest, finding the silky-soft pubic hair. She clutches him, too rough in her enthusiasm. He cries out, breaking the seal. He soon regains it, his teeth clamping her nipple as his tongue attacks it with more urgency, sucking like a wild animal devouring its prey, spurred on by her increasingly frantic whimpers.

His hand moves down, fingers slipping effortlessly through the slick hair and swallowed by her swollen, cushioned lips. He revels in the fact no man has explored this hot, tight space. She allows his tongue to delve deep into her hungry mouth, relishing what's to come.

His middle finger slips further into her. She sobs. He cannot tell if it's pain or pleasure, but he's soon in no doubt; as he withdraws, she forces his hand back, guiding a second finger deeper. By touch alone, she's showing she's more than ready, determined to be taken. He thrusts, pushing harder and further, preparing her for what's to come. He doesn't want to hurt her, which, from his few previous encounters, he fears is a possibility. From the jealous side glances of men in communal showers, he realises he's in possession of a significantly larger specimen than the norm.

A desire to taste her wetness overwhelms him, he removes his mouth from hers. She protests. He runs his tongue down the length of her stomach. She gasps when she realises what's coming. Removing his fingers, he parts her lips, exposing her most intimate place.

He raises his head to take his first look at her. He blows softly, taking her to another level of exquisite torture. Frantic now, she grabs his head and pushes it, forcing him down with such ferocity he struggles to breathe. The heady smell is intoxicating. He sucks her, drinking her essence. She loses herself, her back arches to an impossible angle, tension at snapping point, she's so close.

He cannot contain himself, pushes her back on the bed. He's lost to his desire. He thrusts apart her thighs, and rears to full height in front of her inviting body. But pauses, desperate to control his breathing and raw lust. She suddenly feels a surge of fear. What *is* she doing? But it's overcome by animal instinct as she grasps for him.

Steadily, with utmost care, he penetrates her. She whimpers as his length slowly fills her. Agony and ecstasy vie for dominance. She has, in secret, shameful moments, dreamt of this, the most terrifying, exquisite torment. He checks she's comfortable, her expression is unreadable and could be either pleasure or pain. But she thrusts upward to meet him and soon both are lost in a carnal delirium.

They wrap around each other. Her long, flexible limbs interlock with his hips and buttocks and squeeze him tight. She has extraordinary strength in her thighs. He couldn't escape even if he wanted to. Their thrusts soon find their rhythm, the penetration so deep they cannot be closer.

He's uncertain how much longer he'll last and is close to losing control when he senses the most intense tightening. She gasps and arches, holds rigid for a few sublime moments, then sighs and collapses. Her internal grip on him loosening just at the point of his own desperate, violent release. He calls out, a short sharp groan, and drops, spent, to the side of her.

They lie in each other's arms, drained of desire, at peace. The statue's battered state is forgotten for the moment. Eliza snuggles up against Jack's sweat-covered chest. She has never felt this protected, this happy in her own skin. Jack, at the moment before reality came crashing back in, was in a state of meditation – no miserable, conflicted thoughts swirling, just quiet tranquillity. His peace does not last. Returning to reality first, Jack is conscious of his now even more compromised situation.

'Eliza. My darling. There's something you must know, something I've been not quite...'

Eliza puts a finger to his lips. 'Shh, my love. Not now. Don't spoil this moment. There's nothing that can't wait a while longer. Let's just enjoy this time.'

Jack complies, but with a heavy conscience. He stares at the ceiling, a wretched guilt engulfing him. How can he tell her the truth after this? In time, exhausted by their exertions, they surrender to a post-coital, blissfully dream-free doze.

THE EMPTY PLINTH, APRIL 1906 – THE OBJECTOR

One particularly unsavoury looking fellow breaks rank from the mob that blocks our way. He oozes a disquieting menace which sends a collective shiver through our group. Gaunt, chest inflated with machismo, he saunters over, towering over us, observing, leering. A sneer splits his harsh, pinched face; a flaccid roll-up dangles from his parched lips. He sniffs the air, as if savouring the atmosphere his mob has created, feeding off it. He takes a slow, deep drag, flicks the butt and grinds it into the cobbles with a hobnailed toe. It feels like hours before he speaks but it's just seconds. His voice is a low, menacing growl.

'A word if I might, ladies.' He steps closer, closer still. His searchlight eyes are undressing us. 'I'd totter off home to yer menfolk where you belong if I were you...' His contorted grin is a parody of childish innocence. He clicks his fingers. The gang casually push back their coats, revealing an assortment of knives and coshes. 'So's we avoid these pretty faces of yers getting slashed in all the chaos we've got 'ere.'

A unified gasp. Sensing, almost tasting, the terror of the women cowering behind me, I struggle to contain a rising tide of vomit. I feel their agitation. Some turn to flee. The ringleader, drinking our distress, laps it up, taunts us with crude insults.

'Mind, for some of you old hags it'd be an improvement, ain't that right, lads?' The mob snigger, and as one, takes a step closer.

A sudden sharp cut of stale sweat and alcohol overlays the lingering odour of rotten eggs. I swallow bile and stumble as the support behind me falls away. There are only the two of us left now; the others are observing from a safe distance, some have run off. She feels for my hand, squeezes it, trying to warn me, to get me to come away. But I find I cannot take my eyes off him; I'm willing him to see me, really see me.

It works. The ringleader double takes, his eyes narrowing; he creeps closer to us. I let go of her hand and step towards him. A cold, calm realisation grips me. We are now almost nose to nose. I can smell his beer-soaked, rancid breath. It is nauseatingly overpowering so close up, but I do not flinch. I cannot show weakness.

213

TWENTY-THREE

The Dog Patrol

THE STATUE, SOME WEEKS LATER

It's late November. Weak autumnal sunshine casts its long shadow over the park's lawns but can't quite erase silvery remnants of overnight frost from the undergrowth.

Fallen leaves provide a crunchy carpet – all ruby reds, muddy brown, shades of purple and deep emerald – that conceals the path leading to the statue. Raindrops form a rivulet down the dog's gleaming bronze torso, which now looks as good as new.

The plinth has also been repaired. To the naked eye there are no signs of damage. It is as if the attack never happened, except... except for the presence of half a dozen policemen, all identically attired in familiar black serge – polished silver buttons glinting like stars – and tall, hard-shelled helmets. They're looking, it must be said, rather bored. Standard issue truncheons are strapped to utility belts They stamp their feet and blow into their hands to help keep the penetrating chill at bay.

Two of the policemen are seated on the nearby bench, tucking into a lunch of meat pie wrapped in greaseproof paper, and juicy granny smith apples. A woman from the neighbouring cottages approaches with a tray of tea and cake. The men shovel in heaped teaspoons of sugar and wrap freezing fingers around the steaming mugs.

The older of the two, Sergeant Albert McDonald, Bert to friends, sports an 'I've seen it all before, son' expression on his age-coarsened, yet still jolly, face. He has taken his luncheon companion, a probationary constable by the name of Stanley Robb, under his wing. Stan is bright-eyed, enthusiastic, and still of the belief there is good in everyone – you just have to search harder in some individuals. It is Stan's first day down at Latchmere and Sergeant McDonald is more than happy to fill him in on the peculiar situation of the 'Dog Patrol' – as the police guard has come to be known. Bert, in-between sipping his tea, holds court to a rapt audience of one.

'You wouldn't Adam 'n' Eve it, son, truly you wouldn't. The trouble this yer lifeless lump of stone's been causing us these past weeks.'

'Aye Sarge, it's talk of the station. But I'm befuddled by the fuss; it's only a metal dog when all's said 'n' done.'

Bert harrumphs and, with a knowing sigh, he prepares to put the young man right on a few matters. 'You might well think that, Stanley, my lad, but it's caused no end of strife. It's not just the crazies and radicals down 'ere in Battersea neither. It's spreading over London like a bleedin' disease. Just in the month I've been 'ere, we've broken up bad-tempered kerfuffles between the locals and 'em medical students every bleedin' week.' He snorts again. 'And all that trouble up in town, I don't know what the world's coming to. Mark my words Stan, someone will get seriously hurt one of these days. Maybe then they'll come to their senses, *and I* can get back to me proper job.'

'You'd think they'd be more civilised, them toffee-nosed types, given their so-called superior breeding, education and all,' retorts Stanley, a proud, paid-up member of the nascent Independent Labour Party. Bert shakes his head knowingly.

'Aye, don't you believe it. No better than yobs, 'em toffs. You should 'ear the language coming off of them, effing 'n' jeffing, likes of which I ain't heard since being down the docks, keeping 'em drunken navvies in check.' He scoffs. 'Well, trying to.'

'But I just can't figure it, Sarge. Don't get me wrong, I'm as fond of my old mutt as the next man, he's a great dog. But why all this fuss over a statue? It ain't doing no one no harm.'

Bert bestows the look of patronising, yet gentle, condescension the old and wise reserve for the young and naïve. 'Ah, young Stanley, you may think so, but it's the principle of the thing! You've these fanatics from the Anti-Viv 'ospital up the road, and then those sufferahs, suffrags, those mad women – y'know who I mean, son?'

'Aye, Sarge, I do. Them's ladies who's getting ideas above their station. Demanding a vote when we don't even have it yet. Bleedin' cheek, I say.' They nod in solemn agreement at this universal truth.

'Then there's 'em animal rights lot, they care more about things wiv four feet than two, that's for sure. Their priorities are well up the spout. Plus, you got the council here, they're bloody lunatics 'n' all! Liberals, radicals, the lot of 'em. You know, I blame 'em councillors more than the rest of the other silly buggers put together, it was 'em who encouraged all this nonsense. Where's their sense, eh? Allowing that thing to be put here, with that bleedin' writing on it. Bound to cause grief with 'em la-de-da medical types.' They both stare ahead, nodding in unison.

'They drafted me in on that Saturday as it happens, for that meeting up on the Embankment that turned nasty. Was s'posed to be a peaceful meeting about women's rights, getting the vote 'n' all, but it got hijacked by the 'anti-dogger' mob. Had to be a couple of dozen at least, shouting and raging. They were very uncouth for young gentlemen, I must say! It was an eye-opener for me. They were baying for blood, so they were, jeering and swearing at the ladies. And that's not on Sarge. However misguided they may be, I'm not 'aving that kind of disrespect. Them's still ladies after all.'

'Too right, my lad. Ladies are still ladies, even if they are deranged.' Again, they nod solemnly.

'Them medical students were chanting about this blasted statue yer, how they was gonna topple it and throw it in the Thames, be done with it for good. This only inflamed the situation. We even had some trade union lads join in, defending the ladies – and there's no love lost 'tween them and the suffras, normal times – but thick as thieves they was. So anyway, it grew out of hand darn quick.

216

Bedlam it were! Punches thrown, stuff being chucked – stones, crackers, whatever people could get hold of. We made plenty of arrests, the fighting got that bad. The cells overflowed that night for sure. You wouldn't believe it Sarge, but even some of them ladies were throwing eggs, and worse! It was bad alright, I was glad to get out in one piece...' Stan peters out; lately, he's been given to pondering whether he'd made the right career choice after all.

'Aye, and look at us now, a twenty-four-hour bleedin' guard. Stopping us doing proper coppering, all to protect a likeness to a dead dog. I don't know what world's coming to, lad. Truly, I don't. In my twenty-five years on the force, I've never had an assignment like this one, beggars belief it does.'

There's a rumbling hum in the distance. Bert flinches, his senses attuned to any unusual sounds. The noise builds, recognisable now as chanting, almost a song they can hear drifting in on the wind. There's no mistaking, there's trouble brewing and it's coming their way. Bert throws his colleagues a 'here we go again' look and reaches for his truncheon. He stands and turns to Stan, who is looking a little nonplussed. 'Gird your loins, Stanley, my young friend. Gird 'em loins.'

The policemen adopt their by now well-practised defensive positions. Stan is quick to fall into line, mimicking his experienced colleagues. They form a circle around the statue, truncheons and whistles poised, braced for trouble, ready to defend, again, the silent, staring bronze dog from all who'd do him harm.

TWENTY-FOUR

The Betrayal

LATCHMERE PARK, SOME MONTHS LATER
There is to be no let up, no dampening of tempers or cooling of passions. Regular, coordinated marches are organised by medical schools across central London, as well as over the river in Battersea. Tutors and lecturers whip their students into a frenzy of indignation at the perceived insult to their profession. The physical manifestation of this outrage is the memorial and its inscription so, inevitably, it remains the epicentre for protestations and trouble. The locals are up in arms about the frequent, often disorderly, intrusions into their otherwise peaceful neighbourhood. They are incredulous at the persistence of the *toffs from up town*, trying to harm their treasured statue – why can't they just leave it, and them, alone?

Latchmere Park is in uproar yet again. The Dog Patrol is overwhelmed trying to hold the opposing factions apart. Bert and Stanley are in attendance, nowadays displaying permanently weary, worn-down expressions. Even Bert's famously jolly demeanour has deserted him. They're desperate to be reassigned. The Saturday night beat in Soho was child's play compared to these relentless, pointless clashes.

Today's protest is shaping up to be eventful, even by normal standards. The students, and their paid-for 'heavies' – an unwelcome recent addition, coarse-looking thugs who don't blend in with the usual well-to-do, medical types – are arriving in force, faces

218

obscured by scarves. There must be around a hundred in snaking lines, piling through the gates at either end.

Distant chanting can be heard. It could not be described as singing. It is their battle cry, by now a horribly familiar sound, their version of a traditional tune popular with children – "Little Brown Jug". Although its origins, truth be known, were not so sweet and innocent: it was composed as a drinking song but doubled up as a cautionary tale against the dangers of alcoholism, back in the fifties. The mob has given the lyrics a sinister new edge.

> *As we go walking after dark,*
> *We turn our steps to Latchmere Park*
> *And there we see, to our surprise*
> *A little brown dog that stands and lies*
>
> *Ha, ha, ha! Hee, hee, hee!*
> *Little brown dog, how we hate thee*
> *Ha ha ha, hee, hee, hee*
> *Little brown dog, we don't love thee*
>
> *Ha ha ha, hee hee hee!*
> *Little brown dog, how we hate thee*
> *When we go rioting in the park*
> *We'll destroy you, not leave a mark*

The mob hides a dark secret in its midst. The bitter chill of winter requires long, thick overcoats. Tucked underneath the garments of the more thuggish types are concealed crowbars, knives and bats. They are primed and ready to attack the statue, and, without remorse, any locals who get in their way.

The encroaching army is equalled, outnumbered even, by the locals amassing. Roused by the chants and police whistles, they have come running from all corners of the neighbourhood. Motives for being there vary. Many come to protect their beleaguered statue peaceably, some prepared to defend it at any cost, others are eager for the chance to give those 'la-di-das' from across the river the kick-in they deserve.

Combatants square up to each other on either side of the monument, as if an invisible battle line has been drawn. With a sense of inevitability, fighting erupts across the park, isolated wildfires sparking from a lightning strike. On Bert's command, Stanley, being by far the youngest and fastest, is dispatched to Battersea Bridge station for back-up. A five-minute sprint if he is quick.

Into this chaotic scene arrive the two women. Eliza dragged from her work by a panicked Lena, who, on returning from a shopping trip to the West End, spotted a group of young men leaving Clapham station. Her suspicion aroused by the demeanour of the rougher-looking types, she followed them part way, soon confirming they were en route to Latchmere Park. She turned on her heel and ran all the way to the library.

They rushed as fast as their inconveniently long, straight-cut skirts would allow. On reaching the gates they stop stock-still, catching their breath, surveying the mayhem playing out before them, horrified by the violence – it has never got this bad before. There are a dozen fights happening concurrently, groups of men tussling each other to the ground. Some are stamped upon with hob-nailed boots, others' faces smashed by bare knuckles, iron bars and chains making short work of the arms and hands that get in their way. Blood and phlegm splatter from noses and mouths, coating the scene in a gruesome scarlet glow.

Local women, enraged that their menfolk are being battered by an armed mob, rush home and fetch whatever is to hand – pokers, warming pans, brooms, rolling pins – and launch themselves into the fray. Lena, with no consideration of the danger, dashes to the nearest fight and attempts to prise men apart, struggling to reason with them. Eliza, more hesitant, joins in too, trying to quell the disorder, placating the furious women, ushering them out of harm's way – persuading them that smashing pokers over the anti-doggers heads would not help the situation. But it is to no significant effect. They stop some scuffles breaking out. However, once one stops, and they pause for breath, two more explode in its place.

As Lena valiantly tries to calm a group of irate men, her eye is taken by a vaguely familiar face in the distance. She racks her brain for a moment and then it clicks. How can she forget that oily, sneering scowl, that haughty profile? It's a face that will forever haunt her – up there on that stage, leering into the split-open torso of that poor dog. He is positioned at the edge of the fighting, far enough away so he isn't in any danger of being dragged into any skirmishes. He appears to be issuing instructions to a mob of crowbar-wielding men, gesturing toward the statue. The gang skulk off towards the memorial. Oscar Latham-Ward stands, hands on hips, surveying the scene, his faithful sidekicks – Hugh and James – in attendance.

A red mist descends, Lena forgets the men, the fighting, the statue. She thrusts through the crowd, shoving aside anyone in her way, no care for her safety. It's as if she's untouchable, indestructible. She has one goal: to get to her nemesis and give it to him with all the bile and venom she's brewing. She draws level. Oscar, his back to her, is holding court, he remains unaware of her approach.

James kicks Oscar's shoe and gestures behind him. Oscar turns and is confronted by Lena, eyes narrowed, fury rising. She glares, not speaking. He is unsure how to break the impasse. No flippant comment comes easily to mind, he's put off by her manic gaze. He's spared, as Lena eventually musters the wherewithal to hiss.

'Oscar? Oscar Latham-Ward. It *is* you, isn't it? I'd recognise that conniving, scheming, evil rat-face of yours anywhere.' She scoffs. 'I should've guessed you'd be behind this … this outrage. Your butcher lord sent you, did he, huh? I can't imagine you've the sense to organise this yourself. You'll never get your way, you know. We'll always repair him, replace it. You can't destroy a statue like you destroyed that poor wretch.'

She stares defiantly, inches closer, goading him to act. She's fearless, blood pounding, no sense of the danger she's facing. Just one slight, young woman facing down three strapping men, though anyone witnessing the scene would fear for the men, such is her aura of ferocity. She's glaring at Oscar, but it's Bayling in her mind's eye. With a cool rage, she takes the baiting up a level.

'You ... you heartless, monstrous excuse for a man. Scared of a lump of metal, are we? How pathetic you are. And a coward to boot. You've only the gall to attack a helpless, shackled creature – tortured and half-dead anyway – or a lifeless hunk of granite with the truth of your barbarity carved into it? You've not the backbone to tackle anyone of your own size, not even a pathetic, weak *woman*.' She gestures down at herself.

'That's quite enough!' Oscar barks, absorbing her bile, simmering. Her taunts hit home; she has nailed the true measure of him. He is a coward, always has been. He has hidden behind his family name, his inherited riches, insulated from harm. Ever the bully master, never the bully. Never having to confront anyone himself. But this time it is different, and he can feel his rage growing, devouring his cowardice and feeding off it, allowing his fury to take centre stage. He feels an overwhelming urge to do something he has never done, physically hurt someone. He cares not that the someone is a woman half his size. They stand defiantly eye-to-eye, not blinking, awaiting their fates with an inevitability.

Eliza belatedly notices Lena's absence. She searches around herself, but there is no sign of her. Worry clouds her brow. She picks her way through the warring factions, scanning the crowd, calling. Her panic grows, but then she spots her, way over on the other side of the statue. She is facing off with someone. But who? She squints against the low setting winter sun. Slowly things come into focus.

'Oh God. Oscar.' She whispers his name, as if to confirm what her eyes are telling her. She senses, almost tastes, impending violence. Her stomach lurches, adrenalin pumps furiously. She must reach Lena before something awful happens.

She makes to move, but finds she is incapable. Her legs have turned leaden. She has the sensation of being rooted to the spot. It is just as in her nightmares where she finds herself trapped, strapped to her seat, unable to escape the torture chamber, or the pleading, agony-filled eyes of that little dog. The harder she struggles, the more rooted she becomes.

Panic overwhelms her, bile rises, she's going to be sick. But no, she *will not* allow it, she *will* move. She consciously slows her breathing, in, pause, out, pause, in, pause, out. She reasons with herself, she's not dreaming, *this is not a nightmare*, and wills her legs to move, however slowly. Yes. Yes, she can do it. She puts one foot in front of another. She sighs a slow, controlled breath of relief. One foot, then the other, faster, faster! She's running, yanking her ridiculous skirts to over the knee – a shocking lack of decorum in normal circumstances – flying now.

After what seems an eternity, she reaches her friend. Lena has her back to Eliza, is focused on Oscar, who tenses, a cobra preparing to strike. Her arrival startles him. Eliza grabs Lena roughly, pushing her sideways. Eliza stands in-between Lena and Oscar, her arms splayed out, protecting her friend from harm.

'Stop right there, Oscar. Don't you dare! What kind of man are you?'

A terrifying calm has descended. He is perfectly enraged, emboldened, feels no fear in this moment. In slow motion, he pulls back his fist, hissing so only Eliza hears.

'I'll show you *exactly* what kind of man I am, bitch.'

With that, his fist smashes forward, destined for Eliza's face. She cowers, eyes shut, awaiting the blow. It doesn't arrive. From nowhere, an anguished cry shatters the scene.

'Oscar... noooo.' A man's figure appears from the undergrowth and, in a flying lunge, launches itself at Oscar, rugby-tackling him to the ground a split second before he makes contact with Eliza's cheek.

Eliza opens an eye gingerly. Two men lie spread-eagled on the ground. Oscar's winded, stunned, he looks around himself mystified. 'What the hell?'

Eliza stares at the men sprawled at her feet, in a state of mute shock. Lena looks on, not quite believing her own eyes. Hugh and James resemble goldfish, not moving a muscle to help their warring friends, they stand and stare, impotent, slack-jawed and bug-eyed.

Oscar, gathering his wits, rubs his bruised shoulder gingerly, looks across at Jack in astonishment. 'For fuck's sake, Jack. What the hell's going on? It's just that crazy bitch we've been battling; she deserves a good smack. Why d'you go spoil my fun?'

Eliza looks as if she *has* been punched. Her eyes dart from one to the other, as if watching a tennis match. Now it is her turn to make sense of it. How the hell does he know Jack's name? She focuses on Jack. Belatedly, she is fitting the random jigsaw pieces together – and the picture that's emerging horrifies her. Jack picks himself up from the damp, claggy ground, dusts himself down. He cannot look at her. Lena frowns, her face resembling a clockwork mechanism, working it through, realisation dawning that this surreal turn of events may be of some advantage to her.

'Jack? What on earth? What's the meaning of this? How does he know your name? He's a medic; you study classics. How d'you even know him?' She hisses out the 'him' and points down at Oscar, as if he's a rotting corpse she needs removing.

Jack stands speechless. Oscar absorbs her words, his eyes pinging between the two of them towering above him. Eventually he cracks a wry smile. It widens as he too realises the significance of this encounter. He cackles: it's a malevolent, triumphant sound.

'Ah ha! I get it. My, oh my! Jack, you absolute cad. What *have* you been up to? Sleeping with the enemy, by damn. I didn't think you had it in you, ol' chum. Thought you were batting for the other side if I'm honest.' Oscar shifts up onto one elbow and, turning his attention to Eliza, leers at her.

'Oh, you poor deluded tart. Is that what he's told you? Classics?

Him? And you believed it? My, what a gullible little trollop you are? Drop your drawers at the sniff of a romantic poem, no doubt. Gosh, if only I'd known it would be that easy, I'd have had a bash myself.'

'Shut your mouth, Oscar. I'm warning you – one more word and I'll, I'll...' Jack howls.

Oscar, beckoning James and Hugh for help, heaves himself to a standing position and lurches right into Jack's face. 'Or you'll *what* exactly, Jack ol' chum? Punch *me*? Rugby tackle me again? Refuse to do my anatomy essays?' He exudes mock horror. Oscar's full of it, realising he is in control, holding all the aces. He sneers, 'Now you're a self-styled *classics* student I guess doing my coursework is no longer an option?'

He circles Jack, eyeing him with menace, displaying dominance over him, not only from his class perspective, but now a moral one too, and he's loving it. He ponders. 'For all your fancy high morals you're just a fraud, Jack. But, curiously, I'm not sure which side you've deceived more – ours, or hers. Hmm?' His fingers strum his lips. Oscar is triumphant, chest flared, looking around the assembled group, mock-quizzically.

Jack hasn't the words to put any of this right. He stares at the ground, frozen in despair.

Eliza appears catatonic. She stares at Jack but is not seeing him. Her eyes remain unfocused as she thinks things through.

Oscar's face is clouded, as if grasping for a memory. Then a long-awaited penny drops. 'Wait a minute. Just wait one God damn minute. Bayling! *He knew*, didn't he?' He's figuring it out as he speaks, his usual dim wit working overtime. 'Knew all about your sordid liaisons with madam here? That explains it. By God, that explains it all.'

Jack looks stricken. He is astounded by Oscar's atypical insightfulness. He risks a glance at Eliza. Her expression says it all. 'Just shut the fuck up, Oscar. You know nothing.'

Oscar scoffs in his face. 'On the contrary, Jack. Ha! I couldn't work out why he's been paying you so much attention. Asking you to stay behind for '*a word*'. Whereas he'd hardly even noticed you before.' He turns to Eliza, throws her an obsequious smile. 'Well, well, my dear. Looks like you've been stitched up like the proverbial kipper by our *mutual* friend Jack here.'

Jack clenches a fist, takes a step closer. 'I'm warning you Oscar, shut up *now*.' But the warning's hollow, they both know it. Jack's shame is complete. He can't face Eliza as it is and adding common assault to his list of sins won't help. Oscar stands, flanked by James and Hugh, unfazed by Jack's impotent fury, basking in victory. He can't quite believe how his luck is turning out today.

Lena hovers at the back of this scene. Although stunned, she fights to suppress an emerging self-satisfied smirk. She adjusts it into an indignant scowl as Eliza turns to her, revealing an expression that is a study in abject betrayal. Eliza steps toward Jack. In her misery, no one else exists, even as her anguish overwhelms her. She's determined to force her words out – her last to Jack – before devastation renders her mute. Her voice a hoarse whisper, she looks directly into his eyes.

'Oh, Jack, I believed in you. In us. I truly did. What a utter fool I've been.' A solitary tear rolls down her stricken face. She is such a picture of despair even Oscar experiences a twinge of guilt.

Silence descends. Eliza turns her back, walks away from the men, from the brutality raging around them, her head held high. They watch her leave. Apart for her retreating frame, the scene could be one captured on a canvas, such is the sense of stillness.

Lena follows her, a cauldron of competing emotions: sadness, yes, compassion, of course, and anger that her dearest friend has been so cruelly betrayed. But she is thrilled she has her Eliza back, all to herself. Jack Forsyth is out of their lives for good, and the thought makes her deliriously happy. She stops and glances back. Jack raises his head and meets her stare, his expression devoid of emotion. She allows herself a triumphant, smug smile. Jack nods in acceptance of his defeat.

She turns and hurries to catch Eliza, sliding a supportive arm around her waist. Eliza leans in and allows herself to be led away.

TWENTY-FIVE
The Mirror

Lena has never seen Eliza so low. Her current melancholia doesn't even compare to those dark, dark days after the verdict went against them, when she fretted herself into a nervous mania over her position at the library, convinced she would lose her job over it. Lena tries everything in her gift to cheer her up. Excursions to the theatre, trips to her favourite shops – Fenwick's and Liberty of London, evenings out at fancy restaurants, but nothing seems to lift her spirits. Eliza accompanies Lena dutifully enough, not refusing an invitation, but her heart is never truly in it. She laughs at the right points in a comedy, tries on exquisitely cut raw silk dresses, allows Lena to pin extravagant corsages to her lapel, makes polite conversation over coffee and petit fours, but her spark is missing. She is a husk, her life force spent. Lena fears that the old Eliza, that beautiful young woman, so full of life and fun, has gone forever.

Lena loses count of the nights she has stood outside Eliza's bedroom, silently listening to the muffled sobs leaking out from the pillows. She loses count of the number of times she has raised her knuckles to that closed door, poised to tap, but lowered them again, unable to summon the words needed to soothe away Eliza's pain. Lena feels impotent, and that troubles her, troubles her deeply. There's nothing she can think of to do that will make this better, make her dearest friend happy again. This isn't like back then. That fateful evening when she resolved to rescue her delightful new acquaintance from that hovel of a boarding house. She'd felt so powerful then. Eliza's *knight* in shining crinoline, as it were, given

227

there's no female equivalent. Lena indulges in a mirthless grin at the recollection, which sours as she remembers what else emerged out of that first evening in Eliza's cramped attic room.

Lena, with nowhere else to sit, perched on the edge of the bed, absentmindedly brushing it down, just catching herself in time lest Eliza saw and thought her ill-mannered. Eliza yanked open her wardrobe and pushed aside various items, searching for something suitable. She appeared anxious, ill at ease suddenly. Lena couldn't help but notice the threadbare state of her clothes as they were, one-by-one, discarded on the bed. Eventually, Eliza settled on a rather unfashionable, dowdy, high-collared white lace blouse paired with a taupe calico skirt worn over a cotton petticoat. The room was cramped, but, bizarrely, contained a modesty screen that she slipped behind to change. As Lena sat, her line of sight was drawn to the wardrobe door mirror, the angle of which happened to reflect a perfectly framed view of Eliza disrobing. She quickly averted her eyes, feeling herself flush at the thought of inadvertently spying on Eliza in her state of undress. It felt wrong, sordid somehow.

She forced herself to scan the room instead, taking in the full extent of its shabbiness. But something, she knew not what then, kept drawing her eye back to that damned mirror.

Eliza was now stripped to her undergarments. The top hooks of her corset were undone, but her modest bosom was still thrust together in that unnatural manner that corsetry dictates, giving a tantalising glimpse of a most perfect cleavage. As she bent over, her breasts broke free of their boned moorings, spilling over the top. The unexpected view of her nipples, erect and proud, gave Lena cause to gasp. She disguised it with a cough. Eliza called out. She panicked and blamed it on dust, moments later realising the offence Eliza may have taken with that careless comment. She wrenched her gaze away. Her face felt poker hot, flushed crimson. She breathed slowly to calm her racing heartbeat. But ... she couldn't stop herself, she simply had to look, her eyes dragged back to the mirror. Eliza was hastily re-hooking the corset. Her knickers, forgotten in the moment, lay discarded at her feet in silken folds. Lena's eyes slid up her bare legs. She was naked from her hips down. Her skin radiated a light olive hue, her legs toned, Lena guessed from the demands of the miles of book stacks. Her most private parts were hidden within a thick forest of chocolate brown curls. Lena felt a sudden, deep anchored ache to bury her face in that mound. Her hands flew to her lap to quell the sensation. Disgusted with herself, she scrunched her eyes tightly and didn't dare open them again until she heard Eliza's sweet, dulcet voice announcing it was time to go.

Lena couldn't wait to get out of that awful house. As she followed Eliza, she caught sight of herself in that damned wardrobe mirror, her face flushed scarlet with a sheen of sweat across her brow. Mortification gripped her as she swiped the perspiration with her sleeve. God, she needed a cigarette!

Their walk to the restaurant, in the blissfully cooling evening air, allowed Lena time to regain composure. Although, in her paranoid state, she convinced herself Eliza was eyeing her strangely. She was desperate to put the incident out of her mind and instead concentrated on her nascent plan to help Eliza escape that hellhole.

They ended up in a rather pretentious French-styled restaurant; it seemed somewhat out of place, located in the down-at-heel Broadway area. An obnoxious maître d' put up a brief resistance at their request to dine: 'At this late *heure*? *Sans un chaperone*?' He clearly thought it '*tout à fait scandaleux*'. Lena put him in his place with her rusty schoolgirl French and it seemed to do the trick as he led them to a discrete corner – out of sight of prying eyes, which suited her just fine.

Eliza's lack of sophistication became increasingly apparent as the evening wore on. Lena adored her reaction to the vichyssoise. 'They heat up leek and potato soup where I come from, Lena,' she whispered indignantly.

Lena ordered a carafe of claret for them both but found herself quaffing most of it as her companion seemed unused to wine. Eliza became as giggly as a schoolgirl after a few timid sips. Although Lena often boasted she could handle her alcohol as well as any gentleman around town, she drank at pace, which she put down to nerves, and found she too was a little squiffy by the time pudding was served. This had the effect of loosening her tongue. Eliza's unacceptable living conditions had been playing on her mind, and it was inevitable at some stage her concerns would surface. And God help her, so they did.

'It's just ... it's your lodgings, Eliza. They're not befitting a woman of your standing for Chrissakes.' The words had been festering her inside all evening and she'd stoppered them until that moment when the whole thing went 'pop'. She could see Eliza swallow hard, and indignant tears formed at the base of her eyelids.

'Well,' Eliza retorted aggressively, the wine now speaking for her. 'It may be small, shabby even, but I keep it clean, and neat, and anyway I'm very happy there, thank *you* very much.' She turned her head so Lena couldn't see the solitary tear snaking its way down her cheek, her face burning with indignation.

'Oh, my dear, no, no. I'm so sorry, I never meant it as a criticism of you. Not at all! Please, please forgive me. I'm so stupid, always saying the wrong thing, upsetting people. Papa's forever chastising me for my crassness.' Lena's face crumpled in the flickering light like a distraught child's.

Lena sounded so penitent, so apologetic, that Eliza's indignation quickly dissipated. 'Oh, don't mind me, I'm just a little sensitive about this kind of thing. I'm not from a well-off family, like you, but I'm sure you've figured that out.' She shrugged. 'I've had to make my own way, and the lodging house is all I can afford. But it won't be forever. I've ambitions. Aspirations to better myself.' She cocked her nose proudly.

'But ... but it doesn't have to be!' Lena exclaimed, a little too exuberantly for the maître d', whose well-travelled eyebrow rose in reproach. Eliza looked at her blankly.

'You can come live with me, in my flat.' Lena smiled triumphantly.

'I've a spare bedroom and the truth is I've been so lonely in that big old flat I've been thinking of finding a companion for a while. And, the best thing is, Battersea Library is just down the road.' She stopped, out of breath, her face flushed, eyes shining, urging Eliza to see how perfect this idea was.

Eliza felt confused, conflicted. Although Lena's suggestion sounded an ideal fit and, even if she'd not dare admit it, she was desperate to vacate that cramped, airless, prison cell. But it was an impossible dream. A share of a flat in Battersea, with a sitting room, a kitchen and even – Lena proudly informed her – her own private lavatory and bathroom, was so beyond an assistant librarian's means as to be laughable. But how to tell her? How to let her down gently, with her staring, all fuzzy with hope and optimism, urging Eliza to say yes. However much the idea appealed, and appeal it did, it could never be.

'Lena, that's such a kind thought. A wonderfully generous offer, and nothing would make me happier. But I'm afraid it's just not possible.'

Lena's hope-filled smile evaporated. 'But why ever not? It makes total sense, can't you see? I'll gain a charming companion to share my home with, and you can leave all that squalor behind.' Her hand slapped her mouth. 'Oh, I'm sorry, I didn't mean that as it came out. I want to help you better yourself, and I can do so, so easily. Just come, come live with me.'

'Oh, Lena, I'd love to, but ... I simply cannot afford it, I'm afraid.' There, the truth was out. Alcohol had loosened her tongue and rendered her unusually forthright.

With that, Lena burst out laughing. Eliza felt it like a slap. How rude. For all her fine breeding and expensive education, she could be rather coarse.

'Eliza. Oh Eliza, my dear girl. You still misunderstand me. I'm sorry, I should have been clearer. Of course you can afford it!' Eliza raised a quizzical eyebrow that could rival that of the maître d'. 'You can afford it as it won't cost you a pound, or the shilling that thief

Carruthers takes for a space not big enough for a cat. It wouldn't cost you a penny. It's all paid for. My Papa, God bless him, covers my rental for the whole flat. So, you can come stay with me and be better off to boot!' She paused. 'You must say yes. Please say you will? We will have such adventures together!'

And that was pretty much that. Eliza left Mrs Carruthers' humble establishment a week later. Much to her landlady's inconvenience – a fact she reminded Eliza of each time she had the misfortune to pass her on the stairs. Eliza was so relieved to be leaving that room, and Mrs C's incessant grumbling, behind. She packed her belongings in less time than it took to boil the kettle. They were deposited into Lena's spacious, fashionably furnished, but shambolically untidy, flat just over an hour later.

Eliza's, and Lena's, new life began that very day. Neither of them could have imagined their friendship would lead one of them to the loss of everything she had come to hold dear.

TWENTY-SIX

Battersea Council

BATTERSEA TOWN HALL, COUNCIL CHAMBER, JUNE 1905

The escalating violence witnessed across London over the months that follow horrifies Lena and Eliza. But the level of vitriol, on both sides of the argument, could not have been foreseen by anyone. The statue's prominence in the debate means it has become *the* emblem against the careless barbarity rampant in the furtive world of medical research. Since the women's infiltration of Bayling's lecture over a year earlier, further evidence of similar practices has been uncovered across the university landscape. Unintentionally, Latchmere Park becomes the place of pilgrimage for those opposed to cruelty in all its guises.

The pent-up anger unleashed in the park that fateful day is just a taster of the explosion of violent protests, running battles, and the continued infiltration and sabotage of vivisection demonstrations and anti-vivisection meetings alike.

The suffragists take the *'Anti-Viv'* cause to their hearts. When they consider how *some* men treat other species – as possessions to be treated with contempt, with no rights to speak of, to be physically abused and discarded as and when the whim takes them – the parallels with women's own situation are obvious.

Trade unionists, often considered opposed to the suffrage movement due to concerns that women, so empowered, would take men's jobs, also offer their support for much the same reasoning. But the mirror *they* hold up is to the cruelty and casual brutality ingrained in the relationship between business owners and their put-upon workers. Working men – and women, they grudgingly admit – are often treated just like dogs, like horses: worked, and flogged, until they drop. Once their usefulness is spent, they are abandoned to their wretched fates. Left to rot, disregarded, forgotten.

It surprises no one that the medical establishment, and the colleges renowned for medical research: University College, King's, Guy's, the Middlesex Hospital and – it must be noted – some veterinarians, are equally vehement in their opposing view, upholding and defending the position that it is vital that animals continue to be used in this way. They argue human medicine cannot, will not, develop if experiments of this nature are banned, just because of a few over-sentimental fools. They decry them as lunatics, even suggesting some be incarcerated in Bedlam, where they can do no further harm to the progression of science.

The clashes become more frequent, ever more vicious. One memorable incident saw over a thousand marching on central London, commandeering the Oxford and Cambridge Boat Race in a vain attempt to expand their numbers with the out-of-town student visitors. They came armed with their effigies of terrier dogs, and banners denouncing the stupidity of the anti-vivisectionists, the suffragists, the working man. They threatened to dump the monument in the Thames – wishful thinking given its size and weight.

The unrest is not restricted to London, either. Sympathisers on both sides begin marching, clashing, across the country, such is the influence of the national press. Moderate folk shake their heads, mystified at how the death, however cruel, of one nameless stray dog can cause so much strife.

At first, the political elite – at local and national level – are indifferent, dismissing it as mere 'stuff and nonsense'. To them, it is an isolated storm in the proverbial teacup that will blow itself out within weeks. But, as the weeks roll by, the violence does not fizzle out, it grows more disruptive. Their indifference turns into bemusement. As the months pass and the unrest grows ever more fervent, that bemusement morphs into a distinct sense of nervousness. Discussions are held at the highest level. Over time, politicians become ever more exasperated. They reflect the moderates' view: that all this trouble over a single, worthless stray mongrel, is intolerable.

After several violent clashes in the vicinity of Parliament Square, a question is raised on the floor of the House. Primarily concerned with the cost of policing the memorial, Parliament also debates the statue's continued presence in a public park. What is to be done to lance this pulsating boil? A satisfactory answer is not forthcoming from Sir Henry Campbell-Bannerman, who, for a prime minister known for his radical, forward-thinking views, disappoints many by deftly kicking the question into the long grass by declaring it a local government matter. Thus, he places the burden of the statue's fate squarely in the hands of Battersea Council, a decision that is to have far-reaching consequences for all involved.

Battersea Town Hall's Council Chamber is heaving; there's not an empty seat in the house. Locals have turned out in force to satisfy their curiosity as to how the new council leaders will conduct themselves. The new-elected Conservative-led council is in session, and the contentious matter of the dog memorial is top of the agenda.

Liberal councillor John Archer Esq. is addressing the room. He considers himself a *progressive* and, to underscore the point, radiates a louche air of indifference to the etiquette and dress code of the day. He's attired in a casual lounge suit as opposed to the formal morning suits of his Conservative adversaries. It's a decision that raises disapproving eyebrows among the elite of the chamber. He is luxuriously moustachioed but forgoes the full beard – popularised by King Edward – that's expected from gentlemen of standing. His twinkly, deep brown eyes belie his otherwise serious expression.

When he holds forth in his mesmerising, treacle-thick baritone, everyone stops to listen, regardless of their political leanings.

He's also a rare commodity within the council's exalted ranks. As rare, or maybe more so, as a sighting of a female councillor which, whilst a possibility, is rarely experienced. For Councillor Archer is a black man, the product of a Barbadian born father and an Irish mother. Born and raised in Liverpool, he travelled the world as a seaman before settling in London, finding more acceptance in the metropolis than up north. He studied medicine before turning his talents to photography. In his late thirties, he developed an overwhelming passion for local politics and was elected council representative for Latchmere ward. Hence, he considers the dog statue as one of his constituents – albeit a most unusual one – to be defended as he would any of his charges. And it's on this very issue he addresses the chamber.

'Sirs, I ask of you. If tables were turned, and anti-vivisection mobs were targeting a hospital, would His Majesty's Government require the hospital to foot the bill for extra policing?' He pauses, but not long enough for anyone to interject.

'In fact, does anyone object to the cost of police protection for Cromwell's statue up at the Palace of Westminster? No, gentlemen, they do not!

'Gentlemen, I put it to you they would not suggest, nay, not even dream of it. So why, oh why, is the Prime Minister, of all people, requiring our council to pay the full costs of protecting the statue?' An equal mix of 'hear, hears!' and booing persist.

'Please, gentlemen. Don't be so naïve as to think we are just protecting a base stone and metal memorial to a nameless dog. No sirs, it represents so much more. This humble statue, paid for by the good folk of this parish let us not forget, has become an icon – the unlikely mascot of our borough's proud, progressive values. Yes, indeed. A tribute to our noble, liberal borough's fight against injustice, wherever and onto whomsoever that injustice is served.' The noise drowns Archer out.

The chair intervenes. 'Gentlemen, ladies, please, may we have some order? Please?' In time, the chamber quietens.

'May I reacquaint my esteemed colleagues with the fact Battersea contributes a staggering twenty-two thousand pounds a year to London's policing budget. So, I put it to you that this government's demand for an extra seven hundred pounds is duplicitous in the extreme. This punitive sanction is not just a request for an outrageous sum of money, it is a Trojan horse, used to force our hand, strong-arm us into agreeing to remove our statue, to placate their old school chums at the medical schools. We must not, we will not, be blackmailed.'

The room erupts again with the usual banter and catcalling, mixed with snippets of low-level racist taunts. It takes several minutes to regain order. When silence resumes, Mr David Ingrams, early sixties, balding, barrel-chested, with an air of unearned superiority, and the new Conservative leader of the council, rises. He executes a short, curt bow to his colleagues before turning, with a victorious sneer, towards his nemesis – Archer.

Since its formation in the late 1890s, when it wrestled independence back from its neighbour Wandsworth, the parish of Battersea had been ruled by Liberals, and had become notorious as a hotbed of progressives and radicals. So, imagine the shockwave that reverberated throughout the district when, less than a decade later, the council changed its colours in a local election. This was to the dismay of the resident working classes, who were rightly proud of their council's fire-brand reputation. The surprised, but jubilant, Tories now held the majority. This unpredicted result was attributed to the area's recent gentrification. From a destitute slum area to be avoided, in the new century Battersea had been transformed into a respectable district, increasingly popular with the emergent middle-class. The swelling ranks of this upwardly mobile sector, who once wouldn't have dreamt of voting Conservative, were now eager to ape those on higher rungs of the social ladder. An important differentiator was voting preference, hence the surge in the Tory vote.

David Ingrams pointedly clears his throat. 'I thank my esteemed colleague for so eloquently reacquainting us with the fundamentals of our council's contributions to the city's policing bill. Similarly, I applaud our coloured friend's valiant attempt to keep us in the *black*.' He grins to himself and the chamber. 'However, I must object to his histrionic sentiments regarding that infernal statue. A statue forced upon us, I stress, by the more radical factions of the thankfully *former* Liberal councillors of this parish.' Archer fumes, but has no response.

'Do I need to remind you, sir, that we are in charge now? And I'm minded to test the depth of the so-called *devotion* to this emblem of which you speak.' He pauses, the tension in the room mounts. 'I wish to table a vote on whether this council decrees the statue shall remain in place or be removed from the borough forthwith and disposed of accordingly.'

The chamber descends into uproar. Archer glares at Ingrams but realises he's powerless. There's nothing to stop this outrageous move, and his sense of impotency overwhelms him. He gathers his papers and storms out in protest, followed by loyal colleagues. Ingrams allows himself a smug, self-satisfied grin and signals to the chairman to bring the meeting to a close – job done.

Later that month, an army of people descend on Battersea Town Hall. A lively, noisy queue snakes down Lavender Hill all the way to the Junction. Posters are plastered across the frontage, declaring a public meeting to debate the council's forthcoming motion on the statue. The doormen, two spotty adolescents, looking as if they'd blow over in a breeze, are struggling to keep count of the folk charging the entrance and clattering down the mosaic path toward the Grand Hall.

Soon, word reaches the doormen that the hall is at capacity, full to bursting; they must stop people entering. The youths look doubtful as they peer down the queue. It's endless. Their agitation increases as they impotently try to stop folk crossing the threshold. They're all too aware of the trouble caused by this blasted statue, and they don't want to be in the firing line of the malcontent that's brewing. As word spreads, the crowd becomes restless. They jostle one another, tetchiness becoming infectious, declaring they'll storm the building if they're not allowed to say their piece.

Eventually, the general manager shows his face. Gerard Turner is a shy, retiring man in his mid-fifties, much more at home with double-entry bookkeeping than dealing with a boisterous crowd. With reluctance, he shuffles outside to witness for himself the escalating crisis.

Chanting and howls of disapproval hit him like a sound wall before he glimpses the mob amassing on the wide pavement outside. It's obvious he has to do something and quickly, to avoid a riot. He calls for a loudhailer. Without thinking too deeply, he addresses the crowd. The sight of him causes a ripple of interest, there's call for quiet so they can hear what he's got to say for himself. He begins, his tone tremulous. The crowd smell blood.

'Ladies, gentlemen, please accept my sincere apologies, but due to overcrowding, I can't allow any more inside the hall tonight.'

The roar of disapproval amplifies. Cries of 'disgrace', 'let us in', 'conspiracy', 'save our statue' echo down the Hill. Scuffles break out. Turner's eyes dart round desperately, his expression that of a rabbit cornered by baying hounds. There'll be a full-on riot, on his watch, if he doesn't think fast. After some tortuous moments, he decides. If this doesn't work, he'll be forced to bolt the doors and call for police reinforcements. He takes a deep breath, bellows over the discordant racket.

'Gentlemen, ladies, please, please let me speak. I cannot help the situation if I cannot be heard.' No effect. 'Gentlemen, please, may I have QUIET.'

His tone cuts through, the crowd quietens. But it's a fragile silence. In his fevered imagination, he sees the crowd as a wild beast – liable to pounce at the least provocation. He has to tread carefully, but it's vital to not show fear.

'Good people of Battersea. Friends, neighbours. I'm sure, like me, you don't want to see more violence shattering the peace of our borough. God knows we've had our fair share.' Rumblings of agreement spur him on. 'Again, I can only apologise that you can't attend tonight, but for *your own* safety, we cannot let anyone else into the hall. BUT, and I give you my word as a Christian, if you leave now, with no further trouble, I promise we'll hold another meeting.' He wavers, he's making this up as he goes along. 'I promise you'll get your chance to be heard. So, I request you depart now and return tomorrow, same time, same place, when you *will* gain entry, my friends.'

There's a murmur in the crowd, the beast seems to be calming. But then, dissenting voices, shouts of, ''E's having us on', 'Why should we trust you sir?', 'And what if we don't, Mister?'

He can't lose them now. 'And if you cannot gain entry tomorrow, we'll do the same the night after, and the night after if need be. You WILL get your say, I promise. Thank you and goodnight.' He finishes with a flourish and steps back over the threshold. There hangs a stunned silence. This was more than they could have hoped for, his pronouncement taking the wind out of their disruptive sails. They peer around at each other, raise their eyebrows, shrug. There's nothing more to be said, or done, tonight. Slowly but surely, the good folk of Battersea disperse into the gloomy night.

Turner's face, glistening with perspiration, crumples with relief. There'll be no rioting tonight. Although how he'll make good on his promise, he has not a clue. Details will have to wait. The immediate crisis has been averted, and he will, with luck, still have a job in the morning. With a final, satisfied scan of the scattering crowd, he swiftly darts into the safety of the foyer, and gestures for the doormen to lock the doors.

As the reassuring thud of the iron bolt promises an impenetrable barrier between him and the beast, Turner releases a deep sigh, leans against a pillar and closes his eyes. When he opens them again, a semi-circle of staff surrounds him, staring, curious to learn how on earth he'll deliver the rash promise he's just made.

BATTERSEA TOWN HALL, THE FOLLOWING DAY

The posters advertising yesterday's event are being updated. Across the top, a new strip banner is being placed diagonally, from upper left to lower right, announcing another meeting that night. Again, on the Latchmere dog issue. Again, all welcome. Tommy Riley, summoned by Mr Turner for yet more pasting duties, can't believe his good fortune. Gawd bless that little brown dog and all who sails in 'im. He gets a penny a time, and half extra on accounts of the last minuteness of the job. He salivates, his black-stumped molars aching in anticipation of the taffy to come.

Lena and Eliza, rather dumbfounded by the kerfuffle their hastily called meeting has generated, remain holed up in the flat all day. Lena takes some comfort in the interest her otherwise permanently morose friend is taking in the proceedings. Apart from the journey to and from the town hall, and her strikingly animated performance on the Grand Hall's stage, Eliza pretty much takes to her bed and refuses to be roused. Lena busies herself with organising extra print-runs of the pamphlets they have produced decrying the council's appalling behaviour. The first batch disappeared like hot cakes, the original quantity being totally inadequate given the number of people that attended the first night. She watches the mantlepiece clock tick round until, once again, it gets to five o'clock. She raps on Eliza's door, and for once she gets a reply.

Evening falls. It's been a damp, cloudy day, with rain spitting and threatening heavier cloudbursts that never arrived. The leaden grey sky hasn't lifted since dawn and is giving way to an equally dismal night. The rain is heavier now and, combined with a brisk north wind, ensures any folk foolish enough to be out will get a jolly thorough soaking. The inclement conditions have not put off the snaking queue forming on the Hill, however, which appears just as lengthy as the night before. The strength of feeling is equally strong, folk are determined to get into that hall and a drop of rain will not deter them. They want to hear their local heroes, the defenders of the statue, and to debate what lengths they will go to, to protect it.

Again, the hall is full. Again, Mr Turner, a different man from the day before – cocky, confident, inches taller, relishing this temporary power he holds over the crowd – baldly announces to the sodden, miserable crowd they must return tomorrow. The unlucky, in no state to protest, squelch off home, shoulders hunched against the driving wind and rain, fighting to control umbrellas and hats.

The following afternoon. Little Tommy, grinning from ear to ear and whistling tunelessly through the gap in his front teeth, is burying the original meeting poster beneath yet another strip banner. This time he decides to place it bottom right to top left. The effect of a perfectly symmetrical 'X' marking the spot gives him satisfaction. After all, that statue is turning out to be a treasure trove of coinage for the young lad.

Later that evening, the crowd dutifully shuffles into the brightly lit entrance lobby. The two hapless youths are back on duty, keeping count. Mr Turner struts out to the pavement, surveying the slow-moving crowd, blurred in the evening's misty rain. His face radiates relief when he spies an end to the queue. At two people deep, he calculates he'll fit them in with room to spare. 'Thank you, God,' he whispers. No more blasted dog meetings, after tonight things can get back to normal at last.

The remnants of the crowd enter the lobby, led by the swarm of bees depicted in the mosaic tiles at their feet. They make the journey down the long corridor, the rain soaked into their coats and hats gently steaming, their way lit by a series of flickering gas lamps. They pass through the splendidly lit octagonal ante-hall, with its beautiful domed roof of sunny shades of yellow stained glass, and into the Grand Hall itself. They scramble for the last seats available, odd ones and twos scattered to the front and rear. The doors shut behind them and the noisy hum of the auditorium fades in expectant anticipation. The third, and final, meeting on the scandal of the Latchmere dog statue is about to begin.

On stage, in a scene reminiscent of the first meeting, sit Lena and Coleridge. This time they are joined by Cllr Archer. It's Eliza who's first to the lectern, and she is a starkly different woman to that timid librarian who hesitatingly proposed the memorial well over a year ago. Replacing her is a campaigner, eyes flashing with righteous indignation, her voice half an octave lower, demanding respect. She's already had two nights of practice and tonight she's on fire.

'Unfortunately, ladies and gentlemen, His Majesty's Government, and our newly elected council leaders, have left us with no choice. They're hell-bent on taking our statue. A memorial paid for by *us*, let's not forget, for *our* park. This abuse of power *will not* be tolerated. We cannot allow this to happen on our watch. We must, we shall, take matters into our own hands. Over these three meetings, we've announced the official launch of the Dog Statue Defence Committee. Membership's open to all. We welcome anyone dedicated to protecting our memorial.' The announcement, although by now three days old, is welcomed with hearty applause.

'I need not remind you good folk, but to be clear, our statue is not simply a remembrance of one stray dog, caged and tortured repeatedly at the hands of butchers masquerading as men of medicine. It's symbolic of all who suffer at the hands of the corrupt, self-serving ruling classes, whether they be children, women, working men or any other sentient species. When we fight for our statue, we fight for them all.'

There's noisy agreement, clapping, the cheering is deafening. The audience, high on atmosphere and, most likely, a beer or two, declare their intention to protect the statue at any cost. Anti-government and anti-medical sentiment is rife. Eliza stands proud. She beams at them, sensing an almost maternal pride, her New Model Army.

Buried amongst the boisterous crowd, toward the back of the room, a forlorn figure slouches in his seat, the one audience member not infected by the jubilant mood. Jack Forsyth sits, eyes glued to the stage, where his Eliza commands the room. His gaze is a muddle of immense pride, desperate longing and ultimate defeat. He hardly recognises the Boadicea-like woman he's listened to, spellbound, for the last twenty minutes. She's metamorphosed into a fighter, a radical – fearless and passionate. His love is now deeper than when they were together, if that were possible. Devotion and longing bursts from every pore, but he knows it's hopeless. She'll never forgive him, she's made that abundantly clear, spurned him each time he's attempted to explain his shameful lies and beg forgiveness. He rises, stumbles to the end of the row and shuffles out of the Hall, tears clouding his vision. A desolate, pitiful sight, he is watched impassively by the doormen, the only ones to see him leave.

THE COBBLES, APRIL 1906 – THE RINGLEADER

I step out from the rest of the gang to get a closer look at 'em. They stop dead and pull sharply into a tight ring, reminding me of those wagon circles from the old wild west stories. I can almost taste their fear; it's giving me a right ol' boner, I 'ave to admit. They are all shapes, sizes, and ages. Some pretty young bitches nestled amongst the typical decrepit ol' battle-axes you get on them women's marches.

I decide I'll 'ave a bit of sport with them, hell, why not? Rile 'em up a tad. I makes some comment or another that puts the fear of sweet Jesus Christ into 'em and I click me fingers to the lads. It was as if we'd rehearsed it. They, all casual like, open their coats to display their wares – silverwares that is, before you be getting any smutty ideas! Oh, the look on those ladies' faces. Classic it is. I'm really fucking enjoying myself now; it's even more fun than punching the lights out of them liberal dandy types. I makes some comment about their ugly ol' boats getting slashed in the fighting going on, and they turn a shade of pale never before seen on a living thing. I take another step closer, scanning 'em. They trip over themselves, some almost losing balance in their rush to get away. I shout after their retreating backs.

'Though, for you old hags it could be an improvement, ain't that the case, fellas?'

The women, all 'cept for the two young lasses up front, are now some distance back. As I stare, I realise I've seen 'er face before. It takes a moment, but then it dawns. Her picture's been in the Daily News. She stares back at me, the lack of fear in her eyes pissing me right off. I get closer, closer still.

Now, I'm first to admit what I do next, I'm not proud of. And in normal times I'd never be so disrespectful to a lady, however misguided they may be. It's just the heat of the moment. But fuck me, she doesn't flinch! All respect to her. She doesn't move a muscle. I hear the lads behind me, when I do it, there's an intake of breath. As I say, I'm not proud of it. But then, when my mind is elsewhere, she speaks.

Now, in normal times this won't 'ave happened, not to me, Sidney

Arthur Thomas. No sir! Let's be crystal clear on that score. But I'm distracted, and the suddenness of it catches me by surprise. It was a loose cobble, I'm clear on that, but that's the very last thing I am clear on.

TWENTY-SEVEN

The Memorial Defence Committee

Latchmere Park has never been so busy, the statue never so well-tended to, than over the following months. Joining the Dog Patrol, and adhering to the timetable supervised by their womenfolk, is a contingent of local men – all members of the freshly minted Memorial Defence Committee which, after the town hall meetings, boasts a membership of hundreds. As a rite of passage, members pledge to join the rota of volunteers assisting the constables.

The arrangement works well – for a time. Dedication to protecting the memorial remains steadfast throughout the warm days of summer and into a mild autumn. A camaraderie develops between members and the coppers routinely assigned to the park. It becomes quite the social affair, the two groups of men often joined by women bringing tea, beers and morsels of food to see them through. The jolly atmosphere helps while away the tedious hours. Trouble from students becomes less frequent, but bubbles up every now and again – and too regularly to disband either the police presence or the unofficial guard.

As the season progresses, and the weather becomes more inclement, the need for a constant presence recedes somewhat in people's minds. The official, 'unofficial guard' dwindles. Locals avoid each other's accusatory glances when they miss yet another timetabled stint. Excuses litter the air as people find more pressing chores to attend to in their spare time. The thought of spending several hours out in cold, wet weather becomes less and less appealing.

Autumnal days merge into early winter. The nights turn from being a tad chilly into finger-numbing freezing, the odd bright winter's day spliced with many more rainy days, cloudy with freezing, soot-infused fog. Over the month, the number of locals peters out until there are frequent scenes of stoic, fed-up bobbies supplemented with just one man and his dog, if that.

Battersea Council is in session once again. On this occasion, it's a closed meeting. The chamber is much emptier than for the first memorial debate many months ago. The Clerk of the Council is announcing the result of the vote. He calls for order.

'On the matter of the dog memorial statue remaining in Latchmere Recreational Ground, on Battersea Council land. The Council undertook a vote by ballot. The result of said vote is as follows. The ayes have fifteen votes, noes seventeen. Gentlemen, I can declare that the noes have it. Therefore, it's decided the structure be dismantled and removed from this borough and thence be disposed of appropriately.' The chamber erupts. The clerk again struggles to restore order. He is losing patience.

'Gentlemen, please, may I have some quiet?' He waits, fuming quietly. 'I have an extraordinary statement that I'm required to read on behalf of the leader of the council.' A murmur ripples through the chamber. 'Given the level of controversy that has manifested on both sides of this dispute and given it's not merely the removal of a statue at stake here...' He clears his throat; it is as dry as sandpaper. He fumbles for a beaker of water. 'Taking into account it has come to symbolise a more conflicted debate on the morality of vivisection, and that passions have been running extremely high, the decision of this chamber will remain confidential until such a time that the monument has been removed and taken to a secure, undisclosed location, whence it will be disposed of. This decision has been made out of a genuine concern regarding the safety of the council workers – as well as the constabulary guarding the statue. The timing of its removal will not be revealed beforehand for similar reasons. No member will tell of what's taken place tonight. If they speak of it, they risk being held in contempt and excluded from this council forthwith – permanently.'

John Archer's face falls. He holds his head in his hands. There is nothing to be done – they've been officially gagged. He despairs at this subversion of the council's duties to its citizens. He's stunned at his feelings of wretchedness, a ridiculous emotion to feel about what was, essentially, a lifeless hunk of stone and metal.

Another unseasonably cold early winter's night, following which the day fails to emerge from its slumber. A leaden, ominous sky rules from dawn to dusk, with blustery winds completing the grim picture. When darkness falls, it is pelting it down. 'Raining cat and dogs' is a most appropriate term for the scene in the park. The wind is no longer blustery, it's now gale force, driving the rainfall sideways, soaking the unfortunate police guard who have drawn the short straw.

There's not a local in sight. The Committee's determination to protect the statue has deserted them. The only souls left are Sergeant Albert McDonald and Constable Stanley Robb. Bert, his conscience nagging him at how drenched and feeble they looked, had sent the rest of his rather elderly contingent home. They wouldn't be much use in a fight anyway. No conversation passes between the two hunched men, rather their faces are mirror images of grumpiness. They have exhausted all topics long ago, and anyway, Stanley is sore that Bert made him stay, when it's obvious there's no chance of trouble tonight. You'd have to be stark-staring-mad to be out in this if you didn't have to be. They hunker down beneath the shelter of the grand old oak, now devoid of its leaves, but the tangle of thick trunk and branches keep the worst of the rain off.

Suddenly they're roused, ears pricked to a distant sound of marching feet. They tense, alert to confrontation – well-attuned to it by now. As the marching gets louder, Bert rues sending his constables home. He'll get it in the neck tomorrow if there *is* trouble. Both reach for their truncheons, squinting into the rain, struggling to make out what the hell's coming their way. Their eyes widen as they realise what it is.

Into the clearing flow a river of policemen. Around one hundred surround the statue and block all entrances to the park. Men line the path leading to the plinth. A group of council workmen march through this regimental line-up, two by two, a perversity of a wedding procession. They're carrying ropes, shovels, pickaxes, jemmies. They stop when they reach the cross-path, surveying the infamous statue. The commissioner himself steps out of the shadows. With a nervous glance over to the cottages, he addresses his team with a hushed tone only just audible above the storm.

'Right, lads. Get to it. And remember, as quiet as you can. We don't want to be waking the natives, do we?'

On his command, the group gets to work, as quietly as is humanly possible when dismantling a solid granite plinth. The inscription is unscrewed and levered off. Others struggle to take the dog down. The moon is just a sliver of silvery light slashing the inky blackness. Any noise is drowned out by the howling wind, sounding uncannily like a pack of wild dogs, whining mournfully into the night.

TWENTY-EIGHT

Loss

ELMFIELD MANSIONS, THE NEXT MORNING

The sitting room is bathed in the gentle tranquillity of darkness. It appears reasonably tidy, except for the lopsided suffrage poster adorning a door and a scattering of pamphlets across the dining table. Mrs P snores gently, silken paws dangling over the back of the settee, all four a-twitching amid some tremulous mouse-hunting dream. Both women's bedroom doors are shut tight. Last night's rambunctious storm eventually fought itself into an exhausted truce. What follows is a calm, cloudless, breaking dawn sky.

The early morning peace is destroyed by a hammering at the front door of the mansion block. It's followed by an insistent rapping on the bay window. This has the result of ripping Mrs P from her dream of mouse annihilation. She's instantly on all fours, back arched, tail ballooned to the size of a fox's brush, hissing, eyes popping, pupils so dilated she resembles a medieval painting of a demonic witch's familiar.

Outside, causing the commotion, is a local lad, no more than about twelve. Not suitably dressed for the chilly weather in just a shirt, open-necked with a kerchief loosely tied, braces desperately grasping at his brother's hand-me-down checked trousers and no coat or cap. He's leaning over the iron railings to reach the flat's window and now adds bellowing to the list of heinous crimes Mrs P is marking his card for. He's doing a sterling job of waking the entire block.

'Miss Eliza, Miss Lena, wake up please, wake up. You must come quick. It's our statue. Please, Misses, wake up. You have to get up!'

He runs out of breath, almost losing his precarious grip on the railings, which would've seen him plummet to the basement several feet below. He scrambles back to the safety of the top doorstep and continues shouting and hammering the front door.

Eliza's eyes open, still full of sleep. She's confused, a little woozy and a lot grumpy. The external kerfuffle infiltrated, and had been absorbed into, her waking dream; she takes a while to realise what she's hearing is not part of her fading dreamscape. She comes around to semi-consciousness, glancing over at her bedside clock. It shows seven-fifteen. Growling and grumbling, reminiscent of Mrs P, she's furious at this early disturbance on her day off.

She feels for her gown – a glamourous, if not practical, silky cream and sky-blue diaphanous creation, another of Lena's cast-offs – and slips it over her nightdress. She pads into the sitting room, rubbing her eyes and frowning. Lena, a picture-perfect study of a groggy somnambulist, has somehow beaten her to the door. Clothed in her winter nightdress and bare feet, Lena ignores decorum as she opens the front door to a small scruffy lad. She takes a moment to recognise him and retrieve his name from her sleep-fogged memory.

'Tom? Thomas Riley, it is you, isn't it?' She receives an affirmatory nod from the suddenly tongue-tied young lad. 'What the devil is it, Tommy? Why are you bothering us so early on a Saturday for Chrissakes? You'll catch your death out here without a coat.' She's gathering her senses as she speaks, realising there's only one plausible reason. Her eyes snap open. 'Oh God, it's the statue? Something's happened, hasn't it?' He nods again, looking despondent. She swivels back to the interior of the hallway, yelling. 'Eliza, come quick, it's our statue, something happened.'

Eliza's right behind her, and frowns at the full force of the shout. They stare at each other, words unnecessary. They hurry back in, Lena ushering Tommy into the sitting room, sitting him down at the dining table. They face the lad, and regard him with such stern expressions he recoils into himself. Eliza, realising they're frightening the child, softens her expression.

'It's ok, Tommy, please don't be shy. We don't mean to scare you, we're just a little anxious. Now take a deep breath, start at the beginning, and tell us everything.'

The women, with Tommy running ahead, approach a tight circle of residents, chattering and gesturing in disbelief. They push through and stop dead in their tracks. In front of them lies an open gaping wound, a torn-up mess of earth, mud and rock. They've left not a piece behind. The women stare dead-eyed, deaf to the outraged babbling and swearing swirling around them.

A man – a stout, hardened labourer in his fifties – stands scratching his head. 'Well, it's a bloody mystery and no mistake. I swear it was there when I took myself off to bed. I remember looking out window, oh 'bout elevenish, thinking those poor bobbies weren't 'aving the best time in that storm. "Rather 'em than me," I thought. Glad I wasn't on the rota last night. Then went to bed and woke up – to this!'

A local woman joins him, eager to add her tuppence-worth. 'That might well be so, Arfur, but when I got up to start my laund'ring it was gone, vanished, and that was before five. Swear I didn't 'ear a thing, me a light sleeper an' all. What a bleedin' shame, I'd grown right fond of our bronzed mutt. He was no trouble. He didn't need feeding, no dog mess, but he looked out for us in his own sweet way. It was those bloody men that were the trouble. The rotters. And to think they're the educated lot, looking down their noses at us for being the ill-bred heathens.'

Another, her husband, joins in. 'It's a bleedin' liberty, that's what it is, plain and simple. Those Tory bounders on the council waited 'til the weather was so bad they could do off with it without our 'earing anything. Bloody toffs, they didn't like we 'ad something of our own, something we was proud of. He was doing no harm, just sitting there, watching the world go by.' He pauses, eyes narrowing. 'Anyway, who was s'posed to be on watch last night – eh?' His eyes scan accusingly; everyone shrugs, pictures of innocence; they've no idea. 'Well, whoever it was should hang their heads in shame. If they hadn't been so lily-livered as to not want to get their blooming 'air wet, then we might've been able to stop this.' He storms off in an indignant huff, conveniently forgetting he hadn't turned up for a shift earlier in the week when weather was threatening. His wife follows, eager to point this out to him. The first man, Arthur, speaks again, louder this time, determined to attract the crowd's attention.

'We defended it against all those student thugs for months on end. We'll not stand for this. We'll get it back if it's the last thing we do. Who's with me?'

A shout goes up, and the rallying cry grows. The women are still standing, pinned to the spot, blankly staring into the already freezing void, the fight drained from them. Lena reaches for Eliza's hand, sliding it into her own, drawing her back. She gestures toward the gate. Eliza nods, and they walk away, hand in hand, heads bowed in despair.

The friends are seated facing each other at the dining table, in the same position as when they arrived home hours earlier. Righteous anger has been stoked from the pit of despair, replacing the despondency. Lena scrapes her chair back and stands. She paces the length of their well-worn, sun-faded Persian rug – a Hageby family cast-off. She's almost growling, raging at the unfairness of the world, the duplicitousness of the council, the traitorous police – more so given she had come to regard the Dog Patrol as sympathetic to their cause. Topping it off, she blasts the medical establishment, and, finally, herself for not being there when it mattered.

Eliza continues to sit. Her face presents a perfect example of someone deep in thought, oblivious to the whirlwind of exasperation and bluster. Her body is in the room, but her mind occupies a different realm. She's reflective, working something out. But it's only a matter of time before Lena's impotent ravings cut through. She glances up, irritated by the incessant high-pitched whine.

'Lena!' No response. 'Lena, stop with the ranting. It's futile, irritating, and won't get us our bloody statue back.' That silences Lena all right, she's never heard her friend swear before. 'We need to alert Archer, and Coleridge too. There's no time to waste. God knows where they've taken it. This can't be legal. The council hasn't declared the damn vote yet, for heaven's sake.' She gets up, strides over to Lena at the fireplace, grabs her upper arms with both hands, and shakes her friend to ensure she has her full attention – she has. 'Can you get a telegram to them? The library's news desk should be open by now. You can use their line, tell them it's an emergency, and that I sent you. I'm going into town.'

'Yes, of course, I'll send them.' Lena hesitates, ponders a moment, then quizzes Eliza. 'But why town?'

'There's something I must do. I've been putting it off for too long. There's a chance it might give us a clue to where they've taken him.' Eliza pauses, considers something that's just dawned on her. 'This isn't about the memorial at all.'

Lena looks at her, puzzled: of course it's about the statue!

'What they really want is to rip the fight out of us, and they think the cause will wither without its icon.' Eliza puffs up. 'But they won't win. We'll never let them defeat us. With or without a statue, we'll carry on. They've unleashed an army who cares, who know we can't progress on the back of the suffering of other creatures.' She's inspired, buoyant even. 'Chins up, old girl.' She smiles, a genuine, optimistic smile. 'There's plenty to be doing. We'll show them their latest trick makes not one jot of difference.'

With that Eliza slips on her coat and hat, grabs her trusty carpet bag and leaves. As she strides across the vestibule to the main door, she spies a shadow approaching. His silhouette comes into view through the leaded glass panel as he ascends the steps. Eliza gasps, flings open the door before he rings the bell. She starts when they come face to face. It isn't who her fervent imagination convinced her it would be.

'Oh, my goodness, Mr Hageby, what a surprise! It's been a while.'

'Hello, Elizabeth, my dear, how are you keeping? Yes, it's been some time, hasn't it? Too long.' He smiles kindly at her, with, she imagines, an air of contrition.

'Is my wayward daughter at home, by chance?'

Lena comes into view. She stands in the shadow of the hallway and stares, impassively, at her father. With a tone dripping in sarcasm, she greets him.

'Hello, father. What a surprise. To what do I owe this unexpected *honour*?' She pauses. As the silence extends into uncomfortable territory, Eliza and Mr Hageby shift awkwardly, not too sure which way to move, or whether to move at all. Lena eventually breaks the tension. 'Please, father, won't you come in?'

Both Eliza and Mr Hageby imperceptibly sigh with relief and, with an embarrassing back-and-forth shuffle dance, pass each other on the threshold.

Eliza heads down the steps. She hesitates for a moment before turning left towards the station, off to catch a train into town for the long-overdue confrontation that she is dreading.

Feeling that exact same sense of dread, Reginald Hageby now sits in his daughter's sitting room. His eyes skim the stacks of pamphlets and suffrage banners propped up in the corner. He waits, his fingers tapping away at the antimacassars covering the arms of the settee, for her to bring the tea. His expression perfectly reflects his sense of foreboding at the thought of the ultimatum he's come to put to his only child.

TWENTY-NINE

Redemption

Eliza works her way along a quiet residential street off the Euston Road. She's squinting at door numbers, then down at a scrap of paper. Halfway along an identical row of yellow-bricked, three-storey town houses, she stops, checks her note again. Her face clouds as she contemplates her next move. As she stands, persuading herself to walk away, the front door creaks open and a young man emerges. He looks over, smiles and politely holds the door. She hesitates, but etiquette compels her to enter. She nods her thanks and steps reluctantly into a dank, gloomy hallway.

She pauses a moment to take in her surroundings. She has never been inside a student residence. It reminds her of Crawford Street. It is a shabby, long, windowless corridor decorated below the dado rail with a Lincrusta wallpaper – a typical, high-Victorian style, intricate pattern. It had once been painted cream, but now sported a dirty beige-brown hue, scuffed by countless students passing through. There's an odd smell, a mix of wet wool and boiled cabbage. Wooden pigeonholes dot the wall. Her eyes scan the names: they snag on one, confirming she's in the right place.

She squeezes past bicycles leaning against the wall to reach the dark mahogany balustraded stairway. Its threadbare runner leads the way to the first floor. Checking name plaques as she climbs, it's not until the third floor she finds the one she seeks. In elaborate calligraphy, on a card posted in a brass holder, she gasps when she sees:

John Forsyth, Esq.
Oscar Latham-Ward, Esq.

Her face hardens, she frowns, shaking her head at the realisation of the depth of the men's relationship. No bloody wonder he didn't want her visiting him here.

This changes everything: she can't bear to face him. She turns away, suddenly claustrophobic and sweaty in the close, dusty hallway. On reaching the stairwell, she takes a step down before pausing. She's come this far, she doesn't have to stay long, and he just might be useful. She must confront him, one last time. She takes deep, slow breaths, steeling herself, retraces her steps and raps on the door.

On the other side of that oak door is Jack; he moves around the room with a distracted air. His spacious sitting room is furnished with a large oxblood-red Chesterfield settee, two matching armchairs and an array of old rugs. Bedroom doors are located either side of an impressive marble fireplace. Bookshelves groan with medical texts, detritus covers every surface, and a human skeleton hangs in a corner. Large windows face the street Eliza has just walked along; they house recessed seats buried under cushions, cosy cubbyholes in which to sit, read, or stare.

He's tying a bundle of letters with string; he does this with care, as if they're precious, century-old artefacts. An inherent sadness permeates every slow, deliberate movement. Startled at the rapping, his face folds into a puzzled frown; he wasn't expecting anyone. He rationalises it with a grimace. At least this'll be the last time he'll act as Oscar's doorman. He strides across and yanks open the door, barking at the person standing there.

'For Christ's sake, forgotten our keys *again,* have we? How many times...' He stops dead, his eyes adjusting to the gloom of the corridor. He can't quite rationalise what he sees: not a shamefaced Oscar with his usual hangdog expression after an all-nighter, but – Eliza! His beautiful, angry, unattainable Eliza, standing there, just like in his dreams, back poker-straight, chin high – a defiant, proud, lovely face. He stares, the door half open, mouth hanging loose.

'Hello, Jack.'

Their eyes lock, expressions giving nothing away. It occurs to Eliza this moment could last forever.

'You going to invite me in? Or are we to spend the rest of our days on the threshold?'

'But yes, yes, of course. I'm so sorry, where are my manners? Oh God, I didn't expect to see you ever... For you to... Come in, please, do.'

Jack opens the door wide. He turns towards his sitting room to allow her entry. He cringes as he notices the general state of untidiness.

She takes a few tentative steps and looks around, then turns her gaze back to him. He's frantically trying to make the place more presentable, hiding magazines under cushions, removing beer and gin bottles from the mantlepiece, emptying ashtrays, sweeping everything into a waste bin that's already overflowing. She regards him with an archly sardonic expression.

'Oh, Jack, I wouldn't bother on my account. I've lived with Lena for long enough. I'm very well acquainted with mess.' She cannot help but soften at his obvious discomfort.

He, grasping at this olive branch, quips back. 'Yes, it's always the upper classes that are the most slovenly I find. Oscar's the absolute worst.' Jack grimaces.

At the sound of that name, her whole demeanour changes. Her eyes cloud with a thickening fog of hatred, and the fragile signs of a thaw in hostilities disappear without trace. He mentally kicks himself for his stupidity.

'But it *is* wonderful to see you, Eliza. I never had a chance to explain, after that awful time in the park. It isn't as bad as it seemed. I never betrayed you. I swear.' Eliza, her face a portrait of cool, dispassionate anger, raises her hand, palm forward.

'Enough! This isn't a social call. I'm in no mood to hear your confession, or absolve you of sin. You have to live with what you did, Jack. You'll find no forgiveness in me, not now, not ever.'

'But why? I don't understand. Why are you here, then?'

'I'm here to find out what you know about our statue. You, of all people, must have known this would happen. Bayling has had the council in his pocket since his *chums* won the election. I want to know where they've taken it. It's the least you can do, after the way you've treated me, used me, *betrayed* me.' A potent mix of anger and self-pity is bubbling to the surface. She struggles to control it.

'But, but I know nothing. I don't understand what you're saying.' He pauses, the implication of her words clicking into place. 'What on earth's happened to the statue? Are you saying it's gone? Who's taken it? How can they have?'

She studies him: there's genuine bewilderment. She senses he's telling the truth.

'You truly didn't know this would happen? Really? Your best friend Oscar not mentioned anything about it? Anything at all?'

'Agh, Oscar?' He snorts. 'I don't think so. He wouldn't tell me anything. He regards me a traitor. We've not been on the best of terms, putting it mildly, since the park. He's no friend of mine, honestly, Eliza.'

'Stop there, Jack. I'm not interested.' She cackles humourlessly. 'How ironic. I never thought he and I would ever have anything in common but turns out we do. We both consider you a traitor.'

'We weren't ever really friends. We only fell in together 'cos we were assigned these rooms, and then...'

'And then... Then what, Jack?' Eliza's curiosity overcomes her.

Jack looks at her, shrugs, what's he got left to lose? He sighs, the burden of his lies still hangs heavy. It will be a relief to unload it.

'I haven't told you the entire truth. About my past, I mean.'

'Not the truth? You *do* surprise me!' His anguished look softens her granite stare. 'But, do go on.'

'My father's not dead. Although he is to me. I've not seen him in over a decade.'

'Not dead? Another lie, then.'

'He was a conniving, selfish man, Albie Hastings, but apparently blessed with an irresistible charm and devilish good looks. The most dangerous a pairing of gifts to bestow on the amoral. He was poor, but ambitious and devious, and he'd set his sights on my mother. She was fifteen, he twenty. He pursued her relentlessly, until she was under his spell. As soon as she turned eighteen, three years from her inheritance, he married her. Her family warned her about him, they'd heard the rumours. But she wouldn't take telling.'

Now he's started, there's no stopping him, this unburdening feels like balm over his raw, lacerated heart.

'When he cottoned on to the fact he wouldn't get his hands on my mother's wealth, he fell back on what he did best. Thieving and conning the rich, declaring it a fair redistribution of wealth. An oft trotted out justification for his actions. My mother fell pregnant quickly and gave birth to me at nineteen. He soon got bored with playing happy families and returned to his womanising ways. But what could my mother do? She was penniless, more or less, cut off from her family and nursing a baby. She was trapped.' He wanders over to the window, stares sightlessly out.

'When my sister was born money was even tighter, so he took even greater risks. Got himself involved in some serious thieving, robbing grand houses. One night a mansion house robbery went wrong. The master of the house, an old gentleman, disturbed the intruders, and he was carrying a shotgun. There was a tussle, and the gun went off. The old man was hit in the shoulder. It wasn't life threatening, but he died of complications shortly after. They sent my father to jail, for a very long time. He was lucky not to be hanged, but his lawyer argued self-defence, and the fact my father was unarmed reduced the sentence to manslaughter. Last time I saw him was the day they found him guilty. Haven't spoken or seen him since. I was ten years old. God forgive me, but I wished they *had* hanged him.' Eliza joins him at the window, takes his shoulders and turns him to face her.

261

'Oh, Jack, I'm sorry. It must've been so hard on you, and your poor sister and mother.' Jack stares at her, his eyes infinity pools of sorrow and remorse.

'The rest of it, what I told you before, is the truth. The affair broke her, she couldn't cope with the shame, she became more withdrawn and confused. In time she was diagnosed a lunatic and it was recommended she be locked away. To keep her from being committed, and to protect our precious family name, my little sister agreed to care for her at home. In return, my 'oh so caring' grandfather agreed to pay for my education, to ensure I didn't end up like that "*thieving ne'er-do-well you married*".'

'Oh, Jack.'

'And so, here I am, doing something 'worthwhile with my life', resolutely *not* following in my father's footsteps. I'm free from the shame of his crimes, but at the expense of my sister's freedom.' Eliza squeezes his arm.

'Anyway, when I got here, to London, I studied medicine. I wanted to do something – anything – to help my mother, my sister, and this seemed the best option. I created a new past, buried all the shame, the guilt. Took my mother's family name, and all was good for a while. But in my second year I started sharing these rooms, and Oscar found out about my background. I've no idea how, but I guess when you've the connections he has, it's easy. He loves having power over people, it's how he maintains his position. He makes people do things for him as they live in fear he'll tell their secrets, ruin their reputation, and it seems everyone has something they don't want aired in public.'

Jack scowls at the truth of this. 'Anyway, Oscar revelled in the opportunity to jib me. Convict dad, working-class roots, all of it. The price for his silence was simple.'

Eliza frowned, trying to take it all in. What could Jack have done for him?

'I just needed him to stop, I couldn't have everyone knowing the truth.' He scoffs. 'My stupid fucking pride got in the way. Oscar, on

262

the other hand, needed help with course work. He isn't cut out for medicine. His father, a surgeon, rather forced him into it. For all the private tutors and expensive education, he's actually rather dumb, you know?'

'Yes, it's often the most privileged who are the dumbest, is it not? Lena's time at Cheltenham Ladies didn't do her much good either, but she, of course, will happily attest to this.'

Jack brightens at her tone. 'I like to think it's life's great leveller. They might have the private education, the connections, the inheritance even. But if they're all as numbskull thick as Oscar, then us working classes will eventually overcome.'

Eliza smiles despite herself, but returns to her hard stare quick enough. 'But none of this excuses what you did, Jack. You lied, and for all I know betrayed me, all of us, to Bayling. Sold out our plans to that rabid mob; they always seemed to turn up to our meetings and rallies, even though we were careful who we told. But you knew, Jack, didn't you? You knew it all, 'cos I told you!'

Jack senses his new optimism evaporate. He holds his hands up, defeated.

'Yes, ok, I confess, I lied to you. And about pretty much everything. But what choice did I have? Really? Truly?' He lets the question hang. 'I had none. If I'd told you the truth from the start, I knew you'd despise me. You would not have given me the time of day. Me, a medical student, exactly the type of person you deplore. If you had known I'd been there at Bayling's demonstration, you'd have hated me for not doing something, you'd never have got to know me for who I truly am.'

Eliza gasps, horrified at the revelation. Jack realises he has made a terrible, terrible mistake. 'You were there? That night?' She pauses, remembering something, something that, at the time, nagged at her but she thought nothing more of it.

'Oh my God, it was *you*. You were the missing witness at the trial. They called for an Albert John Forsyth, it's you, isn't it? John, Jack, the name's interchangeable. Oh, how could I have been so bloody

263

stupid?' She places her head in her hands, not wanting him to witness her tears.

'Yes, I was. I'm so, so sorry. Albert's my father's name. I've never used it. I hated myself for misleading you, but I'd got myself into such a mess. It trapped me, what could I do? I wanted to tell, confess it all, and I nearly did on so many occasions, but I just lost my nerve. I was falling for you Liza, and I couldn't risk you never wanting to see me again. It would've broken my heart.'

Eliza's thinking hard, going over all the odd things that have happened over the last eighteen months, all the random jigsaw puzzle pieces belatedly falling into place and revealing a stark, unrelenting portrait of deceit.

'You didn't break your leg, did you, Jack? You're a medical student for Christ's sake, you could plaster your own bloody leg. Oh, what a fool I've been. I was in love with you, Jack. The first man I've ever felt anything for.' She whimpers. 'I gave myself to you, completely. Trusted you. And now look at us.'

Eliza's world crumples away, the full extent of Jack's deception has devastated her. Unable to control her sobbing she turns to leave. He grabs her arm and pulls her back; she resists, pummelling him. He holds her, gently but with a grip she finds impossible to shrug off. Slowly she runs out of steam and collapses into his chest.

'I didn't betray you, Eliza, I promise you that. Bayling tried to get me to, but I didn't let him. She saw us together, his blasted secretary, Dunratty, when we were in the tea rooms that time. She went squealing to her master. He confronted me with it, and I couldn't deny it. He warned he'd get me thrown out of college, and threatened to tell you the truth about me, if I didn't keep him informed as to what you were planning. About the court case, meetings, things like that. But I didn't tell him anything – well, nothing of use, anyway. Just stuff he couldn't do anything with, or I changed a detail or two to make it worthless. I had to pretend to help, otherwise he'd have told you everything, and destroyed any chance of a career – he's so well connected I would never have been able to work in medicine. Please believe me, forgive me. I'll make it up to you, do anything, there'll never be secrets between us again. I swear to you.'

Eliza looks up at him incredulously. 'But how, how on God's earth, did you think you'd get away with it? It was inevitable I'd discover the truth at some point. You couldn't keep up with your lies. And I'd have despised you then, just as I do now. What were you thinking?' She's exasperated now, insulted. How could he think she was so dumb?

'I guess I hoped, in time, when this had all blown over, that I could explain it all to you. Try to get you to understand my position and why I *had* to lie. I never dreamt, I don't think anyone did, that things would escalate the way they did. That Bayling would take such umbrage to Coleridge's childish bloody name-calling, that he'd follow through with the court case, then incite his students against the statue. It all sounds unbelievable really, but it's what happened. And I just got so caught up in my initial stupid fucking lie that, as time went on, I couldn't see any way out that wouldn't destroy our relationship.' He shrugs, an air of defeat clinging to him. He looks down at her. No hope left, just resignation. 'I'm not like the others, truly I'm not. I loathe the methods Bayling and others like him use. They're unnecessary, barbaric, and have no place in modern science. But if there aren't people like me taking up medicine, with the motivation to challenge the status quo, then what chance have we to change things? You can do so much from the outside, Eliza, and what you've achieved is astonishing – you've sparked a revolution. But you need allies on the inside too. Can't you see that?'

She stands silently, but his logic is getting through. A spark of hope ignites in his chest. 'I've secured a junior position at the Anti-Viv hospital; I'm continuing my studies and practical work there. I've quit the university – Bayling cannot do me any more harm, I'm free of him. I start next week. I'd hoped I'd be able to redeem myself, that you'd forgive me in time. I still do, Eliza. Please give me a chance, together we can defeat these butchers, we'd make an invincible team.' He gestures at the open bedroom door. 'See? I'm moving out. I've had it with Oscar and his lot. I've secured a room a few streets from here – I'm leaving – today!' Her eyes follow his hands. She scans the room, sees the half-packed suitcases, the piles of textbooks tied with twine.

She returns her gaze to him, mulling it over. The pain in her eyes is fading. She throws him an inscrutable look. Eventually she speaks, choosing her words with care, conscious of what she's offering him.

'So, if I, just in theory, mind, were to give you another chance, how'd I ever be sure of you? You've lied about everything since we first met. We can't build a future on mistrust, Jack.' Her eyes search for his truth.

'Eliza, give me this one chance and you'll never have cause to doubt me again. For starters, I'll find your statue. We'll get it back in its rightful place. I'll guard it night and day.' Eliza smiles at his nonsense, thumping his chest.

'Now you're being silly, but finding my statue would go far in returning you to my good books. After that, we'll just have to see...'

They have run out of words, staring, seeking each other's true soul, trying to decipher whether this was it, they'd made it through. Neither is brave enough to declare it, but both feel it. Jack bends, kisses her softly, she tenses, but then gives in to him, willingly.

They remain enveloped in each other's arms, oblivious to the world about them when, suddenly, the door smacks open with an almighty crash. Oscar, with several cronies in tow, come tumbling in. They all seem worse for wear, glassy-eyed and swaying. Some collapse on the Chesterfield settee, some onto the floor. Oscar's in a jubilant mood, and only partially due to an excessive intake of spirits. He staggers, not able to walk a straight line. He's waving a champagne bottle around erratically. He spots Jack's profile at the far end of the room. Eliza, standing behind him, is hidden from view.

'Jack!' No response. 'Jacks, ol' chum. How are you doing this fine day, huh? I'm doing just fine, so I am, thanks for askin'.' He pauses to release a melody of loud belches. 'Hey Jack, I'm sorry we fell out, it was all so silly, and over a stupid, worthless bitch too.' In a stumbling, meandering walk, he makes his way over.

Jack, still with his back to Oscar, freezes, tense with horror at what is about to unfold. 'Let's forget all about it, 'cause I come bearing the best news we've had in absolutely ages, my ol' friend.' Oscar sways precariously, takes another swig, upends and throws the empty bottle away in disgust. He spins three sixty on one foot with remarkable balance. He assumes a dramatic pose, wobbles, clears his throat, and, with a booming circus ringmaster-like tone, slurs.

'For your delight and delectation, I'm proud to announce that we've finally triumphed over those annoying fucking women and that infernal doggie statue. It, my friend, is gone, vanished, disappeared. Never to be seen again. On its way to the knacker's yard, chucked in the Thames, melted down for scrap – who the hell cares? Good ol' Battersea Council, I knew they'd see sense as soon as the adults took over. We did it, we bloody well did it, old chum.' He cackles triumphantly, his entourage chiming in from their horizontal positions, snorting and honking with inebriated mirth.

Jack takes a deep breath and looks down at Eliza; her face is impassive, but he senses her rage. He turns to face Oscar. As he does, Eliza steps away from his shadow and into full view. The room plunges into a deathly silence.

Oscar stares, slack-jawed, his alcohol-soaked brain slow on the uptake. He wordlessly moves his mouth like a goldfish until it dawns on him what, exactly, he's just walked into. Sobering up quickly his face drops and his mood sours. 'What in God's name is that bloody tart doing here? What the hell you playing at, Jack? You swore you'd have nothing more to do with them Anti-Viv bitches! Yet here she is, flashing a bit of cunt and you're acting like a lovesick puppy again. For Christ's sake, Jack, grow a fucking backbone, not just your cock, for once.' He takes a step closer to Jack, changing tack. 'C'mon, put that bitch down and come have a drink with your chums. We won, and with no small help from you. You should be proud.'

Oscar tries to put his arm round him. Jack shoves him back with raw aggression. Oscar staggers backwards and falls over the arm of the settee, landing heavily on top of Hugh. Jack turns to Eliza, fearful of her reaction. He should be: her face speaks volumes. He focuses on her, willing her not to say it. She appears composed, devoid of emotion. She addresses Jack as if no one else is in the room.

'I'm sorry. It could never work. I'd never be able to truly forgive you, nor forget all that's happened.' And with a brutal finality that breaks both their hearts, she whispers.

'Goodbye Jack.'

She loftily ignores Oscar, still lying on the sofa, ignores the stares of the others. Holding her head high and her shoulders back, she sweeps out of the door and out of Jack's life.

THIRTY

A Proposal

Eliza trudges up Lavender Hill. Lost in misery, her stricken face reveals her turmoil. She endlessly replays the scene in her head. Could she have handled it better? Said things differently? Has she done the right thing, cutting Jack from her life forever?

She turns into her street, glances up as the main door to her mansion block opens. Lena and her father appear on the top step. They appear to be in the midst of an uncomfortable exchange. Not wanting to intrude, she hangs back, inadvertently spying from behind a lilac bush.

The farewell is formal and strained, neither party smiling, no hugs or kisses. Mr Hageby descends the steps. Lena stares after him, a picture of despondency. She exhales a long, exasperated sigh; one Eliza can hear from down the street. Lena retreats from view and the front door slams shut.

Reginald Hageby lumbers away, hunched over. Eliza waits until he turns the corner. Only then does she resume her steps, picking up her pace, a new determination gripping her. She needs to get to Lena. Her own despair is forgotten in the midst of concern for her dearest friend.

Eliza rushes into the sitting room to find Lena at the window staring glumly out, the cat in her arms. Lena doesn't react to the sound of the door opening or clicking shut. When she turns, her face displays the epitome of despair.

'Lena! Lena, *cariad*. What's on earth's wrong? What's happened? What did he say to you?'

269

Lena says nothing for the longest moment. Then, a tad melodramatically, she exclaims, 'Oh, Eliza, it's ghastly. Papa's given me an ultimatum. He's being so unreasonable, heartless.' She wails. 'He says he'll continue to pay the rent, and my allowance, only if I promise him something, one enormous thing. If I refuse, well, then I'm on my own. I'll have to "stand on my own two feet for once in my life".' She concludes with her uncannily accurate impersonation of her father.

Eliza sighs heavily, attempts to arrange her face into a sympathetic pose, but cannot for the life of her see why this is so terrible. After all, Lena's had it easy for every one of her twenty-seven years; it's about time she learns to get by without daddy's help. Eliza's had to stand on *her* own two feet, pretty much from the age of nine. She forms her words with care though, not wishing to deepen Lena's morose state.

'I see. But I guess you may have been expecting this? At some point?' Lena looks nonplussed. 'You can't have thought your father would fund your – let's be honest, Lena – your rather indulgent lifestyle forever now, could you?' Lena shrugs nonchalantly. She thought exactly that! 'So, what does he want you to do? What on earth can be *so* bad?'

At this Lena looks Eliza straight in the eye, her expression so despairing Eliza just wants to reach over and hug her.

'Oh, Eliza, it's ghastly, inhumane. He wants me, requires me – me, of all people – to find myself a … a *husband* for Chrissakes.' She spits the word out as if it is a bitter tasting poison. 'He wants to see me engaged within a twelvemonth… *Engaged,* Liza! Only public conveniences should ever be engaged!'

This was not what Eliza was expecting, not at all. She works hard to stifle her grin. She focuses on Lena's stricken expression, struggling to regain her earlier empathy for her friend's plight.

'Oh, Lena. Lena, my dear, that isn't so bad, surely?' There are worse injustices happening in the world, as we know only too well. And anyway, it's a fate that might befall any of us if we're not careful.' The irony is not lost on her, given recent events, but she shuts down such thoughts. She smiles encouragingly, trying to lighten the mood, but Lena's having none of it.

'Eliza! You know only too well that neither matrimony nor maternity hold any fascination for me.' Shuddering melodramatically, she pauses before launching into her well-rehearsed demolition of the revered institution. 'Marriage has the unfortunate side effect of reducing a woman's position from a free-thinking individual into a mere possession,' Lena rants. 'What use is education, free will, independence, for Chrissakes, if you squander it all on the first man that offers a sparkling bloody ring, huh? Answer me that?' Her pompous indignation comes across as rather comical. Eliza's cheek twitches: she's fighting to contain her amusement.

'Only to find yourself stripped of your property, your inheritance, even your voice. Shackled to the tedium of managing his household for the rest of your mundane life. A life, don't forget, you cannot escape unless *he* divorces *you*. Oh, and let's not forget the intermittent misery of pregnancy, torture of childbirth, then the unrelenting slog of child-rearing.' Her voice reaches the highest note in her range. She's exhausted her supply of oxygen. She intakes a huge breath, concludes with a resolute, dramatic flourish. 'It is truly, honestly... Not. For. *Me.*'

With that she sits down with a thump on the chaise, still gripping a squirming Mrs P, who manages to wriggle free of her grasp and flee to the safety of the sideboard.

Eliza takes a seat and folds her hands over Lena's, and says softly, 'I guess most of that's only an issue if you've received an education *to* throw away, possessions of any worth or an inheritance to speak of.' Lena narrows her eyes, glares at her friend. She still doesn't get it; she still doesn't understand her real self. But Eliza's quiet eloquence has managed to poke a small hole in Lena's self-absorption. She can't help feeling a little silly, and a lot over-privileged. The realisation her rant was insensitive bubbles up and silences her. Why can't she just tell her the truth? Explain the real reason for her horror of marriage.

271

'After all, we can't live here like a pair of eccentric spinsters forever, can we? Although at our ripe old ages, I'm not sure anyone would want us. I mean, we're only a handful of years off thirty, that's positively *ancient* in the marital stakes.' Eliza pushes her shoulder against Lena's affectionately. 'If we're not careful we'll turn into crotchety, cat-obsessed old maids. That's if we're not already, hey Mrs P?'

Mrs P, now luxuriating on her back, legs stretched out, regards them with an inscrutable expression.

Lena stares at Eliza, a look of deep longing in her sorrowful blue eyes. 'But would that be *so* awful, Liza?' Her voice acquired a slightly whiny tone, pleading almost. 'I'd be content turning into an old maid if I'd you by my side. We bump along together pretty well, don't we?'

Eliza, unnerved by this change in pitch, and by the unsettling undertone, examines Lena as if seeing her through a new lens. Something long buried, an intuition, a nagging doubt, has been unearthed, exposed, and cannot be reinterred. Eliza, shocked by the sudden realisation, panics. She loves Lena, but not like *that*! The thought horrifies her, it's against nature, at least that's what the Bible tells.

'Oh, Lena, *cariad*, it cannot be. I don't have—' she begins, before Lena cuts in. She doesn't want to hear it. As long as Eliza's objections are not voiced, then there is always a chance.

'But you don't understand, if I can't find someone for myself then... Then he already has someone in mind. And it's dreadful, Liza, truly dreadful.'

Eliza is shaken out of her whirlwind of emotions by curiosity.

'Who? Surely no one's that awful? After all, he wouldn't marry you off to a monster for heaven's sake, or worse still, a Tory!' Her attempt at levity falls as flat as a drop scone onto the griddle. Lena's solemn face contorts into a decent impersonation of a gargoyle.

'Well, if I can't identify a suitable candidate myself, he's dead set on marrying me off to ... to Theodore Ponsonby, of all people.'

The name sounds vaguely familiar; Eliza frowns, thinking hard, but can't quite place it. Then, without warning, his face – thin, long, weaselly – pops into her head. How could she have forgotten? 'Oh goodness me, yes I do remember dear old Theodore.' She explores his image in her mind's eye and an empathetic grimace develops. 'Well, at least you couldn't call him a monster.' Although trying to find the positives, whichever way she tries to sugar-coat the situation, it's clear to them both that Theodore Ponsonby could not be considered, by any right-minded, modern-thinking woman, to be 'an eligible bachelor'. Rich? Yes. Of solid upper middle-class stock? Of course! He'd have to be for Mr Hageby to even contemplate him for his beloved daughter. Apart from those attributes, neither of his making, poor old Theo has precious little else going for him. He isn't a bad man by any means, he just isn't much of, well, a man. Maybe that's why Lena's Papa has suggested him? Lena's such a force of nature, no man could control her. At least Mr Theodore Ponsonby wouldn't waste his time trying.

'Oh, Liza. The horror! He exudes a persistent aroma of boiled kidneys and is continually under the weather, complaining of his countless ailments. He has a perpetual sniff, but never a handkerchief to hand. Mummy hides the Doulton when he calls; his donkey's bray could crack an entire tea set at ten yards. God help you if you're sat with him at dinner, he bores for England. Mother places him next to dear aunt Mauve, her deafness spares her him droning on about his wretched stamp collection. I swear it's the only thing he is passionate about. It'd be a true living death being shackled to him for life.'

Eliza stifles a giggle and shoots Lena a ridiculous pantomime 'how ghastly' look. Lena, wallowing in her melodrama, responds with an equally exaggerated grimace.

They continue pulling ever more ridiculous faces, each more absurd than the last. Then they take turns imitating the hapless Theodore until hilarity overtakes them. They guffaw, giggle, shriek and snort, hugging each other until the tears flow. Tears of mirth or grief? It is impossible to tell.

As they embrace, Lena's mouth finds Eliza's. She kisses her with a passion that cannot be misinterpreted. Her tongue searches for the crease in Eliza's lips and forces entry.

Eliza is stunned into inaction. She opens her mouth to voice her shock, but this only encourages Lena and she forces her backwards onto the cushions. Eliza now gathers her wits and pushes feebly against Lena's bodyweight.

Lena holds her down with an unusual show of strength, absorbed in her own passion, ripped open after so very long under careful, secure wrapping.

Eliza struggles, panicking against the weight. She gets a hold beneath Lena and shoves her with more force than intended. Lena falls to the floor with a bump. The shock rouses Lena from her delirium. Her face can't hide her mortification. What the hell has she done? Jeopardising years of friendship in a single, unguarded moment. Shamed and devastated, she picks herself up off the floor. She cannot look Eliza in the eye. She flees to her bedroom, slams the door and locks it.

Lena presses her back against the closed door. She looks to the heavens, for the first time in her life pleading with a god she'd never believed in for help, her face disintegrating into a portrait of misery. She chokes on a raw, guttural sob, her hand flies to her mouth to silence it; she cannot have Eliza hear her anguish. She knew it, knew it all along, ever since that first evening, but now, only now, and in the most appalling way, has her true nature revealed itself. She has gone and spoilt everything. Her friendship with Eliza is the one, the only, genuine friendship she's ever had. And now... and now she has the undeniable, irrefutable proof that their relationship would never, could never, be anything more. She collapses slowly to the floor, tears running down her cheeks in rivulets at the realisation that she almost certainly hasn't even that friendship anymore.

THIRTY-ONE

The Offer

BATTERSEA DOGS HOME, SOME WEEKS LATER

Henry James Ward, director of Battersea Dogs Home, sits in his cramped, dingy office overlooking the exercise paddock. Documents, letters, and invoices litter his desk. The accumulation of bills is by far the largest pile, and he eyes it with despair. His secretary informed him five minutes earlier that his visitor had arrived, but he's left him waiting, to both prove a point and to steel himself for what he imagines will be a rather disagreeable encounter. He takes a long breath and calls to Mrs Whittaker to show his guest in.

Ward stares, blinking – as is his habit when about to confront something unpleasant – at the closed door. Moments pass before the door swings back and William Bayling strides in, wafting an air of unwarranted superiority that Ward recalls from his schooldays. Whatever his misgivings about the man – and he has many – Ward rises to greet him with deliberate civility, and a studied coolness.

'Why, William, it's such a surprise to see you, of all people. What on earth could bring you to my humble refuge?' As he extends his hand, he adds wryly. 'Seeking to give a poor, abused creature a loving home perchance?'

Bayling attempts a smile, but it doesn't reach his eyes. In fact, it barely reaches his lips. He reaches out his large, elegant hand and shakes Ward's with far too much vigour and for a little too long.

'Henry, my old friend, how the devil are you? It's been such a long time. I take it your delightful family is well? It surprised me to hear that you were still here, if I'm frank. I imagined you would have

275

moved onwards and upwards by now!' He raises an eyebrow, condescension etched into its arch. Ward repays the courtesy by ignoring his jibe.

With the required niceties and forced small talk quickly taken care of, Bayling gets down to business. 'Henry, I'll get straight to the point, we're both busy men.' Ward nods agreement, only too happy to keep it brief.

'I'm here to make you an offer. If we can be rational about this, we could do each other an invaluable service. One that will benefit both our chosen vocations, however far they deviate from each other.' He smiles obsequiously. 'Now, I'll not beat about the bush, I've heard the talk of your recent money troubles, no doubt exacerbated by the controversy over that infernal statue. It's polarised opinion, that's for sure. I'm assuming donations have suffered as a result?'

Ward riles at the mention of his financial woes, a topic that is monopolising his every waking hour. His eyes flicker toward the pile of overdue bills. 'Our present *temporary* difficulties are no secret, William, and I am dealing with them in my own way. We'll be fine. But I don't lay blame on the anti-vivisection protesters, most certainly not.'

Bayling raises his hands. 'Henry, please, excuse me for presuming...'

'And I must say William, *your* students have been acting more in the manner of brutalised savages than gentlemen of science. The news regarding the removal of the memorial, without notice or the right to protest, is deeply worrying. The council seems to have mislaid its moral compass in recent times.'

Some of the veneer of Bayling's camaraderie is already wearing thin. 'Ward, please, enough of this fake liberal outrage. We both know full well what's gone on these past months, and that these protests will achieve nothing, change nothing. The statue's gone, and that's an end to it.' He speaks with such finality Ward cannot think of another word to say about the subject. He waits, assured that Bayling will get to his point soon.

'I'm wrestling with a dilemma; one I lay at the feet of Coleridge and his cronies.'

'Go on!'

'Now, in present times we're finding it increasing difficult to find suitable, how can I put it ... *volunteers* for our research work. Yes, finding volunteers is becoming an acute problem. We require a steady supply of suitable specimens, or progress in key areas of our research will stall. And that, I'm certain you'll agree, helps no one. No one at all. I'm at a critical stage with my work on hormones, and without our vital pieces of the experimental jigsaw I cannot progress.'

'Are you implying what I think you are? You're out of your mind, man!'

'Come on Henry, see sense for heaven's sake. This could work out well. Now I've money, plenty of it. And you've plenty of the resource I need. If you could see your way to agree to supplying us with, shall we say, some of your more hopeless cases, I'll see to it you'll have more money than you could dream of. Much more than you need to secure the future of your little refuge here.'

Ward stares, dumbfounded, not believing his own ears.

'So, what do you say? The forfeit of a few hopeless waifs and strays in exchange for saving hundreds, if not thousands, of other tragic, abandoned creatures. There is always compromise in the world, Henry. You more than anyone must realise that?'

Bayling opens his jacket pocket, revealing a chequebook. He makes a show of placing it on the desk, then unscrews the top of his expensive looking fountain pen. He sits motionless, pen tip poised over a blank cheque.

'C'mon, Henry, old chap. Don't be sentimental. Surely you can be objective about this? It's a simple trade-off. What in life isn't? It's for the greater good, after all. It's the obvious solution for both of us.'

Ward's initial outrage is subsiding. He *can* see the logic, however perverse, in Bayling's argument. After all, he can't save them all.

Now, with the current financial quagmire the home's experiencing he could soon be in a situation where he won't be able to save any.

Involuntarily, his eyes flick to a letter. It's from the bank, warning of foreclosure on a debt unpaid. The sum is large, and he has no immediate means of paying it. His eyes revert to the blank cheque, and then to Bayling, who is sitting patiently, willing him to name his price, pen poised. He falters, his conscience spinning cartwheels, weighing the pros and cons of this deal with the devil. The end justifies the means. The sacrifice of the few for the good of the many. Glib, clichéd sayings flow unbidden. With regret, he speaks. There's a sad, desperate tone to his voice.

'And I'd have your word that no one would ever hear of this? This potential little arrangement of ours?'

Bayling smiles his first genuine smile of the meeting. He has him, he's won. 'Oh, absolutely, Henry. It'd be just between us two. I'd send my boys to collect whenever's convenient. And I'd, of course, never, ever, reveal my source. You have my word, as a gentleman, and as a friend.' Bayling taps his nose conspiratorially, starts to write out the cheque. 'Could we start with a consignment of, ooh, how many? Shall we say twenty specimens? That should last me a while. I'll pay you a down payment of twenty pounds, and another twenty when delivery is complete.' He signs his name with a flourish and holds out the completed cheque without looking up.

The item remains in his hand. After an awkward moment, he glances at Ward, shakes the chit of paper at him. Ward reaches over and slowly eases the bill from Bayling's fingers. Bayling smirks, but his smug expression soon fades as he's confronted by a stark, icy expression.

'I've heard enough. You can take your sordid little deal, your blood money, and get the hell out of my sight.' With that he rips the cheque in two, in two again, and again, then flings it back into Bayling's shocked face. 'What you're suggesting is not only absurd, it's beyond despicable if you imagined I'd ever agree to something so abhorrent. We weren't friends at school. You were a vicious, odious bully even then, and we're certainly not friends now. Get out. Out of my office now, before I set *my* dogs on you!'

Bayling doesn't flinch as the cheque flutters around him like confetti. He calmly puts away his pen, replaces the cheque book, rises from his chair. As he reaches the door, he stops. 'You disappoint me, Ward. I hoped you were better than this, that you'd grasp the sense in my offer. But I see you're no better than those illiterate, heathen idiots protesting for the statue's return. My proposal could've worked well for us both. But so be it.' He reaches for the door handle.

'Bayling, one last thing.'

Bayling freezes, spins around, raises an inquisitive eyebrow.

'The statue, where the hell is it?'

Bayling grins enigmatically. He still has something over his childhood nemesis. He opens the door, steps through, but thinks again, turns to face Ward. 'You'll probably not believe me, but honestly ... I have no idea. Safe to say however, I don't think we'll be troubled by that wretched bronze mongrel again. Goodbye, Ward.'

With an ever-so-smug smile, he sweeps out. As he strides away from the Home the smirk seeps away like slime down a gutter. His face contorts into a grimace as he recalls the countless rebuffs he suffered throughout their school years. He could never prove it, but he just knew Ward was behind them. He hoped to dispatch those memories, redress past indignities, through demeaning Ward with his blood money. He has failed, and failure cuts deep; it bothers him far more than he'll ever admit to himself.

NELSON'S COLUMN, APRIL 1906 – THE CONSTABLE

Me and the Sarge is first alerted to something a bit iffy going on by a gaggle of ladies descending on us like a flock of excitable seagulls. Dressed in white, all 'eaving bosoms and eyes a poppin', their faces scarlet and perspiring in a way I'd never considered ladies capable of. It's nigh on impossible to make out what the Dickens is occurring, them's squawking and caterwauling away like the bleedin' banshees they are, making no sense whatsoever.

Eventually the Sarge weaves his old gent magic and gets 'em to calm themselves – I've a lot to learn from that old charmer, so I 'ave! – and we finally make out that something calamitous is happening up at the top plinth: the one that's been empty since forever, the one we are forever pulling scallywags and well-pickled young gents off of. Everyone finks it dead clever to climb atop it and hold 'emself in a stupid pose, like they're bleeding Napoleon or King Bertie. Daft 'apeths. Those we throw in a cell to sober up soon come to the realisation it ain't so damned clever after all.

The Sarge instructs me to pull a few of the more frightened looking constables out of the particularly fruity fracas we was embroiled in and to follow him up toward the fancy art gallery. I cannot lie, it's a blessed relief to get away from this lot of ruffians – I swear they are getting meaner and more violent. It ain't the students so much anymore, but the ne'er-do-wells they've recruited into their ranks recently. And the weapons we are confiscating are getting nastier too: cudgels with nails and glass embedded; knuckle-dusters with sharpened edges. It's enough to make you despair of mankind, so it is.

We dash – well at least some of us do – up the side of the square, our destination a rapidly increasing crowd loitering at the base of the plinth, all staring at something.

We force our way through the crowd, ten-deep in parts, the Sarge is wheezing like a flipping steam train by my side. Eventually we break through the front row to be confronted by a sight that stops us in our tracks. We just stand, blinking in confusion. It is the most extraordinary scene – one I've never come across in all my days of coppering. Sarge slowly turns to me, his expression one of gormless disbelief. His mouth opens and closes silently until he gathers the wherewival to form a sentence.

'Righto, Stan, my lad. What the bleedin' blazes are we to do with this little lot?'

THIRTY-TWO

The March

APRIL 1906

If Battersea Council thinks its clandestine removal of the memorial will be the end of the matter, it is very much mistaken. The outrage caused by its actions simply adds fuel to the fire, giving rise to more disturbances, larger demonstrations and seemingly ever-escalating violence – across London and beyond.

The Memorial Defence Committee, dismayed and embarrassed by what occurred under its very nose, remonstrates vociferously with councillors and officials and organises regular demonstrations and pickets at the town hall. Its members' call is straightforward, they demand the return of their statue, forthwith, to its rightful home in Latchmere Park. But the campaigners are met with an equally vociferous anti-statue lobby, and their tactics increase in both intimidation and aggravation. The 'anti-doggers' are far better funded and organised and, worryingly, seem to know exactly where the next Defence Committee meeting or demonstration will be held, turning up with effigies to be burned at hastily assembled bonfires, letting off stink bombs, fireworks and, more often than not, carrying makeshift weapons, concealed about their person.

Battersea Council remains resolutely tight-lipped throughout. Its sparse statement on the matter simply reiterates the fact there was a legally binding vote, which ruled in favour of the memorial being removed. Hence, it will not, under any circumstances, consider replacing it. Councillor Archer's protestations fall on deaf ears; his influence in the chamber is much diminished since the election. With a heavy heart he turns his attention to the host of other pressing matters in the borough, problems he feels he at least has a fighting chance of resolving. The brown dog affair is, to all intents, abandoned, filed under 'lost causes' and left to gather dust in the underground vaults of the town hall.

Lena and Eliza, their issues with each other placed to one side for the time being, throw themselves into the fight for the statue's return. They speak at rallies, meetings, any opportunity they are offered. They are often booed off stage, pelted with eggs and other foul-smelling liquids – the composition of which they dare not question – when meetings are infiltrated by the students and their recruits.

The increasing animosity, the mindless brutality they witness, has far-reaching effects on the women. Lena, her true feelings for Eliza now painfully out in the open, as well as the ever-present threat of marriage, retreats into herself, her vibrancy fading day-by-day. Her flame of rebellion flickers weakly where it was once a wildfire. So much so, she fishes out the abandoned twee 'Home Sweet Home' embroidery her mother gave her all that time ago. Eliza, arriving home early one day, has the shock of her life to find Lena, curled up in a chair, cat on her lap, absorbed in her needlework.

Eliza, in contrast, becomes ever the more emboldened. She hardens her heart to the very idea of love, friendship even, and instead devotes herself to finding her statue. She finally severs her long-time alliance to the law-abiding suffragists and falls in with the newly christened *Suffragettes* instead, a transfer in loyalties from the Union to the WSPU that gives the perpetually morose Lena cause to smile secretly to herself. At bloody last!

The *incident*, although never referred to overtly, takes a heavy toll on their relationship. The women start behaving in a stilted, formal manner in one another's presence. An unnatural politeness imbues their daily interactions. It is as if the years of harmonious intimacy have been washed away in a flash flood, to be replaced by a foreign landscape neither knows how to navigate. Eliza, wary in

Lena's presence, flinches at her slightest touch, making a point of locking her bedroom door each night. Lena, in return, regards Eliza with a studied nonchalance, a forced casualness. It is a vain attempt to convince her *it* was just a silly mistake, *it* meant nothing. Not a word is uttered, no salve applied, so the open wound continues to fester. Mrs Rumple often adopts an acutely befuddled expression whenever she observes the two women together; she senses something catastrophic has happened, but try as she might, she cannot worm the gossip out of her beloved Lena. All appears painfully civil on the surface, and they work well together when involved in activities regarding the missing statue, but the friendship, that seemingly unbreakable bond between them, appears torn beyond repair.

The Defence Committee is ploughing all its energy into organising a march through central London. It will start at Hyde Park and finish with a rally in Trafalgar Square. It will be the biggest, most ambitious demonstration yet, with thousands of supporters estimated to attend. There are genuine worries, however. The Committee fears a traitor in its midst, such is the level of disruption to private meetings and the secretly organised gatherings – the anti-doggers are always there, despite the Committee being extremely careful in its communications. But members are determined, nothing will stand in their way – certainly not a few dozen rabble-rousing students and their hired thugs. Eliza, a key figure in the masterminding of the march, even manages to persuade a reluctant Lena to give up her regular art class to join in.

The day of the demonstration arrives, and the weather is kind to them. It turns out a warm, still afternoon, no sign of the forecasted April showers – a perfect day, in fact, for a protest. A patchwork army of the most unlikely band of recruits advances up Whitehall. Disparate factions of society, who seldom see eye-to-eye on any matter, march in a rare display of solidarity. Trade unionists in threadbare tweeds rub grubby shoulders with demure, tightly corseted Suffragettes, who struggle to stifle their disdain of the men's unfamiliar, pungent odour. The ladies shade their porcelain complexions with silk parasols, while juggling neatly embroidered protest banners. Middle-class, jovial progressive types stride cheek-by-jowl with sullen anarchists. Socialists and Marxists bicker amicably as they stroll. Harassed mums scold their over-ebullient children who skip alongside, oblivious to the reprimands. Young boys clutch frayed rope leads on the ends of which strain a battalion of rangy mongrels. A convenient breeze breathes life to the cloth flags they hold aloft, depicting slogans like: '*Justice for our dog*', '*Give him back NOW*', '*Battersea against the Butchers of Bloomsbury*', '*Student Swine*', '*Where's our statue?*'

A febrile, skittish atmosphere permeates, but the newfound spirit of camaraderie keeps it calm – for now. The handwritten placards and cardboard signs bob gently above this undulating sea of strange bedfellows, a fair few thousand in total. The sound of discordant singing fills the air, clashing tunes sung with no attempt to harmonise. Workers' songs, bawdy drinking ditties, songs of suffrage, anti-government chants, and the dogs enthusiastically barking accompaniment all collude to destroy the peace of this warm Sunday afternoon.

The first wave of protestors reaches Trafalgar Square. As they pass Nelson's lions, their nostrils are assailed by a pungent, eye-watering stench. It's the students' favourite trick, a sulphurous potion concocted in their laboratories for this very purpose. A moment later, they catch the first faint notes of a chillingly familiar rallying cry. The war song gets louder, more ominous. Tension permeates in tandem with the cloying malodour saturating the crowd, causing the ladies to gag into lace hankies and men to wrap scarves to keep the putrid stink from invading their noses and mouths. A collective shiver ripples through the ranks. Mothers nervously grab for their boys and the men feel for the iron rods they've concealed inside their coats – just in case.

In a trice, from left and right, counter-protestors appear. At their head is an effigy of a dog, paraded by a smartly dressed young gent, in a morning coat and top hat. Behind him, a disorderly procession of ruddy-cheeked student types, exclusively male, intermingled with jeering and cussing ruffians. They too have placards and banners. As one – harmony in voice if not in appearance – they chant their bastardised version of "Little Brown Jug", with more than just a hint of victory in their tone.

As the vanguard of each rival group moves to within spitting distance, flashes spark within the crowd, accompanied by a series of loud, sharp cracks reminiscent of gunfire. The shock disperses the protestors. There are no guns. The students are lobbing fistfuls of Chinese crackers into the crowd. An almighty charge by the mob and the opposing sides face off – just inches apart. It begins, as always, with heated words and hurled obscenities, but it isn't long before a first punch is thrown, then another, until everyone piles in brandishing bars, bats and bottles. In the blink of an eye, the scene descends into barbarous, bloodied chaos.

Women scream and yell, panic-stricken, yanking their children from danger. The dogs become frantic, barking, straining their leashes, some breaking free. They lunge at the students, but their teeth and claws are no match for the mob and their weapons. They are kicked, beaten with rods and stamped on. Many lie injured or dead in the gutters. Yelps and whimpering cut through the background noise, children screaming for their pets, men swearing and charging their enemy, their wooden banners now makeshift weapons. Pandemonium reigns.

The police are in attendance but, as ever, they are hopelessly outnumbered. Their feeble whistles are drowned out by the cacophony. Small groups of coppers pile in to separate the warring factions. As soon as they break up one fight, three more start. The police look on, helpless, resigned – they've seen this so many times before they now feel numbed to the violence surrounding them.

They stand impotently, praying for reinforcements – their horse-mounted colleagues – to bring some kind of order back to the scene.

At the outermost fringe of the fighting, a gaggle of prim-looking ladies make haste towards the steps of the National Gallery. The group has avoided getting embroiled in the blood-soaked carnage unfolding in the Square. To the casual eye, they could be on their way to a genteel gathering at the nearby Lyons' tea shop. If it were not for the chanting, that is, as their purpose is made plain by their clear, loud voices, and the placards and banners proudly hoisted aloft as they march.

As they pass the statue-less plinth in the north-west corner of the Square, their path is blocked by a dozen men who appear as if from nowhere. They wield sticks, bars, cricket bats, whatever they could lay their hands on when they left home that morning. They are definitely not your typical student demonstrators, there's something far more sinister about their demeanour.

The women are forced into a dead stop and instinctively form a tight circle. One of the men steps forward from the nucleus of the mob and approaches the women; he radiates a cruel aura that sends a shiver straight through them. Gaunt, chest proud like a pigeon, he stands observing the group, a smirk spreading across his pallid, hollow cheeks. He wolfishly sniffs the air, savouring the atmosphere of fear his lads have created. He takes a final, satisfying drag on his cigarette and grinds the butt into the ground. Several seconds pass before he speaks. It's a low, menacing growl.

'That's quite far enough, ladies.' A contemptuous sneer replaces the smirk. 'A word to the wise, if I might?' His searchlight eyes scan them, leering at the pretty ones. 'I'd totter off home to yer menfolk where you belong if I were yous.' He grins, clicks his fingers. The gang push back their coats, casually revealing an assortment of knives and coshes tucked into their belts. 'So's we can avoid those pretty little faces of yers getting slashed in all this chaos we've got going on 'ere.'

A unified gasp. The women clutch each other, their fear palpable.

The ringleader drinks in their distress, lapping it up. His tone drips malice.

'Although, for some of you old hags it would be a distinct improvement, ain't that right lads?' The mob sniggers and, as one, takes a step closer to the women.

A sudden sharp cut of sweat and stale alcohol overlays the lingering odour of rotten eggs. The ladies fall back, stumbling over each other in their urgency to get away. All except the two young women leading the group, that is, who do not move, their faces defiant, their stance resolute.

The ringleader's attention is caught by one of them. He double takes, then gets right up close, almost nose to nose, and, on recognising her, snarls, his ale-soaked breath hot on her face. She doesn't flinch.

'Hold a bleedin' minute, I know you! I've seen yer face in the papers. You're the demented tart that started all this effing nonsense, aren't yer?' With that, he steps back and casually spits, a gobbet of yellow-tinged phlegm splatters below her left eye and meanders down her cheek. She refuses to wipe it away.

The woman stares straight back, a mask of defiance and loathing disguising the revulsion and fear that's churning the pit of her stomach. Two long years of bottling up an incandescent rage at the horrific exploitation and gross inequality in the world explodes in this moment. She's not quite in control of what she will do next, but calmly accepts the inevitability of it. She says nothing for what seems an age. Gradually all becomes quiet. The ladies, from a safe distance, hold their breath, aghast at what's unfolding. The mob stands as still as the statues surrounding it. When the woman speaks, it is without emotion, her tone calm, her pitch low, enunciating each word. She holds his eye with a provocative glare.

'Yes, that's me.'

Her smile is acid sweet. She steps backward while raising her arm, as if to wipe away the spittle, but in a lightning-fast streak lands the most impressive left hook square to his face.

'And I'm the demented fucking tart that's going to finish it.'

Her companion gasps, wide-eyed in disbelief. Caught unawares by the force of the blow from such a fragile-looking creature, the ringleader stumbles backwards over a loose cobble and drops heavily to the ground. As he falls, his nose explodes, spraying blood over the woman's face and dress. He smashes his head on the kerb.

Lena, finally regaining the power of speech, screams at her friend. 'Nooo. Eliza, stop! For Chrissakes, what *are* you doing?'

Moments later, a squad of police, truncheons aloft and whistles screeching, blunder in. Among their company is one Sergeant Bert McDonald, wheezing with the effort and, ahead of him, his protegé Constable Stanley Robb. They come to a clattering halt, bemusement writ large across their flushed, sweaty faces. They are confronted by the bewildering spectacle of a respectable, primly dressed young lady, her coat and face splattered crimson, standing over an unconscious male, blood obscuring his features. Unnoticed, the rest of the mob quietly melts into the growing crowd of dumbfounded bystanders.

The police slowly get their bearings, taking statements and dispatching a boy to fetch the St John Ambulance Brigade to attend the fallen man. Given the severity of his injury, they have no choice but to arrest Eliza. To his dismay, Constable Robb is given the task. Stanley's face betrays his horror at having to do this to someone he considers almost a friend – given their frequent conversations back in Latchmere Park. He reluctantly frogmarches her to the Black Maria, a horse-drawn van waiting patiently on Whitcomb Street. As they approach, the back door opens and a dishevelled-looking lad with a cut lip – he can't be older than fifteen – is shoved into the bowels of the cab. Stanley catches a glimpse inside. It is already crowded with the most unsavoury bunch of reprobates he's seen in a long while – and he's seen some sights in his time. His stride slows to a crawl. Eliza, her mind reeling, senses this change in pace. She glances over. His horrified expression causes her to follow his line of sight. She gulps as her eyes focus on the van and its inhabitants before the door clangs shut again. She understands all too well his sudden reticence. The van is her intended destination. She halts, digging her heels into the cobbles. Jolted by a tightening in the chain that connects them, he too stops, turns back to face her. Stanley's sad pale-grey eyes, regret flowing freely, lock onto hers. Eliza, openly displaying fear for the first time that day, pleads silently, her eyes black pools of terror – please God no, don't make me, please. Stanley cannot bear it. He turns away and, more abruptly than intended, resumes walking, yanking Eliza, who stumbles with the force, along with him.

They approach the rear of the vehicle and stand quietly, waiting to be noticed. The police officer in charge raises a quizzical eyebrow.

'Seriously, Constable?' A frown deepens even *his* permanently worried expression. 'Surely this young lady isn't to ride in my van. Have you *seen* what's in there?' He glances from despairing constable to terrified woman.

Stanley glances back, back to the crowd that has formed at the empty plinth. He spies his superiors watching him closely. He shrugs, resigned to the fact this deed will weigh heavily on his conscience for the longest time.

'Orders are orders, Sarge. I'm afraid Miss Blackwood here is responsible for an act of violence that 'as to be accounted for. Regrettably, she must be placed in custody.' He releases the handcuffs binding them together and gestures to the Sergeant. He then turns to Eliza, but cannot meet her gaze.

'I'm sorry, Miss Eliza. I truly am. I'll see to it Miss Lena knows what's 'appened and where they're taking you, I promise you that.' He hangs his head and walks away, more ashamed of himself in that moment than ever before.

'Stanley,' Eliza shouts after him, unable to disguise the tremor. 'Know I don't blame you; you had no choice. And please tell Lena I'm fine, not to worry, and I'll be back with her in no time, I'm sure.'

With that, the Sergeant puts a hand to her back and firmly, but not roughly, encourages her towards the door. He fishes out the large iron key from his pocket and turns it in the lock. The door swings open silently. Eliza, with as much dignity as she can muster, steps up to the gaping hole, one foot on the metal step. Her eyes water at the stench of stale urine and testosterone-drenched, soured sweat that hits her. Her eyes adjusting to the gloom, she stares in open-mouthed despair as she gets her first close-up view of the origin of the stink. The occupants, hardly believing the turn in their luck, whip up a frenzy of depravities. She is encouraged to enter the wagon by a guiding hand, which unbalances her. She topples forward, reaching to steady herself. She finds herself pawed by one of the van's vile-smelling occupants. She smacks his hand away, only to be groped by another. An officer follows her inside, and the door is locked and bolted from outside with an ominous, metallic thud.

THE FOUNTAINS, APRIL 1906

'Take that, Jack. You wanker.'

The cudgel comes crashing down, my skull its intended target. Lucky for me, Oscar had clearly spent the last hours supping his way through a barrel of Dutch courage. The weapon's trajectory destabilises him and he's thrown forward by the momentum. I step to one side. The weapon – a rounders bat by the looks – and its wielder crash to the floor. Oscar, taken unawares by the suddenness of his descent, lies winded on the ground, too inebriated to register the injuries that will find him black and blue tomorrow. I stand over him, a fine mist covering us from the wind that scutters across the fountains. I don't know what comes over me, but I feel an irresistible urge to harm him, make him pay for all he has done, the irreparable harm he has caused us. It matters not that he lies there, pathetic, and now unarmed; I feel no compassion, no compunction to help him. Instead, I draw my leg back and land a sudden, vicious kick into his ribs. He feels that – barrel of gin or not! He barks out an involuntary scream of pain, doubles up and starts sobbing pathetically, a whining, grizzly child. Shockingly, I feel no remorse. I kick him again, with greater force.

'That's for Eliza.' He lets out a grunt and curls into a tight foetal position, pleading with me to stop.

'And this is for that wretched dog.' One last strike and I give it everything I've got left, aiming straight for his groin. I stand impassively, watching him writhe in pain, a creeping sense of guilt at not feeling at all guilty. If that makes any sense?

I'm distracted by a commotion over the way. I cannot make out what's going on but am aware of a foreboding sweep through me. I step over Oscar's prone body, blocking my ears to his pathetic mewling, and break into a run. Something terrible has happened, I just know it.

I reach the edge of the crowd. I force my way through. So deep and tight-knit is the crowd that has gathered to gawk. I break through, ignoring the tutting and sharp elbows around me, and see two St John Ambulance orderlies crouching over a body that's laid out on the cobbles. I gasp in horror, but breathe out a sigh of relief when I realise the body they are tending to is an adult male. I break from the crowd, instinct kicking in, shouting as I go.

'Please. Let me through. I can help, I'm medically trained.'

I reach the unconscious man, a rough-looking fellow. There's blood coating the cobbles surrounding his head. I check for a pulse. He's alive, at least. As I attempt to stem the bleeding, I glance up, my eye caught by a silhouette of a couple walking away. The sun's rays fire straight into my eyes. I shield them and squint at the couple. The man is a constable, the rounded dome of his helmet a giveaway. In step beside him is a woman, a lady by the looks, her gait familiar. They appear to be holding hands. It takes a moment to register, but then I spot the glint of metal at their wrists. Suddenly, the policeman slows his pace. The woman glances over at him; her profile stands out against the afternoon sun. I gasp in disbelief.

THIRTY-THREE
Number Thirty-Seven

NORTH LONDON, JUNE 1906

Although it was their mutual passion for women's suffrage that brought Lena and Eliza together – involving them in countless foolhardy escapades that could have landed them in trouble – to Eliza it seems incongruous it would instead be their concern for the plight of other species that alters her life's course so profoundly. As she allows her mind to wander, revisiting her last three extraordinary years, it still baffles her how she ended up here. But now she has plenty of time on her hands to reflect, to dissect and forensically examine the sinewy chain of circumstance that has led her to this fate.

Eliza often wakes sweat-drenched, disorientated by the stark, whitewashed stone walls that mark the boundary of her diminished new world. In just three strides, she can traverse the entire width of it. Her darting eyes are drawn to a single, natural light source: a barred ten-inch-square of blue sky that breaks the monotony of white. The window is positioned so high she can only peer out if she drags the stool – the only piece of furniture besides the wooden base that makes up her bed and a table – along the flagstone floor and clambers up onto it, teetering on tiptoes. Her view of the *outside* world is the mirror image facade of another wing reflected back at her. Occasionally she spies a woman engaging in the same activity, and they wave forlornly at one another. It takes her sleep-coddled brain a panicky minute to recall she is now the unwilling resident of London's notorious 'Holloway Castle', so very far from her own cosy home, her beloved cat and her dearest, her *only*, friend.

Regrettably, that single punch had had appalling unintended consequences. The man she struck, a stevedore by the name of Mr Sidney Thomas, twenty-five-years-old and a father of two, was stretchered off, still unconscious and bleeding profusely. Soon after he arrived at the hospital, he slipped into a coma. After a week he regained consciousness, and the extent of his injuries became clear. As he fell, the impact of his head smashing into the kerb had fractured his skull, resulting in a tear to the membrane which subsequently became infected. Doctors also detected bleeding on the brain. The prognosis was that he would suffer a low level of permanent brain damage, with a high probability of developing epilepsy. Eliza's single act of mindless vengeance that day had caused a man's disability and incapacity for the rest of his life, and she felt as wretched as anyone could.

Eliza was found guilty by an almost unanimous verdict and convicted on the charge of inflicting 'grievous bodily harm'. Eliza's counsel lobbied for her to carry out her sentence in the Surrey House of Correction, situated in Wandsworth, almost a stone's throw from her former home, but it wasn't to be. His Majesty's Prison in Holloway was decreed to be her new abode. HMP Holloway had converted to female-only status some years before, so mercifully she did not have to suffer the indignity of having to serve her time in the company of men. Men, the likes of which she had the misfortune of sharing that squalid police van with on that dreadful afternoon back in spring.

Once she had been deposited into the Black Maria, and the door bolted behind her, the occupants clambered to make room for their *special* guest. A cajoling, weaselly wall of sound hit her, a chorus of gruff voices jostling for dominance, pleading for her to 'sit next to me, darling', 'why dontcha come to daddy', 'I'll look after you, sugar lips.' This was shut down quickly by the guard. Her eyes swivelled frantically, desperate to locate the least odious specimen, but concluded they were hewn from the same vulgar rock, each as vile as the next. The driver snapped his whip and

Eliza stumbled as the cart jerked into life, the momentum forcing her head back against the side of the cabin, hitting an iron strut. The shock elicited a strangled squeal, which only aroused the men further. She slid down the cabin wall, her backside finding a space on the narrow bench. She perched uncomfortably, eyes lowered, surreptitiously observing her nearest neighbours. The lascivious, sideways glances, the proximity of their bodies, the grimy clothing; she'd picked her seat unwisely. An overpowering stench of unwashed armpits and crotches invaded her mouth, and she couldn't disguise her gag reflex. Eliza flinched as a vision of lecherous intent came into sharp focus, just inches from her face. The man, delighted at this sudden turn of fortune, pretended to be jostled by his neighbour in a blatant move to nestle into her bosom, openly touching himself all the while. Eliza could not fail to notice the rise in his stained, grubby trousers. Her vomit rising, she shrugged him off roughly, squeezed her eyes shut, and shallow-breathed through clenched teeth so as to not inhale any of their filthy, airborne lust. To her shock, she found herself praying for the first time in years.

Mercifully, the ride to the holding cells, at the eastern end of The Strand, took only around ten minutes. Although to Eliza it seemed like ten hours. There, they were unceremoniously turfed out, and she was led off, lewd invitations still ringing in her ears.

The female holding cell comprised a long, narrow, windowless room, featureless except for mean wooden benches that ran along the walls and the four existing occupants lounging upon them – each identically hollow-eyed, pallid and wretched. Pick-pockets or street-workers most likely. Women that, in normal times, Eliza would have been wary of passing by too closely. She would, undoubtedly, have given them a wide berth, averting her conflicted gaze from their pleading eyes and out-stretched palms.

Despite the cramped, dismal conditions, and the inevitable taunts from her new cellmates, she felt such a wave of release from her anxiety that she curled up in a tight ball and promptly fell asleep, secure in the knowledge that her friend would soon come to release her from this waking nightmare.

As she stepped from the prison van, Eliza shuddered at her first glimpse of the building where her fate would be decided: The Central Criminal Court of England and Wales, universally known as the Old Bailey. The Portland stone frontage of the freshly minted courthouse stood starkly against the sooty griminess of the older buildings flanking it, a single porcelain tooth in a mouth of otherwise decaying coal-black stumps.

Eliza raised her hands to her forehead; the metal chain clinked taut as she stretched out her wrists to shield her eyes from the building's glare. She peered skyward, intrigued to view close up the much-talked-about recent addition to London's skyline: a twelve-foot-high statue erected at the pinnacle of the court's central dome, a gold-leaf-adorned, classical figure of Lady Justice standing astride the earth's globe. The precious metal glinted harshly as it reflected the summer morning's rays. There was a distinct aura radiating from it, and not one she could warm to. Eliza imagined she was staring into the inscrutable face of a landlocked Siren: a merciless wraith intent on luring her onto the awaiting rocks of retribution.

Unusually, both of her arms were outstretched. She held a set of finely balanced scales in one hand and an unwieldy-looking sword aloft in the other. The silhouette it created reminded Eliza of the crucified Christ. Was this a conscious merging of the most famous miscarriage of justice in the ancient world with the ultimate symbol of modern justice? At least they didn't have the audacity to blindfold her. Oh, the irony of it! That earthly justice is represented by a female, yet women still have no say in its delivery. Where, *exactly*, is the justice in that?

The prison van guards, impatient to offload their cargo, encouraged her to walk on. She was taken to an inconspicuous side door, the only giveaway to its function being the constables flanking it: the defendant's entrance. As she crossed the threshold, a second irony occurred to her. The building she was about to enter had been designed by the same architect responsible not only for her former workplace, but also the venue for the public meeting that was to be the genesis of her plight. She chuckled mirthlessly as she was led to the courtroom, eliciting suspicious, side-eyed glances from the guards.

At her trial, the defence counsel's main case – that she acted in self-defence – didn't quite make its mark, as Mr Sidney Thomas had not laid so much as a finger on Eliza before she lashed out at him. This was something an extremely reluctant Lena, under intense cross-examination, had to attest to. Instead, an argument raged as to whether Eliza's actions were taken 'with intent'. Her barrister argued, successfully it turned out, that the assault was not carried out with any intent, premeditated or otherwise, and was utterly out of character. It was simply a tragic, momentary lapse of judgement and self-control, under intense provocation, if not violence. This minor victory went someway to help with the sentencing. Additional factors were considered such as an otherwise unblemished record, respectable profession and lifelong, law-abiding behaviour – at this description she glanced across to Lena in the public gallery and risked a wry smile. The judge ordered a prison term of two years. A light sentence, by all accounts, given the severity of the man's injuries.

First division is where every prison inmate prays to be placed. If assigned to the first, you're allowed your own clothes, can request food be brought in, and the sanitary facilities are of a socially acceptable standard. There's even someone to clean your cell. It is considered a breeze compared to the alternatives. First division in Holloway is reserved for non-criminal type offences, the likes of libel, slander, contempt of court, or petty crimes committed by ladies of the middle- or upper-classes whose first offences are judged unusual and out of character. It is in first that so-called *political* prisoners are housed. As a rule, women found guilty of *any* kind of violent act are denied the possibility of first. Eliza didn't have a prayer.

Eliza is destined to carry out her sentence in second division, in the company of women the authority considers of low rank, and/or questionable morals: the working classes; lower middle-class ladies who have fallen on hard times; the divorced and disgraced. In second, are the street prostitutes, women who have committed serious, occasionally violent, crimes and first offenders, often very young girls, banged up for trifling misdemeanours such as stealing stale bread or the odd bruised fruit from a costermonger's barrow. Even those who have attempted suicide end up there; their true crime being simply that they are poor, illiterate and, more often than not, destitute. Although second is tough, Eliza thanks God she was not assigned to third, the lowest division before one reaches the realm of 'hard labour' – which does not bear thinking of. Third is where you find the basest, crudest examples of womankind. In third, fester the women convicted of the most heinous crimes imaginable, often one step away from the gallows: the poisoners, murderers, abortionists, baby farmers and other repeat offenders from the unspoken-of underbelly of society.

Eliza arrived at the gates of the Holloway House of Correction for Women on the twentieth day of June 1906. She gaped in wide-eyed awe as the imposing front entrance came into view through the barred rear-view window of the cabin. To the casual eye, it was a medieval fortress, albeit one that had been built just fifty years earlier. It had been designed to a brief that instructed the architect to '*strike terror into the hearts of evil-doers*'. The prison van – a Black Maria identical to the one Eliza had travelled in two months earlier – pulled up in front of the main gates. Although not sharing with male prisoners on her journey north, their putrid ghost-essence was still apparent. Their lingering odour flooded her senses, causing her to gag as she settled onto the bench. Her anxiety burst and, in panic, Eliza found she could not catch her breath; she was drowning in a fug of sweated onion rancidity. She smacked herself manically, convinced those grubby, gnarled hands were pawing her once more, grasping at her breasts, snaking up her thigh; she felt the hot, foul breath on her face. She started screaming, yelling to be let out, panting shallowly, eyes wide and brimming with terror. A sudden, stinging crack across her left cheek silenced her, but forced a deep gulp of the sullied, fusty air, her first in minutes. She glanced up. A wardress stood astride her; contempt clear in those merciless, grey eyes. Eliza flinched at the sight of the woman's raised palm. She closed her eyes, passively awaited the inevitable second slap. It didn't arrive.

'Just shut the fuck up, Blackwood.' The wardress, a Miss Ethel Havers, hissed malevolently. 'Who the hell do you think you are? Lady Muck? Creating a scene, disturbing everyone. Just pack it in. Behave yourself – you hear? Or you'll suffer much worse than the back of my hand.'

Eliza gingerly opened one eye, then the other. She glanced around at the impassive, bored faces of her companions. They had been here before, and the hysterical ravings of a first-timer didn't bother them much. One woman cracked a fractional, sympathetic smile, her expression indicating she should just do what she's told. Eliza heeded the warning and remained silent until she stepped from the cab to view the gothic immensity of what was to be her home for the next two years. The solid brick wall that encircled the outer defences of the gaol was over eighteen feet high, its expanse broken up with almost fairy-tale turrets and battlements. The outer gate that faced her was utterly impenetrable: two solid oak doors, riveted with countless iron studs and reinforcements. She imagined an enormous ironwork key turning the lock and the door cleaving open to reveal an outer circle of hell beyond, so was almost disappointed when a small wicket gate to the side opened with no fanfare, and the posse of fresh interns was herded towards it.

Eliza was the last of the five to be ushered through the narrow, low opening. As she straightened up, she was confronted with a barren brick and cobbled courtyard, where she imagined row after row of wretched-looking, dead-eyed women would line up for inspection by the prison Governor. Directly across the way, she spied another enormous wooden door, set into a protruding castellation, and guarded by two impressive stone griffins raised high on plinths hewn from the walls. One held a giant key, the other a leg iron in its talons, both poised in readiness to swoop down on any prisoner foolish enough to attempt an escape, their claws flexed in anticipation of dragging them back by their scruff. Eliza was captivated by their fearsome majesty. The group was frogmarched in between these two sentinels. As she passed, Eliza reached up and stroked the griffin's claw. For luck – I'm going to need it, she thought. She was led down a long, soulless corridor that ended at the reception desk. Here she was relieved of her few remaining belongings – all housed in her faithful, if somewhat tatty, carpet bag. The women were then bundled into what appeared to be a large storage room, packed floor-to-ceiling with continuous racks of wooden and metal shelving. Upon them perched piles of clothes, each shelf meticulously documented as to whether it contained underwear, stockings, frocks, aprons, caps or footwear. Eliza was instructed to choose her uniform, watching with fascination as her more seasoned companions squabbled over the rare, newer-looking items.

However thoroughly she ransacked the shelves, the pickings were slim. In haste, as she was being hassled by Havers, she grabbed random items from the stacks. She followed the other women into a bleak, bare, stiflingly close room, where they automatically removed their outerwear; Eliza followed suit. There was no privacy afforded, and Eliza stood in cotton vest and drawers, her arms wrapped around herself as if frozen to the core, in a vain attempt to preserve some modesty. One-by-one, they were led into an adjoining bath house and made to strip naked. Eliza stared in horror at the dank grey water. It stank of carbolic soap and Jeyes Fluid. She had to be *encouraged* to enter the tepid bathwater, its surface swirling with the pubic hairs and the oily residue of its previous occupants.

Once a helping hand had completely submerged her, Eliza, eyes stinging and nostrils leaking the murky bath water, clambered out and rubbed at herself with a damp, grey-white hand towel hanging on a rail. Then her uniform was thrust at her.

The prison uniform was an absolute horror: undergarments fashioned from rough, itchy hemp. To Eliza's disgust, closer inspection revealed she was not the first to be wearing them. The green serge frock buttoned up tight from neck to ankle, and caused her skin to break out in red raw, painful welts. The black woollen stockings, with red hoops, were shapeless and baggy, forever bunched at the ankles as they shuffled endlessly around the exercise yard. They were forced to wear pointless white starched cotton caps tied at the chin and pinnies in a crude parody of Lyons' tea shop waitresses, the difference being the tell-tale downward arrows that adorned the apron. Each prisoner was given a badge to stitch onto their dress: a bright yellow roundel displaying a unique identifier, denoting both the wing the inmate belonged to and her prison cell number. Eliza, on arrival, was handed the number thirty-seven. From that moment on she was addressed solely as a number: dehumanised and anonymised. Just one in a roll call of digits by which the wardresses summoned her and her cell neighbours for their once-weekly bath, nit check and their regular turn to slop out D block.

The prison food was not recognisable as such: tasteless, lumpy, salty porridge, slabs of sinewy, green-tinged meat with blanched out vegetables, and grey and greasy stews were standard fare. On repeat. Refusing a meal meant you went hungry for twenty-four hours as punishment, so Eliza forced it down, gagging on every mouthful.

Her toilet comprised an earthenware bowl that squatted in the furthest corner of the cell, to be emptied once a day. She was allowed a bowl of tepid water with which to conduct a 'cat's lick' wash, as her mother called it, but otherwise she just got used to her body's increasingly distinctive aroma.

Conditions were harsh to say the least, but what could she do but bear it as stoically as she was able? She could not claim innocence, imprisonment for a crime she did not commit – unlike the tediously predictable, whiny refrain that seeped into her cell. There was no denying her culpability, her guilt. Eliza endured it all with remarkably good grace, determined the experience would not break her. However humiliating it might be, she would learn from it, come out stronger. One small mercy was that at least she could read during the long, solitary waking hours; she was painfully aware that the luxury of reading was not an option for many of her neighbours. She took comfort in immersing herself in the lives and loves of a host of fictional characters. On picking up her old favourite *Vanity Fair* she found, to her shock, that she began to empathise with the incorrigible Miss Sharp and her morally dubious antics. The thought worried her.

THIRTY-FOUR

New Friends and Old

Although Holloway life is undeniably grim, Eliza soon finds herself in good company. Just as she settles into the monotonous prison routine, a familiar name joins her on D Block. Prisoner fifty-six, the Suffragette formerly known as Miss Teresa Billington, has long been a thorn in the side of the authorities. Obstreperous, fearless and defiant, she personifies the new breed of campaigner that is causing the fresh-minted Liberal government so much grief. They'd resisted jailing her, in fact any Suffragette, for as long as they could, knowing full well it would simply add fuel to an already raging fire, but Miss Billington's latest transgression had upped the ante considerably. She was finally detained for affray outside the home of the Chancellor of the Exchequer, exacerbating the situation by kicking the arresting officer hard in the shin. Mr Asquith was not in residence, but the unconscionable act of ringing the doorbell of a government minister could not go unpunished. Consequently, she was sentenced to two months at His Majesty's pleasure. She is the first to be imprisoned in Holloway for a suffrage-related crime, but no-one would bet she'd be the last. She could have avoided gaol by paying a significant fine, but she refused on principle. As a working-class woman the amount was well beyond her means, anyway.

Eliza and Teresa, on nodding terms only before, are delighted to be re-acquainted – despite the unfortunate circumstances – and spend many a thrilling hour sneaking notes and other contraband items to one another right under the wardresses' noses. Moral arguments, that may have prevented Eliza from entertaining thoughts of such wanton rule-breaking, have been left at the prison gate along with her belongings, or so it seems. She revels in the frisson of danger she feels when almost caught with a cigarette – a habit she has recently adopted, encouraged in no small way by Teresa. This leads her to seek more thrills, she becomes more daring, ever bolder – but always careful, mind – in her small, but satisfying, acts of rebellion against the authority.

However, just as Eliza is getting used to her newly discovered subversive streak, and her new friend, Miss Billington's fine is settled by an anonymous benefactor. Rumours swirl that the twenty-pound fine was paid by a member of the Government. It's common knowledge Asquith has become increasingly exasperated by the continuing publicity surrounding Miss Billington's incarceration. So it seems someone has taken matters into his own hands. This unusual move has left the Governor no choice: he has to release her. Teresa is dragged from her cell, resisting every step, bellowing her indignation at not being allowed to serve her sentence. Eliza watches, horrified, through the peephole in her cell door as prisoner fifty-six is hauled by her armpits from view. She permits herself a self-indulgent tear, the first since she arrived.

Eliza isn't lacking good company for long, however, as Miss Billington's cell is soon to be occupied by a stalwart of the suffragist movement. Mrs Charlotte Despard had been held whilst protesting outside Parliament – *peaceably* she is at pains to inform Eliza. By now the authorities have changed tactic, no longer fearing bad press. They instruct the police to arrest, with impunity, any woman causing trouble – rich, poor, they aren't fussy. Countless are charged that day and given the choice of either paying a fine and being bound over to keep the peace or being incarcerated. Although Mrs Despard, an extremely wealthy widow, could afford the ten pound fine without blinking, she chooses not to. Hence, at the grand age of sixty-two, she's carted off to Holloway to serve her first sentence. It is considered an outrage that a lady of such good standing and blemish-free conduct should be gaoled for such a trivial offence – if an offence it even was.

To add insult to injury, she, and her co-defendants, are placed in second division when, it is argued, they can justifiably claim to be political prisoners, just as the Fenians did decades earlier. But, for now, such protestations fall on deaf ears and in second they remain.

Despite the fact that Holloway's system is based on 'separate and silence', a regime that sees prisoners confined to their solitary cells for much of the day and forbidden to speak to one other when out, the rule is broken so often it's become a running joke. And Eliza, put to work in the prison library, finds more opportunity than most to mingle. Mrs Despard, or number seventy-two as she is now known, in a concession to her age and standing in polite society, is permitted to spend much of her time in the library. Consequently, the women get to know one another well. Despite her stern demeanour and ostensibly serious countenance, to Eliza's delight Charlotte turns out to be a rather wily old lady with a wicked sense of humour and razor-sharp intellect.

The time flies by, and two months later Eliza is once again bereft, having to say goodbye to yet another friend. It's selfish of her, she knows, but Charlotte's company was a blessed comfort, and she will miss her terribly. It is a hardened, brutalised woman Eliza waves off, however. Mrs Despard had taken her incarceration badly and was no spring chicken to endure such harsh conditions. Word gets back to Eliza – through the stream of Suffragettes who are now flowing through at an ever-increasing rate – that Charlotte has defected from the more peaceable National Union to the WSPU after her release. Inevitably, her subsequent protestations become more aggressive, daring, and most *definitely* unlawful. Eliza, with a wry smile, remembers her words distinctly, 'If I'm to be arrested again, Elizabeth, it'll jolly well be for a proper, *illegal* act!'

True to her word, Mrs Despard is arrested twice more. Her most serious offence, leading a march on Parliament which ended in a pitched battle between police – a good number on horseback – pitted against hundreds of angry, determined women.

It is during Charlotte's third incarceration a year later that she persuades Eliza to join her breakaway group, the Women's Freedom League. Charlotte had had an early falling out with Mrs Pankhurst – a woman about whom Eliza had always had misgivings – regarding the way the WSPU was being run. Rumour had it that it had turned into more of a dictatorship and Charlotte, a staunch democrat, could not condone the Pankhursts' actions and had no hesitation in telling them so. Taking a dim view of her insubordination, Emmeline Pankhurst, seemingly oblivious to the irony of her own actions, gave Charlotte a stark ultimatum: either fall in line or leave the WSPU for good. Charlotte promptly upped and left and took a good number of disheartened, newly disenfranchised WSPU members with her, including the irrepressible, and newly married, Mrs Teresa Billington Grieg. The League, of which Charlotte was voted president, was a much more peaceable movement, and its members, to differentiate their approach from that of the ever more destructive antics of the Suffragettes, labelled themselves 'militant suffragists.' The more Eliza learns of it, the more the League sounds a much better fit. She feels increasingly uneasy about the WSPU's escalating acts of violent disobedience and so willingly swaps her allegiance. Her one nagging concern is how on earth she will break the news to Lena, who she knows will not be best pleased at what she will see as a betrayal. Eliza will not have long to wait.

Second division prisoners have meagre allowance regarding visitors – just one a month. Eliza had received the odd visit from library colleagues in the early months, women with whom she'd shared tea breaks, or helped with a double shift when they needed time off. And even a visit from Mrs Rumple, although she suspects it was more to satisfy her morbid curiosity as to how Eliza was faring, rather than any true sympathy for her plight. But it is only Lena who comes with any regularity, and lately even her visits have tailed off. She has missed three in a row now and, in her darker moments, Eliza questions whether Lena has deserted her too. Today, however, such thoughts have been exiled and Eliza is thrilled by the news that she has a visitor. She is so excited at the prospect of seeing Lena, to regale her with tales of Charlotte's latest *holiday in Holloway* as the good lady euphemistically calls her detentions. Yet, there is that nagging worry, a reticence regarding her need to confess her desertion to the 'other side'. But what the hell. She's sure it will be fine; it's not important. They'll just have to agree to disagree. After all, they are fighting for the same cause, it's just the means by which they conduct themselves that differs.

She misses Lena's visits so very much; she can admit that to herself at last. And, although things have not been quite right since the unfortunate *incident,* Eliza is determined that when she gets out – in less than a year now – they'll be able to repair the damage. They'll carry on as it was *before,* put all that unpleasantness behind them, start afresh. Just the two of them. The thought of curling up on the settee, all cosy and warm, Mrs P purring contently on her lap and Lena's head resting on her shoulder, fills Eliza with such joy she could burst.

THIRTY-FIVE

The Visit

The allotted hour arrives and Eliza, awash in equal measure of nerves and excitement, is unceremoniously frogmarched over to the visiting room. It is an unwelcoming, barren space, with soulless white lime-washed walls and little ventilation to speak of. Consequently, it remains stifling in summer and bone-chillingly cold in winter. The meagre natural light sneaks in through mean, letterbox-slit windows clustered high on one wall, and does little to dispel the sense of despondency that clings to the place. There are two rows, three deep, with facing chairs divided by a wide expanse of table, the arrangement chosen to limit any form of contact; the room houses six prisoners, a visitor apiece. Six granite-faced wardresses sit stiffly, backs to the wall, silent as nuns, positioned strategically to keep a beady eye on all. God help any visitor or prisoner suspected of passing something between them. For, if discovered, the visit is brought to an immediate halt, for all in the room. The chairs are designed for discomfort, but that is of little consequence, given visiting time is an hour maximum, the dreaded horn blast heralding 'time up'. Eliza is led in by her least favourite of all wardresses Miss Havers. The woman took an instant dislike to Eliza from the off, from that first day in the prison van, believing prisoner thirty-seven to have 'ideas above her station' and needing to 'be brought down a peg or two'. Havers hustles Eliza over to her allotted table, roughly pressing her into the seat. In a raspy whisper, she orders her to sit in silence, *no fidgeting mind*, until her visitor arrives.

Eliza is kept waiting for what seems a lifetime. The other prisoners have received their guests by now, and the low-level buzz of intense, whispered conversation permeates the room, temporarily lifting the gloom. Eliza's expression softens, gaining some second-hand comfort from absorbing their joy at being reunited, however briefly, with loved ones. She gives up peering round in anticipation of Lena and stares ahead blankly. What on earth is keeping her? Her foot agitates, tapping away on the flagstone. Keeping time with the lapsed, lonely seconds that turn into minutes, minutes of lost company fated never to be made up.

Her heart leaps as finally she hears footsteps behind her. Curiously, it is a heavy step. She frowns, the sound amplifying a suspicion that something isn't quite right.

'Hello, Eliza.'

She catches her breath, then utters an involuntary cry that pierces the room and results in turned heads, sixteen narrow-eyed stares focused on her. She recognises the voice instantly. Two simple words triggering an avalanche of painful memories.

A shadow passes to her right and then a tall figure looms, facing her. Eliza raises her head, her eyes reluctantly following suit, and she finds herself staring into a handsome, but serious, face. He appears older than when she last glimpsed him – in court, during the trial. He would turn up in the public gallery each day, smiling down at her encouragingly. But she could never look at him, acknowledge his presence even. The shame of her actions, the sight of how low she had fallen being reflected in his eyes was too much for her to bear.

'May I?' He tilts his head in that oh-so-familiar way Eliza could never resist.

She gathers her wits, replying in a reedy, high-pitched tone she hardly recognises. 'Yes! Yes, of course, Jack. Do take a seat.'

He drags out the chair and they sit facing each other in an awkward, question-ladened silence. Eliza's hand moves, unbidden, to her hair, suddenly acutely conscious of her slovenly appearance. It feels greasy and heavy to the touch. She hadn't bothered fussing with it, or even checked her face for smudges, so convinced was she it would be Lena visiting. Oh God, how she must look to him. She cringes inwardly, prays for the ground to open and swallow her whole, to relieve her of this unbearable humiliation.

'So, how are you keeping? You look ... well.'

'Oh Jack, please! How do you think I'm keeping? Fourteen months in this hellhole. Wearing these flea-ridden rags, eating the foulest slops you wouldn't even feed to pigs. Rats keeping me up half the night, every night. And not to mention the cockroaches.' She shudders at the thought. 'If nothing else, I think we can agree that I'm most certainly not looking well!' This flowed out in a torrent, a gush of emotion bubbling up from nowhere, and much louder than expected.

Havers rises like an apparition and glides towards their table. She glares, black eyes narrowing to pinholes. 'Any more histrionics, thirty-seven, and I'll not hesitate to cut this visit short. Am I making myself understood?'

'Yes, Miss Havers. Apologies.' Eliza nods curtly, scowling at her receding form. She turns back to Jack, not able to vocalise the one question ricocheting around her brain – what on God's earth is he doing here?

'I'm sorry, that was crass of me,' he whispers, eyeing Havers warily.

Eliza feels a pinch of contrition. After all, what could he say in the circumstances? 'No. It's me that's sorry. You make the effort to come all this way, and all I do is snap. Forgive me.' She stares across at him, taking him in for the first time, his gentle eyes brimming with concern. She feels her resolve melt a little. 'Anyway, how are you? You must be qualified by now, I guess. How have you taken to work at the Anti-Viv? Assuming you're still there.'

'Yes, still there, and now officially a doctor, very junior of course, but they let me loose on patients.' He smiles shyly, but she notices his chest swell just a little. The same old Jack. Eliza senses a thawing under his warm gaze, but steels herself to not allow even a modicum of fondness show through.

311

'I'm happy for you. Honestly, I am. And pleased it's working out there. It's truly an inspiring hospital.' She stretches across and pats his arm. Havers clears her throat, and she snatches her hand away. 'To be honest, I *was* expecting Lena today. She hasn't visited in months. No word by letter, neither. I'm becoming concerned for her.'

'Oh, don't be. She's fine.' Jack responds with a breezy confidence Eliza finds disconcerting. He colours a deep pink as he catches her puzzled frown.

'And how d'you know how Lena's doing, Jack?' She scrutinises him. 'You two haven't become friends in my absence, have you?' She cannot suppress a low, derisive snort. The idea is so unlikely as to be laughable.

He coughs awkwardly, clearing his throat. Eliza feels a first sudden pang of alarm.

'As a matter of fact, Lena and I have, um, buried the hatchet, so to speak.' He gauges her reaction. It is unreadable. 'I bumped into her on my rounds one day. She'd started volunteering on the wards. It was frosty at first, as you'd expect. But we got to talking, and, eventually, given the choices I made, quitting university, working at the Anti-Viv and all that, she saw it in her heart to forgive me.' His uncertain smile, his rapidly bobbing Adam's apple, betraying his disquiet.

Eliza's slackening jaw and incredulous eyes speak for her. Not in her wildest dreams could she imagine Jack and Lena as friends. And Lena... Lena of all people, *forgiving* Jack for all he did: the lies, subterfuge, the betrayal. It quite beggars belief. She searches his face for a clue he is joking, but has to conclude – his earnest expression unwavering – that this is, indeed, the case.

'Well, I never did,' she splutters.

'That's one reason I've come today.'

Eliza cocks her head, curiosity eating her up. 'Go on.'

'Well, my other news is my grandfather has died.' His face takes on an oddly bland, emotionless hue, which confuses her. She reaches out her hand to comfort him, but noticing Havers' beady eye removes it hastily.

'I'm sorry to hear that, Jack. Truly. I hope you were reconciled before his death.'

'Oh, no,' he retorts, rather too cheerfully. 'Not really. But the old man must've felt some remorse for the way he'd treated me – us, my family, I mean – as he left me his estate.' Jack continues to regard her with an expression she just cannot fathom. Eliza's bemusement grows. It's too much to take in, her mind is awhirl with it all. His unlikely new friendship with Lena, his indifference to his grandfather's death, the news he's become a landowner and, presumably, a wealthy man into the bargain.

He shrugs. 'I don't think he'd much choice in the matter. I'm the eldest surviving male of the Forsyth line, and he wouldn't leave anything to my mother, given her condition, and my cousins are all female. I was, by default, his one true heir.'

'Oh, well then, I'm happy for you, Jack'. Eliza cannot work up a tremendous amount of enthusiasm. It all seems a tad cold hearted – but there again, the old man treated Jack, his mother and sister, appallingly for years, so who was she to judge?

'That's the other reason for my visit.' Again, Eliza cocks her head, aware her features are in danger of appearing permanently gormless at this rate.

'Well … given Lena's found it possible to forgive me, and now I am a man of means, I was hoping, well – praying, truth be told – that you too could find it within yourself to forgive me. Forget the past and, when you leave here, we might try again?' His words end on a rather mournful down note, as if he has lost confidence just as his proposal is leaving his mouth.

Eliza finally gathers the wherewithal to alter her expression, now cultivating a splendid visual representation of the term 'agog'. After everything they've gone through. All the lies. That she should forget, forgive, just because he's a man of means. Does he think her so shallow?

She hisses, almost inaudibly, not wanting to give Havers the satisfaction of shutting her down.

'How dare you! How bloody dare you Jack, or Albert, or whatever you call yourself nowadays?' Annoyingly, she feels herself reddening. 'Do you think you can waltz in here, throwing your new-found wealth around, and expect me to fall at your feet? What the hell do you take me for? A whore? A harlot for sale to the highest bidder? To be bought with your undeserved shillings like the poor wretches I share this place with. Is that how little you think of me? Well? Is it?'

'Oh, God, no. Of course not, Eliza. Not at all. How can you say such things? I can't believe you'd think that of me.' Jack's body slumps, deflating like a stepped-upon balloon. 'The money means nothing. I can afford to get help for my mother, and set my sister free at last, but that's all. It'll have no bearing on my life and how I'll choose to live it. I just thought you'd...' He falters, acutely aware that whatever emerges from his mouth will simply inflame the situation.

She's too riled to see sense in his argument. A red mist descends, she fights to keep tears at bay. How dare he come here and insult her in this way. She's finding it hard to breathe. She glances at her hands, to her horror she spies a tremor, she whips them off the table, slipping them under the coarse fabric of her frock. She must get out of the room, away from Jack, away from the thought of Lena – *the traitor* – cosying up to him as if the past didn't matter one jot. She works hard to calm herself, concentrating on articulating a suitable parting riposte. She eventually meets his gaze.

'I'm sorry, Jack. Thank you for taking the time to visit. I appreciate the effort, but I've nothing more to say. Please leave now, and don't bother coming back, as I will not agree to see you again. You can take your riches, your cosy new friendship with Lena, and have yourself a thoroughly privileged life. Goodbye.' She scrapes the chair back, the sound reverberating harshly across the flagstones. She stands. Her legs feel as though they've been stripped of their

314

bones, the remaining flesh jellified and untrustworthy. She grasps the back of the chair to steady herself.

Jack follows her movements, his face a picture of despondency, but unsurprised.

'Lena cautioned me this would be your reaction. But I hoped that, after all this time, we could put the past behind us and move on. I still love you very much, Eliza, and want only to be with you, to make you happy. And now I've the means to do so.'

Silent, hot tears are streaking down her cheeks. She bristles at the thought of the two of them discussing her in such an intimate manner, it twists the knife a little further. She cannot answer him. If she tried, she would just blubber incoherently, and that would be unconscionable. She makes a tremendous effort to stand upright, shoulders back, chin pushed high. She releases the chair back, her focus blurs as she forms an image of his face so she can recall it late at night, when most in need of comfort.

He takes her continued silence as confirmation. He stares up at her, unblinking. His face dips. He takes a breath, steels himself. What he says next will fracture her heart into a million tiny pieces.

'As you wish, Eliza. I must respect your decision. I just needed to give it, give us, one last chance, to convince you I am a changed man. But Lena warned me it would be pointless.' He exhales wearily, careful how he forms his next sentence. He takes a deep, endless breath. 'So, the other reason I'm here today ... and it was, of course, utterly conditional on your response. But, as you've made your feelings crystal clear, then so be it.' Another deep breath.

'The other reason for my visit is ... to tell you Lena and I are to be wed.'

THIRTY-SIX

The Meeting

ELMFORD MANSIONS, THE SAME AFTERNOON

Lena, worry etching a permanent crease in her brow, paces endlessly back and forth, back and forth, sending up little puffs of dust from the rug each time she turns on her heel. Why, oh why, did she agree to it? It should have been her visiting today. After all, she'd missed so many opportunities recently, because of her cowardice, to explain the situation to Eliza. She was determined to tell all this time around, but as visiting day drew nearer, she became increasingly anxious, and her gutlessness, combined with an easy way out – in the shape of Jack offering to go in her place –eventually won the day. It was always such a bittersweet experience visiting that frightful building. In Lena's dreamscape it takes the form of Rapunzel's castle, with Eliza trapped within its circular battlements: a prisoner in the tallest tower, no windows except one, positioned below the parapet. Lena stands at its base, calling endlessly, to no avail. But finally, just as Lena gives up hope of seeing her, Eliza comes into view, framed by the small square window. The sight of her shatters Lena's slumber, and she snaps awake in a film of cold sweat. A final vision lives on in her waking moments as a haunting portrait of despair. It is of Eliza, shorn of her tumbling chestnut brown locks, her wan, skeletal face reflecting her desolation, her hopelessness at being so utterly trapped.

But, despite it all – the endless, tedious journey across London, the feelings of revulsion as she passes down the miserable corridors, reeking of carbolic and bleach – she lived for those precious minutes with Eliza in that purgatory of a visiting room. So, why... Why the hell had she agreed to Jack's suggestion?

This past year has been the loneliest she has endured in her entire life. The flat is so empty, so quiet – not to mention untidy, as the extent of Mrs Rumple's slap dash efforts have become plain – without her dearest friend by her side. And Mrs P. She has not been herself since the day of the riot. Moping about, her gammy little ear perking up whenever she senses movement, only to return to the same listless state when realising it isn't her beloved mistress back at last to scoop her up for a *cwtch*. Oh, how Lena misses that strange little word. It was Eliza's peculiar term for a hug, but represented more, so much more than that.

That foul man, a ruffian of the first order, goaded her gentle Eliza into lashing out. It was not her fault, not at all. She was provoked way beyond anyone's endurance. If only they had not gone on that damned march. Lena was not keen, she'd had her fill of protesting, of being spat at, eggs, and worse, thrown at them in meetings. And after all, it had done blessed little to get their dog memorial back. Ironically, for once it was Eliza who was doing the persuading; Lena only agreed to please her. She had a world of making up to do after that unfortunate encounter the day the statue was taken. Lena has still not forgiven herself for losing control in such a crude way. But there was no taking it back. Eliza now knew the extent of her feelings, feelings Lena herself was barely aware of. Or, more honestly, was unwilling to admit to. It left her mortified, with no clue of how to behave in her friend's presence. She had handled the situation appallingly. She understood that now. Treating Eliza with indifference, disdain even, in a vain attempt to show Eliza meant nothing to her – when, of course, the exact opposite was the truth. She had behaved so, so badly. Their friendship seemed mortally wounded, with faint hope of it surviving Lena's shameful abuse of Eliza's trust.

So it was that they ended up leading their local Suffragette division of the protest. Oh, why wasn't it her he picked on? It *should* have been her! She should have thrown herself at him, torn at his filthy, pock-marked face, but she did nothing. Nothing at all to help her dearest friend, her secret beloved.

In a split second, it was done. Lena couldn't believe her eyes. Her ever sensible friend, the one continually pulling *her* up for her impetuous behaviour, chastising *her* foolhardiness, had knocked out a hulking great brute. Competing with her horror was a secret pride, and yes, a stab of jealousy that *she* hadn't been brave enough to do the same.

This was not the Eliza she had met five years ago in that musty old hall. That timid slip of a girl kowtowing to officious battle-axes, fretting over a little perspiration. In front of her stood a warrior queen, a Boadicea as brave as the one immortalised in bronze who they had passed an hour earlier on the march through Victoria Embankment. At the time they had no idea of the wretched consequences of Eliza's transformation; however, now her dearest friend is rotting away in that pit of Hades, where they mistreat women like Eliza with such petty cruelties she cannot bear to imagine.

In the months following Eliza's absence, to distract herself from the loneliness of the flat, haunted by memories, echoes of joyous chatter and laughter, Lena began volunteering at the Anti-Viv. Over recent times, with all the trouble, the hospital had been on the receiving end of more than its fair share of disruption, vandalism even. It was never proven, but they all knew who was behind it. Feeling a sense of guilt over the attacks, Lena pledged to help. Discovering she swooned too easily at the sight of open wounds, blood even, her duties were confined to visiting patients, those with no one to keep them company, or who needed help with reading and writing. She found, somewhat to her surprise, she enjoyed her visits; they proved a welcome distraction from her own ongoing predicament – her papa's placid, unwavering insistence that she commit to marriage. That insistence intensified after Eliza's court case. This time he made it to court. Seems he's willing to when it's Eliza in trouble, Lena noted wryly. When Eliza was sentenced, he appeared almost as devastated as Lena and it only strengthened his desire to see his only child settled, or *controlled* as Lena saw it.

To Lena's horror, he hadn't given up on the idea of marrying her off to the tedious Mr Ponsonby. Her only hope was to find another candidate, a man she could bear to share a life, and home with. *And* a man willing to accept her true nature; a nature she was slowly coming to terms with. An impossible quest then, or so she'd imagined.

When she first spied Jack on the ward, absorbed in attending to an elderly patient, it was all she could do to stop herself marching up and slapping him full in the face. She was convinced it was Jack's face Eliza was seeing when she hit that ruffian. Lena would simply finish what her friend had started. But for once common sense prevailed. She had no desire to stoop to Jack's level, and instead, made do with a malevolent glare as she glided past.

If looks could indeed kill, Jack would have been in serious need of an intensive care bed that day. He turned a most marvellous shade of puce and dropped his stethoscope as she passed the end of the bed, snub nose in the air, chuffed she had given the bastard such a turn. She smirked as she continued along the ward, on the lookout for a suitably compliant patient to inflict Tolstoy upon.

Jack must have excused himself from his rounds, because she'd barely sat down when she sensed a heavy presence at her shoulder. She paused mid-sentence, set her shoulders back, and swivelled in her chair to discover him towering above her. She threw him her most withering glance, before turning and continuing to read, loudly and determinedly, to an old man laid flat on his back, half-asleep despite Lena's best efforts.

'Lena?' She ignored him. 'Lena. I know it's you. I'll not leave until you at least speak to me.' She didn't turn.

'I've nothing to say to you, Jack. Please leave me alone. You've done enough damage to last us a lifetime.' To her dismay, her voice acquired a tremulous tone.

The old gent was now wide awake, and sat up straighter in his bed, wide-eyed with befuddlement and curiosity at the intriguing scene unfolding in front of him.

'Please, Lena. Allow me a moment, just one, then I'll be gone. At least tell me how Eliza's coping in that wretched place and then I'll not bother you again, I promise.'

'I think we've had quite enough of your promises, Jack. They've proven worthless.' She wanted to sound cold, callous, but she could not help but be touched. He sounded so ... contrite. After all, he was working here, rather than at one of those torture chambers up in town. She sighed heavily. 'So be it, you may have a few minutes. But not now, I've a story to finish. Don't I, Mr Ridley?' She stared at the old man pointedly. Mr Ridley, slightly terrified by the forceful young lady who often read to him – whether or not he requested it – nodded in vigorous agreement. 'Meet me in Latchmere Park at five, and you may say your piece then. But don't go expecting any sympathy from me.'

And so, it began. They met later that day in the park. They sat on the same well-worn bench where Lena and Eliza had spent so many happy times, and stared into the void where the dog memorial once proudly stood.

There it all came tumbling out. He appeared relieved to confess, as if he hadn't had the opportunity before. How the deception started, how it grew and grew until he could no longer control it. How Bayling found out and was blackmailing him with the threat of expulsion and of telling Eliza the truth. To begin with Lena had very little sympathy, why should she? He deceived them both so badly. He broke her beloved's heart, although she could not deny she wasn't privately jubilant when he was finally out of the picture. But as he talked – and talk he did; the five minutes turned into fifty – she found herself beginning to soften. To her consternation, she began to see things from his point of view: the unenviable, compromised position he had placed himself in. She even understood how the lie would have developed, taken on a life of its own, become its own truth in a way. After all, hadn't she been just as deceitful, just as false in deceiving Eliza about her own true nature? Against her better judgement, she agreed to take tea with him the following week. And their unlikely friendship grew. She confided in him about her impossible situation, her impending 'death by marriage'. She suspected he had already guessed her *inclination*, and, surprisingly, she found it comforting, talking about Eliza with him, both of them so very much in love with her, both destined never to possess her.

She meant to tell Eliza about her meeting with Jack on her very next visit, she truly did. But when it came to it, sitting in that airless room, surrounded by soulless gaolers watching, listening to your every utterance, she found she simply could not form the words. Eliza seemed so broken-hearted still, not to mention bitter, that even Lena confessing to *speaking* with Jack would have been a betrayal in her eyes. So, the months rolled by, and each of their visits ended with Lena not quite confessing to her blossoming friendship with Eliza's former love.

Last spring, Jack had confided in Lena the news of his grandfather's will. Peculiarly, he didn't appear overjoyed at becoming a man of not inconsiderable means. His newfound position in society meant nothing to him without his Eliza at his side. Lena genuinely felt for him to an extent that surprised her, given she was well aware of her selfish trait. She recalled it was soon after this announcement that he first mentioned his idea, completely out of the blue.

Lena was lamenting, yet again, her father's growing impatience with her lack of any progress regarding marriage plans. 'He's saying my time's up, Jack. Papa gave me a twelvemonth to find a suitable alternative. Of course, there's isn't anyone, so now it looks like I'm rather stuck.' Her shoulders sagged as she picked away determinedly at a shard of wood that had come away from the bench strut. Her morose expression perfectly reflected her demeanour. She was resigned to her fate; she couldn't string her father along any longer. There wasn't ever going to be a palatable alternative to Mr Theodore Ponsonby, so Ponsonby it would have to be. Jack, troubled by the sorry sight of his typically resilient friend, was determined to cheer her up.

'I know, Lena. *We* could get wed. I'm a man of substance now. So, I guess I'll be in the market for a wife soon – isn't that what polite society dictates? And you're in desperate need of a husband – of some sort at least.' Her finger slipped on the wood, embedding a sliver under her skin – she yelped in surprise and pain. She shot him a startled look. The mischievous twinkle in his eye put her right. A wrinkle of a grin, the first that day, invaded her face.

'Oh, very droll, Doctor Forsyth. The very thought! What a marriage made in hell that would be.' The grin widened and then expanded into a raucous guffaw. Jack smiled back at her, pleased to have his new friend back on form. He took her hand in his and proceeded to extract the splinter as she chuckled away at the very thought.

For the next few months, they laughed it off as the absurd idea it was. But Jack's jesting got her thinking. Why the hell not? She'd wager a sovereign that half of society marriages in London were not a love match, nor hewn from mutual respect or desire. They were contracts, plain and simple, with both parties gaining from the deal. And so it could be for them. Jack was aware of Lena's proclivities and understood there'd be nothing physical between them – *heaven forfend*! They'd each be free to follow their own path – discreetly, of course. Papa would not tolerate any more scandal. But, otherwise, why not? It made total sense.

So, when they next met, she put it to him – came right out with it. Would you do me the dishonour of agreeing to become my husband, Jack? After Jack had recovered, and Lena had convinced him she was being entirely serious, he slowly came around to the idea. How they laughed at the absurdity, the unlikeliness of it. Of course, there was one unsettling aspect of this plan – an aspect Lena shied away from probing too deeply, not wanting to face the reality of what it could mean.

There was one condition. The very thing that Lena had been studiously avoiding. Jack wanted the opportunity to ask Eliza's forgiveness one last time, even though he held out little hope of a reconciliation. If Eliza relented, and would consider taking him back, then the deal was off. Of course, Lena agreed. For although her heart would surely break to see Eliza with another, it was the undoubtedly right thing to do. Thus, it was arranged. Jack would take Lena's place on the next visit to ask for her forgiveness one last time. Lena was to stay home, anxiously pounding the dusty Persian rug in her gloriously messy sitting room.

And so, it is done, Lena reflects. Eliza now knows of their arrangement. And according to Jack, she couldn't have taken the news any worse. Lena knew she should have spoken to Eliza herself, explained the situation; she'd have listened to her. Lena could have made her understand it was not at all how she perceives it. You simply cannot leave this type of delicate conversation to a man.

THIRTY-SEVEN

Acceptance

Jack and Lena to be married! Once more, Eliza's legs give way. Once more, the chair provides support. She could not have heard him right. She is aghast.

'Please, Eliza, I beg of you, don't be upset. It's not what you might imagine – *honestly*.'

She gapes, incredulity growing as she processes his words. If what he's just blithely announced goes ahead it would be the ultimate betrayal by the two people she loves, loved, most in the world. And he's surprised she's upset? The man has lost his mind.

'Not what I imagine?' She laughs mirthlessly, sits back down with a thump as she feels her knees buckle beneath her. 'Do go on. I'm all ears.'

'You know of Lena's father's insistence she secures a husband?'

Eliza nods.

'Well, the situation's come to a head, as Lena's done blessed little to find any chap she could bear to be in the same room with, let alone marry. She's stretched his patience to breaking point, and he's now dead set on a match with this Ponsonby fellow. Lena's beside herself. But with no other suitors, she hasn't many options.'

'But … why you? How do you come into this, for Christ's sake? You *do* know what Lena is?' Eliza croaks, feeling a flush of shame at even bringing the subject up.

'If you mean a sapphist, then yes. She confessed as much when she first broached the idea.'

Eliza's eyes grow as large as sovereigns. To come right out with it,

324

to say that ... that word. But then her attention is snagged by the second half of his sentence.

'Lena asked *you*?' she splutters. Reality is closing in on her. Nothing makes any sense anymore. It is as if she has fallen through Alice's rabbit hole. 'To marry *her*?' His face tells her all she needs to know.

'Truly there is nothing between us in *that* way, Eliza; you must believe that.'

She nods mutely. She *does* believe him on that point.

'It's just ... since I've come into my inheritance. I seem to have become respectable in society's eyes.' He snorts derisively. 'A man of substance, apparently. A man Lena's papa might potentially accept as a plausible alternative to Ponsonby. It started as a joke, honestly it did, but then I came around to seeing the sense in it. It would be a marriage in name only, but her father need not know that. It would be a means by which I could make it up to you both, for all the hurt I've caused.'

He attempts a weak smile, but it is obvious he is finding what he is saying as ludicrous as Eliza does. He pushes on, desperate to make her understand. 'When Lena suggested it, I made it clear. It could only be an option if you turned me down again, something that could only happen if there was no hope of us ever being reconciled. Naturally, Lena agreed to this: she would never stand in our way. That's why I'm here, instead of her. I had to give *us* one more chance.'

Eliza stares at him, stupefied. She appears to have lost the power of speech, of rational thought. This cannot be happening. His face betrays his disappointment; he looks down to his hands, his fingers tapping manically on the metal table. He glances up, willing her to say something, anything that might change the direction he was proposing his life would now take. But Eliza remains silent, her expression a dead end. Eventually, he sighs.

'You've made your feelings plain enough. And I understand and respect your decision. But you must know I regret my stupid lie more than anything ... anything in the world. And I will make amends for it for the rest of my life.' The corners of his lips turn up in the ghost of a smile, but his face remains a portrait of resignation and regret. 'So, I'll accept Lena's proposal. It's the next best outcome under the circumstances.'

Eliza remains glued to her chair, her limbs no longer under her control. She's haunted by the images she's conjuring. Lena and her Jack, playing at happy families. It's absurd.

'I can only hope, once you've had a chance to think, we'll get your blessing.'

That is the final straw. It jolts Eliza into her new reality. She feels her heart pounding to be let out of her chest, its last stand before dropping to the ground and smashing into a thousand pieces like a glass bauble. With every ounce of resolve she can muster she rises, this time with control and, she prays, a modicum of grace. No more emotion or hysterics, just a cool, dignified acceptance.

'You have my blessing, Jack. I hope Lena and you will be very happy together.'

She turns with a curt nod to her gaoler. Havers appears by her side in a trice, and she's escorted from the visiting room. The metal door clangs shut with a ferocious finality.

She has all the time in the world to absorb this unbelievable news. Back in her cell, the vision of the two of them, happy together, occupies her every waking hour. Even sleep cannot provide respite, for the vision's spiteful tentacles pervade her dreams too. Her mind is awhirl with unbidden, hateful images of the two of them: laughing at Mrs P's antics, walking arm-in-arm through Latchmere Park, sharing scones at her favourite table in Lyons' tea shop. It's taken a fair few weeks for her to absorb Jack's words, each one carving itself into her flesh: 'Lena and I are to be wed'.

How could they betray her in such an appalling way? The two – the only – people who have meant anything to her since moving to London have contrived to crush her. Break her heart so resolutely she doubts she will ever find the strength to piece it back together again.

Eliza cries a lifetime of tears in those weeks after his visit. Finally, the well runs dry, and her heart – or what is left of it – turns to granite, like the stony hardness of the statue's plinth. After months of torturing herself, the raw wound of betrayal begins to heal over, providing some protection from the pain, until irresistibly she is drawn back to it; she cannot help but pick at the metaphoric scab until visceral flesh is exposed and her torment returns, as unbearable as it was on that first day.

Lena attempts to visit Eliza the following month, and the months after that, but Eliza steadfastly refuses to move from her cell. She simply cannot face her betrayer. She cannot bear to listen to Lena's pitiful excuses – her shameful, selfish reasons for how this will be the *best for us all*. Eliza cannot trust herself to stay in control. She worries she will lash out, tear at Lena's face, her hair, clawing back some relief for the impotent rage still swirling inside her.

By early December, Eliza arrives at a sort of truce with herself. She realises she cannot sustain this level of rage, keep it stoked so high, indefinitely. It quite wears her out, leaving no space for other feelings. She worries the fury will absorb her until she becomes the sad, angry banshee everyone tries their best to avoid.

Her rational side is awakening and making itself heard above the rage, its calm reasoning pouring soothing balm over her wounds. After all, was it not she who had rejected Jack? Not once, but twice previously. He had come to ask, plead even, for a third, last chance, and she spurned him yet again. So, wasn't he free to pursue whomsoever he liked? But... Lena? Of all the women! She'd never, in a thousand years, have predicted his choice of wife. This is the maddening, crazy new reality she cannot quite bring herself to accept, not in her head or her heart. Lena all but demonstrated her shameful feelings towards her – her sapphic lust. She had always held men in such disregard – and Jack in particular – that the thought of Lena turning around and asking him, *him*, to marry her beggared belief.

When she hears Lena is here again, for a third month running, she relents. By now, her curiosity is getting the better of her and she is able to trust herself: Lena is no longer in any physical danger at her hand. She will remain calm. She will carry herself with dignity. She will treat her civilly, but with a coolness Lena cannot mistake for anything but utmost disdain for her appalling, selfish behaviour.

It is Havers who comes to collect her. She suspects the woman swaps with the other wardresses simply so she can bestow more petty indignities upon her. Havers cannot know what went on between her and Jack, but it was obvious it didn't end well, and she revels in making sly digs every chance she gets. Her beady eyes rake Eliza up and down. Her mouth twists into a smirk as she barks her orders.

'Thirty-seven, your visitor has arrived. Do try to make yourself presentable, woman. You don't want to scare another one off.'

Eliza pulls on her heavy, woollen overcoat – however much she airs it, she is unable to rid it of the must of damp cellars – to walk the bitterly cold journey to the visiting room. It has snowed overnight; the flakes flowing thick and fast, blanketing all with a sanitising coat of white, turning the complex temporarily into a fairy-tale castle.

After lights, Eliza had dragged the stool over to the window and watched entranced as the fattest flakes slowly drifted past the icy metal bars.

The last time it had snowed this heavily, Eliza had forced a grumpy Lena out of bed early, wrapped them both up warm as could be and had proceeded to slip-slide precariously all the way to the park, giggly as schoolgirls. There, they were confronted by the memorial, a four-foot drift partially covering the inscription, and the bronze dog glinting magnificently in the bright winter sunlight, highlighted by the snow that had settled into his folds. They joined in a vigorous snowball fight with local children before finally wending their way home, all rosy-cheeked and soaked through, frozen to the bone but brimming with a joy for life. Eliza made them rich, steaming mugs of hot chocolate and they dried off, toasting marshmallows in front of the fire.

She had only just torn herself away from the window when she heard the tell-tale clanking of the key-chain the wardresses wore around their waists. She couldn't be caught out of bed after curfew – that was a sin grievous enough to be paid for by a week of slopping out the entire wing's chamber pots. She drifted off to sleep easily that night, despite the bitter cold, her dreams full of happy memories – for once.

She has to traverse the exercise yard to reach the wing where the visitors' room is located. No inmates have been called for their daily trudge around the square yet, and the snow lies undisturbed, perfect and glistening white, as if shards of diamonds had been hidden amongst the flakes. The scene almost makes a walk around the bleak stone yard look inviting. Eliza deviates off the path and takes childish pleasure in stomping through the virgin snow, delighting in the sharp crunch underfoot and the perfect footprints she leaves in her wake. Havers scowls impatiently, her face disappearing behind a mist of frozen breath, yanks at Eliza's arm, hurrying her on.

Havers smiles malevolently as she positions Eliza at the same table as where the fateful meeting with Jack took place months earlier. This time she is not kept waiting and Lena is the first visitor to enter. Before Eliza has a chance to compose herself, Lena is there, standing in front of her, shuffling from foot to foot – with cold or nerves, Eliza could not tell – her face a picture of anxious concern as she studies Eliza.

'Hello. Eliza. It's so wonderful to see you. Thank you for agreeing to meet with me.' She sounds breathless, her body hunched over, slightly cowed. Sheepish is the word that comes to mind.

Eliza nods coolly and gestures for her to sit. Lena does what she is told without a word. A silence, as frosty as the room, lingers. Eliza holds her gaze, wanting the other woman to appreciate the pain and hurt she has caused. Lena cannot bear it, she looks away, guilt corroding her still pretty but – as Eliza registers with malicious pleasure – more careworn face. The icy air is creating a perceptible veil between them as they breathe out.

'So, how is Jack?' Eliza mutters sarcastically. 'Your fiancé now, I believe! If what I've heard is true.' She spits the words out with as much incredulity as she can muster. Lena's face crumbles.

'Oh, Eliza, please. You must believe me, us. This is purely an extremely kind favour. Jack's helping me out of a dreadful predicament, and ... well, I couldn't be more grateful to him. But that's as far as it goes. You, of all people, know where my true feelings lie.' Lena shrugs hopelessly. 'But as it turns out, neither of us can have you, so, I guess, we're making the best of things.' Lena reaches across and clasps Eliza's bone-chilled hand in her own. Havers harrumphs loudly and Eliza snatches it away as if a flame had licked it.

'I don't care to discuss that further, Lena,' Eliza fires back. 'You and Jack are free to carry on however you wish. So please, don't fret on my account. I couldn't care less, I made my feelings plain to Jack, months ago.' She is lying and they both know it. 'Anyway, how's Mrs P? It's she I'm interested in hearing about – not your sordid nuptials.'

Lena battles to disguise her dismay, manages a small smile at the thought of their cat. 'Oh, Mrs P's fine, but misses you dreadfully, of course. She settled in well. No need for butter on the paws or any such old wives' tales, which is a relief.' At this Eliza's forehead concertinas as crisply as a sheet emerging from a mangle.

'What do you mean ... settled in well? Where the hell is she?'

Lena gulps visibly, realising her mistake. 'Ahh, yes. Sorry, Eliza. I forgot you didn't know. I've had to... I mean, I've... Well, the thing is, I've given up the flat and moved back home. It seemed pointless

330

keeping it on, on my own. I was so lonely without you. And I would have to have moved out anyway, when we...' She hesitates, but Eliza's expression demands she continue. 'When we move into the home that Jack's bought... After the wedding, of course.'

'I. See,' Eliza says, her tone emotionless, but looking more dejected than Lena has ever seen her. 'Well, I'm glad she's doing well. I can imagine she's loving the countryside. The resident rodent population won't know what's hit them.' Despite herself, her mouth twitches upward at the thought.

Lena sees the hint of a smile and seizes upon it, greedy for any relief from this excruciating exchange. 'Oh yes, she's turned into a right little mouser. Cook's thrilled. "I swear Miss Evelina, my larder's never been so free of vermin, so it ain't".'

Eliza smiles weakly, Lena's impersonations were always spot on. Silence follows, neither sure what to say next. Eliza cuts it with another question that has been playing on her mind over the months.

'Is there word on the statue? Its whereabouts? Are we any closer to finding it?'

Lena grimaces, shakes her head, hesitating, not wanting to be the bearer of more unwelcome news. 'No, I'm afraid not. There's not been a single lead since... Well, you know when. There was a rumour it was thrown in the Thames, off Chelsea Bridge, but nothing was found.' She retrieves a handkerchief from her sleeve and twists it around her fingers. 'To be honest, the fight has all but gone out of the Defence Committee. It's been over two years now and still no sign, not a whisper. They're still protesting, but there hasn't been a proper march since the one on ... well, on Trafalgar Square.' She glances at Eliza. 'There are other causes people are getting stoked up about – you know all too well what the WSPU is up to, given half of them have ended up in here! Our statue's a fading memory, I'm afraid.' Eliza looks so forlorn that Lena's heart breaks. She cannot help herself, her hand twitches, reaches out, takes Eliza's in her own, then snatches it away as Eliza's eyes flash a warning. The women glance nervously at Havers, but she's distracted by some commotion at another table.

'Oh, I'm forgetting. There is one positive to come out of this.'

'Oh yes,' Eliza replies dully, but cannot keep the curiosity out of her tone. 'Do tell.'

'Well, due, and not in a small way, to all that's happened, the government has ordered a new commission. To look into standards in live experimentation.' Lena searches her eyes, delighted to see a flicker, a glint of her lost friend, the woman she'd loved so dearly – a lifetime ago. 'It was supposed to have released its findings by now, but it's been endlessly delayed.' Lena hesitates, unsure whether to mention, but what the hell. 'And Jack, oh Liza, he's done us proud. He volunteered to give evidence. And he was extraordinary! It was a different man up there in the witness stand; I've never seen him so passionate, so fervent. He laid into Bayling and his fellow butchers. Demolishing the pathetic excuses they regurgitate to justify their barbaric practices. His arguments were so compelling. And his evidence really mattered, given he'd studied under Bayling for four years. You'd have been so proud of him.'

Eliza sighs, the mention of his name all but extinguishing the fragile light that was flickering into life. 'But what difference will it make, Lena – truly? Will it have even a hope of stopping the likes of Bayling and his cronies?' She shrugs. 'There's already laws in place, have been for decades, but that didn't make a ha'pence of difference. What difference will a new set of unenforceable pronouncements make now?'

'Well, it can only help,' Lena retorts, a little more gruffly than intended. 'According to Mr Coleridge, the rumours are they'll announce a raft of recommendations that'll tighten up procedures and increase inspections of laboratories such as his. I guess it'll be impossible to completely eliminate it, but more stringent laws can only help, surely?' She sounds bullish but cannot stifle the hint of doubt in her tone.

'Oh well.' Eliza sighs. 'I guess it's something. If anything changes for the better, then these past four years, my being here, won't have been completely in vain.'

Lena reaches over, takes her hands in her own, wilfully ignoring the wardress's sharp throat-clearing.

'No, Liza, of course it hasn't. We did everything we could, and it *did* make a difference. We showed people what was going on, mobilised thousands to take to the streets. We, *you*, fundraised the memorial and we bloody well got it built. *And* put the wind up those torturing bastards. Us, mere women for Chrissakes, against the entire establishment. We should be proud, Liza, we really should. And you'll be out of here soon, the next six months will fly by, and then we can start again, put all of this behind us.' Lena, breathless in her enthusiasm, pauses. As she looks up, Eliza is shaking her head; her look says it all. In that moment, any scrap of hope Lena had left, dies.

Eliza lets her hands linger in Lena's for a moment longer, secretly delighted, yet pained, by her touch. She then delicately extracts them and wraps them around her body. Her eyes focus on a chink of missing paint on the tabletop, resembling a heart. She picks at it.

'When I get out, I'll be moving away. I don't want to set eyes on you, or Jack, ever again. I'll make a fresh start, somewhere far from here. Somewhere no one knows me or what I've done. I hope you both will respect my wishes.' Eliza allows her gaze to drift up, Lena's expression almost melts her resolve. She's heartbroken, that she can tell, but this gives Eliza a small, vindictive spark of pleasure knowing Lena now has some inkling, some understanding of how wretched she has felt these past months. Lena nods slowly, a solitary tear escaping. She dashes it away.

'I understand. And, of course, Jack and I will respect your wishes, if that's what you really want. But Eliza, I beg of you, if you do change your mind, if you can find some way to forgive us, then please, please let me know. You're part of my family. That will never change, and we'd welcome you back with open arms. There'll always be a place for you in our home.'

Eliza feels herself cracking; she is in danger of losing control of the well of tears that sit just behind her eyes. She has to get away before she gives in.

'Thank you for the offer, Lena. But I very much doubt I'll take you up on it. Now, if you'll excuse me, mine is a very busy schedule in here, as you can imagine. And I need to get back.' She hears the self-pity in her voice and despises herself for it.

Eliza rises slowly from her chair, pushes it back neatly under the table. She looks at her dearest friend for the last time. 'Goodbye, Lena.' She turns away, then thinks better of it, her venom dissipating and the need to part amicably rising in her soul. 'The time we spent together will always have a special place in my heart. But we all move on, change, and we're not the same people we were back at the Tooting Ladies' meeting. We can never regain that time, that innocence, it's gone forever, just like our statue. But please know I did love you. You were the sister I'd always dreamt of having, and I'll not regret a single moment.'

With that she turns, waits for Havers to dart across and glue herself to her side. They march, perfectly in step, out of the room, as solemn as a funeral cortège.

THIRTY-EIGHT

The Yard

A chilled, bright winter's afternoon is retiring into a sharp, frosty dusk. Two sturdy men, no strangers to manual labour, stomp through a deserted blacksmith's yard, foggy breath announcing their arrival. The place has a neglected feel about it, having been abandoned for many a year. Littering the place are decaying wooden skeletons of old broughams, less in demand since the rise of the motorised engine and electric tram, rusting bicycle frames, iron scrap and other discarded junk. It has the look of a forgotten cemetery for inorganic corpses.

The workers make straight for a large brick-built building – the old forge. Given the desolate look of the place, it is disconcerting to see dense smoke pouring from its chimney. As the smoke rises, it blends with the misty, bone-chilled air. One of the workmen blows into his hands to get movement in his frozen fingers before delving into his greatcoat pocket to retrieve a set of keys. His companion sparks up a conversation, something is weighing his conscience.

'I'll tell you summing, Jonny, I'll be relieved when this job's done, an' that's for sure. Ain't liked it one bit, it's like we're traitors to our own kind, with all that's gone on up in Battersea these past years. I can't tell the wife what we're up to down 'ere, I'm that shamed. She's been on 'em marches, you know, demanding they return it. She'd 'ave my guts for her garters if she knew what I was up to. It's a rum ol' situation and no mistake.'

John O'Connor rolls his eyes, tuts impatiently. 'Ah, will you be cutting the griping there, Michael? They're paying us well, are they not? Triple time and a whack extra to keep shtum. More than I make in a month normal times, so I ain't grumbling, and neither should you.' He throws Mick a look that shuts him up. John does not want to hear any more. Deep down his conscience is pricking at him too, but it would not do to admit to it.

They arrive at the forge's door and John sighs as he starts on the inordinate collection of new, shiny locks that keep it fortified – the clanking of keys the only sound. There is no doubt it is safe from prying eyes or opportunist thieves, even though there's nothing here worth nicking. He is on strict instruction to keep it secure, even when they pop out for a quick tea break. He cracks open the last padlock and pushes open the creaking door. There is no lighting, only an amber glow emanating from the far end, so it takes their eyes a while to adjust to the darkness. The cavernous space is empty except for a stacked pile, at least four feet in height, of smashed-up rock and stone. A closer view reveals it to be a pile of granite – large chunks with smoothed, rounded surfaces. An even closer view exposes a water fountain bowl, intact, placed at the pinnacle of this pyramidal shape. The mound resembles a stone Christmas tree, with the bowl taking the place of the fairy.

Leant against the wall is a mess of metal oddments – a tap, metal strips, copper piping – and, propped up and still in one piece, a battered inscription plate.

At the far side, in an open forge, there is a substantial fire burning: the source of the eerie light that gives the whole place its flickering, shadowy feel. A large vat sits above it, held in place with a metal support structure. The men stride the length of the room to reach it. The heat forces them back a few steps – it has taken many an hour to reach this temperature. They peer into its interior, both on tiptoes. A bubbling, swirling golden lava of liquid metal confronts them. The men appear like witches, casting their evil spells around a frothing, steaming cauldron. In the centre of the molten metal, sinking fast, is the soulful, placid face of the little bronze dog.

The men stare silently, their faces impassive in the amber radiance, both feeling wretched at the thought of what they are doing, what they are destroying. They've a pact that neither will speak of this again. The mournful bronze eyes stare back at them with a reproachful gaze that will haunt them for the longest time – much longer than it will take to spend the money they earn from this grubby little job. They reel backwards as the heat becomes too much to bear. The next time they peer in, only the top of the head is visible. Gradually it too disappears, absorbed by the molten surface, no trace left. Jeff is the first to speak, in a melancholic tone that betrays him.

'Well, Mick. I guess that's about the end of that.'

THIRTY-NINE

Release

Christmas does not really register in Holloway. Eliza hardly notices the holy day pass. It has the same grinding monotony to it as every other day. The only concession is a portion of Brussels sprouts, boiled to a grey-green mush, and carrots. At least, Eliza assumes they are carrots; they appear remarkably devoid of any colour, not to mention taste. These were added to the typical fare of grey-brown slabs of meat and boiled-dry, desiccated potatoes, and what purported to be gravy: a liquid of dishwater consistency, stained with browning. She eats it all without complaint, suppressing her gag reflex, in the vain hope it might just be followed by that rarest of treats – pudding and plum sauce. Of course, it is not to be, and Eliza must make do with the imagining of such delights. She closes her eyes, lays back and can almost taste the gooey, treacle-like richness of the rum-soaked sultanas and glace cherries – *almost*.

The Governor, brimming with uncharacteristic Christmas spirit – of the liquid variety, the wardresses gossip – had granted the inmates a carol service on Christmas Eve, this being remarkable as the only occasion where all inmates have been present together in the same open space. By now, dozens of Suffragettes are incarcerated with Eliza in east wing: a weekly conveyor belt of women gliding past the griffins' unflinching stare and outstretched talons. Well, the working-class women at least, as by now the authorities have bowed to pressure and are allowing well-connected *ladies* first division status. Eliza draws much comfort from their close physical presence and the soaring harmonies they create on the passageways

338

and stairs of the east wing – its long, thin, high aspect providing unexpectedly good acoustics. The carol service is jolly enough and raises the women's spirits somewhat, but it is over all too soon and the wardresses, seemingly untouched by the season of goodwill, are roughly hustling them back into their solitary, freezing cells before they know it.

The singing continues unabated, notwithstanding the muffling qualities of solid oak cell doors. Eliza leads the way with a defiant change of tempo and spirit, moving from festive tunes to evoking songs of the suffrage movement. She can't resist a cheekily subversive rendition of 'Onward Christian Soldiers', inserting the lyrics of the 'Women's Battle Song', so pertinent, despite the bittersweet memories it evokes, this being the tune they were singing when she and Lena encountered the mob that day.

> *Forward sister women!*
> *Onward ever more,*
> *Bondage is behind you,*
> *Freedom is before,*
> *Raise the standard boldly,*
> *In the morning sun;*
> *'Gainst a great injustice,*
> *See the fight begun!*

> *Forward, forward sisters!*
> *Onward ever more!*
> *Bondage is behind you,*
> *Freedom is before.*

The wardresses, begrudgingly tolerant of the continued singing until then, suddenly shut it down. The implied insurrection in the words is simply too much to bear, even though a good number catch themselves humming along under their breath.

Eliza hears the cover of her peephole sliding across. She glances at the sudden stab of light penetrating the solidity of the oak door and then darkness again as the beady black eye of Havers glares at her.

'I know it's you, thirty-seven,' she hisses. 'Stop this racket right now, or I'll make sure you won't see another living soul until Easter.'

'Yes, Miss Havers. Of course, Miss Havers. Apologies, Miss Havers.' Eliza does what she's told, her sickly-sweet smile of condescension infuriating Havers and dissolving any remaining Christmas spirit. But to Havers' disgust she could not discipline her further, as Eliza remained as silent as the grave, and meekly obedient, for the rest of Christmas.

Since her meeting with Lena earlier in December, Eliza has done a lot of thinking – calm, rational thinking – for the first time in an age. Truth be told, she had not decided on what she would do upon release until the very moment she revealed to Lena she wouldn't be seeing her, or Jack, ever again. But once the words had formed themselves – straight from her subconscious without passing her brain – and hung heavily in the frozen ether between them, she came to the stone-cold realisation it was her best, *her only*, option. After all, what else could she do? Her best friend and her former beau had gone behind her back and betrayed her in the cruellest way possible. She almost accepted that theirs would be a union based on convenience – mostly Lena's of course, everything was for Lena's convenience – but even so, surely Lena could have found another willing party to help deceive her father. Why in God's name did it have to be Jack? It was almost as though Lena had done it to punish her, for rejecting her advances that time.

Her pride took over from that point on. It was unconscionable that she could have anything more to do with either of them. If she did, she would look such a fool, a *cuckold*, wasn't that the term? And there was no way she'd allow that. She, Elizabeth Siân Blackwood, was better than that, stronger than that. And over the coming months she consoles herself with imagining her new beginning, away from all the hurt and betrayal, away from the painful memories of that wretched little brown dog. She has a bright future ahead of her, she knows that, but it is up to her, and only her, to make it happen.

Just as winter reluctantly releases its grip on the frozen earth and morphs into early spring, Eliza allows herself to thaw out long-buried thoughts of her forthcoming release. The powers-that-be decreed this to be the second half of June, as long as she didn't spoil her unblemished record of exemplary behaviour in the meantime. Eliza smirks. How little they knew of what she'd got up to. She is dead set on moving back to Glamorgan, where she was born and spent her entire life, without so much as leaving the county, until, aged twenty-four, she took herself off to London with the lofty ambition to better herself. And look how well that worked out. She chuckles mirthlessly to herself.

Now the Battersea flat is no more, Eliza ponders how to get her belongings back, concluding she'll worry about that when the time comes and if she cannot retrieve them, then so be it. After all, she'd arrived in London with very little, and survived well enough, so she'll be able to do so again. And besides, the years she lived with Lena – rent free and clothed in her cast-offs – had furnished her with a tidy sum she had the foresight to squirrel away for a rainy day. I'll cope jolly well thank you very much, Miss Evelina Hageby!

June arrives, and with it comes hot, sultry weather. Eliza swears time has applied its brakes, the nearer it creeps to her release date. The days before she is to be set into the world again seem never-ending, her cell stifling and now suddenly unbearably claustrophobic. Her impatience threatens to explode, she simply cannot bear the wardresses barking orders at her, the petty indignities they bestow upon her. She has to watch herself; her temper, a rare thing in her former life, constantly hovers just below the surface. She does not want to give Havers the pleasure of hauling her up on a trifling misdemeanour or the Governor grounds to increase her term. Even a day or two longer would be unconscionable now her heart is set on freedom.

SUNDAY, 21st JUNE, 1908

The day of her release finally dawns and Eliza awakes to hot sparks of excitement clashing head-on with an icy dread. After two years, it's inevitable she has become institutionalised to a degree. The very idea of untethered freedom is simultaneously exhilarating and terrifying. She snatches the pile of clothes Havers hands her, discarding her prison garb, subtly tearing it when Havers isn't looking, so the next unfortunate through the gates will not have to endure the indignity of wearing another's soiled undergarments. *Good bloody riddance.* She dresses quickly, eager to be reunited with the clothes she arrived in. To her horror, they hang loosely about her frame, faded and shapeless. It is the first time she has had cause to notice such changes, the horrific realisation of what effect prison life has had on her body. Nevertheless, it's comforting to see them, feel their touch against her skin, even if the fustiness from two years festering in damp storage, coupled with moth damage, has rendered them unsuitable for polite society. Hello, old friends. Prison life has taken its toll on you too, huh?

She tidies her cell for the last time – old habits and all that. She carefully folds the rough, scratchy blanket, placing her brown-stained, flaccid pillow on top. Perversely, she feels a sense of regret to be leaving the pillow behind. It was the unflinching, patient recipient of countless futile tears over the last nine months and has almost come to feel a part of her.

Havers – *who else?* – is to escort her out. Much to Eliza's astonishment, instead of her usual jibes, her gaoler attempts to engage her in a civilised conversation.

'You know what day it is today, thirty-seven?'

Eliza, her mind elsewhere, shakes her head mutely.

342

'Well, it seems today's the day *your lot* will be out in force.' Havers' disapproval seeps from her words. Eliza, curiosity piqued, shoots her a quizzical glance. She's far too slow on the uptake for Havers, who adds, huffily.

'Apparently, thousands of *ladies* with nuffing better to do are marching to Parliament Square this afternoon. What good it'll do 'em, mind you, is debatable. What's not debatable is there'll be another bumper bloody intake of over-petticoated, moaning madams come the morn, you mark my words!' Havers fixes Eliza with a loaded stare.

Despite the veiled warning, a twinkle sparks in Eliza's eye. She had heard the rumours, of course. But had no idea that it was to be today, *her* release day. It feels like fate. She is sorely tempted to join them. Why not? She's nothing else to do. But memories of the outcome of the last protest come flooding back and quickly engulf such foolish thoughts. Oh no you don't, Eliza Blackwood! Your marching days are well and truly over!

As she approaches the front desk, a male guard proffers the release register, and fountain pen. As she signs her name, she feels the corners of her lips rise – this is it, this is finally it, *freedom*. By the time she looks up and hands the pen back to the lad – heavens, he cannot be more than nineteen – she is grinning widely. It must be infectious as he returns the grin, his smile as genuine as any she'd encountered in two years. A second, surlier guard arrives and places a battered wicker basket on the counter. The young guard checks the label matches her name, 'Elizabeth Blackwood.'

"Ere you go, Miss Blackwood. Now mind 'ow you do out there, Miss. We don't want to see your face back yer in a hurry, no matter 'ow pretty it may be.' He winks at her. Eliza blushes, but senses Havers at her shoulder, tutting loudly.

It is the first time she has been addressed by her full name in two years, and it sounds weirdly formal to hear it spoken out loud. She peers into the basket, not knowing quite what to expect.

Recognition jolts her. It contains the few belongings she entered Holloway with: a hat; her tapestry bag containing a comb; a lace handkerchief; several leaflets decrying the statue's disappearance; her purse with its meagre coinage and the crumbly remains of what she deduces was once a Garibaldi: oh, what she would have given for such a treat! Eliza thanks the guards – the only men, apart from Jack, she has conversed with during her time inside. The smiley young guard attends to the ritual of unbolting the wicker gate. He pulls it towards himself and stands aside, twitches his cap at her in lieu of an instruction to pass through. She turns back one last time, catching Havers' eye. There has been an imperceptible thawing between these two adversaries over recent weeks and Eliza feels a perverse twinge of sadness to think this will be the last time she'll see the cantankerous old witch – well, she certainly hopes it will be. To Eliza's surprise, Havers speaks; it's in her usual curt, clipped tone, but Eliza detects a softening.

'So, Elizabeth. This is goodbye. I hope you'll not think too unkindly of me. I was only doing my job after all's said. And don't think I didn't cotton on to some of your more obvious indiscretions, young lady!' With that, and Eliza isn't entirely sure she didn't imagine it, Havers winks at her.

'Goodbye, Miss Havers.' Eliza stares at her, caught unawares by the sound of her own name on her gaoler's lips. 'Please don't take this the wrong way, but I hope we never have cause to encounter each other again.' With that she smiles, not unkindly, at her tormentor, and turns her back on 'Holloway Castle' for the very last time.

Eliza bends to fit through the mean wooden door. She clambers out. Not the most dignified exit, Eliza! As she straightens, her hand raises in salute to shield her eyes from the glare of the sun. It momentarily blinds her. So fierce already, and it's only just gone ten. It takes a minute to open her eyes fully. She drops her bag, stretches out her arms and takes a deep gulp of air, sighing it out with a deep, earthy sense of relief. Freedom at last. It is only then she takes in her surroundings. They have emptied her out into a side road, rather than through the portentous front entrance she arrived at. She's saddened she will not see the griffins again. The street sign displays Dalmeny Ave. It is narrow, pot-holed and faces onto the back gardens of a row of two-up, two-down workers' cottages. She stands, staring up at the bedroom windows. They appear strangely familiar. She takes a moment to recall why as she lights the cigarette that a fellow inmate, with a wink and a conspiratorial tap of the nose, slipped into her pocket as she left D Block for the very last time

She had been on duty in the library, late last autumn it must have been, when she heard an almighty racket coming from behind the boundary wall. She rushed over to the window and, to her amazement, spied a gaggle of women hanging precariously from the bedroom windows of the cottages beyond, waving suffrage flags and banners. Eliza, from her vantage point on the fourth floor, watched mesmerised, as the ladies sang and shouted encouragement to the latest batch of Suffragettes, of which sixty had been incarcerated that very day. This went on for a good few hours before they were shut down by the authority. The women had commandeered the bedrooms of sympathetic residents for the afternoon and had to be dragged out, kicking and screaming. The scene lifted Eliza's mood no end, and she regaled her fellow inmates with the story for weeks after.

She finishes her cigarette – resolving to give up her habit now she's out – and turns to her left. The lane appears to culminate in a dead end, with no obvious way through. That settles it. Her only option is to the right, which appears to lead onto a junction, around fifty yards away. She's sure to find an omnibus request stop on a main road. That will take her into central London at least. Then, who knows?

In the middle distance, framed against a fine-looking motor vehicle, she spots two figures getting out of the car, silhouetted against the stark morning sun. As Eliza approaches, and her eyes adjust, she makes out a man and a woman. The woman is wearing a white frock with a bright sash that catches Eliza's eye. It is striped white and green – colours she's familiar with from suffrage campaigns – but, intriguingly, it's also shot through with a bold flash of purple. She shifts her focus from the sash upwards. The woman's face is obscured by the shadow of her wide-brimmed hat. But the gent, sporting a fashionable peaked driving cap, slowly turns and his profile comes into sharp relief. Eliza halts and cries out in shock. Her exclamation triggers a ricochet of high-pitched yelps, and only then does she notice the man is cradling something. She squints. It's a puppy, a Jack Russell, couldn't be more than a few months old. The man places the squirming dog on the ground. He's a coarse scruff-ball of black and tan, with absurdly large ears and a purple bow tied to his collar. The pup growls at Eliza, almost taking off with each bark, displaying much bravado for such a tiny thing. 'Ernie, please. Stop that racket,' Lena scolds. 'Eliza is our friend.' The dog, suitably chastened, takes cover behind Jack's feet, staring out at Eliza with mistrust apparent in his liquid black eyes. Eliza smiles wanly. I know the feeling, little one.

Lena and Jack wave tentatively. She can sense they are wary of her reaction. And rightly so. She looks from one to the other. Lena's cornflower blue eyes flash with a passion she once knew and loved so well, in what feels like a lifetime ago now. And Jack – her handsome, sensitive, traitorous Jack – stands perfectly still, as still as their lost statue, observing her. To Eliza's astonishment, she feels only a controlled calmness, a sense of serenity where anger once resided. And, although loath to admit it, a secret gratitude that they made the effort. But what are they... Why *are* they here? An image flits unbidden across her mind's eye. The audacity quite takes her breath away. Is it possible... Could they, the *three* of them, create a life together? Ignore convention and somehow make it work? Heavens, whatever is she thinking? She flushes crimson, reeling at the imagined obscenity. The idea is preposterous, Eliza exorcises it from her mind. She stands rooted to the spot, with a sudden, crippling, crisis of confidence as to what to do next. Instinctively, she turns back, but the prison door has long been shut and bolted. There's nothing else for it, the only way is forward. She takes a deep breath, holds her head high and fixes her gaze on her erstwhile friends. She conjures up a broad, self-assured smile and marches defiantly towards them.

POSTSCRIPT

Battersea Park

THE PUMP HOUSE, 1985

It is a blustery, arctic-chilled winter's day in December. Battersea Park has been stripped of that vibrant, autumnal colour palette that makes it such a visual delight. Now it's only devoted dog walkers, dressed in thick layers, wellington boots, stripy scarves and woolly bobble hats who visit, occasionally overtaken by the hardened jogger in Dayglo Lycra.

But today is unusual. Today a large crowd has gathered, so muffled up against the penetrating chill it takes on the look of a Michelin Man convention. People have congregated around the back of the park's ramshackle Pump House and are joined by many dogs, off their leads, racing around, oblivious to the cold, chasing each other and their own tails.

The Pump House was built in 1861. Battersea Park itself was created a decade earlier from derelict ground and reclaimed marshland from the Thames. The thirty-foot-high tower housed a coal-fired steam engine to drive circulation and to power the artificial rock water cascades of the lake. It also irrigated the park's many exotic plants. The years after the Second World War, during which the park was given over to allotments, saw the park woefully neglected. A fire, in the 1950s, destroyed the roof and many windows of the Pump House, which only added to the general sense of decline. It was now in a dismal state of disrepair, with nature recolonising its brickwork and open-air interiors. Its appearance earned it a reputation for spooky creepiness, the locals nicknamed it 'The Haunted House'.

At the centre of this frozen tableau stands a familiar figure: English actress Geraldine James, a household name thanks to her role in the popular TV drama *The Jewel in the Crown*. She is addressing the assembled crowd. To her left, a shroud covers something tall and oblong-shaped.

'Ladies and gentlemen, on behalf of the Anti-Vivisection Society, the British Union for the Abolition for Vivisection, and almost seventy-five years since the original statue was torn from the heart of this community, it's my great honour and privilege to be here to unveil this new memorial to our dearest little brown dog. Long may he watch over this park and all the dogs, and the dog-loving humans, who visit it.'

She pulls on the cord and the shroud, with a little encouragement, falls from the object, revealing a second incarnation of the dog memorial. This version is a five-foot-high Portland stone pedestal. It is a simple rectangular shape, with minimal carved adornments, and four slate inscription plates set into the stone. Sitting on the pedestal is a bronze sculpture of a dog.

The new dog has a very different pose to the original. Instead of the upright posture and a proud, distant gaze, this terrier appears to be cowering, ears down. Most unsettling is his subservient gaze upwards at his master. Or is it his torturer?

An enthusiastic shout of applause slices the frigid air. Other speeches are politely listened to, with much stamping of feet and blowing into hands to ward off the icy wind. Formalities over with, everyone gratefully moves off into a warmer environment where they toast the new memorial, the little brown dog and each other.

THE PUMP HOUSE, 1992

The statue, with a selection of dried posies laid at its base, stands glinting in weak winter sun. The bronze dog has witnessed a renaissance in the Pump House over the intervening years. No longer a derelict building with weeds growing through the walls, it has been restored to its former glory. The roof has been replaced, windows refitted, and there is a buzz about the place. It is now a popular centre for education and exhibitions. Those who pay a visit cannot help but notice the statue of the dog and wonder at its provenance, its painful history explained in the inscription plates. All the while the dog watches over the scene with his cowered, distrusting expression.

It is a quiet afternoon as the Pump House is shut on Mondays. A diesel engine can be heard in the distance. It gets steadily louder. A Wandsworth council liveried work van pulls into view. It makes a handbrake stop, skidding on the gravel.

Two workmen pile out of the front compartment and two more jump from the open-top trailer. They grab a ladder, shovels and rope and dump them near the statue. They get to work. They remove the bronze from its plinth and lower it, with much effort, onto the lorry. Then they turn their attention to the pedestal. This needs a hoist, it's decided. They reverse the van up to the statue, as close as they dare, affix the ropes and tackle, and hoist it, with much huffing and cussing, onto the trailer. Once secured, they squeeze into the front cab. They pull off, but quickly crunch to a halt. The foreman jumps out, reaches into the back and pulls out a board attached to a wooden stake. Then he returns to the freshly exposed patch of ground, and drives the stake into the earth with as much force as he can muster. Once satisfied it isn't going anywhere, he jumps back in the cab and they drive away.

A pack of professional dog walkers watch this unfold from a distance, their unease increasing. As the van turns out of sight, they stride toward the Pump House, a canine army of various sizes and shapes in tow. They read the board. It makes little sense.

Removed as part of Park Renovations
By the order of Wandsworth Council

The walkers look around at each other, faces frowning in puzzlement. Why would they need to remove the statue now? The Pump House was renovated years ago. Then it would have made sense to remove it to prevent damage – not now. They collectively resolve to 'get to the bottom of it' before dispersing into the frosty morning.

The van draws up outside a vast warehouse, a council storage facility. The workers sigh inwardly as they contemplate the task. They unload the dog and the plinth onto a reinforced trolley and wheel the entire ensemble to the warehouse entrance. The foreman cracks open the bi-fold doors and the team enters. The workers look around, awed at the dimensions of the vast echoey hangar-type space, packed with boxes, wooden crates, objects draped with tarp, defunct machinery. It is a view, one remarks, reminiscent of the closing scene in *Raiders of the Lost Ark*.

They find a spot that will fit the statue's dimensions and get to work unloading it. They place the dog back in his rightful place, on the top of the plinth, and cover it with a dust sheet. Job done. The workers walk towards the light, the sun low enough in the sky to dazzle them. The foreman waits impatiently at the concertinaed doors, ready to count the men out and secure it. The last of the men turns on his heel. Hidden by the deep shadows within, he creeps back to the shrouded object, and lifts up the sheet. He looks into the pleading eyes of the little brown dog one last time. He gives his nose a rub, leans towards a bronze ear, and whispers 'Sweet dreams, old boy'.

Author's Note

This novel exists solely because of a chance encounter at Battersea Arts Centre. It was a Saturday, 15th September, 2018 – a date that would later resonate. The event I stumbled across was part of a series of celebrations marking the Centre's re-opening after the awful 2015 fire that all but gutted its Grand Hall. Ian Mursell was one of two speakers retelling stories of the building's early twentieth century social history, when it served as Battersea's Municipal Town Hall. He had been researching the building's archives and unearthed a curious entry. It was a record of three public meetings, all held within one week, hosted in the Grand Hall. Residents packed out each event and the meetings addressed the same single issue, a row about a local statue – a memorial to a nameless, stray dog.

Ian's curiosity was piqued, and that drove him to investigate further. In doing so, he rediscovered an extraordinary series of events that made up the 'Brown Dog Affair'. This was the story he told us that day.

He ended with an apology. He hadn't been at all sure whether to tell this tale, whether it would be of any interest to us, but the peculiar little story had got under his skin and he couldn't shake it off. Well, that peculiar little story got under my skin too, and continued burrowing until it reached my heart. I couldn't shake it off either. In fact, it became an obsession. My first idea was to recreate the original memorial, with the terrier looking tall and proud, rather than cowed and fearful, and return it to where it belongs: Latchmere Recreational Ground.

Then a second idea struck. This incredible story has been all but forgotten in the century that has passed, except for an excellent recounting of events by author Peter Mason. And that is not right. I determined the world needed to hear this story, its central theme as relevant today as it was then – even more so, one may argue. This fictional retelling started its life as a screenplay, and I still have ambitions for a feature-length film, but in the short-term getting a novel published was a more likely prospect.

This isn't simply the tragic tale of one stray dog, appallingly treated and abused in a less enlightened age. Nor is the hysteria, violence and bewildering behaviour directed at a lump of stone and metal – so feared by the authorities it drove them to steal and destroy it – the main focus of the novel. It's more complicated than that. The whole sorry episode is an echo, a mirror, reflecting the endless injustices and evil carried out by humans on other species throughout history.

We are currently staring over a precipice, on the brink of a biodiversity crisis. A sixth extinction, in this, supposedly civilised, 21st century. We have lost half of the planet's known species in the last forty years, whilst almost doubling our human population. It might be inconvenient to state, but there is likely to be a direct correlation between these two trends. As Lena points out, 'Our humanity is defined by how we treat, respect and nurture other species, not just our own kind.' Can we say, hand on heart, we are any more 'humane' today than we were one hundred years ago? Indeed, an estimate of the number of vivisections, carried out in the UK alone, on various sentient species, was reported to top 300,000 in 2014, over 20,000 of them on dogs. This is in a time where humane alternatives to animal experimentation exist and are proven to be effective.

So here we are. Although this novel is a fictional reworking, I've based the backbone of the story on the actual events that took place across London between 1903–1910. The vivisection of the dog, the ensuing legal fight and protests, and the fate of his memorial are described broadly as they happened. I've remained faithful to the fact that there were two female protagonists and one main male antagonist. However, I have fictionalised all three, to one degree or another, for dramatic purposes. The idea of Lena volunteering at the Dogs Home is also a fictional construct, for two reasons. The first is that Battersea did not have volunteers at that time, and the second is that, even if they did, they would not have been women, as it was 1960 before women started working at the kennels. I've also contracted the timescale, again for the needs of the fictional narrative.

Here are the facts. There were two women who sat in on a live vivisection demonstration at University College London. They claimed to witness acts of appalling cruelty on a brown terrier dog. They were, in actual fact, Swedish, upper-class, educated, strident feminists, early Suffragettes and passionate animal rights activists. I salute their bravery, their compassion, their tenacity to do what they believed was right. Leisa Schartau and Louise Lind af Hageby have become two of my most admired heroines.

Dr (later Professor Sir) William Bayliss was a celebrated, successful medical academic with several important scientific breakthroughs under his belt at the time of the incident. He performed the disputedly illegal vivisection demonstration alongside another academic, a Dr Starling, who was not only a colleague, but also Bayliss's brother-in-law. They were not the only medical professionals to perform such brutal live demonstrations: the practice was apparently widespread. But it was Bayliss alone – Starling refused to be part of it – who brought the libel case (it ended up as a libel case rather than slander as Coleridge's words were published by the press) against Stephen Coleridge: barrister, director of the National Anti-Vivisection Society, and descendant of Romantic poet, Samuel Taylor Coleridge. The case was heard at the Royal Courts of Justice by Judge Alverstone. Coleridge lost the case and was fined the sum of £2000, equivalent to over £200,000 in today's money.

The first memorial was the brain-child of a third woman, Anne Louisa Woodward, founder of the World League against

Vivisection. She raised the money through voluntary public donations – an early example of crowd-funding. They unveiled the statue in Latchmere Recreational Ground. Battersea Council, led by Liberals, welcomed it and what it represented as, at the time, Battersea was a vibrant melting pot of radicals, activists, and animal rights protestors. It also housed the capital's first anti-vivisection hospital, the Anti-Viv, up on Prince of Wales Drive, near Battersea Dogs Home. The Home was founded by yet another remarkable woman, Mary Tealby, in 1860, and was originally based in Holloway, where it was known as the *Temporary Home for Lost and Starving Dogs'*, before it was moved to Battersea.

Over the next four years, the statue became much more than a symbol against vivisection. It became an emblem of class war – and the war of the sexes – as well as the fight for improved animal welfare in general. It became a lightning rod for continuing disturbances, riots, and rallies across London. It suffered repeated attacks by outraged medical students. It was defended by the equally outraged working-class locals of Battersea plus a cast list of feminists, suffragists and Suffragettes, trade unionists, radical liberals, and anarchists. The situation became a national talking point and was debated in Parliament. The statue was protected, at great expense, day and night, by the police.

In November 1909, the balance of power within Battersea Council tipped in favour of the Conservatives. Despite the protestations of the Progressive Liberal politician, the councillor for Latchmere Ward John Archer, amongst others, the decision was taken to remove the statue. Cllr Archer later defected to Labour and became the first black mayor in London. The removal was carried out in a clandestine operation in the dead of night in March 1910. Over 100 policemen were deployed to protect the workmen. The statue's whereabouts were unknown for years, but, much later, it was revealed that it had been broken up and melted down years earlier.

The one positive to come out of this sorry tale is that, influenced by public outrage, a Second Commission on Vivisection convened in 1906. After many delays, the Commission reported in 1912. The findings led to the laws being tightened and regular checks were made on the procedures of vivisectors and laboratory practices.

In the 1980s, the Anti-Vivisection League and British Union for Abolition of Vivisection (BUAV) commissioned a new statue. The Greater London Council granted it a home, pride of place near the Pump House in Battersea Park. As if history was repeating itself, in 1992, the statue was removed after a change of Council leadership to Conservative, with the weak excuse of 'park renovations'. In an echo of the situation eighty years earlier, the unannounced, sudden disappearance of the statue did not go down well with the residents of Battersea, nor with regular visitors to the park. The Anti-Vivisection societies who raised the funds for its commission, and wider animal rights campaigners, were furious at the council's action. They were determined they *would not* allow history to repeat itself.

They launched a vociferous campaign, this time without the accompanying violence, to persuade the Greater London Council to return the statue. The Council, in due course, relented and, two years after its removal, agreed to replace it. It was only a partial success however, as they would not agree to return it to its original location. The little brown dog would no longer look out, pride of place, from the Pump House grounds. Instead, his new resting place was to be in a far less prominent area of the park – a short walk away from the quaint Old English Garden, a walled area, accessible through large wrought-iron gates. A prominent 'No Dogs Allowed' sign is displayed beside the gate. The statue is not, as I describe in the prologue, hidden away and neglected, however. He is in full view, set back from a path, and is often to be found adorned with flowers and other items.

All other characters are fictional. Exceptions are Henry James Ward who was Director of Battersea Dogs Home at around the time, Teresa Billington-Greig and Charlotte Despard, whose own exceptional stories are ripe for the telling. And, of course, George Bernard Shaw.

A fascinating and reassuring fact about Battersea Dogs Home, related to me by their archivist, is that Battersea has always been concerned about the possibility of its dogs being used for vivisection, and went to great lengths to prevent this. During Queen Victoria's reign, they went to the extraordinary level of hiring an investigator, more than once, to follow members of the public who had bought a dog, to ensure that they were bona fide dog lovers. Anyone buying a dog from Battersea had to sign a form confirming their intentions. The conditions of purchase, as quoted in the annual report from 1905, state: 'The purchaser also receives the animal on his promise that it shall not be used for physiological, pathological or toxicological experiments, and on his statement that the animal is required for ... [insert purpose for which the dog is required]'.

I intend to set aside a percentage of the royalties from the sales of this book to kick-start a campaign to recreate the first memorial's design. I have no idea how much such a statue would cost nowadays, but I'm figuring we'll need to add a fair few zeros to the end of the original £120. Where it will eventually reside is a decision for the future. Back in Latchmere Recreational Ground? The Pump House? Or even at Battersea Cats and Dogs Home?

Oh, one final thing. When I was researching the facts of the story, I came across the date of the unveiling of the statue, in Latchmere Recreational Ground. It was a Saturday. Saturday, 15th September, 1906.

References and Further Reading

The true events depicted in this book relied heavily on several sources, some contemporaneous accounts by eyewitnesses, newspaper articles of the time, British Medical Association journal articles, and a number of more contemporary retellings of the events. In particular, Peter Mason's version of the whole affair, published in 1987, is a comprehensive, thoroughly researched account.

Ford Edward K. 1908, The Brown Dog and his memorial – eyewitness to the conflict, A facsimile published by Euston Grove Press

Bayliss L.E. 1955, The Brown Dog Affair, privately published

Lansbury Coral, 1985, The Old Brown Dog – Women, Workers, and vivisection in Edwardian England The University of Winsconsin Press

Mason Peter, 1987, The Brown Dog Affair, Two Sevens Publishing

Cain Joe, 2013, The Brown Dog in Battersea Park, Euston Grove Press

Acknowledgements

As bizarre as it may seem, the first two things I must acknowledge in the creation of this novel are climate change and a local wine producer – yes, believe it or not, wine production has come to south London. Had 2018's exceptionally hot, long summer not caused the grape harvest to be brought forward two weeks, and had the guys at the Urban Wine Company not asked us to deliver our back-garden-grown grapes to a venue on Lavender Hill in Battersea, this book simply wouldn't exist.

There are a great many people I need to thank for their help, encouragement, gentle criticism, patience and brilliant ideas, which have made this book what it is. I'll attempt this in some sort of chronological order.

First, I must thank both Jeanne Rathbone and Ian Mursell, the wonderful speakers at Battersea Arts Centre that day in September. Jeanne for her extraordinary tales of the amazing women – Charlotte Despard in particular – that lived and campaigned in and around the area, back in the day. And Ian, of course, for introducing me to the poignant tale of a stray terrier dog. They were both early readers of my first attempt at the story – sorry! – and provided invaluable feedback and ideas on how to improve it.

I have to thank Mark Speed, who also read an early version, saw the potential and valiantly offered to grapple with my worst abuses against the English language. Also, thanks for all the useful, typically droll, insights into fiction writing and the publishing world, and aviation!

Next, I must thank all my friends who bravely agreed to be beta-readers and have all, in some shape or form, contributed to the story's development. I can't thank you guys enough for putting up with my obsession over the past three years. So, thank you: Tracy Avison, Anthony Browne, Kristin Cooper, Mark Fletcher, Paula Higgins, Sadia Khan, Lydia Makin, Maggie O'Neill, David Picton, Karen Potter, Georgina Stevenson.

And a shout out to all at Curtis Brown Creative, whose three-month novel writing course kept me sane through lockdown #1, and my fellow Summer 2020 cohort who contributed to the refining and shaping of the story through their helpful and insightful comments.

Huge appreciation goes to all at Honno Press for taking a chance on me and my strange little story. It is extra special to me that Honno is a Welsh women's press, the longest running independent women's publisher and a not-for-profit cooperative. So, thank you, Caroline Oakley and Helena Earnshaw. Thanks, in particular, go to two members of the Honno Committee: Gwyneth Tyson Roberts who advised on historical aspects of the period and put right some of my worst anacronyms, and to Eurwen Booth who proofread the book. Thanks also to Harri Roberts, who copyedited the manuscript so thoroughly. However, the biggest cwtch of all goes to the wonderful Rebecca F. John, my editor, who championed this story from the moment she set eyes on it, and wrestled it into the fantastic shape it now inhabits. Although, at the time of writing this we have yet to meet in person, I consider Rebecca a good friend, as well as a brilliant editor and amazing writer.

Last, but not at all least, I have saved my biggest thanks and heartfelt appreciation for Robb, my long-suffering partner. Robb has had to share me for the last three years with a long-dead dog, and has done so with patience and humour. I have inflicted countless versions of the manuscript upon him, which he has read with good grace and a wealth of invaluable suggestions and comments – I appreciated them even if it didn't seem that way at the time. And, of course, not forgetting the last jigsaw puzzle piece of the number of coincidences that led to me hearing the story in the first place. This story would never have been told if it wasn't for a certain condition which led us to venture into Battersea Arts Centre that fateful day. I will say no more to save his blushes.

Thank you all, so very much for being part of this journey. I'm sure there is a little brown dog looking down on all of us, wagging his tail and barking his most hearty approval!

About the Author

Credit: John Duffy, Zuma Creative

Paula is the author of several environmental non-fiction publications. Her first book, *Decommissioning the Brent Spar*, was released over twenty years ago, and is the key source reference material for a forthcoming TV drama series. Paula is acting as consultant to the show.

In her other life, Paula has a doctorate in atmospheric science and – when not writing – spends her days campaigning, speaking and banging on to anyone who will listen about climate change and sustainable living.

Little Brown Dog is her first foray into fiction writing. She is currently working on the sequel. She lives in London with her partner and a posse of rescue animals.

You can find Paula on:
Tw: @PaulaSOwen

To learn more about the story, and the campaign to re-cast the original statue, follow or visit:

@L1ttleBrownDog
@LittleBrownDogTheNovel
www.facebook.com/groups/387789955994600
https://littlebrowndog.london

ABOUT HONNO

Honno Welsh Women's Press was set up in 1986 by a group of women who felt strongly that women in Wales needed wider opportunities to see their writing in print and to become involved in the publishing process. Our aim is to develop the writing talents of women in Wales, give them new and exciting opportunities to see their work published and often to give them their first 'break' as a writer. Honno is registered as a community co-operative. Any profit that Honno makes is invested in the publishing programme. Women from Wales and around the world have expressed their support for Honno. Each supporter has a vote at the Annual General Meeting. For more information and to buy our publications, please write to Honno at the address below, or visit our website: www.honno.co.uk

Honno, 14 Creative Units, Aberystwyth Arts Centre
Aberystwyth, Ceredigion SY23 3GL

Honno Friends

We are very grateful for the support of all our Honno Friends. For more information on how you can become a Honno Friend, see:https://www.honno.co.uk/about/support-honno/